PRAISE FOR

"This dystopian tale skillfully balances delusion, disillusionment, and disdain. Readers are in for a dark, difficult trip down the rabbit hole."

—*Publishers Weekly*

"A work of unbelievable creativity and imagination. Han Song has taken Kafka's institutionalized horror and endlessly reproduced it with trillions of 3D printers, enough to fill the entire universe. Taking the image of an AI machine gone haywire or a cancerous growth spreading out of control, expansive yet utterly devoid of hope, it 'clogs every possible escape portal and blocks any possibility of running away, leaving behind nothing but a devastating and overpowering feeling of grief.'"

—Lo Yi-Chin, author of *Faraway*

"Han Song stands out among Chinese science fiction writers. His exuberant imagination engages history in total earnest, speaking to the darkness and perversity of the human condition. *Hospital* is his masterpiece and should be a landmark in the terrain of contemporary science fiction."

—Ha Jin, author of *Waiting*, *A Song Everlasting*, and *A Free Life*

"China's premier science fiction writer."

—*Los Angeles Times*

"The kind of science fiction I write is two dimensional, but Han Song writes three-dimensional science fiction. If we look at Chinese science fiction as a pyramid, two-dimensional science fiction would be the foundation, but the kind of three-dimensional science fiction that Han Song writes would be the pinnacle."

—Liu Cixin, author of *The Three-Body Problem*

"Han Song's fiction has a uniquely 'dark consciousness' that offers deep reflections about history and keen observations about our contemporary world, all of which comes from an otherworldly perspective. *Hospital* is part of a stupendous trilogy, which is filled with a seemingly inexhaustible series of ghoulish episodes, grotesque figures, and sublime scenes of the wildest kind."

—David Der-wei Wang, professor (Harvard University) and author of *Why Fiction Matters in Contemporary China*

"Han Song's Hospital trilogy is the second most important Chinese science fiction trilogy after Liu Cixin's *The Three-Body Problem*. Han Song is the Philip K. Dick of China. *Hospital* reveals strange visions from a fantastical universe, yet the true secret remains hidden under the skin of contemporary China. His twisted surreal vision seems removed from the everyday world of reason, and yet it is able to reveal a truth impervious to traditional realist narratives."

—Mingwei Song, professor (Wellesley College) and coeditor of *The Reincarnated Giant*

"Han Song is an important part of the legacy of critical humanism, from Lu Xun to the Chinese avant-garde writers of the 1980s."

—Yan Feng, literary critic

"The darkness contained within *Hospital* expresses the author's desperation with mankind's attempts at self-treatment and salvation. The novel's completely unbridled narrative path sets out in the direction of science fiction but ultimately arrives at the spiritual abyss lurking in the reality of today's China . . . and the rest of the world."

—Yan Lianke, author of *The Day the Sun Died* and *Hard Like Water*

"Demented, delirious, and one of a kind . . . 'Kafkaesque' doesn't begin to describe this cunning labyrinth of a novel. Nothing I have read has captured so incisively (and searingly) the unrelenting institutional brutality of our contemporary world."

—Junot Díaz, author of *The Brief Wondrous Life of Oscar Wao*

"In this era in which the epidemic rages, Han Song's *Hospital* has presented us with a delirious Kafkaesque vision of the future where the relationship between disease, patients, and (technological) caregivers has become enshrouded in a new level of complexity and dark enchantment. Thanks to Michael Berry's brilliant translation, this unforgettable literary experience can now reach a new group of readers."

—Chen Qiufan, author of *The Waste Tide*; coauthor of *AI 2041*

DEAD SOULS

DEAD SOULS

HAN SONG

TRANSLATED BY MICHAEL BERRY

AMAZON **CROSSING**

Previously published as *Wangling* by Shanghai wenyi chubanshe in China in 2018. Translated from Chinese by Michael Berry. First published in English by Amazon Crossing in 2025.

Published by Amazon Crossing, Seattle

www.apub.com

Amazon, the Amazon logo, and Amazon Crossing are trademarks of Amazon.com, Inc., or its affiliates.

ISBN-13: 9781662507717 (paperback)
ISBN-13: 9781662507700 (digital)

Cover design by Will Staehle
Cover image: © Dotted Yeti, © wacomka, © Independent birds / Shutterstock

Printed in the United States of America

If a person can make peace
with their past memories,
all shall be released
—Ci Cheng

Table of Contents

PATIENT VIOLENCE

1

DAY OF RESURRECTION

Your nose and mouth seal shut. Your instinct to survive drives you to do everything you can to prevent the water from entering your body. But once the first mouthful starts to go down your esophagus, your throat responds by automatically closing up to prevent more from rushing in. After two or three minutes, your blood oxygen level begins to decrease, your throat muscles relax, and large amounts of water surge into your body. Stripped of your energy, you are rendered helpless. The level of carbon dioxide in your blood rapidly rises as your lungs and airways fill with water. Your engorged body rapidly becomes bloated, and you feel the weight pulling you down. You figure: *This must be death . . . my time among the living has come to an end.* One after another, complex feelings of pain, fear, regret, sadness, and longing rise to the surface. A red constellation appears suddenly, floating on the face of the crimson water. The shadowy reflections of the stars congregate like a row of malevolent spirits, welcoming you . . . you want to run away. All around, you are surrounded by darkness and enveloped in an even greater sense of fear. But it doesn't take long for all those emotions to disappear. Your consciousness leaves your brain . . . and in that final moment, you rise up from the body of water as if passing from one side of the world to the next.

A fishnet-like object ensnares you. You are on the ship, right? But you cannot see the sea. All you can make out is a billowing cloud of purple-black smoke as it churns in the sky. You look up to see a woman dressed in white. Her complexion is like glazed jade, her body like a porcelain vase. She extends her long arms through the haze and pulls you in from the net, dumping your body on the ground. You have died and been resurrected. You cannot help but struggle to stand up. You want to embrace her, but she evades your touch. She looks familiar, and you try calling out the name of a woman you once knew.

"Hey, what did you just say?" she responds sharply.

"Who are you? Are you the Bodhisattva Avalokitesvara?" you ask in confusion.

She appears to think there is something laughable about your question. Then, as if coming from a distant other shore, her voice responds, "What is Avalokitesvara?"

You assume she must be yet another person in this world suffering from memory loss . . . even so, you feel like you have just been reunited with a long-lost sibling, and you feel even closer to her.

"Not bad," she says. "You survived."

"Thank you for saving me."

"How can I look death in the face and not make an effort to help?"

"What exactly happened to me?"

"You don't know?"

Only then do you remember the boundless sea, its waters raging, vicious waves crashing down, the ship torn apart . . . you saw a guinea pig jump into the sea, and you leaped off the deck after it. You again see the woman in white who saved you, a gold-plated red cross hanging from her neck, and she is wearing a coarse green uniform beneath her hospital jacket. She appears a bit exhausted, yet there is a look of bravery about her. You realize that she is a doctor, a military doctor, a famous one at that! And you? You are nothing but a patient. You start to remember more: all under heaven is one big hospital. The doctors organized themselves into a war brigade. The world has already transitioned from the Age of Medicine and is now in the middle of the Medicinal War. You became enveloped in the Second World War. The main player in that war was the hospital, and the primary weapons were artificial viruses. The ship you boarded was called the *Peace Ark*, a hospital ship sent to the front lines by the Allied forces. The war dragged on without any clear winners or losers, but the casualties were immense. Many people sacrificed their lives, including Dr. Norman Bethune. The woman who saved you put her own life at risk to do so. Not knowing what else to do, you keep expressing your appreciation.

"Remember, this is your day of resurrection," the doctor declares.

"Resurrection?" There is something troubling about the way that sounds. The fact that you didn't die leaves you feeling both extremely fortunate and uncomfortable.

"What's your name? How old are you?" she asks, as if you are in an outpatient clinic.

After taking a moment to think about it, you respond, "Yang Wei. I'm forty years old."

"Then how come you look like you're fourteen?" she asks. "I'm actually two years older than you. You're like my little brother."

You are extremely embarrassed. Even though she looks at least ten years younger than forty-two, she is more like a big sister in terms of your actual ages. She has delicate, distinct features and firm lines extending down from the corners of her mouth. Her gaze emits the warmth of soft jade, but something else cuts like sharp thorns. You see the net she used to fish you out of the sea, but for some strange reason, it gradually disappears before your eyes.

"We need to do an inspection to check if you are suffering from any aftereffects from your drowning," she says.

There is something odd about her words. You look around in terror, but nothing is familiar. You have no choice but to follow her. Together you enter a thick fog that appears out of nowhere. The path ahead is full of twists and turns and ups and downs; the ground is littered with splattered blood and leftover remnants from various animals' internal organs. A series of white structures that look like stacked containers forms a small mountain, with rows of circular windows and the mark of the red cross. You arrive at what seems to be a treatment room. It is devoid of people, and the furnishings are in utter chaos and disarray. She has you lie down on the examination bed, where she takes your temperature, measures your blood pressure, and listens to your heart and lungs with a stethoscope.

"Let's get you an infusion!" As she speaks, a strange look appears on her face. She grabs hold of you and pulls a sheet over your body. Then she suddenly orders, "Hurry up! Let's go!"

Something about the way she speaks sends a chill down your spine, but you nevertheless follow her even deeper into the fog. The mist envelops your body like a carpet, wrapping tightly around you. What exactly happened? Did the enemy launch an attack? You don't know what to say, so you just repeat, "Thanks again for saving me."

"It's not like I did it just to be a Good Samaritan!"

"Then what do you want from me in return?"

"Help me carry this oxygen tank."

"It seems like the conditions here in the sick ward are quite serious. The patients wounded on the battlefield are in desperate need of oxygen."

"Little Wei, from now on you need to start thinking of yourself. The hospital has already sounded the fire alarm. The flames will absorb all the oxygen from the air. Without oxygen, people die. Aren't you afraid of dying?"

Oh, so there is a fire . . . no wonder there was so much smoke. You feel so moved by the fact that she referred to you as "Little Wei." That's right, the hospital is the foundation of the entire world; if it should burn, all will be lost!

"Okay then! Let's all work together to save the hospital!" you offer bravely.

"No! Only an idiot would try to save the hospital," she retorts. "Those with the ability to save the hospital should save themselves first!"

You momentarily choke as you take another good look at the woman before you. She may be past forty, the year that Confucius said people begin to leave their troubles behind, but she has somehow managed to take really good care of herself. She has full breasts, perfect posture, tight muscles, and firm thighs; she looks like a peach tree in full bloom. She has a straightforward, trustworthy manner about her. You take another moment to make sure that she isn't just a figment of your imagination. She is like a replacement guarantee that allows you to continue living. She is your savior, a woman who behaves like the big sister you never had. But she also seems different from the other doctors you saw previously. You follow her orders and pick up the oxygen tank.

2

RUSTY FLAMES

The two of you arrive at a towering white structure just behind the sick ward. It looks like some kind of sacrificial altar. A raging fire spews out, and the flames appear as a fiery cross in full bloom. Yet it is mottled and old, coarse and unkempt, seemingly covered in rust, and yet it does its best to crawl out from the lower strata of time itself. The entire area is enveloped in a strange putrid smell. This is the crematorium. You wonder, *Is this the roaring flame that will destroy the hospital?* Yet it is every bit as gorgeous as the flame burning at the Olympic Stadium. You have never before been to this place lying suspended above the Hospital Ship like a lantern illuminating the entire world.

There is a boy with the body of a child and the face of an old man. He has a mouselike nose and eyes that resemble a river deer's. He wears a white lab coat over a green military uniform. You remember his name—Malnutrizole. He was selected from the patients suffering from premature aging and assigned to oversee the crematorium, where they referred to him as the Funeral Artist. Malnutrizole once said, "Only the crematorium can save the hospital." Excited to see your old friend, you call out to him, but he doesn't respond.

The woman introduces you to Malnutrizole. "This is Weber. He is a fireman."

Weber casts a serious look your way. "So you're still alive? How about your old buddies from the sick ward?"

Your face suddenly changes. "Oh . . . they're probably all dead."

That's right, the Hospital Ship sank. No one could have survived that. Perhaps Malnutrizole also died, and now Weber has replaced him? "Our souls crave peace," Weber explains. "We are all better off dreaming of paradise . . . How do you plan on dying?"

You remain silent. Seeing how the situation is unfolding, the woman tries to explain. "The crematorium is a crucial strategic site in the inevitable coming war between the doctors and patients. Life and death are of the utmost importance. We must all contemplate how we are going to die!"

Somewhat startled, you ask, "A war between doctors and patients?" Meanwhile, you wonder, *Isn't the war between the Allied and Axis powers?*

"Don't you know the patients have revolted?" asked Weber. "They have been attacking the hospital! The patients are our most dangerous enemies! They have thrown themselves into politics, but their motivation is certainly not to ensure that the people live better lives."

The ship has sunk, the patients are all dead—how could they possibly wage an attack on the hospital? Could they also have been saved like you? Perhaps this day of resurrection is not just for you . . . you can't help but feel depressed, realizing that you will need to start interacting with patients again, which makes you realize that you, too, are still a patient. You glance in fear at the massive, queerly shaped rusty flame and try to run away.

But the woman stops you. "All the patients are running toward the crematorium—they plan to throw themselves into the flames, spontaneously combusting and blowing up the crematorium in an effort to burn down the entire Hospital Ship. There is nowhere to run."

You pause in frustration. A torrent of smoke shaped like a series of interlocking fish scales rises, sweeping up skull fragments, which reassemble into a new humanlike form before settling back to the ground. A faint sound of thunder can be heard in the distance. The hospital has transformed. It is no longer the place you were once familiar with.

"There is a patient named Einstein," Weber explains. "He is the main instigator of the riots that have been breaking out. He claims that there is no such thing as an ideal that can be scientifically proven. If you happen to see him, be sure to tell me right away. He must be captured!"

You seem to remember having heard the name Einstein back when you were in the sick ward. He was no ordinary man, but "a patient among patients." You are about to say something when the woman suddenly asks, "And what is the situation like now?"

"The last few that broke in have already been arrested and cremated by the firefighters," replies Weber. "Fighting fires is among the most important tasks of the hospital. The Fire Department has taken the place of the Medical Insurance Office as the single most important office in the hospital. Given the current crisis we are facing, I have been appointed Fire Chief, to oversee the situation."

Sure enough, the crematorium is filled with fire extinguishers and fire hoses, and its steel frame is painted with red characters against a yellow background:

INSPECT FREQUENTLY TO ELIMINATE RISK OF FIRE!

IMPROVE THE DEPARTMENT'S ABILITY TO STAMP OUT FIRES EARLY!

HELP ORGANIZE PERSONNEL SO THEY CAN ESCAPE FROM DANGER!

IMPROVE TRAINING AND EDUCATION ABOUT FIRE PROTECTION!

Weber has a tall nose, large sunken eyes, and sharp pointy ears. He is balding but has clumpy patches of hair, and his entire body is covered with wrinkles. He starts yelling orders to direct the firefighters' work. That's when another round of patients rushes in through the smoke, releasing a series of strange howls and cries. The patients set to be burned are bound and thrown into the crematorium, where they are to be melted down into the ultimate works of art. Everything is repeating, again and again . . . and yet something is different about the atmosphere this time around.

Gazing at the mushroom-shaped clouds rising into the sky, Weber observes, "The true face of the world is one of flame. A soul that has not endured the flames of loneliness and suffering is unable to become a vessel of any true value or meaning." He is so consumed with leading the firefighters and dealing with the patients that he doesn't have time to provide you and the female doctor with a proper welcome. You become concerned about your predicament, but since your body is still covered in a bedsheet, you remain helpless to differentiate the doctors from the patients.

Unable to find any oxygen tanks at the crematorium, the female doctor leads you away. A blanket of thick smoke envelops the earth, which is trembling and shaking as if struck by a tsunami, an earthquake, a hurricane, or an erupting volcano. Sweat soaks your body, and you are assaulted by a feeling of utter exhaustion. You look back to see a mirage-like vision of burning flames as Weber's words echo through your mind: *The true face of the world is one of flame.*

"Little Wei, you might be feeling a bit confused by the current state of the hospital," the woman addresses you, with a tone of understanding. "But no matter what happens, you must face it. There are those who say that our troubled times are now behind us, but they are gravely mistaken. That era of chaos has never left us. We normally look at going to the hospital as an everyday occurrence, like going to the movies. You line up at the window and pay the fee. You pick up your medicine like buying a bucket of popcorn. And as you are sitting there blissfully munching away, a sudden boom erupts, and the entire building collapses. You may be taking the best medicine in the world, but what are you supposed to do when the entire hospital collapses? Suddenly the doctors are forced to save themselves. In the past they were too full of pride to imagine that they themselves might one day need saving."

"Understood." You don't actually agree with her metaphor, but you nevertheless feel like she is a very rational woman. Women's brains may be smaller than those of men, yet their ability to think through complex issues is quite sharp. You grow dependent on her, like a gift from God. If she hadn't saved you, you would have drowned. What was left of your remains would have been sent to the crematorium to be burned to ash. But the one puzzling thing is this: Don't the doctors have the power to control everything that has been playing out? In the Age of Medicine, doctors are the rulers of the world! They are superhuman, omnipotent. There is no task beyond their abilities, so how is it possible that they would be unable to handle a few patients? Since when were patients more powerful than the doctors? Perhaps it was not just pride and vanity holding the doctors back. What else could be standing in their way? The thought is enough to strike fear into one's heart.

The doctor leads you to a place that resembles a finance department. Quite a few people wearing long white medical jackets are lining up outside the door. The woman leads you directly inside. Sitting behind a counter are two women, around thirty-six or thirty-seven years old, who look like cashiers. Something about their faces looks dirty and unkempt. They look familiar, but you can't remember where you might have seen them before. You try to say hello, but they ignore you. The female doctor flashes them a strange, knowing smile before whispering something to them. You are struck with a sense of déjà vu but can't figure out why all this feels so familiar. The doctor who brought you here hands the cashiers a wad of cash and receives a stamped form in return. She then directs you to a warehouse to pick up an oxygen tank. A sleepy security guard keeps watch over the warehouse entrance and takes a cursory look at you before letting you in. The warehouse is filled with a mountain of pharmaceuticals and medical equipment. You pick up an oxygen tank and follow the doctor to the morgue.

3

THE BLADE OF DEATH

There are already more than a dozen oxygen tanks stacked up in the cold, dark room. Looking at the piles of torpedolike objects, you are struck by the following paradox: Since there can be no fire without oxygen, how could the patients possibly burn down the hospital? The flames of the crematorium will eventually burn themselves out. Just thinking about how the flames have been used to burn the bodies of the deceased and those on the brink of a lonely death, you are overcome by a deep sense of terror. No matter what happens, this is one catastrophe from which there is no escape. What should you do?

The morgue has now become a private space to be alone with this woman. "Aren't the oxygen tanks the public property of the hospital?" you ask. "If we start hoarding the oxygen, there will be a shortage for the patients, and there is no telling how many of them will die." You assume that by expressing how deeply invested you are in patient care, you might be able to get on the doctor's good side so she will continue looking out for you.

But that is clearly not how she sees things. "Little Wei, how is it that you are still wasting your time thinking about other people's deaths? It's not like patients are some sort of low-end fringe group! They can be pretty damn fierce! They started killing each other over bed space, medicine, and food back when they were still confined to the sick wards! You must have witnessed things like that, no?"

You begin to recall more from your past. She's right, you indeed witnessed those things with your own eyes. The scenes of violence that used to play out in the sick wards were unusually brutal. You your-self were killed during those struggles. That is the inner nature of the patients: they have always been a bunch of lowly bastards. As the say-ing goes, "Three feet of solid ice cannot be formed by a single day of cold weather." The crisis at hand has been brewing for a long time. The undercurrent of violence has long been festering in the hospital. Chemical drugs only temporarily keep things under control. But now the patients have gone from simple infighting to open attacks against the physicians. The very nature of the violence has transformed, as if whatever inhibitions had been keeping them in line have now been completely removed. How could this have happened? Why would she even *want* to save you?

Your feelings toward doctors have always been complex. You look up to them, seeing them as the ones with their hands on the steering wheel of your life. Standing before them, you feel inferior and devoid of self-confidence. You didn't come to the hospital voluntarily, and this place has never brought you an ounce of happiness. It has done nothing but make you aware of your own physical and psychological defects, which is why you are now in such dire need of being set straight. Do you still remember that initial series of exams when your clothing was stripped away? At first you felt humiliated: ashamed by everything about yourself, ashamed to expose your private parts, ashamed by what the doctors and nurses might think of you, ashamed by the fact that your illness sets you apart from normal people. Yet none of the medical workers gave a damn about the fact that you were naked. In fact, they never bothered to give you a second glance. To them you were nothing but an unadorned clothes hanger, dangling there helplessly while they giggled and gossiped about their own lives. You realized that the other patients felt the same way. When a patient suffering from hemorrhoids complains about his ailment, the doctor usually takes a look at the affected area, but he never tells the patient what he sees or what he has discovered. The patient is always naked, left there without his clothes on even after the examination. On one occasion, a nurse went ahead and shaved all the hair around one patient's anus without even telling him what she was about to do. The patient felt more like a "thing" than a human being. One patient who underwent induced labor said that a nurse had grabbed her, pulled her legs apart, propped them into the built-in stirrups on the delivery bed, and strapped her in with a set of restraints that looked like handcuffs, her legs sticking up into the air. Meanwhile, a middle-aged male doctor towered over her, gazing down between her legs. He rattled off a few orders to the nurses with a tone of complete indifference, like the commander at the National Space Administration speaks when you hear him on television. Even if the moon were to fall from the sky, that voice wouldn't waver.

Patients are unhappy about the inordinate number of exams and treatments they are expected to undergo. Some of the bolder patients might make some requests of their doctors, but only a very small fraction of patients would ever dare to resist their treatment openly. At most, they might refuse to follow their doctors' advice or secretly throw away the pills administered by the nurses, but that is always viewed as extremely ignorant. In the end, patients like that only hurt themselves. You must have heard about the movement to get rid of all the medical records? But that is something different, a true exception to the rule and an extreme example of what happens when the contradictions between doctors and patients are taken too far. After all, who doesn't want to be a "good" patient? Patients might hate one another, always jealous of each other and contending to get the upper hand over their fellow patients, but none of them dares challenge the authority of their doctors. Nor would they ever openly accuse their doctors of doing anything wrong. All patients are afraid of being mocked by their doctors. They can't stand the thought of a doctor saying, "Hey, have *you* gone to medical school?" or "In that case, perhaps it's best you seek out another more skilled doctor to treat you." But more likely, patients will be forced to face divine retribution for their insolence—God's punishment for those

who desecrate the sacred is death. Here in the hospital, you might die
at any moment.

The connection between patients and doctors is not a normal relationship. Once the field of medicine took over the entire world, the
supreme status of doctors was further solidified, and today we find
ourselves in a situation in which, surprisingly, patients are engaging
in widespread acts of collective violence. They seem to be releasing a
deep-seated anger that has been long repressed. They want to overturn
the rule of the "angels in white" and tear apart the long-standing agreement between patients and doctors. The whole thing is actually quite
unbelievable.

Seeing you sitting there with an empty stare, the female doctor
grows anxious. "As a doctor, it is extremely painful for me to see all of
this unfolding, although I, too, have some mixed feelings. But since you
have not participated in the riots, you should have nothing to worry
about."

"Are you really a doctor?" you ask with a sense of apprehension.
There is something strange about her, as if she comes from another
world. Who is she? Why does she insist on saving you?

She seems upset. "What's wrong? I don't look like a doctor? The
whole point of the patient riots is so that they themselves can be doctors. They think that if they assume control of the hospitals and clinics,
they won't have to worry about how hard it is to get an appointment,
or how expensive medical care is. When it comes right down to it, they
have no faith in their doctors! All they want is to become specialists
in whatever ailments they happen to be suffering. They think that by
achieving their goals, they will be able to smash the dualism between
doctors and patients. But doctors are not so easily replaced! They put in
a decade of hard work at medical school, not to mention the complex
set of contributing factors behind various diseases. It is ignorance that
makes the revolting patients so fearless. But . . . How can I put this?

Little Wei, when I told you to take an oxygen tank, I can assure you that you were not stealing it. We left an IOU."

You figure that leaving an IOU falls broadly under the category of mathematics. That was, after all, something you were always good at. Back in the old days when you were still in the sick ward, you offered math lessons to your fellow patients, leading them down the path to becoming qualified soldiers so they could eventually participate in World War II. Mathematics is the foundation of medical weapons. Weren't you, too, one of the patients who participated in the riots?

"Do the two of us really need all these oxygen tanks?" you ask nervously.

"No one knows what might happen next. The hospital is in a state of emergency. We also need to bring some for Spring Tide and Autumn Rain."

"Who are Spring Tide and Autumn Rain?"

"Those two working in the Finance Department."

"Does Professor Eternal know about all this?"

"Professor Eternal?" The female doctor places her index finger under your nose to make sure you are still breathing. You realize that you shouldn't have mentioned the professor. Professor Eternal is your primary care physician. But where is he? How come *he* didn't save you?

Lugging those oxygen tanks around soon wears you out. Before entering the hospital, you were a songwriter and rarely engaged in any kind of physical labor, but now you find yourself short of oxygen, and sometimes you feel like you would be better off dead. You know damn well just how important oxygen can be. You have suffered from a poor constitution and multiple ailments ever since childhood, which led you to spend almost all your time here in the hospital. But you are more curious than most of the other patients, which led you to study some basic medical knowledge on your own. You know that Hippocrates once said that "man is an obligate aerobe." These words contain the mystery of life. Back in the late eighteenth century, scientific researchers discovered that oxygen (and not air) was the key to sustaining life. Breathing is the primary sign that humans are alive. Every time a human takes a breath, 10^{22} oxygen atoms are taken into the body, bonding in a covalent structure. Cells die without oxygen, and humans are, after all, composed of cells. When blood flows through the lungs and begins to absorb oxygen, it immediately transforms from a dark, deathly red to a vibrant, bright red; and then, after its long journey bringing oxygen to tissue structures at the far reaches of the human body, it eventually turns a cold blue. You feel shocked, confused as to why life would have been designed in such a way—it is as if the Creator has had a master plan from the beginning.

Yet oxygen is not a standard component in all worlds; it is actually a rare resource in the universe. Even on this planet, it only began to appear around 2.4 billion years ago. And it was a mere two hundred years ago that humans even discovered it. Oxygen created this richly diverse biological world, but at the same time, it paved the road to death of all life-forms. It integrates both life and death; in other words, it restricts life, preventing people from living their lives with wanton abandon. You are quite clear about what happens when people are deprived of oxygen: the brain is the first part of the body to suffer—as the core engine of the human body, it requires large amounts of oxygen to sustain itself. If the oxygen supply to the brain is cut off, nerve cells become irreparably damaged in fifteen to thirty minutes. After one hour, vital brain tissues lose all functionality. Even if a patient should be revived at this stage, he will inevitably suffer from irreversible brain damage: speech and visual impairment, paralysis, sensory loss, and abnormalities in balance.

In reality, the cause of death—no matter how one might interpret death—is always, in the end, "loss of oxygen." Death may be caused by various diseases and conditions, but in every case, the oxygen flow to the body is disrupted, leading to the same outcome. Cells are deprived of their oxygen supply and unable to exchange materials—death wins.

Living people immediately transform into corpses that are unbearable to look at. No wonder some refer to death as "taking one's last breath." When we breathe, we are human, but without breath we are nothing but corpses. Oxygen deprivation is like a blade of death hanging over the heads of all patients.

You look down at the withered hands and feet protruding from your own emaciated body. Just the thought that they rely upon oxygen in order to continue functioning makes you feel sick. Your ability to move forward with your life is controlled and torn apart by this external factor. Your assumptions about the world turn hypocritical, and you have lost yourself in a sea of pain. You feel inferior. You also believe that doctors are the only ones who control the natural laws, so any patient rebellion is destined to come to naught.

Therefore, the sole reason for the hospital's existence boils down to preventing the sword of death from falling down and slitting open the patients' throats. The doctors' mission is to fight this. It also makes sense that the female doctor making you lug oxygen tanks around is also related to this basic instinct. Related medical technology has been constantly advancing. Ventilators and artificial lungs are in widespread use. Even if someone is brain dead, machines can artificially maintain heartbeat and blood circulation. You have also learned that some patients have surgically implanted devices that automatically break down oxygen molecules in the body. Others have received oxygen-supply stents, while another group has undergone genetic reconstruction and organ enhancement in order to become hypoxia-resistant organisms. However, you seem never to have been offered such an opportunity. And yet you console yourself with the thought that even if you had received this special therapy, in the end, how long would it really extend your life? On this road between life and death, sooner or later the blade of death will eventually fall. We are destined to stop breathing one day—in the end, there are no exceptions. We shall all become dead souls.

As a doctor, this woman must know all about the ups and downs of life, and yet she doesn't immediately ask you to inhale the oxygen. Instead, she tells you to lie down flat on your back, propping your head up on her lap, as if that might somehow help you breathe a bit easier. This is clearly not your typical doctor-patient relationship. You lie there, frozen in horror. Yet something about this experience leaves you with a sense of déjà vu. It is indeed quite unusual. The doctor caresses your head, as if ironing out all the uneven emotions running through her own heart. You can sense that she is anxious about the state of the hospital. This is, after all, her longtime place of work, and her entire existence is closely linked to its fate. In this sense, she has an even closer connection to the hospital than the patients do. She must be having a hard time adapting to the changes taking place around her. Having just carried those oxygen tanks, her muscles are taut, her slender thighs firm and tight like two loaded cannons. The various fluids running through her body slosh and gurgle as her strong, exquisitely crafted bones join together in a chaotic disarray. As a eukaryotic organism, is she also hypoxic? Is she beginning to encounter challenges related to her mitochondrial metabolism?

But you don't have the luxury of giving any of this too much thought. She is a doctor, her judgment informed by her professional training and expertise. It seems that she is waiting until the last possible moment before taking more radical steps. Instead, in an attempt to preserve what precious resources remain, she holds off on using the oxygen. Maybe that's not a bad plan, as long as the other patients don't discover what she is doing. You know a few other women in this hospital. Hopefully they won't show up and see you sleeping like a stray dog with your head in her lap!

The thought of being discovered makes you want to get up, but the doctor easily pushes your head back down with just one arm. "What are you doing?" she admonishes you. "Don't move. If I hadn't pulled you out of the sea, you'd have been a goner for sure! Little Wei, since you have already given yourself over to the hospital, you must never forget the debt of gratitude you owe. Even though that can be difficult for patients." She has superhuman strength, reminding you of those female astronauts who work out every day and are also soldiers. It is a strange feeling to be held down by someone with such unusual strength. Is this *Peace Ark* actually a spaceship? After all, there is no oxygen in space.

You decide just to lie there in that strange position, maintaining a frozen, corpse-like pose. You don't dare suggest having some oxygen from one of the tanks, but as an alternative, you wonder if you and the doctor might engage in some mutual therapy treatment? This involves entering the other person's body, a flesh-on-flesh arrangement. You could borrow the fluids circulating in her body to complete the breathing process. Perhaps the therapy might even save you, blocking the blade of death from crashing down upon you. It is not entirely clear when this habit of engaging in mutual therapy first began to take control of you, but it became an addiction, like a drug. In the past you engaged in mutual therapy sessions with many women. During times of crisis, they used their bodies to help you get through difficult times. Perhaps this is an alternative therapy treatment. You feel like you are no ordinary patient . . . then you get a whiff of a disinfectant-like smell coming from between the doctor's legs. The smell makes you restless. The urge wells up inside you, but you are afraid she might not be willing. After all, she hardly knows you. And so, you hesitate . . .

"Hey, are you feeling any better?" the doctor asks. After you have gone so long without saying a word, she gently pats you on the cheek. You think about all the different women you have engaged in mutual therapy treatment with over the course of your life, but that only exacerbates your sense of shame. You were not only unable to protect any of them but actually relied upon them to save you. It was only thanks to those women that you survived, yet you were never able to establish a stable, long-term collaborative relationship with any of them, at least nothing that went beyond that of a doctor and patient relationship.

You look at the perfectly intact oxygen tanks sitting there beside you and can't help but begin to cry uncontrollably, your tears soaking the doctor's thighs. This makes you even more upset with yourself. Even she can't stomach the sight of you like this, so she props you up, and you go back to transporting the oxygen tanks. The intense physical labor helps you forget your pain and frustration.

Meanwhile, the blanket of smog around you grows thicker. It feels like the air is going to explode. It's a good thing it doesn't appear to be poisonous. And although the oxygen seems to be thin, it hasn't completely dissipated. But visibility keeps getting worse, and you still can't figure out where you are. Are you on the ship? Or on land? As the female doctor said, everything has been brought on by the troubled times in which we live. But this seems different from the chaos brought on by the war. Doctors may be able to treat disease, but they are helpless when it comes to coping with the turmoil of war and unrest. Perhaps this is where the field of medicine's limits lie? You need to be more tolerant, instead of being so cynical and angry at the world. But the most important thing is quickly adapting to this hospital, or whatever new reality takes over after the hospital completes its transformation. Because when it comes down to it, patients are never able to extradite themselves from the hospital.

4

DEATH OR SURVIVAL

As you pass by the Thoracic Surgery Department, you catch sight of several doctors packing up their scalpels. They resemble a pack of hoarders squirreling away their most prized personal possessions. Never before have you seen such a rich and varied assortment of scalpels, shiny and dazzling, like those expensive high-level imitations you find in a store that sells cultural relics. Some of the scalpels are inlaid with gold, silver, and diamonds; others have been meticulously carved from bone. The doctors scramble to put scalpels and surgical blades into their bags like an elaborate magic trick, probably preparing to sell off the blades in exchange for basic material goods to get through these chaotic times. After that, a crowd of doctors from the Neurology, Respiratory Medicine, and Gastroenterology Departments frantically packs their bags as they prepare for their escape. Their faces are obscured by black oxygen masks, but you can still hear the waterfall-like sound of their heaving breaths. They remind you of a band of defeated Stormtroopers from the Galactic Empire in *Star Wars*, and you almost feel like you could be on a movie set.

"From the look of things, the main patient forces are coming," the female doctor warns.

"How exactly did the doctor-patient relationship become so fractured?" you ask. "Why weren't steps taken earlier to prevent this from happening?" Of course, you already know the answer to these questions, but you ask anyway. In the face of death, doctors and patients should be down in the trenches, fighting side by side. Who betrayed whom?

You also wonder, with the hospital in such a state of internal chaos, how they will battle the external enemies trying to invade. Perhaps all is on course for this Second World War to end in defeat, and the tide of history is set to change. If that's the case, it will affect the fate of all humanity—so how come no one has been talking about this?

"Sooner or later, we knew this day would come," the female doctor says, in a tone filled with regret. "Doctors have spent their entire lives researching patients, yet they still have not figured out what their patients are actually thinking. There are a lot of questions that the field of medicine cannot answer. Of course, that's not what people used to think. Early on, the entire medical establishment assumed that once they mapped out the human genome, everything would be solved and their work could come to a successful end."

Yes, that's exactly right. You remember back during the Age of Medicine, when there was no problem the field of medicine couldn't solve—medicine was the ultimate weapon against illness and death. Doctors established a program for genetic and cellular engineering and discovered the mathematical foundations behind them. As one of the patients who took an active role in research, you were assigned by Professor Eternal to teach mathematics to your fellow patients and help popularize relevant knowledge. In the end, diseases, patients, and treatment can all be boiled down to numbers and transformed into parts of a larger algorithm. Armed with that knowledge, one can accomplish anything. You and your fellow patients joined forces to seek out a special patient named Einstein, in an attempt to use a formula hidden in his mind to assist doctors in bringing a major upgrade to the field of medicine, which could then be used to defeat the Axis powers, win World War II, and bring peaceful unification to the entire world. This displays the way in which the field of medicine is not only broad but all-encapsulating. At that time, elite physicians still had faith in their patients. They never imagined that one day Einstein would lead a violent rebellion against the hospital. Could the doctors really have been wrong? Had the hospital fostered Einstein as a future savior, only to have him turn on them? Then you realize that perhaps you yourself have done things to support this revolution. Perhaps you are in fact an accomplice to the crimes being committed. But you can't remember. Instead, you grow increasingly fearful. This female military doctor is still unclear about all the things you once did. Otherwise, she could never treat you this way. You try to conceal your true thoughts by pretending like you can hardly breathe, squatting on the floor like a child and pleading, "I feel terrible . . ."

"Your old symptoms are acting up again?" She has all kinds of prejudices toward patients, but she manages to display a flash of professional intolerance. These doctors seem to be forever living in a world of self-contradiction. In her eyes, patients are a bunch of devilish children who need to be constantly taken care of.

"That's right . . . I'm in so much pain . . ." You rub your throat in an exaggerated way as your arms and legs convulse, like a student subjected to corporal punishment.

Yet she still refuses to give you any oxygen. Instead she removes the first aid kit strapped to her back, takes out a syringe, and gives you an intravenous injection. "Lidocaine. The last two doses I have. Hey, how come your veins are so thin? I can't even find a pulse! Come here, get a little bit closer."

You can feel her warm breath, and through your anxiety, you begin to feel a flash of excitement. *After all this time,* you think, *I'm finally getting some proper medicine! Now this is more like a real hospital!* To help her find a vein, you clench your fist like a good little boy and, in your excitement, momentarily brush up against her breast. It feels like a car's inflatable airbag, exuding a soft elasticity and a firm chill, a completely different feeling than her thighs. She doesn't respond to your touch, and your hand begins to fondle her. You blush, and as the needle enters your body, you silently look up to steal a glance at the green military uniform she wears beneath her white lab coat. The area around her breast has already been soiled by your dirty hands, smudging the beautiful red cross emblazoned on her clothing.

The innate sense of compassion that led her to save you comes through in her voice. "Little Wei, you really shouldn't be so hard on yourself. Does anyone really feel good these days? Of course not! Not even the doctors. For some time now, we have all been treading on thin ice, looking down into the abyss. But we must pull ourselves together and push through. We all still very much treasure the glorious dreams of the angels in white, but those dreams are now being destroyed. From now on, no one will ever pursue this profession again. All the doctors suffer from depression. Don't you think for one moment that only patients get sick. Last night, I, too, dreamed of death. I dreamed of a sharp object entering my neck; I couldn't breathe, blood began spraying out . . . patients aren't the only ones who have nightmares like this. As a physician, this was the first time I had ever felt true fear. That vision in my dreams was coming true. I really shouldn't be telling you all this, but the hospital is indeed an extremely dangerous place. It's not just the patients running amok; there is something wrong with the hospital itself. The doctors are unable to keep things together any longer, yet somehow, I still risked great peril to save your life. Why do think that was? Don't tell me that I somehow still remember my professional obligation to my patients? That I still recall the oath I took when I first began working at the hospital? That I somehow managed to hold on to my early aspirations? I see the kind of comfort that a simple hug or some consoling words can provide to those gravely ill patients in the sick ward who have yet to find salvation, and that's given me the courage to face death calmly. Even a veteran doctor like me cries when I see patients suffering. Little Wei, you need to treasure what you have."

You can't tell if her words are true or an exaggeration, but you sense something clichéd and artificial about what she is saying. She is probably used to speaking like that to everyone she saves. But in reality you feel like not even she understands why she saved you. Perhaps there is a deeper, more complex reason for her actions. You also don't understand why the doctors would insist on describing themselves as an underprivileged group. They are like Jesus Christ, who allowed His enemies to crucify Him even though He was clearly gifted with boundless divine power; instead, He hung there on the cross, staring at the very people He was there to save, quietly neighing with indifference. You are worried that the doctor will collapse under the pressure, which would mean the end for you.

You nervously gaze at the liquid inside the syringe being injected into your vein and try to flatter her. "Although I still don't know your name, I must commend you on your skills! As a doctor you are in the same league as the legendary obstetrician Dr. Lin Qiaozhi. I'll be sure to write a letter to the Hospital President, praising your professionalism. Please rest assured, there is nothing to be afraid of. I, too, have long contemplated the question of death. Here in the hospital, what does death mean, anyway? After all, isn't the hospital a place explicitly for the dead? Even I understand this. The only difference is the method by which death comes." You repeatedly try to encourage and console her, but you wouldn't necessarily say all these things if she were a man.

"Little Wei, is that what you really think?" she asks with a bland smile. "I'm actually no model doctor. The way I treat my patients is nothing more than a kind of professional response I have developed over a long period of time. But given the larger environment we are living in these days, I'm not sure what purpose it serves anymore. I'm just worried that I won't be able to return to the sick ward. Saving you was the final professional responsibility I needed to fulfill as a doctor. There are some things that you will understand in the future. Anyway, maybe we will survive . . . then again, perhaps we, too, will die. Just look at the two of us, crossing paths as though it was determined by a chance set of circumstances. At the very least, we won't be so lonely. Doctors and patients now share the same fate." She pulls the syringe out, heaves a deep sigh as if she has just delivered the first true treatment session in her life, and pats you on the shoulder like a big sister taking care of her little brother.

You are sweating profusely, as if you've just finished having sex. You crave more and reach out for the needle, pleading, "But . . . I don't think I can die." In this respect, you are very different from the other patients. Time and time again, you throw yourself into the jaws of death and yet, each time, somehow manage to escape unscathed. As far as the hospital is concerned, a man who cannot die is of little use.

"What's all that nonsense you're babbling about?" She flashes you a cold gaze and bluntly announces, "Here in the hospital, there's no such thing as a patient who cannot die! Unless you are already a dead soul."

The injection of lidocaine provides a temporary release from the pain. The two of you look for your oxygen tanks, but doctors from all over the hospital have already carted off all the oxygen tanks stored in the warehouse. The doctor doesn't utter a single word of complaint as she leads you off to the emergency treatment room. The medical workers inside have fled, and you arrive at the sickbed of a patient who is fast asleep. The female doctor tells you that all the patients here were taken to the emergency treatment room after being injured in the riots, displaying the hospital's great spirit of benevolence toward its patients. She stands there in silence for a full three minutes before asking you to remove the oxygen mask from the patient's face. This request takes you off guard, but you obey without uttering so much as a peep of resistance. You figure this probably means you won't have to leave an IOU for this one, and you wonder whether Spring Tide and Autumn Rain might end up getting put out of their jobs. The placard at the head of the sickbed reads EDDINGTON. You commit the name to memory. The doctor doesn't offer a single world of explanation, and the two of you take the oxygen tank and leave.

On your way out, you run into the Editor in Chief of the official hospital newspaper, *Geriatric Health News*. He is leading an entire crowd of men carrying oxygen tanks. As they huff and puff down the hallway, the Editor in Chief orders you and the female doctor to hand over your oxygen tanks. You dare not disobey his order, and the Editor in Chief rewards you with a copy of *Geriatric Health News*. The front-page editorial is about the Hospital President leading the entire medical staff on a mission to deepen reforms, eliminate obstacles, and realize the hospital's great revival as the curtain rises on an exciting new era! As soon as the Editor in Chief and his men have left, the female doctor throws the copy of *Geriatric Health News* into the garbage and leads you back to the sick ward to steal more oxygen tanks.

By the time you get back to the morgue, you are utterly exhausted. You collapse to the ground, still clutching the oxygen tanks, and fall into a deep sleep. With the hospital in a state of such utter chaos, the doctor doesn't worry about appearances and falls asleep next to you, her thick, frog-like thighs wrapped around your waist. Half-asleep, you want to push her legs off you, but you dare not do anything that might be construed as impetuous. Instead you lie there without moving a muscle. Even with her on top of you, you gradually begin to feel comfortable . . . in fact, you grow to like it.

You start pining for another injection, but she sleeps like a dead pig, snoring loudly. Unable to fall asleep, you begin reflecting back on your experiences, trying to make sense of everything that has happened, the strange circumstances you now find yourself in. You remember back when you were first admitted to the hospital. You were a songwriter who had gained a bit of recognition for your work. Your idol was a singer-songwriter named Bob Dylan, but in the society in which you live, no matter how talented a person might be, no one would ever be allowed to be a Bob Dylan. And unlike Dylan, your music never had the power to change the world . . . let alone turn it upside down. You spent the majority of your life walking on tiptoes, constantly afraid of offending people, always cautious with your words, careful never to commit the wrong ones to paper. All the songs you composed were well within the censorship standards that dictated what was permissible for public performance. And yet you were still deemed to be "sick" and ended up being forcibly admitted to the hospital. From that moment forward, your fate was inextricably tied to that of the hospital. The hospital had saved you.

But how long ago did all of that take place? You can't remember, but you still have a murky image of the hospital, at that time, as a majestic and imposing structure at the peak of its powers. The doctors were incredibly imposing and insufferably arrogant, and the patients groveled at their feet, servile and obsequious. There in the inpatient ward, you experienced all kinds of trials and were tortured to the point that you didn't want to go on living. You did not dare resist; all you could do was try to escape. With great effort you finally made it out of the sick ward and found your way aboard the Hospital Ship, on which you traversed the oceans, seeking out a place beyond the sea where you would finally receive more advanced treatment. Who could have imagined that the entire world would be turned upside down with the sudden outbreak of World War II? The sea became a battlefield, the ship was unable to make it to the other shore, and the AI program controlling the sick ward collapsed. You were assigned by Professor Eternal to serve as the Team Leader of the Red Label Commando Unit, leading the patients in a people's war that would break through the viral sea created by the Axis powers. But then your contact person, Zi Ye, died . . . the Hospital Ship capsized and sank deep into the sea. With no other alternative, you threw yourself into the water, hoping to end it all, but then you were unexpectedly saved by this female military doctor. You can't be certain what exactly happened, nor can you tell where you are. The strangest thing is the fact that you are still alive—or at least you *feel* alive.

5

THE SEA OF ANGER

Curled up like a bug between the doctor's thighs, you finally drift off to sleep. By the time you wake up, she is gone. All the oxygen tanks you collected are gone, save one, which she apparently left for you. You wait for a while, but she still doesn't return. You begin to grow paranoid: Could this doctor have been a hallucination all along? You look around at the silent smiling corpses surrounding you and, overwhelmed by sadness and loneliness, begin to cry. But you know that tears are of no use, and you are afraid that some of the rioting patients might come after you, so you pick up that last oxygen tank and bid farewell to the morgue. The thick black smoke in the corridor now seems imbued with a strange, hostile atmosphere. Large particles of red matter float, suspended, through the smoke, wantonly invading your nasal passages and making it difficult to breathe. They seem to be embers falling from the crematorium, gradually covering the entire world like a blanket of volcanic ash. A series of shadowy figures surrounds you, some of them roaming, gliding, and falling to the ground, never to rise again. The howls of the dying occasionally break out, like ghosts crying. You don't want to risk anything and inhale a bit of oxygen from your tank. At this most critical moment, the oxygen tank you stole from that patient has proven to come in handy. Eddington's death has saved your life. You are filled with gratitude for the doctor. She must have suffered terrible psychological pressure in order to save you.

You are indeed no ordinary patient. In times of trouble, women have always appeared to help you. Had it not been for the decisive role they played during those critical moments, you would never have made it this far. When it comes to the most important things dictating one's life, it seems that the single most decisive factor is gender and not medicine. It is very difficult to imagine how lonely and helpless humanity would be if everyone were the same gender. And what would the world look like if all doctors were men? This insight has allowed you to understand the purpose of evolution. For billions of years, evolution has been preparing for this very moment. But exactly what kind of destiny is this?

You suddenly remember something. Didn't all the women in the hospital disappear? During the war, a genetic-engineering bomb wiped out all female life-forms. That doomsday weapon proved to be more powerful than any nuclear bomb. In a state of utter shock, you feel cold sweat soaking your clothes. Just who was that woman who saved you? Where did she come from? The more you think about it, the more frightened you become. You can't help but grow suspicious of that thing strapped to your body. You are using it to help you breathe, but it has also allowed you to enter this world of thick mist, in which the difference between the living and the dead is difficult to discern. But it is unreliable. It arrived uninvited, but now that it is here, it is difficult to unload, yet it can be snuffed out at any moment like a cigarette. Then again, perhaps "strange" is the first precondition of life. The hospital exists to provide a place where all kinds of different people obsessed with "living" can come together, regardless of their individual differences, opposing interests, and contending fates. But what next?

The Editor in Chief of *Geriatric Health News* reappears. Your oxygen tank is again confiscated. You cry silently. Walking becomes increasingly difficult until you are no longer able to take a single step forward. That's when a series of flashing black-and-white lights shines through the mist. You force yourself to take a few more steps, until you can make out a row of LCD screens that resemble a series of surveillance monitors. Back when the hospital was still controlled by the AI algorithm, it used this surveillance system to control the patients' each and every move. Back then the patients suppressed their anger, and none of them dared to revolt openly. The image of a doctor appears on-screen. You seem to recognize him. Isn't he Dr. Meloxicam? The doctor's eyes tighten in on you like a wrench, following your every move, as if ready at any moment to take defensive measures to guard against a possible attack.

Putting everything on the line, you cry out, "Help me! Help me! I'm not one of the rioters! I was entrusted by the hospital to help restore patient autonomy. I need to report back to Professor Eternal!"

"Is Professor Eternal not dead?" Dr. Meloxicam asks sternly. "Whatever you might have to say, you can certainly report to me directly."

Professor Eternal is dead? The news strikes you with a feeling of deep sorrow. You feel like a thief who's failed to get away with his crime. "I fell into the sea and almost died," you utter in shame. "And now . . . I can barely breathe . . ."

"The sea?" This critical word captures Dr. Meloxicam's attention. He cautiously examines your pale-blue complexion and, after thinking for a second, begins to climb out from the monitor. Actually, that's not right—he doesn't climb out—he is 3D printed. From a flat two-dimensional image, he transforms into a moving three-dimensional man of flesh and blood, wearing a green military uniform beneath his white lab coat. With a sudden twirl, he dances through the air, arriving right before your eyes. You recoil in shock.

"No need to be afraid," Dr. Meloxicam says in a magnanimous tone. "Since the crisis first broke out, you are the first patient who's been able to articulate the situation you are in. You are our only hope!"

You gaze at him, flinching. "That's right . . . I have always been a loyal patient. I have always followed the rules and stayed in the hospital. I would never betray the doctors."

This version of Dr. Meloxicam presses a button on the red cross hanging from his neck, opening the door to the treatment room behind him. You both go in. The room is filled with a thick mist, and the floor is littered with 3D printed blood vessels and biochemical fingers. An oval pool in the center of the room is full of a thick, mushy, brain-like substance that churns with red waves, seething with resentment and anger. The light-yellow bubbles floating on the surface look like chunks of dirty fat, and thousands of snakelike pipes protrude from the thick mucus. Most of the pipes are broken, but many are still connected to a series of rusty iron cabinets.

"Behold! This is the sea into which you fell!"

Dr. Meloxicam must be pulling your leg.

"This is the sea? The sea from which I came was boundless . . . no matter how far our ship sailed, we could never arrive at the other shore." You glare down at the pool as if confronting a mortal enemy.

"That's because you have been caught within, sailing in circles. How could you ever expect to get out?" The doctor's explanation is smooth and logical.

"What the hell are you saying?" Fear wells up inside you, as if your entire world is being ripped apart. The sun has fallen, and the stars are shattered. Heaven and earth have been turned upside down, and the worlds of the living and the dead have become one. That body of thick, dark-red liquid continues to wriggle before your eyes like an angry monster. Did that female military doctor really save you from *this*? You take another look at Dr. Meloxicam, trying to figure out if he is indeed a real person.

"It looks like water, does it not? But it is actually a liquid polymer, a medical material. The ship you were aboard was nothing more than an imaginary space created by electro-nerve structures." Dr. Meloxicam reaches out his hand and gently points at your head. "My dear patient, all you have been experiencing is nothing more than your own neurons firing. Look, the substance has hydraulic characteristics, which when looked at through an artificial cortex can create the appearance of a diseased red sea. It is but a concept. When you describe the sea as 'boundless,' that is nothing but your subjective consciousness swaying. If the sea had been composed of real water, you would have long ago died from pulmonary edema. Professionally speaking, the Pool of Dead Souls is a model built on a medicinal liquid base. Thanks to the feedback it provides, patients can develop a sense of the world."

The Pool of Dead Souls? A sense of the world?

You take another look at the pool. It looks like a massive piece of gauze soaked in blood and pus, but it is actually composed of droplets from a malleable substance that resembles molten metal. A rush of burning cold surges up your spine. You know that the hospital is capable of playing all kinds of tricks, but you never imagined there might be something behind this.

Dr. Meloxicam opens one of the iron cabinets, and inside are clusters of nerve-like wires connected in a series, some of which are charred. He lazily scans the empty treatment room and observes, "The patients have all escaped. They have scurried off to join the rebellion."

You are stunned. Could that cluster of nerve wires be yours? According to the doctor's analysis, it seems that it was through these nerve wires that your brain and "the sea" were connected. Perhaps something akin to the "medical intermatternet" is at work here, forming the legendary consciousness circuit, which created that watery thing called "experience," which allowed you to perceive so-called "existence." Your "experiences" of going to the hospital, receiving treatment, escaping, seeking out death, and taking part in World War II all occurred right here in this pool. So, who are you actually? What is the world?

You frantically feel your body: your muscles tight, your bones tense, your blood vessels throbbing, your lips trembling. It all feels so real, and yet, perhaps all of this was simply 3D printed like Dr. Meloxicam. After all, isn't so-called "life," or "living beings," nothing but a mass of clay that can be manipulated according to how it was designed? You have long heard stories about how modern medical technology can now create gods. The concept of "life" has long been replaced by "information."

All kinds of strange things can be created on a whim, not unlike the way you used to write pop songs.

"So then . . . what should I do?" you ask.

"Continue your treatment. Naturally, you need to continue your treatment. This is, after all, a hospital."

"What exactly am I suffering from?" This was always, of course, the key question.

"You are suffering from multiple ailments. But the most serious is amnesia. The source of all illness is forgetting. If you can't even remember whether you are alive or dead, coming to the hospital will do nothing but waste the doctors' time."

You heave a deep sigh. "Am I already dead?" You think back to what the doctors have said about "Dead Souls" and the "aftereffects from your drowning."

The doctor examines you as if meticulously analyzing a lab specimen, then flashes you an empty and terrifying smile.

"I heard that the world was afflicted by a great catastrophe, and many people died," you utter mournfully.

"That's right, the great catastrophe," Dr. Meloxicam responds, with a tone of disgust. "But what is there that is not a direct result or continuation of that catastrophe? The doctors created this profession of medicine as a means of cleaning up the mess after the great catastrophe!"

The idea of a "mortician" suddenly flashes through your mind. You can't help but think back to when you and your patient buddies went beneath the "sea," and there, between the coffin-like structure of the rotting ship and a group of floating corpses, you found the original version of yourself. Was that an early memory from the Pool of Dead Souls? Subconsciously, you probably realized that you were already dead.

The doctor standing before you again appears like a dark, two-dimensional image from beyond the horizon. The sound of his voice, which resembles the narrator of the documentary series *Animal World*, eventually makes its way to your ears. He speaks with excitement and passion, his face alternately blushing and turning pale. "Not bad, right? The sense of the world that patients have has been completely reconstructed here in the Pool of Dead Souls. Without this, we would have nothing left. That's why you must understand just how joyous it is to feel pain. This is the gift of baptism that the pool has given all of you. What is death, anyway? It is a state of complete forgetting, an eternal dreamless sleep, your memory completely erased—*that* is the most terrifying thing. Resurrection is actually quite different from ordinary memory reconstruction. It is difficult to achieve the desired goal with conventional memory-enhancement compounds, nor can it be achieved by controlling neurotransmitters related to long-term memory. Instead, what is needed is a kind of imaginary medical technology. This thing called death is not like Alzheimer's disease, depression, schizophrenia, vascular dementia, or cognitive decline. Even more serious is the fact that the world of yesterday can no longer be found. You mentioned the great catastrophe? Of course such a thing occurred! Boom! Everything was destroyed, people's bodies and minds were completely obliterated. That is precisely when the Pool of Dead Souls was created—it is here to re-create people's memories. Memory is what makes the patient. That is how we can create life from death. Patients have a responsibility to sense the world around them, for only then can they articulate their own suffering. The more painful the experience, the better they will remember it. If they forget the great catastrophe, it will be like forgetting everything. Here in the hospital, what could be more dangerous than forgetting your own pain? If a patient is unable to dictate his medical history and clearly articulate where he is feeling discomfort, the doctors will never be able to treat him, and even the best medicine will be a waste. Health insurance is an indisputable human right. Everything we do is to protect the welfare of our patients. In the name of our patients' happiness, medical science must closely observe what is happening in the real world. We cannot afford to be satisfied by mere lab data. That is why we must reconstruct the entire process of how patients seek treatment in the real world, including how patients describe their symptoms to their doctors and how to understand and follow the medical advice that doctors provide to their patients. The Pool of Dead Souls must feel one hundred percent authentic. Only then will the dead have the opportunity to return to the world of the living. Only then will patients know who they really are, what they fear, and what they want. They will then fully devote themselves to the practice of medicine, allowing themselves to transform into part of the doctor-patient collective, to serve as their physicians' most loyal allies, and to bear the historical responsibility they are destined to carry. Patients are the reason the hospital exists, and it is only within the hospital that doctors can help their patients achieve happiness. So even if patients are nothing more than Dead Souls, they, too, deserve to be saved. This is the hospital's most fundamental mission: to save the living but also to save the dead. Do you understand?"

You don't entirely understand, and a lot of what he's said leaves you stunned. He seemed to be saying that when you commit to saving someone, you need to follow through to the bitter end, but there is something absurd about the whole thing. Patients exist so that the hospital can exist, and that way doctors can carry out their professional responsibility to make their patients happy? And so even the dead must be saved? Could this really be the life that you and your fellow patients have been living?

Dr. Meloxicam's tone of voice grows darker and more ambiguous. "I never imagined that as I was bringing my patients happy suffering and delivering social welfare to a society in the throes of a great catastrophe, I somehow awakened your tyrannical ambition. Perhaps this is simply a tragic medical accident, and not even the most experienced doctors could have predicted what would happen. The patients began to remember the ignorant things they did during the great catastrophe, reflecting on the difficulties they experienced prior to their deaths. They began to feel fear, regret, and shame, leading them to grow rebellious toward their doctors. They refused to continue their treatment and ran away from the Pool of Dead Souls. The riots you patients launched drove the hospital down a dark path, toward an even greater catastrophe. The economic losses came first. You are not ordinary patients. You come with a cost . . . the whole thing is dreadful indeed!"

"That is really bad news," you reply. "It could give our enemies the opportunity they have been waiting for . . ." As soon as you hear the doctor mention "cost," you immediately feel like you have lost the ability to communicate with him. Perhaps you should remind him that it is actually World War II that poses the greatest threat. The great catastrophe? That was created by the Nazis. Patients should never be the hospital's enemy. The cost that the Pool of Dead Souls paid for them can always be repaid. But what if World War II was nothing more than a "minor incident" that "took place" inside the pool?

You find yourself utterly speechless. You look back at the gleaming reflection of waves on what appears to be a body of water. It may not be a cauldron of flames, but the pool contains the spirit of fire, dancing up and down, rushing from side to side, hinting at a sense of indignation. You can feel the accumulated rage and resentment that has been building within the rising, angry tide, a manifestation of the patients' long-standing dissatisfaction with the hospital. How could the knowledge that you, too, are but a dead soul not drive you mad? This wellspring of pent-up resentment is the real reason behind the riots that have broken out.

"As for the enemies . . ." Dr. Meloxicam shrugs his shoulders in resignation. "When it comes to the hospital, it made staunch enemies as soon as it decided to do battle against death. Given their natural dispositions, the patients decided to stand on the side of death, taking a position contrary to the doctors. The patients are unable to understand anything the doctors say, and the doctors have no way of comprehending what is going through the patients' minds. The danger of open conflict between them is ever present. Saving the injured and healing

the wounded has become a bloody, never-ending battle. One false move
is all it takes to destroy a career or even take a life. No exaggeration—
thanks to the patient riots, all research and production related to the
Universal Treatment Machine have been brought to a standstill! Like
the old fable about the farmer and the viper tells us, kindness to evil
will always be met with betrayal."

6

THE STORM GODDESS

The most difficult thing about being alive is being unable to recognize the environment in which you live and the self that exists within that environment. Overnight, all kinds of new things appeared in the hospital—including the Universal Treatment Machine—all of which deeply troubled many people. Your system of knowledge, life experience, and reading background simply could not keep up with the changes. According to Dr. Meloxicam, these new things were "created" by the Pool of Dead Souls. By this time the efficacy of medicine had expired, and pain and suffering once again descended upon the hospital, leaving you feeling disoriented, weak, and alone, as if frozen and tucked away in some airtight container. Everything turned pale and barren. You might still be alive, or perhaps you have been resurrected and are living another life; there is no way to determine which is the real you. You are deeply disgusted and resentful of this new reality, which has unexpectedly been thrust upon you, and yet there is nothing you can do.

There was a time when you underwent narrative implant therapy. "The Hospital" was a story directly implanted into your brain. But now you learn that you have been "living" in an artificial pool of "liquid," in which all of your experience has been condensed, the true sick ward in which you have spent your entire life. Are you really dead? How many times have you died? Who were you before you died? How was this body that you now inhabit assembled? Is your fate merely the result of a bunch of electro-neurons vibrating? Who is the real farmer, and who is the viper? You raise your arm and take a deep whiff to see if you can smell the stench of death—but there is nothing.

That is when Dr. Meloxicam makes a strange movement, like he wants to push you into that fiery pool of burning anger. Your conditioned response is to block him.

"What?" Dr. Meloxicam responds, shocked. "You, too, are joining the resistance?"

You look away for a split second and discover that the doctor is gone, disappeared without a trace, like a ghostly spirit. The only sign of him left is the flickering picture on the monitor, which keeps switching between the images of different doctors, some of whom you recognize. You see Dr. Bauchi, whom you met when you were first admitted to the hospital. You see Dr. Ornamental Rock, Dr. Artist, Dr. Violinist . . . you want to call out to them and ask what is happening, but they just stare blankly at you. You raise your fist and smash the screen. *Smash, smash, smash!* The monitor emits a series of sparks, followed by darkness and silence. You can't even make out the Pool of Dead Souls. Assaulted by a biting cold, you can sense the gaze of many eyes staring at you through the darkness, but you can't see them, so you run, slipping into the thick smoke.

You are still in the hospital, this vast entity from which you are unable to escape, like a dream within a dream. Right now, the most important thing is to stay alive, no matter what form that might take. You don't have the luxury of worrying about anything else. A gust of wind rises up around you, creating a surge of chaotic energy, transforming the thick smoke into a turbulent vortex. In a fit of panic, you don't know which way to go and end up slipping inside one of the sick wards. Patients lie in their sickbeds, completely still. You're not sure if they are connected via electro-nerve structures to the Pool of Dead Souls, repeatedly dying and being reborn. You scan the room for oxygen tanks, but they have all been removed. Something flashes in the corner of the room, but you can't tell if it is a mirror or a screen. You approach, only to discover that there, reflecting back at you, is an elderly version of yourself, with glowing skin and white hair—but there is something demonic about its appearance. This must be the real you. You remember being forty years old, when you were first admitted to the hospital, and although you were suffering from a terrible disease, you still maintained a decent appearance back then. Could that female doctor who said you were just forty years old be right? Could that be the real you?

You find the childish appearance of this old man horrific and shocking, and you feel deeply ashamed. Perhaps, like Funeral Artist, you, too, are suffering from premature aging syndrome. In some ways, facing this is more difficult than facing death itself. You are well aware of the suffering that geriatric patients must endure, many times worse than being eaten alive by a tiger. You pull a few white hairs from your head, hoping that might make you appear younger, but dark blood begins to ooze down all over your face. Even the screen is covered with blood. You can barely catch your breath, the bridge of your nose turns blue, and your appearance grows hideous. Facing the image of your nearly bald head, you imagine yourself as a young monk who has just taken up vows, and the hospital as a massive temple where you shall embark on your journey of self-cultivation. That helps make the blow a bit easier to stomach.

The image of someone else gradually appears on another screen. It is the female military doctor who saved you from "the sea." She is the only person in the world who feels like family. She quietly materializes and stands behind you, but you cannot figure out whether she is real or just a reflected image. She flashes you an eerie, seductive smile, haunting and majestic. Her uniform appears shiny and clean, but it also has an ethereal quality, as if she's completely naked. You are reminded of the Storm Goddess, who breathes the living air into idols, imbuing them with life. You immediately recognize the oxygen tank on her back and heave a sigh of relief. You and she are now in the same frame. You want to gaze directly upon her but dare not move, afraid that she might

disappear under your gaze. Filled with resentment, you instead whisper
to the figure on-screen: "Where did you go?"

"Did you use the oxygen?"

"I did . . . but then someone stole my oxygen tank."

"Oh my, how could you be so careless at a time like this!"

"By the way, I just saw a doctor. I think it was Dr. Meloxicam. He
told me that everything that has occurred here actually took place in
the Pool of Dead Souls. The patients' lives are all artificially created,
and there is an economic cost . . . those painful memories of the great
catastrophe have been awakened by artificial nerves. This is the only way
to treat illness and allow us to go on living . . . Is this the true face of the
hospital? Why did you save me? I wasn't consciously trying to escape
from the Pool of Dead Souls! And I had no intention of forgetting the
great catastrophe . . ." You try your best to apologize, as if washing away
your sins to prove your innocence.

"Did you mention Dr. Meloxicam? He was beaten to death by the
patients during the riots. Would you believe the words of a dead man?"

"I'm not lying, but then again, perhaps it wasn't Dr. Meloxicam?
Maybe it was some other doctor. I thought I saw a lot of familiar faces,
but it seems like something might be wrong with my memory. There
are a lot of things I can't quite recall. My mind is all jumbled like a ball
of sludge, but one thing I do remember is the fact that doctors cannot
die." What you really want to say is that, here in the hospital, perhaps
we should have more faith in the words of the dead.

The doctor looks at you with a questioning and pitiful gaze, as if
you are speaking incoherently after suffering the aftereffects of drowning. You feel like something out of Pu Songling's *Strange Tales from a
Chinese Studio*, but you don't remember any fellow patients who went
by that name.

"No matter how many unimaginable things you may have witnessed, none of them qualifies as strange," she says. "Everything the
hospital does is in order to 'survive.' The methods it uses to achieve that

goal are irrelevant. This is extremely difficult. In the end, no one can really save anyone else—all you can do is save yourself."

You muster up what courage you have left. "Did I really die?" You assume that, as a doctor, she must know all about the Pool of Dead Souls. There has to be a reason why she has been unwilling to bring it up.

"What's the difference between life and death?" she asks. "They are simply two different stages or states of life. It all boils down to a simple medical proposition. You can also ask, 'What's the difference between water and ice?' From the perspective of microphysics, it all comes down to a simple rearranging of particles. By the way, can you sense your own existence right now?"

". . . I think so." You feel weak and utterly exhausted, but you can still sense the flesh hanging on your bones, your blood struggling to circulate, your brain functioning, just barely anyway. You feel the pain every time you take another breath. All these sensations are created by the arrangement of particles within your body. Is this not how "reincarnation" is decided? Even if you are a dead soul, you are clearly still alive . . . or at least you *feel* like you are still alive. This medical technology works like magic, a fait accompli that doesn't require you to do anything. But then how is consciousness restored to the brain? Could it be the same method that witches employ when they blow on clay to imbue it with a soul? I wonder how much it costs each time this black magic is used? Those women you previously encountered really seemed like they could shape the times, though they were unable to relieve you of your pain, sadness, and fear. And what exactly does the Universal Treatment Machine do? Is it more effective than the Pool of Dead Souls? Is it more expensive? This hospital is turning out to be much stranger than you imagined. No matter how many thousands of times you live or die, you will never understand its true face.

"That's good, Little Wei. Look, everyone is carting off oxygen tanks, storing up water and food and anything of value to store in their own secret places. Would Dead Souls need that stuff?" She lectures you like a kindergarten teacher.

"I suppose . . . they probably wouldn't need that stuff," you utter, worried that she is leading you into an even deeper labyrinth.

The reflection of the doctor's face flashes across the screen for a moment, like a star shooting through a sea of flames, revealing a trail of gorgeous broken ripples. It is hard to differentiate between what is real and what is merely a reflection on the screen. All at once, the real and the fake seem to merge. With greedy eyes, you pine after her oxygen tank, afraid that she might suddenly disappear again, taking the oxygen with her. This world seems fundamentally unable to maintain its own stability.

"Are you okay?" She seems most concerned with her ability to save her patients.

"Not really . . . but it's okay." An overwhelming urge to faint screams from every pore in your body, but you need to be strong in front of your doctor if you want to leave her with a good impression. After all, she turned your life around, pulled you out from that bitter sea, interrupted your painful memories of the great catastrophe, and prevented you from joining the violent patient riots. You have no one else to rely on.

The doctor casts her cold gaze down your back as if inspecting a newly cast piece of iron before imprinting it with her stamp. As soon as you stand up, you collapse to the floor. The lack of oxygen has left you with low levels of hemoglobin, no longer enough to support your body or your will. You seem to be dreaming. You are drowning in a dark-red flood, pulled down toward death. A strange monster grabs hold of you. You beg the doctor to help you. You still want to live—you don't want to be a Dead Soul. It seems like your father is beating you, and you beg your mother to protect you. The doctor embraces you, but then she suddenly extends her hand to rip your heart out of your body. You don't resist and instead call out to her, "We are one! We are one!"

You suddenly awaken to discover the woman on the screen clutching her oxygen tank, her head tilted as she frantically inhales oxygen like a *Deinonychus*. After taking in oxygen, she eats a snack and takes out a bottle of alcohol. She resembles those women you once knew, so much so that she might be their reincarnation. She sees you staring at her but has not even the slightest sense of shame.

"Give me a hit," you plead. She sticks the oxygen tube in your mouth, and the sweet fishy smell of fresh oxygen rushes down your throat and into your windpipe. You are overwhelmed as you feel your addiction taking over. You ask her for a swig of alcohol, and she wraps her arm around you from behind and places the bottle directly to your lips.

"Whoever said you were my patient?" she asks.

You taste the alcohol and immediately feel the blood rushing to your head. Someone must have mixed it with medical disinfectant. The people here are not your typical doctors and patients. Unable to take it anymore, you fall backward onto the woman's trembling breasts.

"Drunks! Drunks! They are all a bunch of drunks!" She points at the shaky image on-screen and laughs.

"Everyone these days is a drunken ghost!" you respond. You think you may be a ghost, but as the alcohol goes down your throat, you discover, to your surprise, that you are a living person and not one of the dead. "Of course, without alcohol, at least half of the intelligent civilizations in the universe would be destroyed. There is no way for the Drake equation, which estimates the number of actively communicating civilizations in the universe, to be true." You take advantage of the opportunity to show off your humor in hopes of getting her to like you—but then you suddenly realize that the Drake formula might be directly related to the hospital. You look back at the image on the screen and see it gradually merging with the physical woman.

"Since you don't remember who you are, I'll call you Summer Stream," you suggest abruptly. "As far as I can remember, that was my daughter's name. As soon as I tasted that alcohol, the name came back to me. Once upon a time, I, too, had a family. I also experienced life as a young man. My daughter looks just like you. She used to work at the hospital, piloting a medical helicopter, and was considered part of the line of Storm Goddesses. After all these years, she must have grown up. But I somehow lost touch with her . . ."

As far as you can remember, the hospital dismantled the family structure, eradicating the very foundation of the nation and tearing apart the fabric of a society that had lasted thousands of years. It now seems that all of that was carried out in order to lay the foundation for the construction of the Pool of Dead Souls. So what exactly was that great catastrophe? Did such an absurd thing really take place? For the moment, you still hold out hope that patients and doctors can be one big happy family, staying together, keeping each other warm, standing side by side to overcome this crisis. The boundary once separating doctors from patients has already been destroyed, anyway. You figure that if you are going to make a move on her, you may as well take it all the way, so you edge closer to the woman's firm chest, pressing yourself against her as if her body is a cushion to catch a spacecraft crashing down to earth. Like a true professional, she wraps her slender body around you.

7

PRINCESS MONONOKE

You smell something. The dreadful stench resembles rotting seafood mixed with formaldehyde. The doctor sees helplessness and pity in the reflection of your gaze. With alcohol in your system and a fresh dose of oxygen flowing through your lungs, your blood begins to boil and rushes up to your brain. You are overcome with feelings of inferiority and resentment. You suddenly turn, throw yourself upon the woman, and, taking her head in your hands, begin smashing it against the ground. You never imagined committing an act of violence against "your daughter," and you find yourself breaking out in a cold sweat. Your hands grow weak as you realize you referred to her as "Summer Stream." She clearly didn't expect that and now appears angry. She extends her legs up and springs to her feet, knocking into you with a bang before straddling your body and slapping you across the face. She then takes a swig of alcohol, but instead of swallowing it, she sprays it into your face!

"You ungrateful bastard! How dare you treat your doctor like that! Didn't anyone teach you how a proper patient should behave? That's not how you act if you want to maintain a harmonious relationship with your physicians! You are really clueless! I guess I saved your life for nothing!"

The alcohol burns your eyes and mouth so bad that you begin to scream madly, but before long, you are crying like a baby. Eventually you reach out to her for a hug, like a desperate child begging for his mother's forgiveness . . . and after that, you begin to copulate like wild animals.

You penetrate one another without even bothering to take off all your clothes. You never anticipated any of this, and you are both pleasantly surprised and utterly shocked. In some sense, it feels like you have gone back to the old days, when you used to carry out mutual therapy sessions with your fellow patients Bai Dai and Zhu Lin. But just like before, the whole affair feels passive, mechanical, devoid of any true pleasure. Cold and barren, she doesn't even feel to you like a member of the opposite sex. Like a drowning man clutching at a straw, you cling to her, close your eyes, and quietly beg, "Please, don't leave me."

She feels more like a cold, slippery fish than a human. But wasn't that also the case with the other women you had relations with? Perhaps they, too, were wandering ghosts from the Pool of Dead Souls? Is it possible that you have been committing necrophilia all this time? But then, perhaps when two Dead Souls connect, they provide comfort and salvation for one another? Together with those previous women—Bai Dai, Zhu Lin, and the others—you attempted to escape from the confines of the hospital, tried to determine whether doctors can really die, to make it to the sea, to stabilize the number of patients in order to defeat the Axis powers . . . and now you find yourself with a middle-aged woman who resembles your own daughter, stealing oxygen tanks like a cunning little mouse, even engaging in mating activity. Such an unexpected course your life has taken; the whole thing is rather exhausting. But hasn't it all been inspired by the same motivation? You hope that the two of you can spend as much time together as possible so you can avoid the overwhelming feeling of fear and confusion and not worry about things like who you are, where you are from, and whether you are alive or dead. As for the discrepancy in age—fourteen years verses forty-two—that can also be put aside for the time being. But due to oxygen deprivation, you are devoid of strength and unable to concentrate. Gradually you find it more difficult to move, and you are increasingly frustrated by how clumsy you are. You begin to worry that Bai Dai, Zhi Lin, or Zi Ye might suddenly appear before your eyes. Spring Tide and Autumn Rain bear an uncanny resemblance to Sister Jiang and Ah Bi, who first brought you to the hospital. You need every muscle in your body to keep breathing. You gradually realize how much this middle-aged woman's body turns you on. At first, she is completely dry, but it doesn't take long for her to release a secretion, and she heats right up like a cup of instant coffee. That little detail makes her seem as real as an actual human. You realize that she can be penetrated from top or bottom, which those fragile young girls can't handle. From up close, you observe how her green military uniform shines. She is a general and has seen many battles. Her hands must have been stained by the blood of countless patients. Is that not what all Dead Souls most crave?

"Hey, do you feel any better?" You fiercely pound her, as if to prove to yourself that you have given her everything you have. Casting aside the fact that you are still not accustomed to this body, and that you are suffering from early-onset dementia, you put everything you have into this act of copulation. That way she, as a doctor, will be better able to get close to you and won't look down on you simply because you are a patient, a child, or a dead man. Yet she still grows impatient.

"Wrap it up already!"

She seems frustrated that you aren't masculine enough, unable to satisfy her desires. You can't help but think of the female demons in *Journey to the West*.

"C'mon . . . let's fuck!" you mutter.

"Hey! Aren't we already fucking?" She indeed seems like an old pro. Perhaps this is how she always behaves in bed. Maybe this is the real reason she saved you.

"Uh-oh . . ."

"Little Wei, I know what you need." She holds you tight against her body, like the women in your dreams. She seems to need you too.

"I don't want to keep scampering around like a mouse with oxygen tanks."

"You really are a naive child. Well, how do you expect to survive if you don't?"

"Isn't there a Universal Treatment Machine?"

"Who told you about that?"

"Dr. Meloxicam."

"So you believe dead people now?"

You have somehow made your way back to that elusive truth. "Yes. Actually, no . . . after all, didn't you say there was no difference between the living and the dead? As for the Universal Treatment Machine, it represents a new form of high-tech medical equipment, born of these chaotic times. Just hearing the thunderous weight of its name—Universal Treatment Machine—one instantly knows that it has the power to cure all patients! It really doesn't matter if they are alive or Dead Souls. From this moment forward, all will be saved! The gratitude that patients will feel toward the Universal Treatment Machine shall be boundless, and with its arrival, the riots and unrest shall be quelled. The relationship between doctors and patients can be repaired!"

"You really believe all that crap?" she hisses. "In the old days, young people graduating from medical school would break their backs trying to get a job in a third-rate hospital, just to bask in the halo of its glory. That's what originally attracted me to this job. Those male doctors really thought they were gods. Their every breath could save a life . . . but as for this Universal Treatment Machine? I heard about it, but I don't dare to believe it. One of the big takeaways I have learned as a doctor is that I no longer believe that anything 'universal' exists in this world."

"Does that mean that doctors can also become Dead Souls?" you whisper, playfully biting her earlobe. As the words leave your lips, images of Dr. Meloxicam and those other doctors' faces that flashed on the screen race through your mind.

"Doctors can never become Dead Souls." She pinches your tailbone as she reaches into her pocket to pull out a copy of the manga *Princess Mononoke*, which she shoves in your face, as if she wants the book to encourage you.

In the manga, a hairy female primate leads a group of male animals away from a lake and deep into the wilderness, in search of something they never find. It seems that if they were to find it, the entire world would be destroyed. And so, while they continue to search, they need to create a barrier between that missing object and the real world. This proves extremely difficult. You never imagined that the doctor would give you a book like this, but something about its dark energy grabs hold of you and gives you a burst of excitement.

The doctor narrates the story. "Everything has become unreliable. I've learned to keep my distance from my superiors and colleagues. I question everything they say. They brag about bringing people back to life, but I know they say that just to impress the patients. There is no guarantee that the Pool of Dead Souls will carry on. Those male doctors love to bullshit . . . some of them even tried to sleep with me, but I refused. I could tell it was dangerous. That's why I chose that critical moment to save you. They discovered something was wrong and ran away . . . anyway, you should read more manga. These things are the hospital's real blueprint. Patients used to be prohibited from reading manga. But you, Little Wei, are different from the others. Even the way you describe things like 'war' and 'the enemy,' it sounds like something right out of a manga. I love comic books. One day, back when I was young, I found myself on a twenty-four-hour shift in the emergency room. From the middle of the night through the early-morning hours, I performed three life-saving surgeries. I finished my shift at dawn, only to discover there were still six regular surgeries waiting for me, two of them to help impoverished children on welfare. I was in the operating room until 9:00 p.m. that night. By the time I got back to my dormitory, I was still so full of adrenaline that I couldn't get to sleep. That's when I discovered that copy of *Princess Mononoke* by my bedside. I picked it up and found it bringing me to tears . . . Little Wei, you are so young. Are you sure you have a daughter? Does she like reading manga . . . ? This is the kind of book you can only find in the hospital. In that sense, it's like alcohol. But let me tell you, manga and booze are going to be much more effective than any Universal Treatment Machine! Doctors may forget their pain, but patients are never allowed to . . ."

The only time you've seen a manga was when Professor Eternal showed you one. You are immediately struck with a strange sense of déjà vu, as if the filth of a former life has suddenly come rushing back. It is a completely different feeling than taking medicine or receiving an injection. You feel much better than before; you are breathing easier too. You go deeper inside her, letting her body become your place of refuge. Your pain and her pain merge. Yet you wonder why she didn't share this manga with you earlier. Would the patients have still staged an uprising if they had been exposed to manga?

"It's such a painful situation to be in!" you plead. "I want to die, but I can't. I used to think that one life was enough, but I've failed even at that! Life is so fucking exhausting. Why do we have to keep on living? Because some strange, intangible thing keeps bringing us back . . . now that things have gotten to this point, one must ask, If a patient can make it out of the Pool of Dead Souls, will he be able to escape from the hospital?"

You hope she might lead everyone out of this strange circle of life and death, even if that means going to that desolate place depicted in *Princess Mononoke*.

But once again, she ruthlessly crushes your fantasy. "Escape? You think you'll be able to escape wearing that cheap patient uniform? Do you have any idea what will happen if you try running away wearing that ridiculous outfit that looks like it's made from an old newspaper?"

With those words, she rolls off your body. But you still haven't cum. Filled with frustration and anger, you reach out to pull her back to you, but she nimbly evades your grasp, as if she's suddenly remembered the proper distance that doctors should maintain. Yet somehow your fingers reach her body, moving up and down and back and forth along the delicate crevice of her dry armpit, as if searching for evidence of silicone implants or machine-interface ports that might reveal her true identity and confirm that the act of intercourse you just engaged in was real and not just another artificial memory. Brimming with remorse, you wonder: If your birth and death are carried out in the Pool of Dead Souls, is there no more need for women in the world? Are they no longer needed to play the role of mother or partner? What then is your relationship with this doctor?

"What the hell are you groping at?" Summer Stream quickly slaps your hand away. "Those are lymph nodes! They're not 3D printed! . . . Little Wei, you just refuse to give up, don't you? Okay then, let's go look for this Universal Treatment Machine you keep talking about! But let me warn you, you're going to be disappointed! But before we go, I want to show you something else. Since you said that you have already freed yourself from the Pool of Dead Souls, I think it's time for you to get to know the real world. Let's find out if it's really just a mirror within a mirror."

8

THE ISLAND OF THE OTHER SHORE

The doctor leads you, and like a pair of lovers, or maybe two comrades in arms, you set out on a journey to explore the world. Only then do you discover what a large area the hospital takes up, much more expansive than the hospital you stayed at previously. At least from the outside, it seems to be a real-life brick-and-mortar structure and not a sheer product of someone's imagination. The hospital is built on a steep orange cliff, extending in all directions like barnacles. At first glance it leaves you with the impression that you have discovered the elusive Peach Blossom Paradise. Stacks of dull gray boxlike buildings rise up through the mist. Each building is a different height, spiraling up toward what are probably the sick wards. The overall impression is of a chaotic pastiche of World Heritage Sites like Angkor Wat, the Pyramids of Giza, and the Great Wall of China. Among the buildings are various reflective white metallic surfaces—those must be the various medical machines—sparkling like a sea of shining stars.

The elevator is out of order, so you climb the fire escape. As you ascend, you see a red, cross-shaped hollow steel frame built into the bedrock like a solitary radio tower. It is marked with the number 301. Not far off, you see the smoke from the crematorium. Violent winds whip across the sky. Then the mist suddenly dissipates, exposing the naked cliff. You gaze into the distance and see a vast open land with natural and artificial structures surging beneath a massive transparent hemispherical dome, which encapsulates the entire mountainous area.

There isn't a drop of water in sight. The plateau beyond the dome burns a fiery red, extending as far as the eye can see, seemingly into eternity. As it descends, traces of sand dunes, gravel, craters, cliffs, and canyons appear in rusty clusters. The horizon comes in and out of sight, eventually revealing a winding black wall. Isn't this the same red planet you saw when you first dove into the water? So, it appears to be real after all.

Although you don't see any yakshas, those malevolent demons might still be hiding somewhere, perhaps in a crack in the dome that protects this royal tomb. Positioned within this enclosure, the hospital seems to have been damaged. A continuous stream of black smoke spews from the crematorium's smokestacks, wisps of mist mixing with thick red dust and seeping in through the cracks in the dome, whipping around violently through the air, propelled by gusts of wind. Groups of robotic termites appear from nowhere and crawl up the surface of the dome to repair the cracks. The image before you feels right out of a manga. Standing amid this expansive space, you and the doctor feel like a pair of tiny insects. You are about to ask her where you are when you hear her gently whisper, "The red planet . . . Mars."

Deep down, you are utterly shocked. A hospital on Mars? No wonder you are unable to leave. You first heard the name Mars a long time ago: a rocky planet, quite well known in the universe, first discovered many years ago by Buddhist explorers. Its mass and gravity are relatively low, and with 92 percent of its atmosphere composed of carbon dioxide, it faces a severe lack of oxygen! Its surface is covered with desert and craters. There are no bodies of water. The air is thin and cold, with low pressure, and strong ultraviolet rays bathe the surface. Dust storms are frequent. These conditions make Mars unsuitable for biological life, yet somehow a hospital has been constructed here, oxygen and medicine have been produced, and the Pool of Dead Souls has appeared, all so the hospital can receive and treat countless patients. The whole thing is strange indeed! And here you are, right in the middle of it. How did you get here? Are you alive or dead? How is this connected to the story of that legendary monk who led a team of explorers to Mars . . . ?

You see another sign that reads **301** and smell the stench of war. You remember back on the *Peace Ark*, when Dr. Linezolid once revealed that humankind had already established a series of military field hospitals on Mars. This was apparently not a myth or some kind of sham. But who is at war, and with whom? The Pool of Dead Souls and the reality before your eyes converge, like life and death, the line between the real and the imaginary beginning to blur.

"Will we ever be able to leave this place?" you ask, wondering what military rank Summer Stream holds. Perhaps a major, or a captain?

"If you are talking about trying to escape Mars, you will need to climb over that black wall in the distance," she explains.

"And from there?" You wonder if the version of hell described in the Buddhist classics might really be Mars.

"On the other side of the sea is a place called the Island of the Other Shore. They say it is a place of *naiva-saṃjñin-nāsaṃjñin*, 'the sphere of neither perception nor nonperception.' But no one knows how to get there."

The Island of the Other Shore? The sphere of neither perception nor nonperception? An image flashes through your mind: a Cosmic Hospital, hundreds of millions of light-years away, woven from the spiral arms of all galaxies. You feel as though you once took a journey through that realm, where you witnessed countless patients struggling in a hellish place, dying only to be resurrected again to face another death, the cycle repeating, again and again. Is that the Island of the Other Shore? Or an even more expansive Pool of Dead Souls?

"Have you been there?" you ask.

"How could that be possible?"

"Why not?"

"There is a rule here on 301 Base: you can only go to places you have been before. But not a single person in the entire hospital has ever been there."

"Would you like to go?"

She stares at you silently, as if looking at a sacrificial vessel.

"Are you afraid?" you ask rudely, though you know she can see right through you. As if your question has upset something hidden deep in her heart, her face suddenly contorts. She whips out another bottle of alcohol from her pocket, like a weapon of self-defense. It seems that alcoholics might be the only ones to survive on this red planet of unknown origin—clearly standard medicine and injections aren't enough. It seems that the doctors themselves are leading the way with this new alcohol-based treatment. You wonder if Summer Stream might be a reincarnated clone, like Zi Ye. That would explain why nothing seems to bother her. Perhaps it's not just the patients in this hospital who are Dead Souls? No wonder a military doctor would also feel fear; they, too, are stranded here on this red planet along with the patients. There is no difference between military doctors and death-row inmates. She must be completely beside herself, losing faith in the hospital and, in her own strange way, betraying it by standing side by side with a patient who's unable to decide his own fate.

In and of itself, there is nothing special about resurrection. It's hard to say whether it is a form of reward or punishment, but the reincarnated body has puzzled humans from ancient times through the present. You know that the apostle Paul discussed this question in the fifteenth chapter of Corinthians: "But someone will ask, 'How are the dead raised? With what kind of body will they come?'" Paul pointed out just how foolish this question was, and today it all boils down to the same thing. You once learned from Zi Ye that reconstructed organs could provide patients with the opportunity to live another life. People could even receive brain transplants, and brand-new bodies could be produced in a matter of minutes. Zi Ye herself was one such example: Professor Eternal conducted computer-based gene editing according to a blueprint of her neocortex from before she died. He then 3D printed a multicellular entity so that she could return to the world after death and have a beautiful face and body to come back to. In simple terms, as long as you control the data, you control the cycle of life; with the right conditions, you can even create gods. By closely connecting the development of quantum computers to the field of neurology, incredible breakthroughs have been made, bordering on magic. Artificial synapses can replicate the brain's abilities on tiny chips. Narrative implant therapy can reshape dying patients' minds through the creation of a fabricated dream world every bit as vivid and exciting as a work of fiction, allowing patients to live carefree lives and opening a portal through which they can escape their disease, suffering, and even death. The process of uploading consciousness is moving from the laboratory to practical application: by scanning everything in a person's brain—including thoughts, memories, and even a soul—and transferring them into a data set, these can be uploaded to an AI machine in order to infinitely extend patients' lives. Consciousness can attach itself to a carrier such as cerebroproteins, so why can't it attach itself to a machine cortex? Cognitive processing can be accomplished through a new kind of cultivation that doesn't involve existing neurons. Life is determined by the mode through which it expresses information, rather than its unique hardware configurations. Re-creating life can be as easy as scribbling a few lines on a piece of blank paper . . .

But it is unclear what method the Pool of Dead Souls uses. It appears similar to the legendary hippocampus prosthesis, but several times its size. But if the hospital can resurrect the dead, bringing their physical bodies back to life, why doesn't it imbue these new lives with healthy bodies? Technically speaking, this should be a simple task, so why force everyone to continue suffering from such torturous ailments in the sick wards? Perhaps the hospital is determined to treat patients as if they're among the living. Only the living can experience pain, and only those in pain seek out medical care and treatment. It is a win-win situation for both doctors and patients and gives them both a true sense of the world. In short, the foundation of the hospital's very existence must never be threatened by potential collapse. Even here on Mars, the magnificent illusion must be maintained. But then what is the purpose of a Universal Treatment Machine?

"So why are we here?" you ask. "Did our spaceship crash?"

"I'm not sure . . . ," she responds. "This is what it was like when I arrived."

"Where did you come from?"

"That's no longer important."

"Okay then, I'd hate to ask you to say something that might put you in an awkward situation." You seem to be assuming a caregiving role, even though you aren't qualified, so you just imitate lines of dialogue you once heard in a movie: "From where did I come? Where do I go? Who am I? I often wonder what's the point of pondering these kinds of questions. There are no answers. If all of us are already dead, perhaps none of this matters anyway. Since we can't make it to the sea, we might as well find this Ultimate Treatment Machine. At the very least, we should give it a try to see just what it can do!"

"You're still hung up on that? Little Wei, you patients always over-simplify things!" She seems to be trying to regain her confidence as an angel in white. "As a doctor, I have seen much death. There's nothing to be afraid of. I'm the one who saved *you*, not the other way around! After all, what's the worst thing that can happen? Maybe you'll die again, but it's not such a big deal. It's no worse than an appendectomy."

You find it strange that she didn't use your earlier mating ritual as a metaphor. But then you realize that the two of you will have plenty of chances for more mutual therapy sessions as you search for the Ultimate Treatment Machine. That's better than nothing, and it will allow you an opportunity to release your frustration, but it is a pity that you won't be able to take your relationship to another level, something more ordinary and long term. What would that be? It would have to be more like the relationship between a father and a daughter, or perhaps between siblings. A slight fear wells up inside your heart. Here in this alien realm, nothing is ordinary or long term. The Pool of Deal Souls has transformed all relationships. But is there some deeper meaning behind dead patients carrying on as the living? Summer Stream probably doesn't even know the answer. The kind of doctor-patient relationship you have been waiting for might only be found in the pages of manga.

Another wave of reddish-black smoke surges up, enveloping the entire hospital. The desert wasteland beyond the dome fades, and the craters, cliffs, and canyons gradually disappear, as if they were part of a painted backdrop, and you suspect that this little island in the universe might be entirely man made. You follow the doctor down from the peak and descend into what seems like the interior of a tomb. You hear an army of the dead breathing in perfect, putrid unison, their breaths rising and falling from every corner. In front of all the patients, the doctor takes another couple swigs of alcohol, her face flush and radiant.

"Do you think I'm cute?" she asks. She smiles seductively, and you can feel her hot breath on your neck. Her combination of the playfulness of a young girl with the weariness of a mature woman leaves you utterly speechless. Could she, too, be contemplating the strange nature of your relationship? Perhaps she can't let go of those beautiful memories from when she was a doctor . . . ? You remember that synthetic human named Zi Ye, a clone based on the model of a female martyr killed by the enemies. You later killed her again and raped her corpse, and you wonder now whether she has been resurrected, and what she might be like in her current incarnation.

You gaze into Summer Stream's eyes. From your perspective, she is no longer simply a physical body that developed from a fertilized egg, but a woman imbued with rich emotions. Then, in an instant, she changes, transforming into something devoid of sensory components, her body consumed by fishnet-like holes. Her entire being becomes an open space, metamorphosing into a pure void. You are completely taken aback. Countless particles dot her material body, which is no longer young. These electrons and atomic nuclei rotate, the distance between them at least one hundred thousand times the nucleus's own volume. This woman is but an image produced by the laws of physics; her "true form" is fake. When you mated with her, it was nothing more than two piles of 6 x 10^{27} atoms rubbing against each other. You smell the scent emitting from her body and feel the warmth coming off her skin. You see the glitter in her eyes and hear the wild ravings dripping from her lips, the result of spinning particles devoid of any consciousness. Their point of origin is a mysterious big bang that occurred 13.7 billion years ago, the single most confounding incident in this world. A long time ago, these particles were scattered across trillions of kilometers of space in which nothing else existed except them. Billions of years ago, there was no indication that these cosmic ashes would one day form human eyes, skin, bones, and the hundred billion neurons that make up the brain. They were like ghostly phantoms roaming the depths of interstellar constellations, separated by extreme distance. As stars began to disintegrate, blasts of hot gas projected these particles outward, where they eventually came to occupy a tiny corner of the galaxy. Hundreds of billions of similar galaxies are distributed over a startlingly broad volume, its diameter stretching over one hundred quadrillion kilometers of space. Some chance occurrence caused these particles to gather in the ocean of a planet and, stimulated by lightning and volcanos, begin to form amino acids, laying the foundation for the birth of life. Over a long period of time, they roamed in the shells of trilobites, inhabited thousands of trillions of bacteria, some concentrated in the compound eyes of insects, where they witnessed landscapes from hundreds of millions of years ago. Some formed the yolks of dinosaur eggs, while others were later exhaled by great woolly mammoths during the Ice Age. Some transformed into sea ice and floating clouds, eventually forming raindrops and snowflakes. But today they have come together to form this doctor's body, giving shape to her eyes, tongue, breasts, colon, ovaries, vagina, and toes, and to her brain, nerves, and consciousness. These are what saved you, these particles that you had intercourse with.

Summer Stream's voice reverberates through your ears: ". . . the only difference is that the positions of these particles have been rearranged."

But is that a completely random process? What are its causes? Is your mysterious relationship with her one of the factors? You believe that the Pool of Dead Souls must be real, just as you have faith in the existence of the Universal Treatment Machine. Humans are nothingness; disease is nothingness. They have no essence of their own, but together they create a colorful and dazzling world. All it takes is a slight tweak in the trajectory of these particles, amid the vast space of nothingness, and shouldn't a new island be able to be created? It might manifest as a star, or a new medical treatment machine . . . or the body and mind of a human being. Now that doctors can manipulate atoms and edit information, they will never squander this opportunity. But what is the difference between what they will do and the choices made by the original Creator?

Once again, Summer Stream seems to be able to read your mind. "Don't think too much," she tells you. "You'll never figure it out anyway. The field of medicine is still quite superficial. Our relationship will never get any deeper or more complicated than it is now. Looking at things from the other side of the universe, Mars itself is the Island of the Other Shore. It just happened to end up here, accidently, an entire planet covered in red and devoid of light. White and yellow pills are scattered all over its surface, along with a series of black oxygen tanks. The red cross is the only source of light. No one is responsible for this. Don't blame the patients; not even the doctors have any control over the time in which we live, its place, form, or method. We are all like Robinson Crusoe. These things go far beyond the scope of medical skills and leave everyone feeling utterly helpless. So people begin to resent one another, yet they are forced to live together. But that doesn't necessarily mean they have more interactions, whether spiritual or physical. The more complicated medical technology becomes, the simpler interpersonal relationships become . . . anyway, as long as there is alcohol to drink, everything will be okay. I'm not like those other spineless doctors who are terrified of the trouble that dead patients like you might stir up. The only problem is that, here on Mars, alcohol is a commodity even more scarce than oxygen! Almost all of our reserves have been depleted. The distillery on the Martian farm is no longer in service. Only after we resolve our alcohol shortage can we begin to talk about things like food and water . . ."

"On the surface you act like a public intellectual," you scream hysterically, "but deep down you are a foodie!" You're not sure if getting that out of your system will relieve the invisible pressure that has been building up inside your heart. All the women you have ever seen have been obsessed with eating and drinking, acting as if consumption was the most important thing in the world, but it seems as if that was just a mask to conceal their reproductive instincts and avoid the topic of marriage. In this world, none of those things are necessary. But this obsession with food proved to be their weapon against reality. Unlike men, they didn't care about quoting the classics, getting into theoretical debates, fighting and killing each other. They were more vigorous and unrestrained, giving them a sense of liberty and equality, but this being a chaotic era, you can't judge them according to the usual standards.

You recall an old movie you once saw. Entitled *Alien*, it also took place in a dangerous, isolated island. A protective carrier, similar to a hospital, was invaded by aliens, and all the men aboard the ship died. The sole survivor was a brave heroine who, in the end, stood alone to do battle with the alien monster and save the world. Summer Stream is petite, is completely addicted to alcohol, and spends all her time lost in pain. Besides having saved you, it is hard to put a finger on what exactly she does, but when things come down to the wire, she will prove to be the strongest of them all, using all her energy to turn the tide, help the patients escape from the Pool of Dead Souls, and find a path to survival. Just thinking about that makes you want to stay close to her; if she could completely encase you within her, you would welcome it. You are terrified by the thought of her leaving you. Your relationship is not that of a father and daughter, or an older sister and little brother, but more like the protective relationship between a mother and daughter.

You again examine the cross hanging from her neck, which emits a red glow that scorches your blood.

9
VIOLATION OF THE DOCTORS
IN WHITE

Struck by a sudden urge to mate with Summer Stream again, you rush forward to embrace her. You absorb the life-force from the particles that make up her very body—the same power imbued in a living person. The experience completely differs from procreation, entertainment, or even necrophilia. But this time, in the middle of the act, someone suddenly grabs your shoulders and flips you over. Bearing the pain and shame, you discover an old man with a medium build standing over you. He has disheveled white hair and an unkempt beard, a protruding forehead, and tiny narrow eyes. A crowd of several hundred patients surrounds the old man. He seems to be leading them. The patients curse, jump, dance, and sing, each one brandishing an oxygen tank. Together they look like a dense forest of fruit trees. The patients dance in a fit of ecstatic release. You realize that these are the rioters who have been revolting against the hospital. Having escaped from the Pool of Dead Souls, they refuse to remember or relive the calamities of the past, and now they want to tear this hospital, which has brought them so much suffering, to the ground.

You feel an indiscernible sense of regret. Afraid that Summer Stream might be in danger, you shield her with your body, surprised that you have the courage. It is as if a fatherly instinct has awakened inside you, but driven by selfishness—after all, Summer Stream is your "daughter."

"Haven't you been wanting to know how doctors die? This is the most gorgeous sight you will ever see on Mars!" The old man starts to have sex with the other patients—tearing off their clothing and jostling around on the floor—as if going out of his way to show off his vigor and health, devoid of disease, certainly not one among the dead. He strips out of his patient uniform and slips into a doctor's gown. Besides the fact that he is not wearing a red cross, he is virtually indistinguishable from the other doctors. Some of the patients hold white doctor jackets, seemingly embarrassed to put them on. Together they break out in song:

> No need to dictate our medical history,
> We can now forget all about our agony!

You wonder if their electro-nerves and artificial cortices were really restricting these patients. And who let them out of their cages?

"Just who are you?" you ask the old man.

"You little bastard!" A patient named Rousseau kicks you. "Don't tell me you don't recognize the Venerable 'Stein?" Rousseau's face is covered with disgusting scabs and sores—he looks horrid. His limbs, torso, and head are decorated with a series of fleshy blue and red tumors, which seem to be rotting. This "Venerable 'Stein" must be the famous Einstein you have heard so much about, the leader of the patient rebellion, the root cause of the catastrophe that has led to these chaotic times. You once expended great energy trying to find this man—never could you have imagined that you would encounter him here.

The old man's eyes light up as soon as he catches sight of you. Desperately panting for breath, he responds with an arrogant tone, "That's right! I'm Einstein! But they like to refer to me as Guevara, an honor of which I am surely not worthy! On account of Mars's tiny size, the type of guerilla warfare we can wage here is child's play compared to what the real Che was able to do! But I'd like to speak frankly and share one of my secrets. I have a son. He has fallen into a bitter sea of disease and suffering and cannot escape from the obsession with death that haunts him. I have been trying to find him in order to rescue him from all of this and make sure he doesn't again have to face the fate of a Dead Soul. He has a bright future ahead of him, but he needs to stay close to me to avoid the glorious future the hospital has planned. It is a good thing that I have finally found this child—and he is you, my brother Yang Wei! I have long been searching for you, wondering why my child does not return. I sent you postcards, promising to send you money to cover your expenses. I said I would visit you, promising never to abandon you . . . but you never wrote back. Where have you been all this time? This dreadful hospital must have made you lose your way. I was so very worried about you."

His words come as yet another shock, yet they also trigger long-forgotten memories. You remember a voice repeatedly whispering in your ear, "My son, come back." It is only natural that you once had a father, but didn't he die a long time ago? How could you possibly be reunited on Mars? Having just escaped from the Pool of Dead Souls, you first met a woman who seemed to play the role of your "daughter," or perhaps your "mother," and now you have encountered your "father." One after another, the old man and the other patients embrace you. But this leaves you with a difficult decision. You don't feel the same sense of intimacy with the old man as you did with Summer Stream. Instead, you timidly address him in a tone of veneration, "My goodness, that outfit you're wearing really gives you a commanding presence. You look even more dignified than the Hospital President!"

This "Father Yang," who seems to have appeared from out of nowhere, addresses you with an imposing tone: "My son, only we are connected in both flesh and spirit, body and soul! No matter how well others may treat you, always be wary of them. Look at this outfit; you, too, shall don these garments. They were taken from the body of a doctor, indeed, stripped off of him like the skin of a carcass. Oh, how delightful and exciting! The doctors have been arrogant and domineering, running the hospital like it's their own personal playground, replacing people's lives with medicine, bringing us all to this ghastly place, breaking up our families and destroying our nation, forcing father and son apart—it is beyond evil! That is why we must tear the hospital down! It must be destroyed! The patients are now enforcing justice and carrying out the will of heaven! We have been hiding out here all this time, just waiting for the day to stage our revolution! The patients outnumber the doctors by the thousands. Why should we be forced to follow *their* orders? People's fates are cast in the hearts of the patients, not in the doctor's consultation rooms! We have emerged from the watery prison of death and refuse to die again! What do you say to this, my good brother, Yang Wei?" The old man is so excited he can barely catch his breath, and his chest sounds like wood cracking.

You gaze at the terrifically odd appearance of this old man and, realizing that he, too, must be a Dead Soul, decide it best not to respond directly. The Venerable 'Stein coughs up two massive wads of phlegm before continuing. "So you still don't believe that doctors can die? Let me take you, so you can see for yourself! They are in fact the true Dead Souls! Hey, what's all this wincing and mincing about? You don't need any mathematics to figure this out. All of those axioms, theories, rules, and formulas are bullshit, anyway! Doctors just use them to intimidate the patients. They have used those tools to construct the prison in which we are being held. The most despicable of all is mathematics. It doesn't even exist in the real world! All those mathematical principles they talk about are constantly changing. It's not like they exist because they were discovered by humans. Mathematics is just an illusion induced by haloperidol, like space, time, and matter—all cognitive illusions! No different than dreams, shadows, dew, and electricity! Under the cover of numerical medicine, the doctors can get rich and kill countless patients in the process. Whoever said I am a mathematician? Guevara would never stand for such an insult! My dear brother Yang Wei, would you ever claim to be a fucking mathematician?"

"Uh . . ." You shrink back, hugging your arms tightly against your chest. You sway from side to side, trying to block Summer Stream from the old man's view, but she gazes out from behind you as a putrid stench of alcohol rises from her stomach. She pushes you aside and steps forward.

Einstein twitches his nose and flashes an obscene smile. "My oh my, nothing to worry about, my dear brother Yang Wei. How could I fight with my own son over some middle-aged woman?"

Rousseau calls another woman over and introduces her to you. "This here is your daddy's girlfriend. Her name is Winter Dew. She holds double master's degrees from the Medical School, where she is one of the top interns and is currently studying for her doctorate."

Winter Dew has a dignified look about her and a serious expression. She clasps Einstein's arm. He takes a piece of candy from his pocket and places it into her mouth like a priest handing out communion wafers. This is already the second woman you have encountered since leaving the Pool of Dead Souls. She stands side by side with the patients. Is she, too, among those who betrayed the hospital? You flash Summer Stream an uncomfortable look. Her eyes are wide, and she gnashes her teeth. Winter Dew must be about twenty years younger than Summer Stream.

"Whoever said we aren't doctors?" The old man beats his chest like a hungry ghost. "Whoever said we are enemies of the hospital? Whoever said we are trying to revolt? This is not an uprising; it is a revolution! Patients make the best doctors! The patients are the true masters of the hospital! The patients will treat the hospital like their real home! The hospital has kept us locked up in an underwater prison, where we were forced to live like aquatic demons, forced to experience one catastrophe after another, giving us endless shots, forcing us to consume pills all the time! And it didn't stop there. Even the dead received no reprieve: every last corpse was drained! Without patients, where would the doctors get those red envelopes filled with bribe money? But who could have imagined that this pain and suffering would awaken the patients. We have decided to save ourselves, save our children, and save our nation! Did they really think they could deceive patients with small-scale reforms, separating medical treatment from pharmaceuticals? Humph! The uniforms are where it's at! Here in the hospital, it doesn't matter who you are. People only pay attention to the uniform! As long as you dress like a doctor, who can say otherwise? If you look the part, you can go right ahead and discuss organ transplants, genetic decoding, stem cell therapy, and all the rest of it! Don't think for one minute that we don't understand how this game works!

"But now that we know the tricks they have been playing on us all this time, we are determined to smash it all to bits! And then the carnival shall begin! We shall sing, we shall dance, we shall make music! It will be marvelous! I heard that the doctors just held their Exorcism Congress, and that they even had a variety show! How dare they treat patients like they're already dead? Everyone knows this is just a big show to please one man—the Hospital President. They allow a few patients onstage to show their faces here and there, but the doctors feel like they are the only ones who are truly alive. They hog the entire stage of life—how the hell can we stand for that? Did they ever once discuss this with the patients? Don't they always say that all are equal before death? These hypocrites in white lab coats have zero understanding of the suffering patients endure! All they do is observe, but we experience it! The doctors use fancy words to dress up bioethics in a flowery package, all the while forcing their patients to live a life worse than death and face a death worse than life! Meanwhile, those doctors spend all day drinking, eating, and having fun, as if they are living in an amusement park! To hell with that!

"Stop treating patients like we are less than human! We may be Dead Souls, but we have human rights! Oh, my son; over the course of my journey, I have discovered that each sick ward has been planning its own performance routines. Since the doctors have gone through the trouble of arranging such an elegant program, we as patients should do our best to show our support. Who knows? Perhaps our performance skills might even be a notch above. But don't ever assume that we are simply a bunch of fucking corpses! Guevara may have suffered from severe asthma, but that never stopped him from summoning his indomitable will to push forward and fight on to the very end!"

A violent fit of coughing erupts from the Venerable 'Stein's throat, like he is being ripped apart. Winter Dew hastily rushes over and gently massages his back. She reaches into his pocket to remove a bottle of salbutamol sulfate aerosol, which she nimbly sprays into his mouth with two good pumps. The old man snaps back to life and promptly rewards her with another piece of candy, then continues his dance, his white lab coat fluttering like a peacock displaying its colors. The patients applaud approvingly.

A strange terror grips your heart, but you are also excited. Something about this performance brings you pleasure, as if the pain of disease that has had such a firm grip over your body has been ripped out by its very roots. You are secretly thankful to be a patient, and to have escaped the Pool of Dead Souls.

Einstein pulls Summer Stream from behind you and pushes her into Rousseau's arms. He flashes her a mischievous wink. "What do we have here? A female military doctor? Not really on the young side, but she still has a cute baby face. Being sent here to Mars must've been tough. In order to take my own job seriously, I'd better let the patients make a good appraisal. She might not be worthy of my son. What do you say, my good brother Yang Wei?"

Shocked, you don't know how to respond. Rousseau rips the cross from Summer Stream's neck, forces her to the ground, and rapes her like he is wolfing down fast food. Rousseau contracted AIDS after selling his blood, and usually when interacting with Einstein in the sick ward, he was extremely even tempered, calm, even submissive. But when he engaged with ordinary patients, he was prone to breaking out in sudden fits of explosive violence, and no one dares to cross him. He bites at Summer Stream's breasts like a wolf, leaving a bloody mess. A thick pus oozes out of her, covering her abdomen; the mix of blood and pus makes her entire body sparkle and shine.

One after another, the patients take their turns. Summer Stream doesn't make a sound, her eyes closed, expressing the kind of strength and courage you remember seeing in movies. You stand there, forced to hide your anger, but another part of you feels as if you have finally been relieved of a burden. You now have a new protector, a "Father." You feel disappointment that Einstein didn't personally mate with Summer Stream, but the way things are playing out, while not perfect, have ended up being okay.

10

LEGACIES OF TERROR

The Venerable 'Stein leads the patients off on their journey. The bed-sheet you were wearing is ripped off your body and replaced with a white lab coat. It takes a little getting used to.

"Where are we going?" you ask.

"We are off to see how doctors die!" Einstein replies. "And to search for the Universal Treatment Machine!"

"Wonderful! I hear it can treat all illnesses and diseases. Once we find it, all the patients can be cured!"

"No. Once we find it, we will destroy it."

"Why would you do that?"

"Because we are not sick! The Universal Treatment Machine is the final veil covering the hospital's lies and illusions! Now that the Dead Souls have been awakened, we know what must be done."

You have no choice but to follow Einstein. The patients took Summer Stream as their prisoner and continued to rape her as they went on their way. They treat Winter Dew completely different. After a while, you lose visual contact with Summer Stream, but you still hear her screams. You feel bad for her but quickly put her out of your mind. Here on this mysterious place called Mars, "holy mothers" and "beloved daughters" are forever transforming, fleeting, part of the transient. For the time being, all power is in the hands of "Father."

Like the towers of the Efang Palace, the hospital buildings begin to shake uncontrollably. The dome cracks, pieces of it fall to the ground, columns and towers collapse, and fissures grow. The exterior walls are constructed from a special glass with the strength of steel. Alumina is injected into the silica during the production process, which should withstand the harsh and uncompromising natural environment of Mars, but even this material is unable to hold out. One after another, the robotic termites trying to repair the dome lose their kinetic energy and fall to the ground like rain. Meanwhile, in an underground chamber, crowds of patients flood in. The wave of them strides forward, stepping over piles of rubble as they take regular hits of oxygen from their tanks. Some of the patients on the brink of death jump down from their sickbeds and join the human train. As they link up with other patients, it is as if their batteries have been recharged, and they skip forward, marching with the rest of the crowd. Some patients wear colostomy bags, while others carry ventilators. Some wear pacemakers, while others ride electric wheelchairs. Almost all have tubes affixed to their bodies, which deliver blood, nourishment, and medicine or expel urine, feces, and contaminated blood. Quite a few seem to be in a trance, bumping into things like sleepwalkers or slow-moving nighttime predators, likely an aftereffect from having just emerged from the Pool of Dead Souls. They are like ghosts that have just been bestowed with a physical form and still need time to adjust, but this makes them seem even more qualified to be the true leaders of this hospital. They wear expressions that seems to say this place belongs to them. None seems to have even the faintest urge to run from the hospital, even though it has destroyed their lives and is now on the brink of being reduced to ruins. The constant jealousy and endless fighting that used to punctuate life in the sick wards has somehow transformed into a united front, partially motivated by a spiritual dimension. Their state of mind has undergone a transformation, as if, for the very first time, they have discovered the meaning of life. This alone proves to be much more effective in controlling the growth of cancer cells than any medicine out there. Moreover, it has triggered the release of endorphins, which have the effect of relieving pain.

Wearing a new set of uniforms, the patients stride into the hall. It is quite a sight to behold. They imitate one another and walk with a unified gait in an attempt to conceal the fact that they are sick, acting as if this is the first time they are able to fight for their own survival. Displaying a sense of comradery, like a band of brothers, they must shake off their previous state, in which they were constantly consumed by paranoid suspicions and factional strife, and begin to cooperate closely. And so they merge together to form a massive centipede. It is a scene never before witnessed in the hospital's history, and yet here it is, playing out on the distant surface of the red planet. The history of this planet is much too short, and an effective long-term treatment system has yet to be established here. But that is not the only reason why things are being overturned.

Many of the patients still have trouble walking, so Einstein tells Rousseau to round up some hearses and garbage trucks. Before long, he returns with a fleet of vehicles, and he and his henchmen call for the patients to climb aboard. Soon crowds of patients sit in rows atop the garbage trucks and hearses like a carefully arranged group of arhats, screaming and slamming into one another. As the vehicles drive along, patients reach up to the bulletin boards they pass and tear down photos of model doctors, vowing to find them and see firsthand just how these so-called angels in white meet their end!

The gang of patients eventually breaks through the layer of thick mist and rushes into the farm. Bushels of lettuce and other grains that look like rye rustle in the wind as if breaking out in song. Amid the trees, the patients discover what looks like a massive birdcage. People are chaotically strewn about within the cage. Waving their fists in the air, the patients surround the cage and compare the faces of the prisoners inside to the portraits of the doctors they have just collected. When they determine a match, the patients demand that the doctors come out, but the doctors are already dead.

But how did they die? The moment the patients escaped from the Pool of Dead Souls, the myth of the doctors' immortality was shattered instantly. Your heart is filled with a mixture of joy and sorrow. You remember your fellow patient Bai Dai, which leaves you with a sense of relief as well as sadness. You first met her back when you were initially admitted to the hospital, and she spent many years trying to figure out how doctors die . . . a pity she couldn't live to see this day.

An overjoyed Rousseau cautiously leans over to look inside the cage, like a hunter observing his prey. Slowly extending his head into the cage, he pries open the eyes and mouth of a doctor's corpse to conduct a closer examination. He takes out one of the photos to compare. "Ah, so this is the once-famous Director of the Emergency Room! In the past, you took care of us. The bulletin board featured your bio, which says that in the hallowed halls of the emergency room, you soldiered though the long march. During those critical moments that decide a patient's life or death, you always remained calm and collected. You made a brilliant split-second decision that turned the tide and saved the entire building from collapsing . . . you are a saint, but just which apostle are you? Alas, now you, too, lie dead. And not a pretend death, but the true, final end. One should never think that doctors cannot die. Once you strip them of their white jackets, their original form will be exposed and their magic will no longer work. Who are the real 'Dead Souls' after all? Shouldn't that be perfectly clear?"

Rousseau curses like he is trying to avenge all the wrongs committed in this world. He strips the doctor of his white lab jacket, rips the cross from his neck, and uses it to poke a hole in the dead man's belly and dig out the intestines. An engorged grayish-white bubble forms under the corpse's skin, and the crowd of patients applauds, but with a look of terror on their faces, like hungry ghosts that are suddenly scared away from consuming feces.

A sudden pain erupts in your stomach, forcing you to double over and collapse, vomiting profusely. It might seem like fear and

DEAD SOULS ✦   79

resentment are driving this response, but you have a look of ignorant bliss on your face. "Do the doctors have to die?" you ask, as if trying to cover something up. Deep down, it is as if you have been secretly waiting for this day.

Rousseau keeps watch over the doctor's corpse, coughing like a vampire before spitting on the dead body. "Hey, it's not that patients chose to live under this terror. The terror chose them. The Pool of Dead Souls left us with a single legacy of terror. During normal times, patients bow down to the doctors like loyal subjects, always submissive, forever living in fear. Is it not their greatest dream to steal the scalpel from their doctors' hands? They could treat their own illnesses in the way they see fit, never worrying about being the victims of excessive medical care. What's more, we weren't even sick to begin with! How could the dead possibly be sick? The doctors proclaimed us to be sick! They defined the standards for illness in the first place! The hospital is the largest terrorist organization on Mars, but it hides in plain sight, referring to itself with pleasant-sounding names like 'the Biopolitical Community.' The hospital controls patients' bodies. They even take DNA strands from rodents and forcibly implant them into us . . ."

"And they extend the claws of capitalism in all directions," Einstein adds, "controlling biomedicine, DNA sequencing, surgical machines, medical equipment, medical techniques, medical researchers, health organizations, medical newspapers and periodicals . . . if the sick are not allowed to go on living, how can this sham possibly be kept up?"

"Even when patients die, they force them to be reborn!" Rousseau explains. "That way they can continue their never-ending regimen of shots and pills. Even if they don't want to go on any longer, they must continue living—there is nothing more terrifying than that!"

"This is indeed the most fundamental social contradiction we face today," asserts Einstein. "Patients have become the hospital's gravediggers."

"Exactly! We must fight terror with terror!" Rousseau says grate-fully. "It is all thanks to your instruction that we have finally awakened! Had it not been for you finally standing up to lead us, who knows how much longer patients everywhere would continue to suffer."

This seems to answer most of your questions. You look at Einstein, who appears refreshed and full of ambition. You see Rousseau with a renewed sense of intimacy. Even his Kaposi's sarcoma lesions feel like your old friends. You now have proof that some patients may have actu-ally died, which sets you at ease. Rousseau flashes you a strange look, as if your relationship with him is even more intimate than the connection you have with Einstein. Feeling a wave of heat across your face, you turn to see the crematorium's flames. Their light is odd, twirling upward amid a cloud of black smoke. The crimson flames spit a series of golden flowers, each one the size of a finger, and emit a low hum that sounds out in all directions like the burning lanterns of the Buddhist Ghost Festival. The flames ignite your heart with a flash of fiery excitement.

The patients storm into the birdcage and begin stripping the physi-cians' corpses of their clothing before clumsily putting it on themselves. They rip the crosses from the doctors' necks and break out in a wave of thunderous laughter, pointing to these silly things. But the Venerable 'Stein is not entirely satisfied with the results of this mission. Now that the patients have seen dead doctors, they are intent on finding some alive. Einstein divides the patients into two groups: one to occupy the strategic base around the crematorium, the other to search for living doctors. You have personally seen living doctors, packing their things and running away, fighting with patients over oxygen tanks, but now they seem to have disappeared like ghosts into thin air.

You look for Summer Stream but cannot find any trace of her. It is unclear if she ran away or is dead. You can't help but wonder whether you really encountered such a woman. Was she even real? Assuming she existed, there is still no way for you to protect her. You will never save her, as she once saved you. The patients quickly lost interest in her;

they needed someone younger. This is the primary objective behind the patients' occupation of the hospital. Back in the Pool of Dead Souls, all sexual activities were strictly prohibited, but now the patients find themselves free to explore their deepest pleasures. They had long heard rumors that women were still being kept in the doctors' camp, likely one of the "special privileges" afforded to them. Feeling lost and resentful, you realize that Summer Stream never even said goodbye. Despite being her so-called "father," you were actually of little consequence to her. Women tend to be moody and unreliable; they are, after all, on a different level than you. You clearly misjudged her. In the end, she proved helpless when it came to your final salvation. If you want to survive, you will need to rely upon the Venerable 'Stein. A world without "fathers" is fragile and weak. Yet you can't help but savor the feeling of having been inside a woman's body. Just the thought of it sends a kaleidoscope of emotions rushing through your heart.

Seeing you in a daze, Einstein admonishes you. "What's wrong? Still obsessing over the little things, are you? Don't tell me you've mistaken the enemy for your father? I guess that last round of death wasn't enough for you, huh? It's only natural for you to feel a bit unfamiliar around me. After all, it's been a long time since we saw one another. We can blame it all on the Pool of Dead Souls. The doctors have a strict rule that prohibits the dead from having families. They really went way too far with that rule! What do you think, Winter Dew?"

Winter Dew looks like a teacher's pet who has just been called on. Brimming with a sense of accomplishment, she speaks as if reciting a text from memory: "Taking the risk of genetics into account, the hospital has carried out large-scale geneticization on all patients, cutting off blood relations and eliminating the ethical ties that bind families together. These might be considered drastic measures by some, but it proved necessary in order to implement a militarized management system for the Dead Souls that would prevent them from forming factions and ensuring they would follow orders and submit to treatment. But how could the deep ties that bind fathers and sons, which have persisted for thousands of years, suddenly collapse overnight? Brother Wei, you share the same soul as your father. Even though you have escaped from this prison, you must now reestablish your original genetic ties. Woven into that network of genetic relationships is a long-standing blood lineage and family memories, which carry with them mutual responsibilities and caregiving obligations . . ."

"I saw through the doctors' tricks a long time ago." Einstein laughs. "My son, I recognized you immediately. A wellspring of love and affection flooded my heart the moment I laid eyes on you. You are destined to take up the baton and lead the patients forward. This is the only way to restore our lost nation, culture, desires, religion, culinary habits, and way of life. Only then can we stick out our chests and walk proudly as new people. That's why I knew I had to find you, even if it meant being beaten to death. I am well aware of the terrible things the doctors forced you to do, even making you serve as the Team Leader of the Red Label Commando Unit. But it's okay, I forgive you. Who could have known that you were my son? But now you have an opportunity to redeem yourself. I may be unable to save others, but no matter what happens, I must save my dear brother Yang Wei."

Einstein's words brim with truth and sincerity. He is full of self-confidence, like an actor portraying a professor teaching an open-access course in a one-man play. He collaborates closely with Winter Dew, and she seems to depend upon him. But she looks at you in a different way, as if she is your "mother." Einstein heaves a deep sigh before reaching out to pinch your face, like he wants to test his son. Or perhaps he wants you to succeed by making you an offer to lead the patients in their search for a living doctor. Though still despondent that you have been torn away from Summer Stream, you are swept away by Einstein's gang of patients, and there is no way for you to act independently. You smell the stench of death from the bodies of the patients, making you even more certain that they are indeed Dead Souls. Dead Souls engage in strange acts. Once resurrected, they tend to come back to reenact the catastrophes that once befell them. You, too, were one of them, and thinking about that helps to ease your guilt.

11

CARNAL DESIRE

The Venerable 'Stein's gang of patients is made up entirely of old men, just like on that Hospital Ship. In your eyes, the two primary characteristics that define patients are (1) being male and (2) being advanced in age. Never are any other genders or age groups represented among the sick. But it seems that the hospital has made some special preparations for their Dead Souls, so all of these old patients smear medicinal ointments on their faces to resemble children and women. They appear innocent and harmless, making them more affectionate to one another and diminishing the terror that aging brings. They have emerged from the Pool of Dead Souls, and, tempered by their intense pain, their performances are natural and adept.

Even so, finding a living doctor proves to be a tall order. The doctors have shown they are not smart enough, and in the face of the patients' attacks, they should have known at least to take off their white lab coats and disguise themselves in patient uniforms. They could have blended in with the patients, but now the patients have started wearing doctor's uniforms—how can anyone tell anyone apart? Things have become so twisted and entangled that a new internal logic is needed to navigate this new reality.

On a few occasions, you catch a glimpse of a doctor, briefly through the mist, but by the time you rush over, he is always gone without a trace, as if someone is projecting fleeting slideshow images of these doctors. You look back at the Mars Hospital and notice that it is built against the side of a mountain. It has a partially cavernous structure riddled with complex curves and enshrouded in a thick cloud of mist. The mirage-like image is like an island floating on the sea. Unfamiliar with the environment, the crowd of patients keeps getting lost. You search everywhere but cannot find any living doctors. Suspecting the haunting effect of the Pool of Dead Souls, you lead the patients back to that television monitor where you once witnessed a doctor materialize. You intend to pull the hiding doctor from the screen . . . but the monitor is dead black and empty, so you have no choice but to return to the farm, where you see what appears to be a physician's corpse freshly sprouting up from the dirt. This doctor, too, is not among the living. His white lab coat has been ripped off, but it isn't clear who did it.

Clearly upset, Einstein admonishes you: "Brother Yang Wei, what the hell is going on? You're much too slow! Someone beat us to the punch! The question is: Who? Which sick ward struck out on its own? How come it didn't submit to our central command?"

You feel completely humiliated.

Rousseau suddenly exclaims, "I know a place!" He leads you and the other patients to one of the nurses' stations. There, several women in white, with red crosses hanging from their necks, appear like a projection, abruptly materializing before you. The patients' eyes light up, and amid a fit of howls and screams, they savagely leap forward like a pack of wild beasts released from their cages. They surround their prey and tie the women together with a long string of stainless-steel wire. You can rest at ease a bit, knowing that these women are medical personnel. There might not be any female patients, but there are female nurses. At least this will serve as something to show the Venerable 'Stein. Rousseau doesn't tear their clothes off. He allows them to keep their white medical and surgical masks on, but their large raven-black eyes remain exposed and seem to speak. Sticking out from under their jackets, their long legs sport tight, flesh-colored silk stockings, which resemble worms under the light of a fluorescent lamp. Everything you see looks correct. In your mind, they are the very definition of what nurses should look like:

always young and female. No other gender or age is possible. The very sight of them burns your eyes, and you are forced to close them, as if the nurses are a reflection of what is in your mind. Yet you dare not compare them with Summer Stream or Winter Dew. Based on your experience, doctors and nurses are two different categories of human, the latter being much more instrumental.

Einstein paces back and forth with his hands behind his back, admiring these newly acquired spoils of war. Then, with a sinister laugh, he addresses you: "My son, you have done well. Take this as a warm-up exercise. Did you think this would be like a dinner party? Take a look at yourself in the mirror! What have you done? Don't tell me you've only got the balls to fuck old ladies?"

You blush in embarrassment. You want to tell him that Summer Stream is different. She bravely saved you. That's when you suddenly realize that your "daughter" actually looks quite similar to the singer and actress Whitney Houston.

Rousseau begins to shout reluctantly:

Doctors! Doctors! Bring them here!
We want to wear their white jackets and hospital gear!

We want to see their corpses decay!
If they really can't die, then why run away?

We want the Universal Treatment Machine . . .
So we can smash it to bits and leave it in the latrine!

The patients join the chorus, screaming at the top of their lungs. One after another, they leap toward the nurses, and as they tear off their uniforms and fondle their breasts and thighs, they feel as though all their pain and suffering is released into the sea.

They viciously interrogate the nurses. "Fess up, where did the doctors go?"

"We don't know."

"They're usually busy saving patients. Isn't that what they spend all their time doing?"

"Their God-given mission in life is to heal the sick and care for the wounded."

The nurses shudder as they respond to the patients' questions, huddling together like a herd of lambs surrounded by a pack of wolves. They have never before encountered a group of such unruly patients. Through this strange game of exchanging clothing, the roles of guest and host seem to have inverted. Actually, no—maybe the medical personnel are the hospital's real invited guests. In the past everyone had it all wrong, but now, thanks to the chaos of the insurrection, everything has been corrected.

"Could it possibly be that only fate has the power to decide who gets to become an angel in white?" asks the Venerable 'Stein. "We are all going to die anyway, so why not break out of the sick wards and play the role of doctor for a while? We can live for more than one lifetime, so why not live it up?" He speaks like a gambler who's just hit the jackpot, flicking nurses in the face. Winter Dew stands by his side the entire time. She is a tall woman—more than double the height of Einstein—and she wears black-rimmed glasses that make her look educated, but her noble expression belies a look of sadness. She chews constantly on a piece of candy, as if to calm her nerves, and looks at the nurses with contempt and confusion. You steal a glance at her and can't help but think about your lost Summer Stream, how unfair life can be.

Rousseau gets right in the face of the nurses and, one by one, recounts the crimes they've committed against patients in the name of the doctors. With pus dripping from his cheeks, he threatens them, saying he is going to rip out their spinal cords and transplant them. The nurses break down in tears, but Rousseau is only trying to scare them and breaks out in a fit of maniacal laughter. He and the other patients lift up their white lab jackets and begin to rape the nurses. The patients are incorrigibly impatient. It seems that Summer Stream alone was unable to satisfy the common needs of the crowd of patients, and for that you feel ashamed. The patients try to imitate the various sexual positions they saw Einstein using on Winter Dew, which is apparently the gold standard. But many of the patients are not in good form. Some, suffering from bronchitis or meningitis, begin to cough convulsively, as if someone is stabbing them in the lungs, but they are determined not to stop because anyone who hesitates for even a second immediately loses his place to another patient.

Einstein gives you one of the nurses, but you are suddenly struck with a fit of performance anxiety. You remember a nurse giving you a shot back when you were in the inpatient ward. She had trouble getting the needle in and had to jab repeatedly, each time saying, "It'll only hurt a bit. Just a little pinch." After surgery, another nurse cleaned out your bedpan, mopped up your vomit, and consoled you with sweet, sweet words. You feel like these nurses are big sisters to you, but you can't help fantasizing about marrying one of them one day.

Rousseau tosses aside the nurse he is straddling and struts over to you. He gently caresses your nose, lips, and ears. "Now, now. Let's not be weighed down by any psychological burden," he says with a charming smile. "This is the coming-of-age ceremony that all patients must go through. It shows that we still have some human dignity left, and we're not just a random assembly of cold, indifferent biological molecules. We need to express our appreciation to all medical workers for taking such good care of us. We need to repay them by treating them the way they treated us." You see the carnal desire sparkling in Rousseau's eyes and try to sneak away from him.

But Einstein insists that you stay with the nurses. He wants them to lead you to the living doctors. Meanwhile, the gang of patients chants, "We're not sick! We have faith! We have strength!" After raping the nurses, the patients seem to have been reborn. They no longer look as strange and demented as before. Even their atrocious body odor and bad breath seem to have improved.

As they continue their journey, a never-ending string of patients drops dead from strokes and myocardial infarctions. Their facial features hideously contort, barely discernable as human. They must have endured extreme pain just before death, and those contortions are a direct result of the serious illnesses they suffered in life, which still continue to haunt them. The living pretend not to notice the pain the others are suffering. Instead they just peel the white lab jackets off the bodies of the newly deceased and put them on. It's always good to have an extra lab jacket. Then they kneel to write on the dead body: *Dead Doctor*. The crowd arrives at another patient area, but still no sign of any living doctors. Assorted medical equipment is strewn all over—electric suction devices, automatic gastric lavage machines, dynamic electrocardiogram machines, cardiac defibrillators, ECG monitors, multifunctional transfer rescue emergency beds, anesthesia machines, anesthesia monitors, x-ray machines, B-ultrasound machines, Doppler imaging machines, EEG machines, cerebral blood flow machines, pulmonary function test machines, ultrasonic diagnostic machines, positron emission tomography scanners, single photon emission computerized tomography scanners, functional magnetic resonance imaging scanners, high-frequency electric knives, microscopes, sigmoidoscopes, ultraviolet spectrophotometers, automatic cell filter machines, and nucleobase sequence cutters, among other assorted medical equipment—but there's no sign of the Universal Treatment Machine. As soon as the gang of patients encounters this wall of medical machinery, it is as if they have reached an impasse. They immediately retract in fear and stop moving forward.

Einstein orders Winter Dew to deliver a lecture to the patients. She takes off her glasses and ferociously wipes them with a piece of medical gauze before pointing to the wall of medical machinery and breaking into her speech: "Behold! These are the tools the doctors have used to blackmail and enslave you! They have handed the patients over to these cold machines. The story of medicine is no longer a tale of humans treating humans; it has become a tale of machines treating humans. Doctors have been reduced to an army of indifferent engineers whose only job is to manipulate the machines. So how could you possibly expect them to show you their good side? Doctors look at patients' brains as nothing more than an internal hard drive or file archive for storing memories. Disease is nothing but a breakdown of information or communication. All this is built on molecular DNA machines, which means only machines are equipped to retrieve information and treat other machines. The human body is made up of countless tiny, irreplaceable parts . . . it is not 'treatment' that one undergoes, but a rearrangement of experience. Doctors utilize computer x-ray axial tomography to analyze your brain structure in order to determine whether you have any natural predilection toward committing sexual abuse. They then use a cortical scan to monitor your thoughts, claiming that you have an instinctual tendency to tell lies. They use brainprint recognition technology to compromise your neural privacy and establish a new business model based on mental illness. They use genetic essentialism and neural determinism not only to reshape your body, but also remold your mind so that no one will ever again feel pain. Then they take what they determine to be the 'correct' system of norms, values, and judgments and interlace them into the neurological drugs they give you. Even ethical standards are worked into the design of these drugs on a molecular level. Once you ingest these drugs, you are no longer the natural human being you once were, and your view of the world undergoes a transformation. Through the process of DNA editing, every aspect of your lives is in the hands of the doctors, who now control how you live . . . and how you die. That's when the doctors flash a bright smile and explain that, although this therapy is expensive, it will ignite a new form of life for all of you, giving rise to a new set of biological values. This is what they talk about when they refer to the legendary 'perverted sick ward'! When it comes to the patient, what is 'the self,' anyway? We are all products of creation! None of you is your true self!"

Winter Dew has the inside scoop on the hospital and exposes all of its dark secrets. At first the patients are completely confused, but they quickly wake up to reality, and once the truth sinks in, they begin to cry. Before long, those cries turn to laughter. You gaze at all those sturdy machines and think that they are simply piles of atoms and electrons, yet for a long time they managed to take over your mind and body. You have trouble believing what happened, and a feeling of disgust wells up inside you. The information that Winter Dew shared is likely the kind of thing that Summer Stream would never dare speak aloud. In a beautiful act of resistance, Winter Dew has gone further than anyone else in her fundamental betrayal of the hospital. She is now studying hard for her doctoral degree, to be awarded by none other than the Venerable 'Stein.

"Everyone complains about how violent the patients are! But who has ever witnessed anything more violent than this?" exclaims Rousseau. "The doctors have used their machines to strip everything from us, leaving us with nothing! And they have a sophisticated explanation for everything! When we suffer the hunger of poverty in the hospital, they call it 'malnutrition.' When we contract HIV after being forced to sell our blood to survive, the hospital blames it on our own 'high-risk behavior.' These machines are proof of the doctors' crimes!"

"What the fuck do they mean when they talk about 'doctor-patient relations'?" Einstein adds, summing things up in his distinctive style. "It's nothing but a relationship built on authoritarianism! Doctors are a special class of people that has exploited its power to transform all the world's problems into 'medical problems'! That allows them to justify medical violence to exert their rule. This is the most dictatorial period of rule in human history. No one in the past ever dared to resist them. But once you strip them of their white lab coats and take away their medical machines, they are nothing! The Age of the Patients has arrived!"

With those rousing words, the patients surge forth, destroying the machines and, in the process, cutting off their last remaining escape route. Now there is no turning back. But then something strange happens: the broken remnants of the machines suddenly melt away and disappear, like the fishnet earlier. You are in a state of shock, but you have no choice, so you lead the patients forward, and like a plague of locusts, you sweep through the hospital in desperate search of a living doctor. Another group strips the clothing off the dead doctors' corpses. Isn't that the Editor in Chief of *Geriatric Health News* leading them? You approach to find out.

"I knew this day was coming! That's why I decided to help the patients!" the Editor in Chief explains, as if trying to curry favor with the patients.

"Just who do think you are?" you ask, in a state of confusion. "A doctor or a patient?"

"Of course I'm a patient!" the Editor in Chief explains anxiously. "I want to be a legitimate patient!" As he speaks, he takes off his white lab coat and respectfully offers it to you.

You have no choice but to accept his gift. "So it seems we are on the same side after all."

"That's right! I despise this fucking hospital! I know all the tricks those doctors play. I want to learn from Winter Dew, the true goddess of wisdom and justice! I want to expose all the misdeeds committed by those devils in white coats! Humph, the medical profession is the most disgusting and perverted occupation in the universe! They are all a bunch of liars! After people saw through their lies on the other shore, they could no longer stay there and had to come to Mars in an attempt to perpetuate their con. I was unable to write down what I saw and publish it in the newspaper. Instead, I was forced to hide the truth and say things that betrayed my conscience, which haunted me with repeated nightmares. I knew that if I continued on like that, I, too, would become perverted. All of this led me to contract a serious illness. Thank goodness I found all of you!"

Einstein approaches and, with an air of magnanimity, announces, "Let bygones be bygones! All who adhere to the path of the Dead Souls are welcome to join our ranks!"

The Editor in Chief is moved to tears. "How could I ever repay such a grand display of benevolence?" As he speaks, he returns a stolen oxygen tank to the patients.

"Where can we find the living doctors?" you ask anxiously.

"I shall lead you there," replies the Editor in Chief. And he pats you on the shoulder.

12

AN ELEGY TO VIOLENCE

The Editor in Chief leads the patients toward the highest peak in the hospital. You and the others follow him up the cliff.

"Behold!" he shouts.

You turn to see a parade of living, breathing doctors! Wearing a peculiar outfit over their large white lab coats, they are like a flock of mountain goats, climbing gradually through the billowing mist toward the peak.

Rousseau grabs one of them. "Hey, where are you guys going?"

"The main hospital building is about to collapse," the doctor responds with a look of horror. He stares in disbelief at the patients before him, Dead Souls who have somehow escaped. Only now do you realize that the doctors are actually in space suits. No wonder you initially couldn't tell what they were wearing. You figure Summer Stream must not have been kidding when she said this was Mars.

"So that's why you are all rushing outside?" Rousseau challenges. "Abandoning all the patients and nurses? Smart move." He extends his swollen tongue, which is covered with ulcers and white fungus, and begins to lick the doctor's face.

The doctor screams in terror. "We can't escape! The dome is equipped with barriers that were designed to prevent patients from escaping. The Directors of the Departments of Ophthalmology, Dentistry, and Preventive Medicine got out before us, and they were all electrocuted." He cries mournfully, begging to be spared. He points toward the burnt corpses hanging from the dome's ceiling. "Perhaps you have some other way to repair the hospital?"

"You must be kidding!" snorts Rousseau with a mocking smile. "Doesn't the hospital belong exclusively to the doctors? How could we ever hope to even lay a finger on it? But one thing is for sure, I will never be a deserter like you!"

You take a close look at the doctor and realize that although he is indeed alive, he appears weak, sickly, and demoralized. You go through the physician photos you have collected and realize that he is none other than the Director of the Department of Gastroenterology. Rousseau circles the doctor twice before stripping him of his space suit, lab coat, and military uniform, leaving his emaciated upper body exposed.

"Hey!" Rousseau calls for the attention of the other patients. "I would like to introduce you all to the glorious achievements of this 'model doctor'! According to the essay that accompanied his photo on the bulletin board, 'He walks slowly, but his gait is firm and determined. His gaze is soft, yet penetrating. He emanates boundless paternal love and the kindness of maternal love. Only a doctor whose heart is filled with the most reverential respect and veneration toward life can win the people's love and adoration . . .' Ah, such moving words! I wonder which apostle he is? Who could imagine that even a saint would abandon a patient in need. Instead, he just took to his heels like the others." The doctor breaks out in a cold sweat, utterly embarrassed.

The Venerable 'Stein personally oversees the interrogation. The Director of the Department of Gastroenterology confesses that the surviving doctors divided themselves into several different factions, which eventually regrouped into gangs that occupied various sick wards. While the doctors stubbornly fought on, in reality, they were preparing for their escape. Violent conflict broke out between different factions of doctors over oxygen tanks. Large numbers of doctors had indeed died, but there was another explanation for their deaths.

"We were suddenly afflicted with a particularly dangerous infectious disease," the doctor explains. "We had no means to resist. It was possibly a mutant artificial bacteria released on Mars by a spacecraft carrying perfluorocarbons, which transformed from environmental modifiers into deadly killers."

"Is such a thing even possible?" Einstein asks in surprise. "How come I never heard of this? How would you doctors like to take a dip in the Pool of Dead Souls to feel what it's like? You have only yourselves to blame. Take a look: you angels in white seem to be living comfortable lives, spending all your time in nice, clean, sterile rooms, conducting patient consultations through online visits, sensors, and TV screens. You never need to touch any actual patients, and in this isolation, your immune systems inevitably weaken, leaving you particularly susceptible to bacterial infections. Meanwhile, living in an environment of dirt and filth has allowed patients to build up ironclad immune systems."

"That's right," Winter Dew adds enthusiastically. "According to my investigations, the doctors were afflicted by a type of bacteria that was specifically designed to attack the unique DNA markers found in doctors. In terms of the anthropological physiology of human beings, doctors are fundamentally different from patients. They have used bioengineering technology to transform themselves to the point that they are now genetically superior to patients. This is a form of eugenics. I am the only one to have rejected it."

"Doctors want to hold on to their superior position," adds the Editor in Chief. "They like to think of themselves as better than normal people. In fact, they don't even consider themselves in the same category as 'people.'"

"Indeed, they really aren't 'people,'" exclaims Rousseau. "They are devils that like to dress up as gods. But they never imagined that they would end up reaping what they sowed."

One of the riddles that has been haunting you has finally been solved. You were always confused about how the patients' rebellion was able to defeat the doctors. Under normal circumstances such a thing would have never been possible. But now you know that the doctors' genes have undergone a remodification process. They are no longer like normal humans; this has left them defenseless against special targeted forms of bacterial attack. They get infected with disease and die, one after another, giving the patients the opportunity to emerge victorious. The suffering that the doctors were forced to endure was all because artificial interventions into evolution went too far. As doctors, they should have been respectful, discreet, and cautious, but instead they became extremely ostentatious and unbridled, leading to the current situation. The patients have won. The weak have conquered the strong. But it was not Einstein who launched the rebellion—it was someone else.

"Once we find the Universal Treatment Machine," the Director of the Department of Gastroenterology utters listlessly, "we will cure all the doctors' illnesses."

Rousseau jokingly smacks him. "Oh, so the doctors built the Universal Treatment Machine for themselves! Once you people are stripped of your white lab coats, what do you have left?"

"Can someone tell me just where exactly we can find this Universal Treatment Machine?" you ask softly.

A look of fear flashes over the face of the Director of the Department of Gastroenterology. "The Hospital President knows. We are waiting for him to arrive."

"No need to wait," says Winter Dew. "Join us. You'll only find the Universal Treatment Machine if you join forces with the patients."

"Humph, let me tell you," Rousseau says, "the patients have immunity, the patients are healthy, the patients are doctors . . . and as soon as we find the Universal Treatment Machine, we will destroy it." He waves a stolen white medical jacket in the air, like a strongman lifting a heavy weight over his head.

The doctor recoils in fear. Without his uniform, he is completely defenseless. Einstein snickers and whispers something to you. As it turns out, they are not going to stop with stripping the doctor of his clothes. You are momentarily in a state of shock, but you dare not go against orders, so you grit your teeth as the patients tie down the Director of the Department of Gastroenterology and wheel him into the decompression chamber. This experimental space was originally created to research the negative effects of outer space on the human body. The doctor knows what is about to transpire and begins to howl like a pig being slaughtered. He changes his tune and expresses his willingness to be a patient, even claiming that he is willing to give up on the Universal Treatment Machine.

"The only thing we are trying to do," explains Einstein, "is to test out the actual differences between doctors and patients. This has been a long-standing mystery."

While you remain apprehensive about conducting this "test," Rousseau hastily smashes the start button, gleefully exclaiming, "Okay, now it's time to enjoy an improvisational performance by a dear member of the intellectual class!"

The air in the chamber is extracted, but not all at once. It is a gradual process accompanied by a low hissing sound. The Director of the Department of Gastroenterology begins to sweat. His neck contorts. He goes into a series of convulsions. His breathing becomes strained and heavy before slowing down. He loses consciousness. His abdomen suddenly expands and bursts open, exposing strings of greenish-black intestines. Who could have imagined that doctors were so filthy inside? Normally their oversize white lab coats cover up the disgusting things lurking within. This is more worthy of showing off than death itself. But for the time being, the doctor is still not dead. His body twitches and convulses a few more times, and the patients gather round to watch. At first, they are terrified by the sight, some of them even afraid to open their eyes, but it doesn't take long for them to grow enchanted by the intoxicating spectacle playing out before them. They wave their arms and stamp their feet, dancing wildly like a primitive tribe of hunters enjoying the sight of a deer being captured and slaughtered. Rousseau is so turned on that he starts masturbating, but that's not enough, so he pushes another patient to the ground, tears off his white lab coat, and mounts him from behind. Other patients begin to gang-rape the nurses. The scene brims with chaos and passion.

You are struck with the sensation of some foreign object being lodged in your throat. You feel as if you yourself are locked inside the chamber, that you are the one who should die and not the doctor. But then, in the blink of an eye, you are struck by a poetic, blissful feeling, as if you are enjoying an unforgettable spring outing. You are finally witnessing, with your own eyes, the process of how a doctor dies. Unlike those illusions in the past, this is the real thing! How easy death comes for this magician who toys with life, like flicking a piece of dust off one's clothing. Although they say that the doctors have evolved into another species of human, in death they are no different from any patient. They are not gods, nor are they demons, nor those legendary extraterrestrials, biochemical humans, or robots. They may have upgraded themselves, but they are still unable to escape the shells of flesh to which they are bound. In your eyes, doctors are mysterious sorcerers who dominate and control the minds and bodies of others, forcing patients daily to face the reality of their suffering and show the courage needed to challenge pain and death, asking patients to seek self-redemption in the Pool of Dead Souls, which the doctors use to upgrade themselves into priests who carry the red cross, transforming the practice of medicine into a heavenly ladder that leads to holy miracles. Standing before these men in those imposing white lab coats, no patient dares to talk back or say anything that might be construed as blasphemous against the Holy Spirit. But in this moment, you realize that they can't even save themselves. Now you know why Einstein insisted on finding a living doctor. This is sure to shatter whatever remnants of the illusion were still alive in the patients' hearts, this scar left behind from the Pool of Dead Souls.

You realize that Einstein is indeed a most unusual man. It was no easy feat to destroy the myths and superstitions about doctors that had so long persisted. Patients are undeniably the most filthy creatures in this world, the trash of the universe. One look at their disgusting bodies is enough to make you want to vomit. Even their family members fear and avoid them! Doctors, on the other hand, look at them as a juicy meal on a plate, like a big, bloated, pus-filled tumor to play with. It is utterly perverted and disgusting, yet somehow, they end up being objects of admiration and respect! Aging and death are part of the natural order, mechanisms by which species are selected and eliminated according to the laws of nature. While the Creator would never give up on them, the doctors remain intent on trying to change these laws so that people can live longer lives and the dead can be resurrected, as if trying to create a perpetual motion machine. The insane human race is the only one ever to attempt such a thing—no other species would even dare!

But Einstein saw all of this clearly. He knew that these insane, unnatural experiments would ultimately come to an end. The fate of the doctors was long decided by their own actions. By daring to resurrect the Dead Souls, they had already broken the natural laws. Once the Dead Souls were reborn, how could anyone expect any other outcome than what you now see before you? How could they not have anticipated this? But don't blame the patients! After all, they view death in a completely different way than the doctors do.

Once the Director of the Department of Gastroenterology has been executed, Rousseau takes out several internists to dissect their bodies. He tries to recruit a few patients to lend a hand, but none of them dares to participate. They simply aren't used to this sort of thing. In the past, the doctors always dissected the patients, but no patient has ever performed an autopsy on a doctor! It will take time to erase the Dead Souls' memories.

The autopsies don't reveal any tangible differences between doctors and patients. Winter Dew carefully observes each autopsy, extracting data and keeping notes, the kind of experience and knowledge that she would never have gained while making her normal rounds. Ultimately, she benefits most from this series of doctor dissections, and she can barely contain her excitement.

The death of these doctors has brought the patients much satisfaction and encouragement. Now that they have finally authenticated this important phenomenon as fact, they can heave a collective sigh of relief, as if, for the very first time, they finally have a renewed sense of self-confidence about their treatments. They are more united than ever before, like tightly packed pomegranate seeds. Their ambition is clearer than ever, driving them to seek out even more living doctors, not only to strip them of their white lab jackets, but to see how they die, to bear witness to the fact that Dead Souls are not limited to patients. All it takes is a little bit of violence, and they can create a catalyst and an adhesive that enables everyone to walk hand in hand toward the future. They fought their way into the hospital, and now their drive has become increasingly focused. The hospital used its inherent and unwavering death instinct to create a confrontational yet unified doctor-patient community, and through the struggle between doctors and patients, they have achieved harmony.

13

FIGHTING SOLDIERS

On the march forward, you walk alongside Winter Dew. Craving a deeper connection with her, you venture, "It seems that the war has returned?"

"That's right," she exclaims enthusiastically. "You noticed too? No wonder you're Einstein's son! The war never ends. But there is a process of understanding one has to go through. The Mars Hospital is actually a military hospital. We work on military medical science."

"That sounds about right."

"That's actually what I wrote my doctoral dissertation on," she announces proudly, gleefully popping a piece of candy into her mouth. "Brother Wei, let me tell you, the fundamental nature of medicine is war. Treatment is a battle. Medical models are identical to war models. Patients always underestimate their own bodies, not realizing that they are actually the most ferocious enemy out there. Just think about how horrific that must be! Here in the hospital, it's all about the division between 'us and them.' Everything boils down to brutal killing in the name of victory. The sick wards are like the battle trenches; seeing the doctor is like going into battle. Just listen to the kind of terminology those of us in the medical field are always using: 'defense,' 'offense,' 'invasion,' 'sneak attack,' 'resistance,' 'eradicate,' and so on. It is a world in which 'you must die for me to live,' and there is no such thing as peaceful coexistence. Patients claim that their doctors are cold and indifferent, but that is the true face of all doctors. In their eyes, patients' diseased bodies have been possessed by demons. Those dirty monsters disguise themselves as microorganisms. They are creatures of ill will that only reveal their true, evil form under the lens of the microscope. They hide themselves away, deep in the folds of your clothing. They enter your bloodstream through your oral cavity, where they wage their attack. The doctors are sometimes also referred to by another name, the 'exorcists.'"

"What you are describing indeed sounds like a very bloody scene." You feel this woman's air of authority, but when dealing with practical matters of everyday life, she somehow comes off as clumsy and ill prepared.

"Only the national defense industry is worthy of being mentioned in the same breath with the medical industry." She looks down at you, her words brimming with confidence and eloquence. "When you look at the pathetic history mankind has left behind, it boils down to a history of warfare, which is, in fact, a history of medicine. Doctors and patients are both soldiers in this struggle. Carl von Clausewitz once said that war is an extension of politics. In reality, it is an extension of the body. Everything that the field of medicine does is aimed at defending the accumulated piles of microscopic atoms and molecules that make up the human body . . . Brother Wei, just open your eyes and take a look—the most amazing archeological discoveries had nothing to do with any pharaoh's tomb, Incan ruins, or Chinese oracle bones; it was instead the discovery of how the ancient Sumerians prevented infectious diseases from decimating their military, how the ancient Egyptians removed skull fragments from soldiers, how the ancient Romans invented tourniquets to prevent their soldiers from bleeding out, and how the ancient Indians amputated limbs of wounded soldiers . . . the single most incredible contribution from the Renaissance period was the employment of gunpowder during military surgery. Without these innovations, humankind would have long been eradicated by war. There would be no great geological discoveries, capitalist revolution, industrial revolution, socialist revolution, or the kind of fiery, passionate lives that we live today. World War I brought diagnostic microbiology to front-line hospitals, World War II ushered in the age of antibiotics, and now doctors everywhere are clamoring for the outbreak of World War III."

"Is what we see playing out now World War III?" you ask, trying to sound as humble and flattering as possible. You seem to understand that, in war, when one side attacks, the opposing side always fights back. If one side is particularly vicious in its assault, the other side is sure to strike with even more ferocity. There are no innocent victims: the two sides' cycle of ever-increasing violence comprises the history of medicine, and so the vicious cycle continues, on and on for all eternity. You have already lived through two world wars, but soon there will be a third, a fourth, a fifth . . . isn't that how it always goes?

"Such a smart one you are!" she compliments you. "I guess the apple never falls far from the tree."

Her kind words leave you embarrassed. "I have seen life and death . . . I have saved people, and I have killed people. In some sense, the act of taking a life is the same as saving a life. Doctors and patients are sworn enemies. The sick ward is a hotbed of terror. To check into the hospital is to approach the precipice of death. But dying once is not enough: one must also die a second time, a third time, a fourth time, and continue dying for all eternity. I understand. Otherwise, where would the Pool of Dead Souls find fresh material? Patients begin to shudder the moment they lay eyes on a doctor, just as doctors are constantly on tenterhooks when face to face with patients. Bound together by a similar fate, these two eventually turn on one another and become enemies. Terror and fear arrive at their tipping point, and once the balance is disturbed, the result is murder, riots, revolution, and war. And here in the hospital, these things happen over and over again."

"That's why being a doctor can become addictive," she says. "The field of medicine doesn't care about objective truth and neutrality. That's what attracted me to this field in the first place."

Confused, you ask, "Then why did you decide to stop practicing medicine?"

She is taken aback; it seems you have asked an inappropriate question. "I simply realized that doctors are not the good soldiers I imagined them to be. They may be ambitious, but they are incapable, devoid of talent, hypocritical, and cowardly."

"How can you be sure?"

"All it takes is one month in the hospital, and you will discover several strange yet common occurrences. For example, doctors in the psych ward regularly prescribe antidepressants to their patients, while they themselves never take them, because they know their effectiveness is only a little bit better than that of placebos. Cardiologists never take statins because they know that they barely have any impact when it comes to lowering the risk of heart disease and strokes, but they do carry a long list of serious side effects. Urologists never test their prostate-specific antigen—PSA—because they know that it is impossible to provide a standard value useful in diagnosing cancer. In fact, its level of accuracy is more or less what you'd get by flipping a coin. Even when surgeons suffer from unbearable back pain, they refuse to undergo lumbar discectomy because they know the failure rate is simply too high. And then there are those doctors from the Rheumatology Department, who personally refuse to have x-rays, and those sleep doctors who never take sleeping pills. These are all things I personally witnessed during my residency. The whole thing is really demoralizing!"

"The more of your life you dedicate to medicine, the more suspicious you become of the whole enterprise! It's all bullshit. Patients, on the other hand, have long grown accustomed to all this." You wonder if Winter Dew has realized all the paradoxes and questions haunting the hospital, like Summer Stream has. Then again, Winter Dew is more of a perfectionist. But the question still lingers: Do all doctors really come from patients?

"When I was doing research under Professor Eternal, I discovered that seventy percent of all academic research is never made public,"

Winter Dew confesses. "Most of the articles written by doctors only reflect the negative and corrupt side of medical science, which would not be in the hospital's interest if published. Take for example a study in which one hundred patients suffering from severe coronary artery disease were divided into two groups: one was sent for surgery while the other was forced to do daily exercise. One year later, the recovery rate for the participants from the first group that underwent surgery was seventy percent, compared to an eighty-eight percent recovery rate for the patients who did not undergo surgery but exercised every day. These statistics cannot be made public because of the high income that doctors get from performing surgery. Other stubborn illnesses like herniated discs can be gradually cured with self-care and home treatment, thanks to the spine's incredible ability to heal. The immune system actually views the dislocated portion of the disk as a foreign body and uses enzymes to dissolve it. But doctors never share this knowledge with their patients. Instead, they tell them that their condition will never improve on its own, and the best option is surgery."

"And that's why you decided to walk away from the battlefield . . ." You can't help but feel it is a bit of a shame.

"I discovered that this is a battle the doctors will never win. They are all charlatans, whereas the patients are the true warriors! I realized that the only way I would ever complete my doctoral dissertation would be to join the ranks of the brave and true patients! Your father helped open my eyes to all of this. And for the first time, I realized that doctors and patients are on very different paths in life. One's perspective on death is completely different, depending on whether one is standing beside the sickbed or in it. Back when I was a doctor, I often handed out orders and made casual decisions that affected whether a patient would live or die—I thought I was a god. But once I found myself in the patient's shoes, I discovered something very different. I finally understood that the pain that patients experience is completely different from what doctors imagine. Those little bits of clinical knowledge that doctors possess might look impressive, but they don't amount to much. Those doctors are basically paper tigers, always talking about how much they want to start World War III, but it is empty talk. Nobody fears death more than doctors. I hate the fact that I used to be one of them! In reality, I was already suffering from a serious disease, and my father was personally treating me."

"Really, he knows how to do that?"

"If I may speak frankly, my father was not a very good doctor. It was because of him that I learned to put up with being repeatedly misdiagnosed. I grew accustomed to being disrespectfully called by my first name. I put up with constant ridicule and neglect. It was precisely this experience that allowed me to understand the kind of frustration that patients feel when they go to the doctor. And it is precisely this sense of frustration that ignites their bravery, spurring them to march forward! The real reason your father launched this revolution was to fight fire with fire, using war to end all war and bring eternal peace to the hospital. Your father was actually a great pacifist. The patient organization here is the largest peace defense coalition on Mars, and now the primary object of my investigation. I want to become a true soldier and inscribe my yearning for peace into my thesis! Brother Wei, I can't tell you how much gratitude I feel toward your father. He has been a mentor for me, not only in my academic studies, but also in life."

14

FLOWER COMMANDOS

Einstein mobilizes the patients with a rousing speech: "We must adhere to a fixed strategy! When it comes to the hospital's future, the patients must be in charge! How do we define who is a patient, you ask? Patients are those who have already been through fire and water, experiencing all the dangers life throws our way, from the cradle to the grave! The doctors have too many attachments to this world and are always busy pursuing simple material things like refrigerators, automobiles, and houses. They claim that they are all-powerful, but when it comes to those most critical moments, they bury their heads in the sand like a bunch of scared ostriches. They understand life too well, always shrewd and calculating when it comes to saving their own skins! But that only makes them a bunch of scaredy-cats when it comes to their own mortality—in reality, they are the ones most deserving of death! But what do we, the Dead Souls, have to fear? We aren't afraid of doctors! Patients who have yet to experience death are restricted by the sick ward's rules and regulations, but none of those apply to patients who have died. That said, we still need to leave a few of the living here in the hospital for later use. After all, there is a reason why curiosity exists . . ." When he mentions saving a few of the living, you assume he is referring to Winter Dew, the Editor in Chief, and the nurses.

As Einstein gives the order to attack the entrenchments where the doctors are hiding, the patients break out into song:

The diplomatic envoy faces down the army,
the governor stands against the bandits.
The soldiers are strong and follow orders . . .

They are in high spirits, bouncing back and forth and making a joyful ruckus like a group of kids visiting Disney World. Once suppressed by drugs, their natural state of happiness is now finally unleashed.

"What part of Mars are you from?" you ask the Editor in Chief of *Geriatric Health News*. He is now regarded as a loyal subject, thanks to his leading the patients in their search for a living doctor.

"The Tharsis plateau region on the western side of the planet, more specifically, the peak of the shield volcano known as Pavonis Mons, also known as Peacock Mountain." The Editor in Chief has to really rack his brain to remember all of that.

"Why would anyone build a hospital there?"

"I'm not sure. But I think they are awaiting the arrival of something . . ."

"What is that?"

"Not sure. Maybe some kind of miracle? Or perhaps the apocalypse? Either one is possible."

"Besides hospitals, is there anything else on Mars?"

"I've never left the hospital, so I'm not sure what's out there."

"You've never once gone out to observe the environment?"

"They don't allow those kinds of observation missions. But I heard there are more hospitals outside."

"Why would they build so many hospitals on Mars?"

"Maybe . . . there are simply too many Dead Souls?"

"Were we really all wiped out in a massive catastrophe?"

"That topic is off limits. They don't allow patients and doctors to discuss it."

"Were there actual historical figures named Einstein, Rousseau, and Weber?"

"I can't say for sure . . ."

"Then who am I?"

"The answer to that question should be recorded in the hospital archives, where they keep blueprints for all of the Dead Souls. But I've never seen any of that."

"Do they really used advanced medical technology to reincarnate dead patients?"

"The process is the first time that life and death have been stitched together."

"Really? The first time? Why is that?"

"Because this is the 301 Base."

"Sounds like you are talking about Los Alamos!"

"That was where they developed weapons used in germ warfare. They make some of those things here too. But the word 'Mars,' in Latin, actually refers to the God of War."

"I heard that the war is still going on, but it is waged in the name of peace." You are gripped by a growing sense of trepidation. The war has become a bottomless hole. But none of the patients, including Einstein, has ever mentioned World War II or World War III. Aren't they all supposed to be soldiers in this battle?

"This battle . . . ," the Editor in Chief mumbles. "The doctors selected to come here are the best fighters. They are soldiers! The Hospital President is actually a Major General. Whenever the doctors' kids get into fights with the neighbors' kids, they always yell: 'We are from 301!' Those words strike a deep fear into the hearts of the neighborhood kids. When members of a doctor's family take a public bus, they don't need to wait for the bus stop—they just tell the driver exactly where they want to go, as if the bus is their own private car. Patients who want to bribe their doctors with gifts don't even have a fighting chance."

"Day after day, night after night, these are the people torturing the patients. Are you one of them?" You aren't sure if you should feel

gratitude toward these doctors, or hate them. After all, they allowed
for your resurrection. But even that failed to save you from the coming
disaster, actually paving the way for even more terrible suffering. All the
while, you remain in the dark about who you were in your previous life,
helpless to decide whether you want to return to this world.

"No, I'm nothing but an insignificant pawn in all of this! I just
spend my days in the editorial office of a newspaper, serving as the
mouthpiece for the Hospital Affairs Committee. Never once have I
been able to express my own opinions about anything. I have only
just discovered what it feels like to be a real human being. I now want
to learn from everyone how to become a model patient." The Editor
in Chief speaks with such passion that he reaches out and grasps you
by the hand, but you feel nothing but a cold chill. Perhaps he, too, is
already dead.

Then the seemingly rock-solid foundation of 301 begins to collapse in upon itself. Does this mean that the Grand Treatment Project
was a failure? You can't be sure whether the patient-led uprising will
really bring about peace. Just like the hospital's being built on Pavonis
Mons, there must be a reason for all of this that even the patients don't
understand. You want to warn Einstein that the danger ahead is much
greater than what anyone has anticipated. But you are also skeptical
about whether the patients will really take out the other hospitals on
Mars (if they exist). Are the patients in those other hospitals revolting
too? Perhaps the current conflict with the doctors is nothing but a small
skirmish, and the true battle will erupt between different factions of
patients? But you dare not mention any of this to Einstein, at least not
until you are clear about the rules governing the Dead Souls. Just like
the hospital itself, they, too, are riddled with instability.

The patients arrive at the Disinfection Room, only to find that it is
locked from the inside. You ask the patients to issue a warning to those
inside: "We've got you surrounded! Hand over your white lab jackets,
or we will have no choice but to use force!" The patients pile on top of

one another, their arms extending from a mass of bodies like a set of pliers, or a horrific multiarmed monster slamming against the door. It is a joyous affair for them, and in a fit of elation, they break down the door. Only a small group of doctors is left alive inside, hiding behind a pile of their fellow doctors' corpses and squirming around like maggots.

No longer hesitating, the swarm of patients follows Rousseau inside. He approaches the doctors, hurling insults and beating them. After landing a few blows, Rousseau takes a step back to let the mob of patients descend upon the doctors. They release a wild convulsion of punches and kicks, stripping the doctors of their white lab coats and putting them on themselves. Once adorned, the patients look like a herd of bulging white elephants. Pointing to each other in amusement, they clap their hands and laugh:

"Check me out! Do I look like a doctor?"

"You do!"

"No, you don't *look* like a doctor, you *are* a doctor!"

"Okay then, let me treat everyone's illnesses!"

"I didn't know I was sick . . ."

"But now that we're doctors, you have to be sick!"

"That's right, we need to treat some illness in order to prove who we really are . . ."

"You're sick! And you're sick too!"

"You all need to be treated!"

In a fit of hysterical laughter, the patients chase each other around the room, pushing their playful carnival toward its climax while maintaining a sense that this is a rite of the utmost solemnity.

That is when another group of living doctors appears. Knowing there is nowhere left to hide, they decide to take a stand. This new group is made up primarily of plastic surgeons but also includes several dermatologists and ENTs. They line up in a strict formation and, moving in unison, approach the patients with a stiff gait and expressions devoid of emotion.

"What the hell do you think you're doing?" Their low voices tremble like the sound of the dying. "Aren't you in pain? Hurry up and return to your sick wards! The doctors will be making their rounds shortly to treat you. You aren't going to survive unless you start taking your medicine again!"

Einstein breaks out in a hearty fit of laughter. "Will you look at these clowns! They are on the brink of death, and yet they claim that *we* are struggling to stay alive! Don't they realize that we all died a long time ago? What's the point of taking more medicine? Nowadays, anyone can become a doctor!"

"Anyone can become a doctor! Anyone can become a doctor!" the patients chant in unison. They charge at the doctors, barking: "Take off your clothes! Take them off!" Several of the patients flail as they prepare to put on white lab coats, singing: "Getting dressed, getting dressed! Just like a doctor!" But then the patients in the front suddenly stop. They notice that the doctors are armed, each one brandishing a golf club. Some of the patients who had died shallow deaths forget that they had once laid eyes on such things, and they seem to think that the golf clubs are a new medical device, more powerful than the scalpel. Set into a panic, they scream and flee before a single blow is exchanged.

"Hey, where are my Flower Commandos?" Einstein calmly begins to issue orders. "We are here! And we shall go after them!" Fueled by a wave of bravery, Winter Dew leads the nurses forward, marching with bags on their shoulders. "Forward, march!" Einstein orders. The Flower Commandos, a unit comprised exclusively of women soldiers, takes the place of the male patients on the front lines. They know the truth about these doctors better than anyone, but they also have a secret weapon. In perfect unison, the women set down their bags and open them to reveal an assortment of objects that they lay out on the ground: wreaths, flowers, fruits, needles and thread, exercise equipment, wheelchairs, cleaning utensils, bedpans, pirated books, clothing originally designed for export but now being sold to the local market, cosmetics, cremation urns, coffins, wigs, firecrackers, quilts, binoculars, compasses, flashlights, notebooks, New Year cards, paring knives, kitchen knives, Buddhist prayer beads, ornamental statues of the Avalokitesvara Goddess of Mercy, nail clippers, used television sets, secondhand radios . . .

The patients see all this spread out on the ground, and they gradually begin to grow nostalgic. Some exclaim, "My oh my! Will you look at that!" The doctors are stupefied by the sight, immediately drop their golf clubs, and begin to pick these objects up. The fact that they fell for this trick so easily proves that they are not qualified to be soldiers. Winter Dew gestures toward the male patients, and they spring forward, ensnaring the doctors in a large nylon net. The patients then pick up the doctors' abandoned golf clubs and begin hitting them, killing many on the spot. But they manage to capture the Director of the Plastic Surgery Department.

"Please, I beg you . . . I'll resign!" the doctor pleads. "I'll let you serve as Department Director!"

"Liar!" snorts Winter Dew. "It's too late for that now. None of us gives a shit about being Director anyway!"

"This is all a misunderstanding . . . ," the doctor pleads. "We had no intention of going against the patients. We were trying to challenge what they were doing over in the Hospital President's office. We are on the same side as the patients. The Hospital Affairs Committee and Secretariat are our true common enemies. They oppress the patients and exploit the doctors. It has gotten to the point where you can't get a military promotion without accepting bribes! That's why we've been unable to wage World War III. But we've had enough!"

"I know that you are the Hospital President's most obedient little dog," the Editor in Chief sneers. "You go around every day kissing his ass and going out of your way to get on his good side. You probably have your sights set on getting appointed as his assistant, right?"

Rousseau strips the Plastic Surgery Director's clothes off and begins to beat him with a gold club.

"Hit him in the balls!" one patient shouts.

"That bastard operated on me once," another patient cries, "but since I didn't bribe him enough, he ended up sewing my asshole shut!"

A third patient grabs a golf club and yells, "We should hit him in the head! He once had a monkey give me a CT scan. When the monkey passed out, he forced me to perform CPR on the monkey!"

"That's right," another patient chimes in. "In order to make that monkey happy, he even forced me to jack the monkey off! He said it was some kind of experiment!"

"Please stop hitting me," the doctor begs through tears. "I have always earned great praise as a doctor. Just look at the bulletin board. For my entire life, I have strived to be indifferent to wealth and fame, instead sharing my knowledge, devoting myself to hard work, and pursuing excellence in medical care. I have saved thousands of people's lives, bringing beauty and vitality to countless patients. Without me, how could all of you stand here today looking so healthy and radiant?"

"You still have the gall to claim that you are a selfless, fearless apostle?" Rousseau continues to beat him.

The Editor in Chief stomps on the doctor's body and declares, "Hold on now, I have something I want to expose about him! Plastic surgery is simply a cover they use to hide who they really are. The doctors are actually a bunch of raving lunatics! This doctor here does nothing but dream of creating a perfect new race. In order to achieve his goal, he abandoned his wife and children and ran off to Mars! For him this cold, desolate place has served as the perfect laboratory to conduct his experiments, because the twisted things he does here would be considered ethically unacceptable anywhere else. I heard that he murdered three sets of twins from the patient population, dissecting their bodies to determine their genetic control mechanism. He injected poisonous toxins into patients' bodies before throwing them into a large vat of ice water, where he could record the process of death, including how they lost consciousness, the way their throats quivered, and the subconscious sounds they emitted just before death . . . okay, that's all I have to say. But *this* is what really happens here at the Mars Hospital."

"Oh, I'm in so much pain," one of the patients mutters quietly. "I already had an appointment with him for a liver transplant."

As soon as Rousseau hears that, he begins hitting the patient. "Are you really sick? Here, let me treat you!" The patient is so scared, he dares not say another word, probably lost in thoughts from his previous life, explaining why he has been unable to catch up with the most recent developments.

Gripped by a strange fear, you wonder: Do plastic surgeons still perform liver transplants? You can sense something wrong and fall back into your dream, as if on the verge of returning to the Pool of Dead Souls. You dare not imagine what comes next. All eyes are on you, pushing you to join in. And so you also start to hit the doctor. Then the other patients start scrambling for their turn, eventually beating the doctor to death. In the process, the patients seem to prove to themselves that they still possess this power. Even the weakest and most cowardly participate in the beating, a kind of performance meant to prove to Einstein, Winter Dew, and the nurses that they are no longer Dead Souls. The patients quickly take over even more treatment rooms and operating rooms; then they discover a set of 3D printers, standing there like a row of giants. The patients proceed to destroy the machines, ecstatically crying out, "This time we are addressing the problem by going straight to the source and pulling out the roots. We will never be cloned again! It shall all end with the Dead Souls that made it to see this day!" It is as if they have finally liberated themselves from the endless cycle of life and death.

The patients then launch an assault on the Hospital President's office. What remains of the physicians from the Allergy Department stay behind to stand guard. They seem to be the only ones left who still remember their original identity as soldiers. With no regard for what injuries they might suffer, they use the corpses of their fellow doctors to build a simple fortification, outfitted with electric-shock devices and barbed wire. You repeatedly attempt to break through their barrier, but each time you fail.

"These doctors are different from the others," you exclaim in frustration. "In some ways, they behave more like Dead Souls!"

"My son," Einstein grumbles in anger, "since when did you become such an artsy-fartsy romantic? Perhaps you have spent too much time writing songs! Doctors have always tried to stitch life and death together, but now we are going to tear those stitches apart. My dear brother Yang Wei, you need to start picking up some tricks from them! After all, we have already boarded the express train that will lead us to a peaceful new world."

The members of the Flower Commandos approvingly clap their hands and shout, "Guevara, Guevara!"

Winter Dew leads the brigade of nurses forward into battle. In preparation for what is coming, they remove all the tools needed to "tear those stitches apart," which include a nucleus pulposus reamer, a bone knife, a bone drill, a bone pry, reset forceps, bent rod forceps, fulcrum forceps, a trocar, a pair of wire scissors, a bending wrench, an Emei chisel, and a tunnel file . . . several young nurses carry torches, which ignite the oxygen tanks the doctors had hidden around them. The tanks explode, instantly killing many of the nurses and blowing up the sick ward. Chunks of flesh and blood fly everywhere, and the hospital dome shakes like it is about to collapse. More robotic termites immediately appear through the thick smoke to begin repairs. You watch with emotional indifference, and gradually, bit by bit, the truth behind the hospital is revealed . . . but it is like a dream, an illusion, a shadow, a flash of ephemeral light.

Following the Flower Commandos' charge, the patients finally break through the doctors' front line of defense, flooding into the Hospital President's office like a tsunami. Once inside, the patients discover a massive cave that has been converted into what looks like a luxuriant restaurant, its walls adorned with all kinds of awards, medals, and ornaments. A portrait of Rockefeller rendered in thick oil paint hangs on the wall near a stack of illustrated foreign-language medical books, each as fat as a brick. Inside, a birthday party is being held. The bloody operating table is covered with all kinds of food and alcohol. Some of the delicacies on display include fried crickets, grasshoppers, and earthworms that came directly from the hospital farm. You never imagined that the doctors would eat these things at a time like this. The main course is a human corpse, which has already been mostly eaten—what's left is barely discernible as human. There is no trace of the Hospital President. Instead an instructor from the 301 Base sits at the head of the table, surrounded by several nurses and the directors from the Hospital's Central Economic Office, Central Accounting Department, and Central Affairs Office. The directors scurry under the table as soon as the patients charge into the room, but the instructor, who is clearly the birthday boy, just sits there, still as a rock.

Without the slightest sign of fear, the instructor laughs. "Have you come to wish me a happy birthday? Please, have a seat!"

Following Einstein's lead, the patients take their seats around the surgery table.

15

NO-MAN'S-LAND

The instructor is a refined-looking doctor with a magenta complexion, graying hair around his temples, and swollen eye sockets. Waving to the guests, he greets them. "This year I am turning sixty, and this is my birthday celebration! This is the perfect time to hold my party! My life-long passion for medicine has been such that I never had interest in anything else. My specialty is breast surgery, but somehow I achieved even greater success in my research on programmed cell death. That said, as an instructor I have spent the majority of my time on the hospital's 'spiritual work.' You came at the perfect time. Would you like to hear the special birthday message that the Hospital Affairs Committee sent?"

Just as you are trying to figure out who would need breast surgery in a hospital in which all of the patients are male, you notice the instructor remove a piece of red paper.

He begins reciting: "'You have worked hard your entire life, paving the way so that we could all witness the birth and development of a new medical discipline. Your devotion to your patients has never ceased. Fueled by your thought, passion, concern, and dignity, your professional dedication has integrated itself into every fabric of your being. On this historic day, please allow us to sing an ode to fertility and wish you a happy birthday!'" Clearly inspired by the crowd of well-wishers, the instructor excitedly encourages everyone to drink. "Please, have a drink! Drinking together is the only way for us to achieve a true meeting of the minds! After all, doctors and patients are all part of the same big happy family!"

"That's right," says Einstein with a smile. "In the past, doctors and patients never had the chance to drink together!" He downs a glass of spirits before exclaiming, "Ah, a good shot of *maotai*!"

"That bottle has been fermenting for fifteen years!" the instructor explains. "The hospital doesn't have many bottles left. It is so rare for you to visit, and we just happen to have the bottle out—a great coincidence!"

Rousseau picks up the bottle of *maotai* and, scanning the room, confesses, "I have experienced enough luxury during my life as an apostle."

One look at his expression, and everyone can tell that Rousseau has never tasted *maotai*.

"There is a theory that puts medical treatment side by side with Dionysian vitalism," explains Winter Dew. "But it isn't about any so-called meeting of the minds, it is all about conquest!"

Einstein squints one eye and looks through his cup like a telescope. "Look at us, are we Dead Souls? Can Dead Souls drink like this? Let's not burden the patients with such an unreasonable label!"

"My apologies," the instructor interrupts gleefully. "There is something important that I forgot to jot down in my medical instructions. But now that we are all finally sitting together at the same table, I can share it with everyone!"

Everyone looks at one another and replies, "Great! We can't wait to hear all the details!"

The instructor looks like a true artist as his long fingers caress the red cross hanging from his neck. Looking at the assortment of corpses laid out on the operating table, he earnestly says, "The Mars Hospital has such an unusual history that I'm going to need to tell you the whole story carefully, so you don't forget any of the details. You could say that we doctors are a bunch of idealists and romantics. The field of medicine is the greatest science in the world. Uh, actually it isn't a science: its history predates the invention of science and is much more complicated. It is also much more wonderous and intriguing than any other science. Have you ever heard of the Nobel Prize? When they give out the prizes each year, the first awards they hand out are for biology and medicine, before the awards in physics, chemistry, literature, economics, and peace. That order is not random. And why don't they simply call it the Medicine Award? Because it stands above all others, representing the most cutting-edge advancements while keeping its feet firmly planted on the ground, all while deeply connected to the most basic stages of life, death, sickness, and aging, along with humankind's most fundamental moral principles. The study of biology encompasses the mysteries of life, but the study of medicine concerns not only illness and disease, but also related topics: politics, economics, sociology, and the humanities. That's what makes medicine the world's most all-encompassing field of academic knowledge.

"How was this field established? For that we must thank the great master of old. His name is Jesus, humankind's earliest medical scientist. In order to atone for the sins and suffering of mankind, He performed miracles, cured the lepers, the deaf, the mutes, and the paralyzed, and He resurrected the dead. Everything we do today is an attempt to reduplicate the earlier efforts of this great healer. Our objective is to take Jesus as our guide and create a world devoid of illness, suffering, pain, death, and evil. And thanks to our tireless work, we have almost reached our goal, culminating in a new era that will bear witness to the reconstruction of the Garden of Eden.

"Under the glorious light of the Red Cross, we have established a welfare fund, an insurance industry, charitable organizations, and various health administration departments. We have promoted broad genetic screening, new reproductive techniques, organ transplant, xenotransplantation, genetic modification, individually coded microchip drugs, and the use of stem cells to regenerate organs. We have developed a new generation of psychotropic drugs to control patients' emotions, feelings, desires, and intelligence. We have expanded the range of medicine beyond the management of accidents, disease, and injuries to include a much wider range of applications, including controlling death, managing reproduction, assessing risks, refining the spirit, creating new industries, improving society, strengthening the military, and consolidating political power . . .

"To sum up, what we are really doing is allowing all of you to tap into the full potential of your bodies and spirits—whether that be strength, endurance, morality, wisdom, or lifespan—and improve them all through divine technological enhancement, allowing everyone to achieve the greatest degree of biological perfection. As such, we shall all become gods!

"But biological control is only one method by which to achieve these miracles. In the end, the real goal is to arrive at a place where the world is perfectly clear and bright, and our pristine human lives are infinitely expanded. Medicine will not only cure any illnesses that might arise, but more importantly, it will guide the entire process of one's mental and physical life. We are talking about the pinnacle of technology. Some might ask: Why does the vitality of life need to be redesigned? But it is not as you imagine. Doctors today still covet their red envelopes, but they need to have faith. By saving patients' bodies and souls, they will achieve even greater joy and happiness.

"Gentlemen, since the moment you were born, you have been waiting to be saved! In the eyes of doctors, all patients are sinners. You have lived your lives never stopping to reflect, and in some sense, the suffering you endure is justified, and it is partially a genetically determined form of original sin, enhanced by other actual sins and triggered by environmental factors. Jesus tells us that cancer is the messenger of evil thoughts, hepatitis is the fruit of anger and jealousy, cardiovascular disease is the reward for immoral eating habits, AIDS is a punishment for social ills . . ."

The second Rousseau heard "AIDS," he jumped out of his seat in anger. "On the one hand, you hide the number of actual AIDS patients, while simultaneously exaggerating the risk of the disease!" he barks at the instructor. "This is all a sham to make it easier to exert political control over the patients!"

The Editor in Chief grows nervous and slips under the table. Thinking of the sins you yourself have committed, you feel somewhat relieved, as if everything has finally been confirmed. You think back to when you were first forcibly admitted to the hospital. You were like a prisoner. You groveled in front of those doctors, sharing all the details of your illness, knowing that leniency would be granted to those who confessed their illness, and that patients who resisted would be treated more harshly. Your sense of guilt lessened only when you were identified as carrying a familial gene for hyperlipidemia susceptibility, which is different from those who develop the gene from unhealthy lifestyle habits. At the same time, you began to develop a new sense of shame that came from personally bearing responsibility for the management of this genetic risk factor. You should have come to the hospital the moment you were born instead of waiting until middle age, when the women from the hotel had you admitted. You can't help but blame yourself, and a feeling of panic overtakes you. You also blame your parents. They knew their child was afflicted with a congenital disease, yet they shamelessly allowed you to be born. Is this not the very definition of original sin? You now identify with the hospital on a deeper level and understand it much better than before.

The patients glance at each other, and the looks on their faces turn to ones of self-shame. Then they go back to drinking.

"I'm sick of hearing all this shit!" exclaims Einstein.

"This is no longer the era when the doctors get the final word!" declares Winter Dew.

The instructor seems unbothered by their objections and continues his lecture. "What is the nature of treatment? Treatment is reform! One thing the hospital has in common with labor camps is reforming criminals into new people. Patients are like lambs that have strayed from their flock, mistakenly going down a twisted path. We doctors have spared no effort in finding you and bringing you back home! Just think of how great a charitable deed we have done! Most people in this world have never studied medicine, which is why they don't understand what a life of sin looks like. Instead, they remain content with letting themselves rot away in a pool of rancid water. But that's precisely why we doctors have come to offer you salvation.

"We've now built an excellent social foundation, but if we want society to continue functioning normally, we need everyone to play their part. If they find themselves unable to assume responsibility for themselves and deviate from society's expectations, two methods can be used to bring them into line: the first is the law, and the second is medicine. Illness is a form of deviant behavior that separates an individual from the rest of society, and the most destructive part of illness is that it makes patients lose their faith. The hospital takes individuals who have deviated from the norm and isolates them, using medical treatment to correct them before returning the healthy individuals back to society after recovery. This is also our way of spreading the Gospel.

"That said, the situation facing the hospital today is much graver than what we went through during the era of Philip the Apostle. The number of sinners has exponentially increased, and the work of doctors is frequently met with criticism and censure. We are left with no choice but to do everything within our means to design better treatment methods, such as stripping medical science down to the molecular level, so that all life-forms can be separated from their relationship with their cells, organs, physical bodies, and species. Once liberated, these molecules can circulate freely, smoothly combining with other natural elements in order to eliminate sin and create a new breed of human. Building upon this new material and spiritual foundation, a new human genealogy shall be written, and a new ode to idealism shall be composed!

"This is an epistemological and ontological revolution that shall reset the themes and content of criminology. Taking embryonic intervention as an example, it is not only a victory in the realm of surgical breakthroughs; it has also resulted in a restructuring of social relationships. People are now considered holy from the moment of birth, eliminating sin and evil from the very source. Education has also become a purely medical issue. The abuse of children has completely ended. Medical advances have created a new economic foundation and a new superstructure that fundamentally corrects all improper behavior. How could anyone ever again contract AIDS from selling their blood? Such rumors are pure slander!

"New life technologies have redefined the meaning and purpose of all human activities. The sins of humankind—exploitation, suppression, corruption, war, unrest, the division between the rich and poor, conflicts between labor and capital—have been swept away into the dustbin of history! Whoever said that medical science tries to blame socially triggered medical problems on individual biological and psychological issues in an attempt to mask deeper social, economic, and political malaise? This malicious tactic is meant to hide the truth. The problem that clinical medicine needs to solve is the malady lurking at the heart of the relationship between capitalism and production—*this* is the true source of all disease! Abject poverty, marginalization, and inequality can only be eradicated by defining suffering as a disease embedded in social relations.

"When everyone is part of the same biosocial group, shares the same biocitizenship, and is managed by the same medical collective, all of the ideals we have been fighting for—comprehensive development, freedom, equality, justice, harmony, friendship, and an appreciation for the beauty of all civilizations—shall finally be realized. If you still need to make a confession, you can proceed directly to the treatment room. And in the event that you find yourself in need of further treatment, you can immerse yourself in the Pool of Dead Souls, where you shall be completely reborn. There your body will be enhanced, and your soul will be upgraded. You shall realize that the great harmonious society we have dreamed about is already right here before our eyes, and that the key to what Jesus described as the beautiful Kingdom of Heaven is already in your hands . . .

"Before you know it, all illnesses will be treated, and all patients will be cured. That will, of course, pose a new problem: medical development will stall and doctors will have nothing to do. This will become a hidden crisis in the new era. When a place becomes too comfortable and familiar, people lose their motivation to innovate. Therefore, in order to continue pushing medical science forward, we must go to a new environment where everything is strange and riddled with challenges. Realizing that, someone suggested constructing a hospital in a vacuum environment, devoid of people—a true no-man's-land. And so the hospital was expanded into outer space, a virgin territory awaiting development.

"After introducing Drake's equation into the field of medicine, we discovered that many living things are scattered across the universe, like the sand of the Ganges. Living things need to be in contact with other living things, but only healthy life-forms can communicate with one another. After this new generation of doctors sets its roots down in outer space, they could shed their identity as husbands, fathers, and sons obsessed with domestic chores, transforming into pure and lofty military doctors, always on call and ready to serve, like the great Dr. Norman Bethune!

"Therefore, our new mission is to travel to a no-man's-land like that! A place devoid of air and riddled with radiation! That's right, outer space may be difficult and dangerous, but it is also filled with excitement and wonder! We need to rescue those patients from various galaxies who have committed terrible sins. This shall be the universe's great harmonious medical society, a perfect Red Cross paradise! There we shall drink even finer spirits! With our grand ideals, we shall head toward this goal, setting out on a sacred journey to build the Mars 301 Base. This is the closest planet where we can find extraterrestrial life. Here we shall establish the universe's first gene bank and create a new civilization unlike anything ever seen before!

"Such a grand endeavor should not be approached like some shady, high-risk investment deal. That's why we need all of you! Then, using our Mars Base as a springboard, we will march outward to other planets in the solar system, to the Milky Way, and on to other galaxies! This sick and ailing universe shall be saved, and all the living creatures from all the thousands of worlds shall be blessed with eternal life! Gentlemen, you should all drink to *me*!"

As he spoke, every wrinkle on the instructor's face lit up bright red, his hands trembled as he clenched the red cross hanging from his neck, and he gestured like he was a spaceship soaring through the universe. The patients force themselves to raise their cups.

"So, you're talking about a new form of civilization," one observes.

You are on the verge of asking how the great catastrophe will come about, but you hold yourself back. You can't help but feel that it's a shame Summer Stream isn't here to enjoy such fine spirits. You really want to discuss the true relationship between crime and illness with her, along with the role that alcohol plays in this great harmonious medical society.

Einstein draws a long face and says, "I'm not drinking. All I really want is a simple life for myself."

"Ha! That's a nice plan," Rousseau says. "A shame, then, that it is doomed to fail! This great harmonious medical society was never established, but at least it gave us a chance to smash the hospital to bits!"

"How come the hospital didn't hold a conference to reflect on what got them to this point?" asks Winter Dew. "Didn't the doctors accept any responsibility for what happened? It seems like they just put all the blame on the patients!"

The instructor is at a loss. ". . . I'm afraid this is something that only the Hospital President can answer. He is the main person in charge."

The patients ask where they can find the Hospital President, but the instructor replies that the President doesn't want to drink with the patients.

That's when the surgery table begins to shake back and forth, knocking dead bodies and bottles of *maotai* to the floor.

"What's happening?" Einstein looks visibly upset.

Rousseau grabs the trembling Editor in Chief, who is hiding beneath the table, and pulls him out.

"Is there something you want to say?" Winter Dew barks at the Editor in Chief with a tone of disdain.

The Editor in Chief stammers, pointing at the instructor and whispering, "He's lying. Don't believe a word he says. He's been secretly conspiring to take the place of the Hospital President. His lust for power has corrupted his heart. He is two faced and corrupt. He even interfered with the hospital construction project and demanded kickbacks. He serves as a trustee for a major pharmaceutical corporation, for which he receives generous renumeration. He owns five private villas on Mars. The hospital farm has a special area devoted to producing a daily supply of grasshoppers and *maotai* for his personal consumption. He lives a depraved, morally corrupt lifestyle. He has his own private harem of fifty nurses, while forbidding his patients from having any form of sex. Half the children you see around the hospital are his bastard offspring. He uses pharmaceuticals to control his patients' emotions and desires, selling their genetic information to unscrupulous businessmen. He even resells medical equipment on the black market . . . he is the devil dressed in white, a criminal through and through. His name has long been on the Most Wanted list, which is why he fled to outer space. The Mars Hospital was established by criminals like him. All these doctors have criminal records . . . I've known this for a long time but never dared to speak out, because anyone who dares speak the truth gets labeled a 'patient,' and some end up dying in so-called 'medical accidents.' Mars is actually an abyss of evil, so far from everything that they can get away with practically anything. There is no one to keep them in check. Thank goodness the patients finally took action, and just in the nick of time!"

"Rumors! Lies!" the instructor barks. He grabs a bottle of *maotai* and hurls it, striking the Editor in Chief in the head and soaking his face.

"How come you're only telling us all of this now?" Winter Dew sneers.

Rousseau leaps forward, knocking the instructor to the ground. He strips the instructor of his white lab jacket and tears the red cross from his neck, then shoves it and the bottle of spirits up the instructor's ass. "You wasted all this good liquor!" he screams in anger.

By this time, Einstein has grown weary of killing people by exposing them to the vacuum of space, so he orders Rousseau to get an electroconvulsive therapy machine. They place the electrodes on the temporal and parietal regions of the instructor's head and begin to administer shock therapy. The instructor goes into a series of epileptic convulsions until he passes out. The Editor in Chief gets in a few good punches; then other patients descend upon the instructor, kicking and trampling him until he is reduced to a pile of thick, fleshy paste. Your reaction is delayed, but all the other patients participate in the bedlam, covering themselves in the instructor's fresh blood, which soaks through their clothes. They look at one another and break into fits of crazed laughter. They take the portrait of Rockefeller down from the wall and smash it. They pull the medical staff out from under the table, where they had been hiding, and execute them all, sparing only the nurses. When they are done, they take their seats at the table again. A few scoop up the meaty paste of the instructor's body and put it on the table to be consumed with the rest of the meats and spirits.

You join them at the table to partake in the festivities, but the food is flavorless. Einstein, Winter Dew, the Editor in Chief, and Rousseau are fixated on eating, but for some reason you can't remember what any of them said earlier. At this critical moment, you have again become a bystander, a depressed thought, as though you have learned that there is no way to escape this hospital. You think back to the Drake equation, which seems to represent your dilemma. The prerequisite is that there must be alcohol to drink. If the universe is indeed a hospital, interstellar dust must be filled with ethanol molecules, not for disinfection, but to satisfy the military doctors' twisted thirst. Lacking courage, they need the alcohol in case they are called to battle. Here in the hospital, no one can say who will die tomorrow, so they drink while they can. Their drink of choice is *maotai*. Molecular biomedicine seems to have solved their production and supply problems, and this is where it most comes in handy.

16

LUSH GREEN LEAVES

The patients have taken over most of the hospital. They destroyed all the medical equipment along the way, but they have yet to get their hands on the Universal Treatment Machine. They took over the crematorium, but Weber the Funeral Artist escaped, and production of the ultimate works of art have come to a halt. The crematorium flames rage, as if burning for their own pleasure. A few remnants of leftover food in the cafeteria are the most highly sought-after items in the hospital after oxygen, and the patients, unable to control themselves, cook whatever leftovers they can find. The instructor's birthday party seems to have sparked a new wave of desire among them.

You ask Einstein for instructions on whether to simply extinguish the crematorium or blow the entire thing up and use the explosion as a catalyst for burning down the whole hospital, as originally planned.

Einstein slurps up half a bowl of meat broth before abruptly stopping, as if his soul has suddenly been torn from his body. "Brother Yang Wei, I've changed my mind," he says, turning to look straight at you. "Let's not change anything. Let the crematorium keep burning. The cafeteria will need the flames for cooking. We seem to have resolved the issue concerning the shortage of cooking materials. Take a look, there are ingredients available everywhere! It would be a crime not to take advantage of all this stuff!" He points to the corpses of doctors and patients strewn all over the floor. "Sorry, I used to be a vegetarian, but that's not possible anymore. If I had to choose a religion to believe in, I would become a Buddhist . . . but what's the harm in letting the fires burn? The primate known as Peking Man long ago figured out how to barbecue his buddies and eat them. If you are going to eat meat, it better be well cooked. This was the earliest form of medicine. Early on, humanoids mostly consumed raw food, which would often lead to various stomach ailments, but fire solved that problem. The consumption of meat stimulated brain development, allowing humankind to evolve. Otherwise, how would we have made it to Mars? Hell, without fire, would they have named Mars the 'fire planet'? Do you understand why the hospital was built here? You need to cook your food if you want to avoid getting infected with kuru. Unlike the doctors, the patients are the truly civilized ones!"

"Once we have taken over the hospital, what should we do with it?" asks the Editor in Chief.

"We will transform it into a brand-new hospital!" declares Einstein. "It will be the greatest hospital under heaven! After everything we have done, *this* is our true mission!"

"Are you saying that we aren't sick?" asks Rousseau. "We're not patients? From this day forward, we will no longer need to take our pills or get our shots? Why do we still need a hospital?"

"Because science is not and will never be something you can close the book on," answers Einstein. "Everything we undertake is in the pursuit of scientific truth!"

The crowd of patients grows agitated. "Okay, enough already!" one blurts out. "If we're going to do it, we should do what we love doing, and what we do best! We all love science, so let's get to it! How do you begin this transformation?"

"It's not about creating strange new medical instruments and devices," Einstein explains. "Those clunky things are simply superfluous objects that get between the doctors and their patients. They end up turning doctors and patients into enemies. Nor are we going to create one of those great harmonious societies—such things are too large and impractical. They might sound nice on the surface, but they fall short in terms of poetic imagination. Scientific thought is often accompanied by poetic elements. True science requires a creative process identical to that of composing great music. That's why we need to establish a rich and opulent Medicinal Empire built on ornate poetic imagery and a detailed artistic vision. Think about it, why did all of those historical empires fall?"

The patients shake their heads in confusion.

"None of them created their own classics!" Einstein announces. "Just look at this hospital, which considered itself the greatest in the world and yet completely fell apart because it allowed itself to fall behind in its theoretical vision—it couldn't keep up with the times. Those doctors took themselves to be the ultimate judges of knowledge and truth, which eventually led to their destruction at the sound of God's mocking laughter. The first step for us is to revise *Principles of Hospital Engineering*. Actually, no. We don't need to revise the book; we need to *rewrite* it! We need to prepare what will become the 'ultimate edition,' which will lead us out of this historical cycle of repetition!"

Einstein suddenly drops to the floor. White bubbles froth up from his mouth, and his face goes blank. The patients don't know how to respond. They grow anxious, but the old man pulls himself up and, after a sharp spasm shoots through his limbs, resumes his lecture in a strange tone of voice.

"The hospital was originally created and founded by patients. But the doctors have long buried this truth, likely intentionally concealing it from us! This has created great trauma for humankind and the universe, where the hospital has always been regarded as a work of art created by the doctors. This is one of the fundamental reasons why the patients have suffered such a miserable fate. We have lost our place as the main characters in the hospital's story. The goal of our uprising is to eradicate this cancerous growth!

"When we talk about the remarkable task ahead, we must begin by going back to ancient times. Back then humankind's productivity was quite limited, and most people faced difficult circumstances daily. Most died of injury or illness in their teenage years. During the Paleolithic Age, the average human life expectancy was only twenty years; in the Neolithic Age it was just thirty. This was only one-sixth or one-fifth of what their natural lifespan should have been. With their rushed lives, littered with pain and suffering, people began to see their own lives like drops of morning dew, and they decided to treasure what little time they had like a flame. This philosophy became the seed that would later flourish into medical thought, setting humans apart from the tigers and wolves. So in this sense, the history of medicine is actually much longer than civilization itself.

"The person responsible for creating the field of medicine was naturally a great man—but it wasn't Jesus. He lived during a time long before Jesus. At the time there was a leader of a group of tribes named Xuanyuan. He had an unusual appearance: the head of a bull and the body of a man, with transparent internal organs. Of course, today most people would blame those characteristics on some form of hereditary disease, but as with Stephen Hawking, these traits affected only Xuanyuan's body, not his mind, which was more brilliant than those of any of his peers. As a child he had a knack for language and keen powers of observation. He thought that asking questions was much more important than providing answers. He grew up to be an honest and hardworking man, and people referred to him as the 'Yellow Emperor.'

"The Yellow Emperor found himself constantly pondering that, between heaven and earth and among the ten thousand things, nothing is more precious than humankind. This observation became the origin of his humancentric philosophical system. Humans exist because they are imbued with the qi of heaven and earth, and they grow according to the laws of the four seasons. From the highest rulers to the average people, everyone strives to maintain a healthy body, but all are afflicted by the pain of disease. The Yellow Emperor wanted nothing more than to find a method by which he could alleviate the suffering of humankind, using what little strength he had to serve truth and justice. Never once did he look at pleasure and leisure as life's objective.

"At the time, a man named Chiyou, the leader of another tribal group, was searching for the same thing. His objective was not to ensure the health of his people but to extend his own life, seeking immortality in order to rule the world for all eternity. He started a war with the Yellow Emperor, who had no recourse but to accept the challenge. It was a long and brutal war that overlapped with a terrible plague. Countless people suffered and died. Consumed with anxiety about these terrible calamities, the Yellow Emperor burned a stick of incense, bathed, and departed for the wilderness of Duguang. There he built the divine ladder of trees, which he used to ascend to the Heavenly Garden. In the garden he encountered all kinds of enchanted plants, and the King of Heaven bestowed upon him a magic whip as a gift. With the magic whip in hand, the Yellow Emperor fought his way from Duguang all the way to Lie Mountain. Along the way he tasted three hundred and sixty-five varieties of wild herbs and began to categorize their different medicinal properties, including which ones generated heat and cold, and the relationships between them. In one day, he encountered seventy varieties of poison, which he miraculously expelled from his body. He recorded the medicinal uses of these various herbs and plants and brought them back to establish a pharmacy, where he cured the people of their ailments and restored the health of his soldiers, who returned to the battlefield and defeated Chiyou in one fell swoop, decapitating him in the process.

"The people were saved, and they rejoiced: singing, dancing, and praising the wonderous achievements of the Yellow Emperor. They declared him the founding leader of the very first empire, the Medicinal Empire. From that point forward, the Yellow Emperor led his people down a new path toward interaction with the outside world: collecting medicinal plants in the mountains, planting medicinal herbs in gardens, setting up medicinal workshops, and creating new medicines.

This is how true civilization was born! Later generations of scholars collected the essence of the Yellow Emperor's medicinal thought, which had been passed down in a sacred tome entitled *The Yellow Emperor's Classic of Internal Medicine.* Yet *Principles of Hospital Engineering* never mentioned a word about this and instead claimed that Jesus Christ was the founder of medical science. That marked the true origin of our suffering and the beginning of historical nihilism.

"Using the study of genomes to reject the medical wisdom of the Yellow Emperor has brought destruction to our race. It has turned us into puppets, parasites relegated to the Pool of Dead Souls, slaves of the Rockefellers. The whole thing is a massive conspiracy. At first everyone was bewitched by the lies. After all, only a small handful of people can think for themselves and see what is happening around them. Think about it. Human beings are an organic whole, so how can they possibly be broken up into particles? So we decided to launch this uprising, to overthrow the rule of the hospital. No matter what the current fashion of the times or social trends might be, human beings can always use their noble qualities to transcend all of that and follow their own paths. This marks a fundamental return to *The Yellow Emperor's Classic of Internal Medicine*! It's the most important canonical work, with a decisive impact on shaping the history of human civilization! Never mind *On Ancient Medicine* by some guy named Hippocrates. That's nothing but a cheap forgery that gained its reputation by deceiving the public. My dear brother Yang Wei, going through such trouble to find you was not simply so that father and son could be reunited, no! More important was to ensure that the great Yellow Emperor had a proper successor to carry on his bloodline and intellectual heritage. Please, never forget that we are the descendants of the divine Medicinal Empire.

"Perhaps you are wondering, Could all of these things I'm telling you be real? Of course they are! At this very moment, the Yellow Emperor is alive and well in my body! Each and every day, at the same time, he comes down to the human world to deliver his daily proclamation to mankind. Leading you in this uprising was not something I chose to do on a whim; I was following the orders sent down from the Yellow Emperor himself! The Yellow Emperor spoke to me: 'Einstein, people live for others, but firstly for those people whose joy and well-being are connected to our own happiness. For those we do not know, their fates are connected to ours through the ties of sympathy. A person's value to society is first decided by how much his emotions, thoughts, and actions contribute to its advancement. That's why you need to step up and lead us bravely forward, like Guevara once did. Under your guidance, people will plant medicinal herbs on every planet in the universe, and we shall again create a Medicinal Empire bursting with lush green leaves!'"

As his speech reaches its conclusion, Einstein falls to the ground. He drags himself back to his feet, and the surprised crowd of patients breaks into an extended wave of enthusiastic applause. You suddenly feel like everything is clear; another riddle that has long haunted you has been answered. You have heard about this "Chinese medicine," and you even asked Zi Ye, your contact person, about it once, but you never got an answer that satisfied you. Zi Ye told you that Chinese medicine was a unique form of medical science—most people actually don't even consider it part of medical science—but rather than being based on the principles of mathematics and physics, it is instead based on the theories of "yin and yang and the Eight Trigrams," which cannot be explained or verified through scientific experiments. But as far as you can tell, there indeed may be a set of secret laws that govern the universe. Perhaps those are the great principles that truly make the ten thousand things function. But the tradition of Chinese medicine is no longer practiced, and no one really understands it.

You realize that your true identity is that of a holy descendent of the Medicinal Empire. Was this what ignited the wave of jealousy that burned through the doctors, leading them to be seen as criminals and ultimately resulting in their relegation to the realm of Dead Souls? Is this why they were imprisoned on Mars? How could they have endured such indignities? It is only natural that they should want to rise up from this disaster. The patient uprising was inevitable. As a wave of hot energy races through your body, you find yourself looking at your "father" with a growing feeling of respect, thankful to have lived to see this day.

17

I AM WILLING TO DIE FOR YOU

The Editorial Committee is established. Einstein personally assumes the role of Committee Chairman, and you are appointed as Executive Deputy Director, but your main task is to oversee the writing and compilation. This demonstrates just how much faith Einstein has in you. You quickly realize that *The Yellow Emperor's Classic of Internal Medicine* was originally written in an archaic language now forgotten. The words and sentences of this ancient tome are extremely difficult to understand, like a strange new treatment program, a discourse system that you have never encountered before, disrupting everything you have been familiar with since childhood. You find the book's broad vision, tight structure, deep allegorical messages, and profound meaning using simple words difficult to grasp. Only after struggling with the text for some time can you read some of the passages, like "A superior doctor treats the nation. A mediocre doctor—that is, practitioners of Chinese medicine—treats individuals. An inferior doctor treats the sick." Another: "Superior doctors treat illnesses that have yet to manifest. Mediocre doctors treat the illnesses we desire. Inferior doctors treat illnesses that have already appeared." What does this mean?

The book also records the ancient way in which the word "medicine," or 醫, was once written, which includes a portion of the word for "alcohol," or 酒. As they say, "Alcohol is the best medicine." But why? The book doesn't explain. The words appear alien to you, and you have many suspicions about what they really mean. You feel an urge to turn against Einstein's plans, but you feel flattered by his favor. And yet the heavy responsibility leaves you terrified.

You are struggling with this confusion when Winter Dew approaches, so you ask her advice. She seems happy to talk with you and suggests that you get a good grip on the relationship between war and peace. Never forget, she reminds you, that the Mars Hospital is a military hospital. Everyone affiliated with it is descended from survivors from the war between the Yellow Emperor and Chiyou. And even today, the war between the Yellow Emperor and Jesus rages on.

"Brother Wei," she addresses you, with a gently intimate tone, "your father is a truly amazing man. He often says that the meaning of life can be found by placing yourself in others' shoes, assuming their joys and fears. Every time we are about to engage in intercourse, he begins by respectfully reciting a passage from *The Yellow Emperor's Classic of Internal Medicine*. That's how I came to realize that this book was the origin of the biological-psychological-social school of medical thought, which represents a major innovation from the military medical school of thought. It denies simple reductionism. It turns trees into a forest, launching a comprehensive and systematic war. On this point *The Yellow Emperor's Classic of Internal Medicine* provides a strategy that combines a sense of ritual with dietary therapy, naturalism with spiritual aesthetics, natural science with a yin and yang style of attack and defense. This was never mentioned in any other books I have read. Your father allowed me to understand that I had always been a failed doctor. He planted a sense of shame deep within my heart, and then he proceeded to treat me. From him I learned of 'dialectics,' which lies at the very core of the Yellow Emperor's medical philosophy, a kind of concept that no machine could master. The foundation of the Yellow Emperor's art of medicine lies with the concept of yin and yang. It is like a binary system, but yin and yang are not absolute, not like 'yes' and 'no.' Instead, there are elements of yang within the yin, elements of yin within the yang, and a fuzzy area in between. In the past they used to say that war was simply a simulation, created by machines, but that's not true. War has existed for a long time, well before machines. Machines simulating war would be a simple binary process, but real war's true meaning lies in killing people. Yet killing people also means saving people. For every person killed, medical science advances one step forward, and every step forward means one more person saved. When one person is saved, we can kill another. The more people are killed, the more innovations in medical science are possible, so we save more people to kill more people. This is how we build the foundation for a lasting peace. War is built upon the foundation of peace; you cannot separate them. You may ask, What is the meaning of benevolence? *This* is benevolence! Only after being inspired by these lessons did I decide to embed myself among the patients, in order to learn from them. I hope, one day, to write an amazing doctoral dissertation on this topic. My greatest ambition is to win the Nobel Prize in Physiology or Medicine—no, what I really want is the Nobel Peace Prize!"

Winter Dew speaks with a confident air, her gaze fixed, her neck swollen with blood, her chest rising and falling. She conveys a sense of superiority, yet she appears nervous when she occasionally glances your way. The fragrant aroma of her armpits combines with Einstein's body odor, and your will is shaken. You get it. Once upon a time, the hospital murdered patients. If they continue functioning according to the old medical system, they will be killed again, so the medical equipment must be destroyed, the medical rules must be broken, and a brand-new model of medical practice must be introduced.

Your doubts are put to rest. In this moment, what you want most is to let yourself go completely, to collapse into the deep valleys of Winter Dew's chest, letting her deep knowledge nurture you for all eternity. Compared to other women you have met, Winter Dew is like a 2.0 version: younger than Summer Stream, with a goddess-like quality, not a goddess of thunder but a goddess of war. Her words have tamed you. You feel almost like she is trying to seduce you. Otherwise, why would she have told you all of this? She even shared that she herself is suffering from a serious ailment, as if simultaneously showing off and displaying her kindness. Her eyes emit an ambiguous luster that speaks of her search for truth, and it takes your breath away.

A sudden sense of deep admiration and terrible fear overtakes you. In order to grasp the depth of *The Yellow Emperor's Classic of Internal Medicine*, Winter Dew has undertaken a journey to explore the mysterious nature of war and peace, and even more miraculously, she has willingly transformed herself into a patient. Doctors rarely do this. You feel like you should follow in her footsteps. Yet she is Einstein's girlfriend, so you dare not even talk to her about it, let alone attempt to mate.

All you can bring yourself to ask is, "How come I've never seen you drink?"

"My parents died when I was still a child," she says matter-of-factly. "I grew up in the hospital, where I survived by eating medicine. But it was so bitter that I began consuming sugar, to balance out the bitter taste."

"But they don't have the Nobel Prize here on Mars . . ."

"That's not true, there has got to be a patient here in the hospital named Nobel!"

Struck with a sudden realization, you muster up your sincerity and begin writing the first draft of the new edition of *Principles of Hospital Engineering*, incorporating the philosophical system of the Yellow Emperor. Using the Yellow Emperor's work as your blueprint, you create a series of guidelines for a systematic dialectical treatment plan: doctors and patients are one; killing people saves lives; living is dying; war is peace. In order to better equip patients with the tools to understand the profound meaning of these principles, you order a patient who is skilled in drawing to create a series of accompanying illustrations. Based on a combination of hearsay, free thinking, and logical assumptions, you conclude that there must be many ancient hospitals spread out across the mountains and hidden beside the rivers, a gorgeous and magnificent series of sites in which the natural world and the human world collapse into an organic whole. You add a footnote explaining: "In the seventh century BC, the State of Qi established a hospital for the disabled. The first hospital to treat leprosy was founded during the Qin dynasty. The Han dynasty's military oversaw the first hospital for infectious diseases. The Sui dynasty created the first plague clinic, and various health clinics, convalescence clinics, and relief centers were founded during the Tang-Song period." This is the official history of the splendid and glorious hospital, a history worthy of demonstrating the might and power of the great Medicinal Empire!

Having stayed on Mars too long, many did not understand this at first. Simply too far removed from the truth to understand this history, they later came to see this history in a fresh new light and were awed by the revelations it exposed. They dropped to their knees and praised the incredible history that had been unearthed. Only then did they realize why patients had been exiled to this impoverished wasteland: they were victims of Rockefeller's doctors, who cut them off from their relationship with the great Yellow Emperor. The patients were moved to tears and swore to bring about the grand plan of a new Medicinal Empire on the ruins of Mars.

You, too, are deeply affected by *The Yellow Emperor's Classic of Internal Medicine*. Never before have you encountered such a transcendent philosophical system, an entire new world suddenly opening right before your eyes. The rebirth of the Dead Souls begins here, in the pages of this book. Yours is the single most thorough round of revisions ever carried out on *Principles of Hospital Engineering*, and the last, for once such perfection is achieved, it can never be surpassed. When you were first admitted to the hospital, you read the edition edited by the Hospital President, which was followed by the AI edition, and later the version edited by the model doctors and the Editor in Chief, but yours is the most authoritative and profound version. Also the most cryptic and challenging version, it will be alternately referred to as the "Dead Souls Edition" or the "Einstein Edition."

You lead the patients in a recitation exercise, dividing them into three "reading groups" consisting of thirty-three members each. You establish an Inspection Committee to monitor the reading groups and ensure proper recitation, but even with that in place, the patients often find themselves unable to remember what they are reading. Having died multiple times—some more than a dozen times!—not everyone is able to achieve the same level of completeness through resurrection. This of course has a major impact on their ability to remember, requiring frequent breaks. During those breaks, the patients are easily distracted, slipping into a state of mind in which they think they are still being attacked by the old hospital. They even go back to debating what the Universal Treatment Machine looks like, putting forth all kinds of suppositions and even placing bets. Some of them think the machine is an energy ring, others believe it is a quantum oscillator, and a few even think it is a magic crystal ball, but it is difficult for them to reach a consensus. Only later do the patients snap out of their crazed state and begin to scream, "We've been possessed!" And then they return to reciting passages from *Principles of Hospital Engineering*, gradually becoming addicted to it. As they recite, a crimson glow of fervent devotion lights up their faces, as if all the fluids in their body are being purified by the process of recitation. But those patients suffering from Alzheimer's disease continue to have trouble memorizing their passages. Finally, Rousseau strips off his white lab jacket and asks everyone to line up and march into the crematorium furnace. Everyone does so willingly.

In order to celebrate the successful completion of the new edition of *Principles of Hospital Engineering*, the patients sing, dance, and play a variety of instruments.

"If everyone had a love for the arts," observes one of the patients, "this world would be a much more humane place to live."

Einstein grabs hold of Winter Dew and drags her off to dance. The old man has a queer, almost absurd dance style, his legs twisting wildly all over the place. Winter Dew bends her body at the waist, giving herself over to the music. The patients embrace the nurses in a wild dance that looks like a coven of witches in celebration. You're not sure why, but you are overcome by a feeling of sadness as you think of Summer Stream. You can almost feel her disdainful, mocking gaze stripping you down, and you can't go on dancing.

Meanwhile, the patients chant in unison:

Looking for too long damages the blood,
Lying down for too long damages the spirit,
Sitting for too long damages the flesh,
Standing for too long damages the bones,
Walking for too long damages the tendons!

They dance until some of them go into seizures and convulsions, and several fall dead to the ground. But none of the patients admits to suffering from any form of illness; instead, they are consumed with fear that they might be punished for not having memorized *The Yellow Emperor's Classic of Internal Medicine*.

"Are you all drinking, or what?" Einstein asks the patients.

"Yes! Alcohol is the cure to all diseases!" they respond.

The patients unload bottles of alcohol from the garbage trucks and hearses, and then they all get to drinking. Since there isn't enough *maotai* to go around, they use medical alcohol as a substitute, consuming the alcohol that only doctors are allowed to drink. They thank the Yellow Emperor for bestowing them with this gift. Amid the excitement, Einstein and Winter Dew begin to copulate. This, too, is an expression of their devotion to the Yellow Emperor. Caught up in the frenzy, the patients imitate Einstein by gang-raping the nurses again, and the room breaks into a thunderous uproar of laughter and excitement.

"Hey, where is that songwriter?" one of the patients cries as the party reaches its climax. "We're sick of those old songs and need someone to write new lyrics for us to sing! We need a new theme song to go with the new edition of *Principles of Hospital Engineering*!"

"My son, come back!" Einstein proudly calls you over. "This is a job for you!"

"That's right, the new hospital needs a new hospital theme song!" the patients exclaim.

"We need a new set of lyrics, a new classic song!"

"I can't do it," you mutter. You can't think of any new lyrics. In fact, you can't even remember the old ones!

Einstein tosses Winter Dew aside and approaches. Pinching your cheek, he says, "The imagination is more powerful than knowledge. This is a rare opportunity for you. Brother Yang Wei, you better put on a good show of effort for the Yellow Emperor! It's your chance to make a good impression on him!"

Looking over at the crematorium's furnace and hearing the patients' cries of ecstasy coming from within, you are reminded of an old song you once heard, so you try to sing it:

North, south, east, and west, the path of heaven and earth.
Spring, summer, autumn, and winter, unity between heaven and humanity.
Twenty-four solar terms, the source of life.
The Yellow Emperor's Classic of Internal Medicine, the natural order.
Ever since ancient times, the great sages have been lonely
And always looking inward.
One's demeanor announces the true spirit,
A person whose great virtue allows him to take charge of the world.

What line comes next? Your face turns pale with embarrassment. Einstein and Winter Dew flash you an impatient look before switching to a different song. You are spared further embarrassment when a fight breaks out on the dance floor, and the patients excitedly rush over to check out the action. The fight is between the Editor in Chief and Rousseau, both of whom have had too much to drink. One of them said something offensive, and an argument erupted, which quickly came to blows.

"You alone think you can renovate the old hospital?" barks Rousseau.

"What, you think you can build the new hospital by yourself?" the Editor in Chief retorts.

"You're nothing but a bunch of hooligan proletarians!" cries Rousseau.

"And you're nothing but a pack of pathetic losers!" yells the Editor in Chief.

The two of them go after each other with golf clubs, and the patients break into two factions, transforming the scene into a battle royale. Watching the chaos, you sense a crisis unfolding. You know that this mob of Dead Souls will eventually break up, so you decide just to collapse to the floor and pass out.

Winter Dew wakes you in the middle of the night and helps you up. Einstein is standing there. He rolls his eyes at you, spits out a huge chunk of yellow phlegm, and announces with an air of mystery: "Shh, the Yellow Emperor has issued his latest set of instructions."

Rousseau and the Editor in Chief pull themselves up and wake the other patients, calling a meeting to nominate Einstein as President of the new hospital. The two of them have already reconciled. Einstein is adamant about declining the nomination, but Rousseau and the Editor in Chief insist, "You are the only one capable of doing the job! No one else can do it! And today we take an oath that we will no longer fight with each other!"

"I won't accept the position of Hospital President, but I'm willing to see patients," Einstein responds humbly. "I'll see between three hundred and five hundred patients a day. What I want most is to spend more face-to-face time directly with the patients, in line with the teachings of the Yellow Emperor. Most doctors spend all their energy pursuing the vulgar things in life—money, vanity, and luxury—but I find those things despicable."

"How is that possible? This is to be a new hospital where the power will be in the hands of the patients!" exclaims Rousseau. "We will transition from taking pills to ingesting medicinal potions. It will be a radical change! But if we don't enlist your help to serve as Hospital President, how can we hope to establish a Medicinal Empire? Actually, no—that's not right. You shouldn't be the Hospital President . . . you should be King, ruler of the Medicinal Empire! You shall shoulder the awesome historical responsibility of overseeing the hospital's grand revival! Although we have all been promoted to doctors, patients are still unfamiliar with the nature of Chinese medicine. No one wants to continue marching into the crematorium furnace. We instead yearn to hear you convey the highest directives sent down from the Yellow Emperor! Only then can we be assured that the correct path forward will be maintained."

The Editor in Chief unfolds a brand-new newspaper, revealing the headline: **Einstein: A Lantern of Universal Truth**. It is an exclusive interview with the Venerable 'Stein. "You have completely transformed our world!" pleads the Editor in Chief, trying to convince Einstein: "Those who contribute most to the elevation of human life should be rewarded with the greatest respect and love. Behold these Dead Souls— their hearts call out for you! The Medicinal Empire needs a man with your knowledge, power, and authority to be our King! To have you as our leader would be the patients' greatest fortune! We must not allow the new hospital to slip into factionalism and disorder, and only you can unify everyone's thoughts and minds! All you have to do is utter a single command, and we will go to our deaths for you willingly!"

The mob of patients breaks into a chant:

To maintain unity, we shall die for you!
To end internal strife, we shall die for you!

After declining the honor three times, Einstein seemingly has no choice but to accept the invitation extended to him. He stands before the crematorium oven to deliver his acceptance speech: "Under the leadership of the Yellow Emperor, the new hospital has been created. Patients are in charge, and this is a critical step forward in reconstructing the Medicinal Empire! I cannot personally take the credit; this monumental moment in human history is instead the result of the collective efforts of the Dead Souls. Only by sacrificing oneself for society can we find meaning in our short and perilous lives. Pursuing truth is much more difficult and precious than possessing truth. I shall work tirelessly to realize the goal of fulfilling patients' ardent yearning for new forms of medicine! I vow never to let you down. I shall find the Universal Treatment Machine—the final shackle that has enslaved patients for so long—and smash it to bits! Our hearts shall be united and never again divided! The Yellow Emperor shall forever be by our side. We shall plant medicinal herbs on every planet in the universe and welcome a new era of true world peace!"

The bell-like sound of Einstein's words makes its way to your ears, but something about the timbre of his voice is solid yet empty, close and yet so far away. You are in an almost trancelike state as you gaze up at the dome. Grayish-red sparks shoot into the sky before transforming into the blurry image of a dead man's face: the Yellow Emperor, the greatest Dead Soul in all of time and space, the leader of all ghostly spirits. He never abandoned the people; he has been with everyone all along. Your body floats up toward the Yellow Emperor. You soar through the air, leaving Mars behind, and arrive at a vast, ocean-like space, where you discover a series of green, white, blue, cyan, and brown floating plants that resemble sea algae. They emit a strong medicinal scent and have long dark tentacles that extend toward millions of other galaxies, weaving a boundless spiderweb structure that ensnares patients like insects in a dense forest where all of humankind's diseases are finally cured. Once resurrected, they shall never die again, achieving the eternal life they have so longed for. This is a moment you have secretly anticipated, or else long ago experienced. Your memory has been completely restored.

Then an even louder wave of sound washes over you. With Rousseau and the Editor in Chief leading the chorus, the patients chant:

> Out integrity is greater than heaven,
> Our faith is higher than a mountain!
> Our loyalty shall never be betrayed,
> We shall die for you!

Heat surges through your body, and you are filled with gratitude. But a feeling of jealousy also rises up within you, as if your "father" has suddenly stolen your place. You should be the greatest king in the universe! Of course, right now you can't let such thoughts be exposed. Perhaps you can share them with Summer Stream, if she ever returns. You find yourself thinking more and more about that middle-aged female military doctor. After all, you'll never be able to lay a finger on Winter Dew.

18

TO KILL OR BE KILLED

The newly appointed President of the Mars Hospital and King of the Medicinal Empire, Einstein establishes a new leadership team. You are appointed to the roles of Executive Vice President, Director of Administration, and Prime Minister. Rousseau is appointed Vice President, Director of Hospital Security, and Minister of the Interior. Winter Dew is appointed Assistant to the President, Director of the Hospital Research Center, and Minister of Development and Reform. The Editor in Chief continues to serve as Editor in Chief, as well as Minister of Propaganda, tasked with controlling all public speech and discourse. The Editor in Chief rechristens *Geriatric Health News* as *Imperial News from the Apricot Forest*, named after the legendary physician Dong Feng, who asked his patients to plant apricot trees instead of paying him. He also reprinted the content about the Yellow Emperor from *Imperial News from the Apricot Forest* in the latest edition of *Principles of Hospital Engineering*. Other key patients are installed as directors of various departments and ministers of various cabinets. They hold a cabinet meeting to devise a top-level plan for the future of the hospital and the empire.

Time waits for no man, and the new hospital administration gets right to work. Einstein decides to abandon the Red Cross and establish a new symbol for the hospital, a dragon-shaped staff made from the bones of dead patients and carved with ornate engravings of toads and geckos—the "Sacred Talisman of Salvation." When the talisman is revealed, the mob of patients drinks and waves it in the air, shouting, "A

new world where heaven and earth are remade! An earthshaking transformation of both heaven and earth! Struggle against heaven and earth!
Heaven and earth are now under our control! A historical moment so
touching that even heaven and earth are moved!" After studying the
new classics, the patients gradually forget their old language.

The most important task for the Medicinal Empire's new government is to stage a large-scale song-and-dance performance to celebrate the founding of the new hospital. At Einstein's request, you are
appointed to spearhead preparations for the event. You examine the
hospital, now in rubble. You cannot even find where the stage is, so in
an almost dreamlike state, you go to the Pool of Dead Souls, where you
finally have a revelation. Everything may have changed, but the Pool of
Dead Souls is as it ever was, marked by incessant waves and the constant
sound of mournful sobbing. You find yourself both terrified and moved.
Did the pool create the Dead Souls? Or did the Dead Souls create it?
You gaze down into the red waves but cannot see your own reflection.
The pool is a huge, boundless, opaque mass with no beginning and no
end, mirroring the world beyond Mars. You think of those doctors and
patients who died in the recent struggle. Will they be resurrected in this
pool? If they are given a chance to live again, what will they remember
of their previous lives? You are again gripped by an unsettling feeling,
unable to get Summer Stream out of your mind. You sit down beside
the pool.

Patients are always overtaken by an uncontrollable feeling of ecstasy
when they see the Pool of Dead Souls. They know that they have
returned to the place of their birth, and everyone remembers the fact
that they are the beautiful fruits, the crystallization, of disaster. Their
births and rebirths are painful, but they draw confidence and strength
from the process.

Einstein seems quite pleased. "This is the place."

The Flower Commandos are called back to duty, led by Winter
Dew and renamed Model Commandos. Waving human bones in the

air, the commandos march in formation around the pool. Einstein paces back and forth, pointing out various details to tweak in his capacity as Stage Manager for the big production, leading by example.

Rousseau dives right into the pool. As his head emerges, he yells, "What's all this business about the so-called Pool of Dead Souls? This is clearly a pool of living water! It's pretty rare to have a pool of flowing water like this on Mars! I'll bet it used to be the former Hospital President's private swimming pool! It's probably the most luxurious place on the planet! Stop trying to scare us with all this talk about ghosts and Dead Souls! You think we patients don't have the right to take a nice bath? As the saying goes: 'The essence of water, the foundation of the kidneys! Water conquers fire, bringing tranquility!'"

One after another, the patients wade into the pool to play in the water.

"Oh, this is holy water!" they cry. "We'll use this to cleanse our bodies and our souls! This is the source of our tears and our sniveling. Life and death are one, forever connected! Once we emerge, the treatment shall begin!"

Sensing that something isn't quite right, you say, "Wait a second, we haven't even begun the song-and-dance show yet."

But the patients are grumbling and growing impatient:

"If we wait for the performance to be over, do we have any idea what time it will be? By then the old Yellow Emperor will have grown angry with impatience!"

"We're just warming up for the performance in the pool."

"All we do is in the name of art!"

"Patients are doctors! Doctors are patients!"

"We need to practice medicine now and immediately start curing disease!"

Then, under the leadership of Rousseau, they begin waving the Sacred Talisman of Salvation and break into song:

Zi is the sign of the rat, *Chou* the sign of the ox,
Yin the sign of the tiger, and *Mao* the sign of the rabbit.
The rhythm of the twelve Chinese zodiac signs,
Is the essence of preserving good health throughout the four seasons.
I open *The Yellow Emperor's Classic of Internal Medicine*,
And with a key, I unlock its mysteries.
Capturing the light and shadows as they move,
I open *The Yellow Emperor's Classic of Internal Medicine*,
And with a key, I understand the origin of all life,
Enlightened to the ephemeral and ever-changing nature of the body!

Hearing their words, you realize that even the patients have mastered this shtick. You no longer have the upper hand. They are using this song to intimidate you. The only reason they still listen to you is out of respect for Einstein, but deep down they resent you. You are frightened by their show of force and worried that something bad might happen, something that could ruin the song-and-dance performance and put your own position in jeopardy. So you agree to participate in their little pilot program and try out this new form of treatment. You, too, are curious about the effectiveness of traditional Chinese medicine, though you remain concerned because you haven't reported any of this to Einstein.

Ecstatic to begin treatment, the patients leap out of the pool.

"So how does this treatment work?" they ask. "Is there a specific treatment plan?"

Rousseau demonstrates by example. He grabs one of the patients and throws him to the ground. Pulling his white lab jacket over the patient's head, Rousseau takes his Sacred Talisman of Salvation and begins beating the patient. Fresh blood and brain matter spurt out, but Rousseau keeps pummeling him until all that is left resembles a pulpy red gourd. The patient's blood trickles into the pool, adding a striking crimson hue to the liquid.

"So, this is how you administer treatment?" you ask, your voice full of sullen sadness. Deep down you feel concerned, remembering something similar you once witnessed in the sick ward, although the Sacred Talisman of Salvation has now taken the place of the Red Cross.

"According to *The Yellow Emperor's Classic of Internal Medicine*," Rousseau says, speaking in an eloquent, matter-of-fact style, like a real doctor, "this is the best treatment method. But keep in mind, this is a treatment plan that targets patients, not diseases."

"But that man you just beat is now a doctor, too, just like us." You watch as the life literally trickles out of the man's body, suddenly remembering that you, too, may once have murdered someone.

"Humph, he was just an 'inferior doctor,'" Rousseau says with a determined tone. "There is no place for people like him in the Medicinal Empire. In order to eliminate disease, we must first implement individualized treatment!"

"Oh . . ." You look back into the Pool of Dead Souls, the water still, like a massive eye staring back at you. You sense the terrible power that has accumulated within it.

"No one wants to remember what it was like to live through a disaster," Rousseau continues passionately, "but when those images appear in your mind, there is no way to exorcise them. What should one do? Memories can really be stubborn . . . well, during times like that, just jump in the pool and go swimming! There you will experience a sense of excitement unlike anything you've experienced before! Ah, now it's all coming back to me. Many years ago, I was a scholar who lived a quiet life, minding my own business, but then a catastrophe befell me. A new ruler took over the country. He launched a war and usurped the throne through conspiracy. Once in power, he murdered thousands of officials from the old regime. But one man was so talented that the new lord couldn't bring himself to kill him, instead sparing him so he could write an edict announcing the wonderous achievements of the new regime to the entire world. But this man, still loyal to his previous master, not only refused to write the edict, but cursed the new lord. In a fit of anger, the new lord announced, 'I will execute you and nine generations of your family!' But the man was stubborn and spoke back to the new lord: 'Just nine? How about ten?' And so the new lord counted the man's students and friends as the tenth generation and had them all beheaded, including the man's family. A total of nine hundred and ninety-nine people were executed. I was one of his students, and I, too, was killed that day. Now, after all this time, I have finally tracked down one of the descendants of the culprit—no, I have found the culprit himself! I just realized it. No matter how much time has passed, all debts must eventually be repaid. This is why the Yellow Emperor had us all reunite here on Mars. There is no escape from this place!" Rousseau waves the Sacred Talisman of Salvation in the air, viciously smashing things around him.

"I remember now too," another patient chimes in. "What happened to you isn't that bad. Only nine hundred and ninety-nine people were killed. I now remember the catastrophe that befell me, and it was much more recent. Everything had been peaceful, but one day the leader suddenly announced that someone had written an essay of a treacherous nature. An edict came down to kill him and anyone involved without prejudice! Not only was the author killed, but large numbers of people associated with him were implicated. In the end, fifteen thousand people were executed! I was one of them. Alas, now the victims can finally face their murderer! But the quarrel between these two parties cannot be resolved through a simple heart transplant, like the old hospital used to do. This time, we need to take matters into our own hands by applying our new treatment methods!" With that, he grabs hold of another patient and smashes in his skull.

As if afflicted by a contagious disease, other patients start offering similar testimonials. "Ah, I also just realized that I used to live under the same roof with the man next to me—I was his son. That year there was a major natural disaster, made worse by poor decisions, and in the end we were left with nothing to eat. As we were trying to escape, he killed me as an offering to the village chief. They cooked me and consumed my flesh . . ." With that, he begins to "treat" the patient beside him.

"Oh my, my memory has returned as well!" another patient chimes in. "When the disaster first broke out, I thought it was a gift from heaven, so I immediately signed up to join the defense brigade. I was ready to fight to the death to make sure the positive results we had achieved weren't taken away. I was wounded in the battle, and when the brigade was eventually forced to retreat, they left me and one other soldier behind. We lay there, waiting for death. That's when I noticed a corpse holding a first aid kit. I was able to grab it and discovered some sulfonamide pills inside. There wasn't much left, and the other soldier killed me so he could have everything for himself. He managed to survive and went on to marry my wife . . . now I have finally found him! He killed me over a dose of medicine, and now I'm going to give him a taste of *my* medicine!" With that, he begins beating the man beside him.

Another patient comes forward. "This guy beat me to death, and I didn't even know him! It was all because I participated in a performance like the one we are doing. But in the middle of the performance, one of the audience members reported us, accusing me and the other actors of trying to incite a riot. Many innocent actors were killed that day. It was horrific. They even pulled out our teeth and skinned us alive, abandoning what was left of us beneath the stage so no one could even claim our bodies. They even hung signs around our necks that read 'Criminal.'" He immediately pounces on his target.

Other patients begin to shout:

"Our relatives are all dead!"

"We're dead too . . ."

"We remember everything!"

"We know where the Dead Souls came from!"

"The source of the injustices we suffered has been revealed, and the person responsible for the blood debt has a name!"

"Let's give them their medicine! We'll prepare a potent prescription for them!"

Acts of retributive violence spread as the patients administer acts of "treatment" alongside the Pool of Dead Souls. Everyone's movements are in sync, delivering violent blows to the same rhythm, like a group of early *Homo erectus* making stone tools together in their cave. These patients lived during different time periods, yet they are all victims of calamity. Suddenly remembering their pasts, they come to realize that their experiences are the true source of their illness. And so, one by one, they use medical methods to find a resolution. It's not that these former enemies can't get along but that this mayhem is the true objective behind the construction of the Mars Hospital. We live many lives, and as long as you continue to be resurrected, you are bound to run into your enemy eventually. You realize this is like the old saying, "The more you try to run away from the source of your suffering, the more likely you are to run into it."

Other patients shout, "After death we can finally do all the things we couldn't while we were alive!" They huddle over their medical charts, frantically writing notes, clearly and carefully, exactly as stipulated in *Principles of Hospital Engineering*. Every illness, every symptom, every medicine, every cause of death is meticulously jotted down without the slightest mistake. The patients learned how to do this a long time ago—who said they aren't real doctors? But this is just a warm-up for the coming song-and-dance performance.

You never imagined that the patients would take to being "superior doctors" so quickly. You gaze back into the waters of the Pool of Dead Souls and vaguely make out the shining golden light of the Cosmic Hospital. You hear Winter Dew's voice echoing in your ear. You don't try to stop any of it, but instead just report back to Einstein, "They have identified a new disease and have already begun the treatment process."

Einstein's ego bursts with pride, his face a bright, burning red. He coughs loudly before addressing you in a thunderous voice. "My brother

Yang Wei, that is absolutely wonderful! As for who's sick and who's not, let the patients decide! Since this is a new hospital, the patients should be in charge!" Then, holding the Sacred Talisman of Salvation in his hand, Einstein leaps into the Pool of Dead Souls, swimming through the bloodred water like a crocodile. Winter Dew takes off her clothes and dives in after him, swimming by his side.

You stand next to the pool and hear a strange scream but do not dare go into the water. You wonder how you died during the catastrophe. Did you die a painful death? Who was responsible for it? Where is he? If he were to appear at this moment, would you deliver his "treatment"? You seem to be the only one who has yet to remember his true past, like the moon reflecting on the surface of the water . . .

Einstein and Winter Dew wave to you from the water, but their image gradually grows hazy, as if they are fading into another world. You have a bad feeling about what is about to happen and grow increasingly worried. Was the objective of this eruption of violence achieved? Where is the Universal Treatment Machine? Has the Hospital President been brought to justice? What exactly is this bacteria that has been killing the doctors? Might it mutate and begin to infect patients as well?

You are on the verge of warning Einstein and Winter Dew, but you bite your tongue. Consumed with a sense of disillusionment, you stare blankly as the mob of patients enthusiastically carries out its new treatment techniques, passionately tossing dead bodies into the Pool of Dead Souls, which is finally living up to its namesake.

Rousseau leads a group of patients to the Martian farm, where they tear out the plants and throw them into a bloody pool, shouting, "Here among the stars we plant Chinese herbal medicine!"

More and more patients leap into the pool, gathering around Einstein. In their white lab coats, they trample the bloated corpses with glee. With their laughing and singing, their merriment moves both heaven and earth. The performance has officially begun!

But none of them notices a group of men approaching.

THE DOCTORS STRIKE BACK

19

SPRING OF THE MONSTERS

Strange humanoid creatures approach the Pool of Dead Souls. They wear white lab coats, their heads wrapped in green turbans made from the remnants of military uniforms. Each holds a white flag with an image of the Mars satellite Forbes. The group resembles a terrifying fireball rolling toward you. Leading them is an old youth like you, with a fat head, big ears, a bird's eyes, a pig's nose, shiny spots on his skin, and a body that resembles an overgrown baby's. He is carried by four strange creatures. Just behind him is Dr. Daptomycin, who leads four doctors from the Gerontology Department. They carry a stretcher, upon which lies the rightful President of the Mars Hospital.

Only later will you realize that those strange creatures in the green turbans are monkeys, absolutely identical clones escaped from a test lab. As model organisms with the same genetic background, they were originally used for drug screenings. Later, when it was predicted that the hospital would enter a period of turbulence and instability, the monkeys were genetically upgraded to deal with rioting patients: the amygdala regions of their brains were remolded to control their instinctual bodily functions. The monkeys were rechristened "Holy Warriors" that would not hesitate to risk their lives fighting sadistic patients.

Unlike the doctors, they experience neither fear or pain. Outfitted with artificial vocal cord implants, they communicate with their operator via headsets that detect the monkeys' thought patterns through a miniature brain scanner, analyzing their neural activities and then sending them instructions in real time. The monsters march side by side with humans, and it is hard to tell them apart. This is the "Greenpeace Army."

The fat child leading the group whistles, signaling Dr. Daptomycin to sit the Hospital President up in his stretcher. The old man can't speak, but he points to the patients playing in the Pool of Dead Souls as if he wants to administer their treatment personally, displaying an expression of wanton desire to possess everything around him that makes the patients tremble and recoil. The monkey army breaks into the chorus of a song, their slurred, desolate voices carrying an almost human quality:

> You are patients,
> And should know your place.
> Escaping from the sick ward,
> Who is it all for?

The boy with the engorged baby body, Dr. Daptomycin, and the four doctors sing the refrain:

> Who is it all for?
> Who am I?
> On whom can we rely?

This powerful song brings the patients' performance to an end, their singing and dancing worthless by comparison. The actors' legs go weak, as if paralyzed. They cry for help and collapse into the pool. Meanwhile, the Greenpeace Army continues to sing, transformed into the main actors in this long-awaited song-and-dance performance. Perhaps they were always the main performers and had simply taken a short intermission.

Hearing the humans and monsters sing together is a hundred times better than any bone talisman or golf club. Their voices are the most powerful deadly weapon of all. The patients piss their pants and strip away their outer shells, showing themselves for who they really are. The song guides the monkeys forward, their bodies dancing and joints cracking as they imitate a doctor performing surgery. Steadily they approach the patients.

You are terribly confused. Where in the hospital could this powerful army have sprung from?

"The moment of truth has arrived!" Einstein tries to remain calm. "We must defend the new hospital to the death! We shall crush the doctors' counterattack! The Yellow Emperor walks beside us . . . there can be no true progress without sacrifice!"

He orders Winter Dew and the Flower Commandos to take the lead, while he hangs back, supervising the battle. The female nurse is immediately torn apart by the monkeys, her limbs and organs littering the ground. Next it is the patients' turn. Worn out by their earlier game of vengeance, and then all that drinking and sex, not to mention all the effort expended on their big performance, how could they possibly be a match for the Holy Warriors? Strong and agile organisms, the genetically engineered monkey-creatures leap into the air, descending upon their opponents with great force. Their legs wrap around the patients' bodies; they grab necks, bite noses, twist heads. It quickly becomes apparent that the patients are nothing but a ragtag crew of pseudo-doctors, and the patient army falls like a mountain collapsing.

Just moments ago, the Medicinal Empire's grand ceremony to celebrate its founding was in full swing, but the entire scene has completely transformed. Not knowing what else to do, you begin silently reciting passages from *The Yellow Emperor's Classic of Internal Medicine* to drive away your fears. But never in your wildest dreams have you imagined the hospital would mobilize monsters to suppress the patients.

The monkeys grab Rousseau and strip him of his Sacred Talisman of Salvation. Under their crushing grip, his body makes a series of strange sounds, his sores and tumors burst open, his chest heaves violently, and blood spurts from his mouth. An acute hemorrhage sends him into hypovolemic shock, and the fatal blow comes via a ruptured carotid artery, which causes an influx of blood to rush into his lacerated esophagus and into his stomach, leading to incessant bloody vomiting. The look in Rousseau's eyes at the moment of death does not speak of pain, but shock. His final words: "Don't . . . let my departure . . . leave you sad! If . . . I were to live, none of you . . . would survive . . ." The monkey soldiers release a cacophony of unbridled chirps and squeals, their bodies covered in blood, which only adds to their excitement.

You have seen many things in your life, but even you are horrified. The death scene you've just witnessed is hard to face, and you are gripped by a sense of terror. And yet, perhaps it is a good thing that Rousseau died, not from causes related to the diseases he suffered—difficulty breathing, uncontrollable diarrhea and incontinence, organ failure, systemic decline—but in a swift, decisive death. Moreover, he avenged himself, thereby fulfilling one of his greatest wishes in life. Maybe this was Rousseau's own way of resisting his own mortality.

As you struggle with this deep sense of shame, one of the monkey soldiers leaps right in front of you. You hold your breath and gaze into the beast's eyes—somehow, you see yourself. The monkey's shiny bluish teeth are sharper than a scalpel. It gazes at you, hard, and in that moment you realize how young this creature is, brimming with a youthful energy, a creature that has truly dedicated its entire life to the service of medicine. You feel incredibly ashamed as you imagine what you will look like after the monkey has torn your body to shreds.

An awkward, unnatural smile appears on your face. Although you have died several times before, it would be a lie to say you are used to it. You know the clock is ticking, and you are gripped by an extreme sense of dread. Your mind races. You wonder what this is all about. The newly re-formed Medicinal Empire has crumbled, and the universe of traditional herbal medicine has disappeared. You are nothing but a Dead Soul, empty as before, and your death is but a tiny drop in the grand ocean of universal destruction. You extend your hand to welcome the Holy Warrior before you. The moment seems to last forever . . . but this is exactly what you have always expected from the hospital.

Someone pulls you away, and as if awakening from a dream, you snap out of your daze, turn, and run. It is Summer Stream! Somehow, at this critical moment, she has returned to offer you salvation. The monkey freezes at the sight of her. Summer Stream sprays it with a dose of anesthetic, and it falls to the ground immediately.

Unsure if you should feel happy or sad, you ask her, "Why did you save me? Did you suddenly remember the task you were assigned to do?"

"Run! Don't give in to the temptation of death. This is very different from drinking!"

There is a *much* stronger hand of fate linking the two of you, you realize.

You and Summer Stream slip into the ranks of the defeated army of patients, now led by Einstein and Winter Dew. The generals Einstein appointed have either been killed, run away, or surrendered. The monkeys leap through the air in pursuit. The Yellow Emperor never appears to save the patients. After all this drama, the hospital remains in the hands of the doctors.

The patients made the mistake of not taking the angels in white seriously enough. They misjudged the situation and severely underestimated their enemy. The rebellion is doomed. Without altering the fundamental structure of the hospital itself, it is impossible to change the relationship between those who receive treatment and those who provide treatment. The current order was arranged long ago, when the earliest monk expedition team first discovered Mars. You can't help but secretly laugh at Einstein, this man who claims to be your father and the so-called successor and spokesperson of the Yellow Emperor, yet who brims with internal contradictions.

You and Summer Stream run, but the monkeys quickly catch up and take you captive.

20

BASTARD CHILD

The child leader of the Greenpeace Army addresses the patients with a tone of bitter anger: "Patients, you have betrayed the trust the hospital invested in you!" He turns to you. "Patient Yang, were you not appointed Team Leader of the Red Label Commando Unit? Have you forgotten that the hospital is currently surrounded by powerful enemies? The entire hospital now finds itself confronting a perilous time. We need to unite against the enemy. You better not betray us or turn out to be a spy!"

The boy is around eleven or twelve years old, but he is not Funeral Artist, who was in charge of the crematorium. He is someone new, different from ordinary doctors. He wears a green turban and white lab coat, but he doesn't wear a red cross, and he rides on the shoulders of a group of monkeys. His arrival marks the appearance of yet another child in the hospital, and you have a sense that the future will belong to these prematurely aged children. They will control the hospital, and old men like Einstein will fade from the stage of history.

Dr. Daptomycin flashes you a crafty smirk. "Do you know the man-child referred to as Zifeiyu, or 'You Who Are Not a Fish'? Only he can save the hospital and restore order after the patients' insurrection."

You suddenly recognize the child as Super Patient's son, the baby who was artificially inseminated, carried to term by a man, and delivered via C-section in the sick ward. You once saved him by carrying him with you as you escaped for your life. You placed him on the deck before committing suicide by throwing yourself into the sea. You haven't seen him in a very long time and are surprised by how large he has grown. His facial features resemble your own. The Holy Warriors look at you in confusion, wondering if you are related. From their expressions, you detect both surprise and respect. The former doctor Einstein led the patient uprising and became your father, but now the Greenpeace Army is fighting back, and they are led by Super Patient's child, who happens to look just like you!

"What year is this?" you ask in a panic.

Someone blurts out, "2049." It is the Editor in Chief of *Imperial News from the Apricot Forest*. He, too, has defected to the hospital's side.

"Isn't it 1976?" you ask in confusion. You remember this being a decisive year in the Second World War. How wonderful if you were still in World War II. Things were so much simpler back then.

"Actually, it is 2066," replies Dr. Daptomycin. "Everything is starting over again."

You wonder, *Could all of this be occurring in the future?*

"Perhaps you were momentarily confused, or someone deceived you?" says Zifeiyu. "You were all held hostage by Einstein and weren't responsible for your actions. But Einstein has always been a member of the antiscience camp! Can you believe it? He once said, 'Life only has meaning when you live for others.' Ridiculous!"

"He was quite arrogant in his youth," says Dr. Daptomycin. "He was driven out from the ranks of the doctors, so he harbors a deep hatred for the hospital. He abandoned science completely and instead embraced the theories of yin and yang and the Eight Trigrams. That's when he started using these superstitious ideas to deceive the patients."

"The instructor was right when he said that patients are all sinners," the Editor in Chief says. "A shame that the patients brutally murdered him . . ."

"Wasn't there some kind of bacteria that did in the doctors?" you ask, with some trepidation. "But now you are using experimental monkeys to—"

"My dear patient," Zifeiyu interrupts, revealing a sinister smirk. "You are weak, ignorant, simplistic, and naive. You have been deceived by an illusion. But had they not deceived you, how could they have coaxed you out of your little hole? Don't you know? Patients are utterly incapable of an outrageous revolt against the hospital."

You are so shattered with sadness that you break into tears and rip out your last few remaining strands of hair. You hand the small clump of hair to Zifeiyu to prove your innocence. You figure he must know that you once taught mathematics. Zifeiyu reacts to your hair like he has just been handed a ball of fire, screaming and throwing it to the ground.

"They may have been kidnapped, but they are still utterly despicable!" Zifeiyu says angrily. "Don't you want to establish a new hospital? I hear you want to be the Hospital President? You even want to be King? That's just wonderful! 'Those soldiers who are not willing to be a general are not good soldiers.' Do you know who said that?"

"Napoleon?" you respond nervously.

"No, it was a patient who said that!" says Dr. Daptomycin.

"His name was Zhu Yuanzhang," the Editor in Chief adds.

"No, his name was Shi Tiesheng," Zifeiyu corrects him. "Shi Tiesheng is a novelist, and the most outstanding patient novelist at that! But that's not exactly what he originally said. He said, 'From the point of birth, people don't want to die, yet as soon as we come into the world, we are already on the road to death. This brings us fear.' But he also said that this gives us the opportunity to achieve happiness. Such a deep philosophical message!" Looking down at the torn-up patient corpses strewn across the ground, Zifeiyu covers his mouth in glee.

Maybe everything that has happened was merely a warm-up for this moment, all part of a massive song-and-dance variety show. Nothing can happen except what the hospital originally programmed. But how did Zifeiyu become the leader? This child seems to have an extremely high IQ and is quite cunning. His large eyeballs spin round as he details what sounds like a well-thought-out plan: "Many have attempted to overthrow the hospital, but all have failed, without exception. The hospital may have a lot of problems, but it has yet to reach its end. And you patients want to establish a Medicinal Empire? Keep dreaming! History repeats itself, over and over, but different paths all lead to the same destination. The hospital was established to prove that patients are merely patients. How could it possibly allow everyone to become a doctor? Would that not be a terrible disaster?"

"Speaking of the Universal Treatment Machine," Dr. Daptomycin jumps in, "it's like a bear trap, specially designed to ensnare patients." He breaks into a fit of arrogant laughter.

"The most important thing is to maintain stability," the Editor in Chief says, with a sense of justice. "We can't carry on like this, or we won't get anything done! The hospital needs to start functioning like a hospital again!"

You look over to the Hospital President on his stretcher, hoping the old man might save you. But he seems to be afflicted with some serious illness, lying there in a semicomatose state, quietly mumbling incomprehensible words.

Full of regret, you decide to speak up. "I was deceived, because of my own naivety. But I don't want to be a general, and I certainly don't want to be a hospital president, a king, or even a novelist!"

All you really want is to find the Universal Treatment Machine and eradicate the source of all pain, to rid yourself of the burden of being labeled a "Dead Soul," to live your life like a normal living person. You hope that Zifeiyu might forgive you, that he's not the kind of person to carry a grudge, but the patients have murdered doctors, raped nurses, destroyed hospital equipment, and disrupted order in the sick ward— can they really be forgiven?

Patient prisoners line up under the watchful eyes of the Holy Warriors. The prisoners report on each other, exposing one another's misdeeds and divulging crimes—who suffers from which illness, who destroyed what medical equipment, who killed which doctor. You join in, clasping Summer Stream's hand, but she lowers her head and doesn't say a word, as if lost in deep thought. Which side will she take?

Zifeiyu pinches one of the monkeys on the cheek before turning to the old man on the stretcher. "The old Hospital President is a highly respected artist who abhors violence and has never coveted power. That is why we all love him so. When it comes to art, our dear monkeys also adore music. Once they start drinking, they break into song, and no one can stop them! When it comes down to it, medicine is an art. How could we expect the patients to understand this? You can't expect someone who hums a few simple notes to compose a great song. That's the real tragedy here."

"That's right," says Dr. Daptomycin: "Thank goodness the Holy Warriors stepped in to save us at that crucial moment! The monkeys are no longer performing 'Uproar in Heaven.' Their professional performances will drive away the demons that have possessed the patients' bodies and souls, the Yellow Emperor and his minions. This is no simple war. It is a struggle between faith and aesthetics."

"That's why the doctors need to come back," says the Editor in Chief, tears of passion running down his cheeks. "They need to bring order out of chaos and restore the correct medical perspective! There is still hope for our hospital yet!"

Zifeiyu smiles and raises a bottle of spirits high in the air. Thinking he is inviting you to drink, you approach him, but the monkeys immediately encircle you and take away the bottle. Zifeiyu thinks this is hilarious and begins drinking with the Holy Warriors, whose hands are still stained with human blood. Zifeiyu and the monkeys are like naive children. You watch them with envy, seeing your own reflection in the alcohol. But deep down you curse Zifeiyu: *Bastard child!*

Dr. Daptomycin leads the prisoners to the morgue, where they are locked up. The Editor in Chief changes the name of *Imperial News from the Apricot Forest* to *Greenpeace Daily* and publishes a supplement with this headline: The Doctors Take Complete Control over the Hospital.

21

A BANQUET IN HELL

You find yourself locked in the morgue with Summer Stream, the other patients, and a host of stored corpses. There you witness firsthand the high level of professionalism displayed by the Holy Warriors as they meticulously search for hidden patients. When they find them, they immediately execute them without so much as a word of explanation. Then they strip the patients of their white lab coats and medical jackets so that they themselves can wear them. They also make military flags from the clothing, which they adorn with the Forbes logo. These articles of clothing have finally been returned to their rightful owners. But things haven't come completely full circle, because many of these white lab coats are transformed into something else. Within the new exists the old, and within the old exists the new.

Guided by this new sea of white flags, the Greenpeace Army expands its reach even further. The patients look like a forest of wooden trees, just sitting there awaiting death. The crazed energy they exhibited earlier seems to have disappeared. The act of stripping the patients of their doctor's uniforms and putting them on feels like an unnecessary step for the Holy Warriors, but it serves as a powerful metaphor for the doctor-patient relationship. You witness members of the Holy Warriors ripping apart human bodies with a level of precision and comfort that is difficult for most patients to imagine. They reach their clawed, hairy hands into the patients' chest cavities, dig around, and remove their organs in one fell swoop. But they only take the important organs, those shaped like eggplants and grapes that can now be used for experiments, transplants, and educational purposes. The monkeys show no interest in nerves and capillaries; only neurosurgeons pay attention to such things. While orthopedic surgeons love the complexity of human bones, the monkeys seem indifferent to them. They handle the dead bodies as if these patients were never alive, with no taboos regarding how they process the dead. Perhaps they are getting ready to create a new army of Dead Souls. You realize that all of this might be in order to prepare material for the new edition of *Principles of Hospital Engineering*. Only dissections carried out according to the principles of modern anatomy can provide valuable content. But the subjects being served are now different.

The Holy Warriors take the remains of the patient bodies, dice them up, and make them into human chop suey, and the monkeys' eating noises resemble a raging tidewater coming to a boil. Before each patient is killed, genetic matter is extracted, and their memories are scanned. A new round of rebirth will begin at the ordained time.

"This is how we will build an exhibition hall for new medical technologies and an arena for new pharmaceuticals," Summer Stream comments. "This will show those doctors who betrayed the hospital!"

You worry about the predicament that you and Summer Stream have found yourselves in. "What should we do?" you ask.

You are hoping she might lead you to the doctors' camp, where you can make a show of repentance, formally surrender, and receive their gracious pardon.

"Even if you want to go back, there is no going back," she responds. "These monsters are no longer the doctors they once were. They are guided by a new faith and aesthetics."

You are disappointed, but also struck by Summer Stream's beauty, and so you decide to stay with her. The two of you run off. She knows the area well and leads you into one of the freezers. Patient bodies stored here have been torn into tiny pieces and are now frozen to the floor. Afraid of freezing to death, the two of you stay only a short time.

As you continue, a thick mist descends, and you can barely make out the path in front of you. You begin to ascend, and when you reach the highest point, you can see many parts of the hospital burning. The fires look like a series of new crematoria sprung up out of thin air. Bursts of magma leap out of the ground, deforming the sick wards and hills surrounding the hospital. The hospital is alive with a cascade of brilliant colors, the dome intact and holding. The desert, rock ridges, impact craters, and shield volcanoes surrounding the dome are all hidden by the thick fog. Patients run everywhere, in a state of chaos, while the monkey soldiers leap after them in pursuit, as if everyone is now on a sinking island with no possibility of escape. A small group of patients manages to stage a last stand against the monkeys.

"Where did all this anger come from?" You shake your head in dismay, but you don't tell Summer Stream about Winter Dew's academic research project. This could be considered an expression of the art of benevolence.

"You are so immature!" says Summer Stream. "Didn't I tell you that it has aesthetic value? It is like a doomsday exhibition, unlike any you have ever seen before. You could also refer to it as an 'out-of-print edition.'"

"Patients are indeed vulgar. But what can we do about it?" You wonder if the war between the Yellow Emperor and Chiyou broke out over opposing literary views.

"Your father is completely out of touch with the times. The medical field isn't for everyone—it is like walking a tightrope. He doesn't understand the true meaning of art. When you end up responding to violence with more violence, you are destined to come to no good."

"But he's not my father. My real father died a long time ago. Einstein simply grabbed some random person—who happened to be me—to satisfy his fantasy of finding an original genetic connection." You want to ask, *And what about you, Summer Stream? Who are you? Didn't you also betray the hospital? Do you really understand medicine and art?* But you do not dare. She has suffered enough. Moreover, had it not been for her, you would have been a Dead Soul a long time ago.

"I'm sorry, I don't know who he really is," you mutter.

"Huh? Isn't he Einstein? He should have a formula in that head of his to prove the universe is beautiful." Summer Stream's voice is filled with regret.

"So he also forgot his original identity? That's the real tragedy?"

"That's right. He will make a much greater contribution to humankind. One day his ideas will change our definition of how the universe was created."

"So it has nothing to do with planting medicinal plants and herbs on all the planets?"

"Einstein will invent a new theory of time and space, completely reshaping the relationship between cause and effect, order, and responsibility. These ideas not only concern medicine, but also spill into politics, art, and culture. This enlightenment movement will be much more important than the Medicinal Empire."

The image of Einstein in his white lab jacket flashes through your mind, spitting green phlegm and ordering Rousseau to deliver more electric shocks to the doctors. "How could you know?" you ask.

"Professor Eternal mentioned it a long time ago."

"Then who am I? How did I die?" You figure that Professor Eternal must be long dead. He was a much more pathetic figure than Einstein. Summer Stream shakes her head. That's when several pieces of the dome start to crash to the ground. Everyone around you screams, thinking the dome is about to collapse.

"There is no way for us to escape," you lament.

"There's actually nothing to escape from."

"If there were only five minutes left in the world, what would you do?"

"You first. What would *you* do?" she asks.

You rack your brain for a moment. "I'd spend those final minutes with you." You figure that if the monkeys came to kill you in those final moments, you could use her as a human shield.

"You are one duplicitous man . . . ," she sneers.

"And you?" you ask.

"I'd spend my last moments eating and drinking, even if I only had five minutes."

"You're still a foodie! Maybe you could use that time to come down with a new illness!"

"You're still a patient! You really know how to get on a doctor's good side. But I can't treat you."

"You're right, I've always been a patient. I should have stayed in the sick ward like a good boy. Only now do I understand that true meaning comes only through illness. My old life was so much better. I no longer appreciate things like I used to. When people are sick, they retract into their own little shells. They become small minded and grow sharp wartlike objects. Patients eventually start to feel like they are nothing but a typo or a deleted punctuation mark. They realize that being illustrious and debonair is meaningless, and they begin to reflect inwardly. As the body experiences increasing amounts of pain, its antennae become more sensitive, allowing you to finally see the situation you are in clearly. After spending so long on Mars, one loses the ability to see the truth. This is proving to be the most painful lesson one can learn, but also the most valuable. Even more important is the realization that disease is a patient's most powerful weapon. Once he has grasped this lesson, he can do whatever he wants, not going to work, acting shamelessly, and spewing whatever bullshit comes to mind. That's why the doctors are intent on removing disease from the patients' bodies—it is the most severe punishment a doctor can inflict. This is what led to the uprising. We simply don't have enough time to spend on getting sick!" You begin to hate Summer Stream. You don't have the same deep connection with

her that you feel around Winter Dew, and the smell of her body is
enough to drive you mad.

"Little Wei, having spent your entire life afflicted with various illnesses, are there certain things you now see more clearly? What are they?
Can you share that with me? Is there any real benefit to you patients
when doctors cure you?" She indignantly punches you in the arm.

You have the urge to talk back to her but can't quite work up the
courage. Just thinking about your own past, and how tenuous the line
between your life and death has been, you feel like you don't have the
right to say anything, so you just sneak a glimpse of her breasts and
whisper, "Summer Stream, my daughter looks just like you. She was
young when I left her. But I still remember her. I have no idea if she is
alive or dead. And my father—if he is still alive—doesn't even know he
has a granddaughter . . ." You think back to when Einstein ordered the
patients to gang-rape Summer Stream and feel a mix of excitement and
envy shoot through your veins. She, on the other hand, seems to have
forgotten that it even happened.

The dark fog grows thicker, and it becomes difficult to breathe.
Summer Stream puts down the oxygen tank she has been carrying on
her back and inhales some fresh air. You take a few breaths. The area
around you is dark and gloomy. You hear only the sound of weeping,
but you can't make anyone out. The crematorium flames continue to
burn bright, like hot lava cutting through the night. You are terrified,
and also gripped by the need for a strong drink. Finally, you just put
your head in your hands and squat.

Summer Stream counts on her fingers. "It's a solar eclipse. Forbes
has blocked out the sun."

Neither of you has ever seen a solar eclipse.

"From the hospital's perspective," Summer Stream continues, "this
is not allowed. Every time a solar eclipse was about to occur, Funeral
Artist would tweak the atmosphere to block it out. I'm not sure why,
but the hospital was intent on cutting off our relationship with nature.

They seemed to think that it was the source of the coming catastrophe. But now that the hospital has undergone such a radical change, there is no one left in charge of things like this, and the light from the eclipse has shone through."

You work up the courage to look up. "But how could it penetrate all of that hellish smoke and fire?" You remember Forbes being named after the son of Mars, the embodiment of cowardice and fear.

"It takes a curved path," Summer Stream responds. "It is said that light curves as it passes by the sun, but we can only see it during the solar eclipse."

"But it is clearly straight."

"The war is not yet over. The only one capable of such calculations is a patient under Einstein's care named Eddington—but he's already dead. Therefore, this supposition will never be proved. Perhaps the war between the doctors and the patients is simply a proxy war." She gazes out beyond the hospital at the Martian landscape with a look of bewilderment. The solar eclipse seems to have triggered a major revelation.

"Does that mean something more serious is still on the horizon?" The name "Eddington" echoes in your mind—you feel like you have encountered that name before.

"That's why we have to make sure we don't die right away. We have to risk living a bit longer to see what happens." She has a profound expression on her face, like a true intellectual or frontline soldier.

You are no stranger to this expression; you have seen it in the eyes of a few other women such as Bai Dai and Winter Dew. But Winter Dew is much more direct and goal oriented. Summer Stream is tougher. You hate these qualities, yet you can't seem to stop yearning for them.

You and Summer Stream are silent for a moment. You squat while she stands, both gazing at the solar eclipse with looks of mourning, because you know that this rare moment is slipping away right before your eyes. You make out a series of unrecognizable silhouettes hovering about three feet above the ground before floating away like ghosts. A chill runs through both your bodies, and you feel embarrassed, over-come with the urge to embrace her, but you hold yourself back.

"If someone were to take this opportunity to stab us in the back, it would all be over." Summer Stream's words are so cool and collected. It makes her even more sexy.

What follows is an almost carnivalesque celebration to commem-orate this great day. Temporarily forgetting the danger around them, the last remaining patients link hands and feel their way through the darkness toward the crematorium. Perhaps the eclipse has reminded them that the place where dead bodies burn is still safe. Indeed, as they get closer, that fragrant familiar scent reaches their noses.

"What's the big deal?" Summer Stream asks, smacking her lips. "Let's go take a look. I'll bet they'll have something for us to eat. You can't live on oxygen alone!"

You are also starting to feel hungry. Those women you knew in the past did the same thing, but Summer Stream is the most courageous of them all. Winter Dew would probably never have taken you out to eat.

The temptation of being a satiated ghost makes everyone tempo-rarily forget about everything else. The remaining doctors, patients, and monkeys all descend upon the crematorium. Everyone collects every last morsel in the cafeteria, puts down their weapons, and sits down to eat. There is no more killing. The grand banquet has begun! The cafeteria is decorated with colorful lanterns and lights, and the doctors and patients toast one another and joke about each other's clothing. The patients break out in song. But when they start reciting passages from *The Yellow Emperor's Classic of Internal Medicine*, the doctors start to heckle them: "You idiots! You're completely out of tune!" That makes the patients a bit more bashful. The doctors distribute leftover cigarettes and alcohol to the patients, who in turn give all the stolen surgical equipment back to the doctors.

You realize that the hospital has returned to its basic essence: eat-ing. After all, isn't treating disease reliant upon maintaining a healthy metabolism? Isn't oxygen intake needed to transform and transport the energy produced by food to the organs that need it? In the final analysis, survival relies upon carbohydrates, fats, and proteins. How can a patient be expected to survive on shots and pills alone? Whether the hospital can be saved is the litmus test that shall determine everything. Jesus was known for breaking bread, and the Buddha was known for begging for food—in this sense, they were both the same. One does not eat in order to survive; one survives in order to eat! Even ghosts need to eat. All of this brings you back to your golden days, when you first entered the hospital. Could that experience have been a projection of what is happening right now? But there is no need to engage in idle talk at the dinner table. Summer Stream urges you to hurry up and wolf down your food, and then you start drinking. It really is a big festive party. Ever since the lunar farm was destroyed, everyone has been eating the corpses of the dead doctors and patients. But the bodies are not consumed raw; they are well cooked and thoroughly prepared.

Summer Stream tries to make small talk as she eats. "Did your father really come to save you?"

"Didn't I tell you? Einstein isn't my father!" you answer, frustrated that she keeps bringing this up.

"The doctors caught us all off guard with their sudden attack. Why won't you admit that? Are you afraid of being implicated?"

"It's not that I don't admit it; I'm just conflicted about what happened . . ."

"But you must have had a real birth father? If you can access memories of him, maybe you will remember how you died."

"That's right . . ." Ever since you left the Hospital President's office, you can't remember eating a single decent meal. But now that you have some food in your stomach, you begin to feel human again. As your body processes those calories, all kinds of buried memories return, and you decide to share them with Summer Stream, hoping she will continue to provide you with compassion and support.

22

THE GATE OF FLESH

"The father I remember was a doctor," you say. "Just thinking about him leaves me somewhat at a loss for words. The world in which I once lived was very different from this place. But I'm not sure if it was that place by the sea. I have childhood memories of my father bringing me to play at the hospital where he used to work. The entire place was like one big nursery school. His intention was clear: he wanted to raise me to grow up and become a doctor. The field of medicine was in dire straits then. There were all kinds of heated conflicts between doctors and patients. Most doctors at the time didn't want their children to follow in their footsteps, but my father was different.

"The facility where my father worked was a small community hospital. You can't compare it to a massive facility like 301. Though it was small, it had all the necessary facilities, including an Emergency Room, Internal Medicine, Surgery Department, Gynecology, Preventive Medicine Clinic, Pharmacy, Laboratory, Radiology Department, and a Disinfection Room. I grew up accustomed to the smell of various medicinal ointments and was no stranger to all those colorful and strange-shaped medical utensils, bottles, jars, sharp objects, medical tape, gauze, medicines, liquids, blood, human bodies, and organs. I was exposed to all of those things from the very beginning. I spent every day wandering this forest of medicine. Many adult patients found this world difficult to get used to. In fact many were terrified by what they saw there, but not me.

"From a very early age, I lived amid a world of suffering. My ears were filled with the incessant sound of patients howling in pain. I thought this was simply the way of the world. I was never shocked or surprised by what I saw, but over time I grew annoyed. I started whining about wanting to go home, which left my father deeply disappointed. The more time I spent in the hospital, the more I began to dislike it there. I loathed those doctors. They looked utterly ridiculous in those large white jackets.

"My father was always good to me. He would often let me sit on his lap, playing while he saw patients. He would even hum little songs to me. But his medical skills weren't the best, and there was more than one occasion when his patients died after being treated by him. Somehow, he always avoided getting into trouble, claiming that his patients were simply too ill to treat, waited too long before seeking treatment, were misdiagnosed by quack doctors, or else their families refused to follow the hospital's suggested treatment plan. He even got the Hospital President to cover for him. The hospital concealed the truth by falsifying medical records, securing media endorsements, and defaming patients' families.

"The hospital walls were adorned with flowers, awards, and commendations. It might be okay for other work units to do this, but it is clearly not right for a hospital to engage in this type of behavior. Hospitals are in the business of saving human lives, not selling vegetables. They need to be one hundred percent free of mistakes. But my father and his colleagues were clearly not up to the task. It wasn't their fault; the Mars Hospital is also incapable of living up to that standard.

"The problem arises that the falsification of information becomes an everyday affair. The more incapable the doctors, the more unwilling they are to admit their mistakes. The patients know they will end up dying here, yet they still blindly flock to the hospital at the first sign of trouble. The doctors control all the information and have the professional advantage of leaving patients with few options. Patients think their lives are precious and valuable, and they truly believe the doctors will prevent them from dying. That creates a space for doctors like my father.

"Although his medical skills were abysmal, he did truly love the hospital. He was eventually promoted to Director of Internal Medicine and hailed as a 'model doctor.' He created an account for himself on social media and collected a huge number of followers. I felt like I was the only one who knew the truth about him, and I couldn't see a single thing he had done to contribute to society or make the world a better place.

"All the lousy money our family accrued came from my father accepting bribes in red envelopes. He sent me to the best private school in town. All my classmates kissed up to me when they learned my father was a doctor, but I knew that deep down they pitied me, even despised me, because my father took their relatives' money and never cured their illnesses. I knew that when the opportunity arose, they would try to get their revenge. I became depressed at school. I was the descendent of a cunning murderer in white. That's my father. How could someone like him lead the patients in a rebellion against the hospital?"

"Wow, I didn't realize you were a 'hospital brat,'" Summer Stream interjects. "No wonder I feel such a strong, natural connection with you. But the hospital isn't as bad as you make it out to be. There are still a lot of bright, highly skilled, honest, and selfless doctors. They used to be the majority."

You suddenly feel much closer to her. "Perhaps I was exaggerating a bit. But I wanted you to know that all those trips to the hospital cast a dark shadow over my childhood."

"No wonder you still haven't grown up!"

You tell her that you once saw a dead body in your father's hospital, during the summer when you were five years old. You developed pneumonia, and the fever wouldn't break, so your father brought you to the hospital. You were put on an IV drip in the observation room while your father chatted with female patients, online followers who loved his posts about topics like "Why Foreplay Is a Required Class for Both Men and Women" and "Can You Achieve Orgasm through Masturbation?" He offered a meticulous medical analysis of these topics, while you just lay there alone, suffering, helplessly staring at the ceiling. The IV drip took three hours, and by the time the bottle was finished, it was the middle of the night. The nurse removed the IV, and you went to look for your father, but he had already run off with the female patients. The nurse told you just to sleep in the hospital and go home the next morning.

"There were no other patients in the observation room," you continue, "which was cold, empty, dark, and completely silent. The nurse stopped coming around. I was so terrified I couldn't sleep. Soon I heard sounds coming from outside. I was nervous, but I couldn't contain my curiosity, so I got out of bed to take a look. In the hallway was a large middle-aged man arguing with a much younger man. I quickly figured out that the young man's girlfriend had drowned after they'd gone swimming in a reservoir. He was bent over on the floor, completely pale, his head buried in his arms. He kept yelling at the middle-aged man, who must have been the girl's father.

"Soon two uniformed police officers came along, one middle aged and the other much younger. They went into the sick ward adjacent to the observation room. I slipped out, walked around the outpatient building, and crawled under a windowsill to see what was going on. The light inside was like a chrysanthemum, illuminating another world. The police officers seemed relaxed and informal; no doctors accompanied them. Something that looked like a beached fish lay in the sick ward bed. The officers walked up beside the bed, glanced briefly at it, and removed the white cloth, which revealed a dead body. It was a woman with pale yellow, almost adobe-colored skin, wearing a tight wet blue bathing suit that accentuated her curves. She was quite young, probably only about ten years older than I was at the time. An odor emitted from

her body and turned the air rancid, like a water snake emerging from
the depths to strike at me for peeking. I lowered my head. By the time
I got up the courage to sneak another glance, that middle-aged police
officer was removing the bathing suit from her upper body, like he was
peeling off a layer of her skin.

"As he removed it, her left breast popped out. It resembled a leather
drum, and the nipple was quite large. It wasn't white or red, but a dark,
dirty gray. I never expected that. I felt like I couldn't breathe. This was
the first time the gate of flesh had opened before my eyes. My fingers
grasped the windowsill so hard that they almost bled. I tried to breathe
through my heels so as to not make a sound. Eventually the snake
returned to where it had come from. The middle-aged police officer
lifted the dead woman's eyelids and leaned in for a closer look, but
there was no sign of life. He patted her ribs, and then her belly, feeling
her body with his hands. Then he rolled up his sleeves and slipped his
hand into her bathing suit, deeper and deeper, until his hand disappeared, as if into some kind of canyon between her legs. He suddenly
exerted force, pressing hard before making a violent pinching gesture.
The younger police officer just stood off to one side, coldly observing
without uttering a word. Neither of them knew I was watching from
the window. Or maybe they knew but just didn't care. Finally, the
middle-aged police officer removed his hand, raised it to his nose,
and took a deep whiff. Then they exited the room, single file, without
a word.

"The dead woman's tightly pursed lips seemed even more pale than
before. The police hadn't bothered to put her top back on, and her
upper body was completely exposed. I could feel my body tremble, like
something was scurrying around my stomach. I wanted to take one final
look at her, but I was afraid that snake would swim back to bite me.
Instead, I just turned and slipped away.

"I tried my best to pull myself together and went back around to the front entrance of the outpatient building. But the middle-aged police officer stopped me.

"'You saw everything, didn't you?' he asked.

"There seemed to be a layer of membrane covering his face. I lowered my head to avoid looking him in the eye. That's when I felt a large hand clasping my neck. At first it wasn't too bad, but I quickly felt like I couldn't breathe. I struggled, but I couldn't break free from his grip. I think I passed out . . . I'm not sure how much time went by, but when I finally awoke, I was all alone. It was as if nothing had happened. I returned to the observation room, lay down on the bed, and stared blankly at the ceiling. I waited for a long time, completely motionless, before I finally fell asleep. The next morning, I walked home alone. I never told my father what happened that night."

"Perhaps he already knew," offers Summer Stream. "Your father or some other doctor probably performed CPR on that drowned woman."

"Would you perform CPR on someone who was already dead?" You think back to what you felt when you drowned. "The hospital was already being run by the police."

"Perhaps those people you thought were police were really doctors," Summer Stream suggests. "Maybe they were legal medical experts."

"Huh . . ." You wonder, *Are doctors still responsible for people after they are dead?* Medical science indeed seems to be a part of every stage of life. Everyone, even the dead, must pass through the hospital gates at some point.

"Do you know how that woman died?" Summer Stream's tone has changed. She sounds like your big sister.

You cast her a strange glance. "She drowned." Is she trying to remind you that this is how you died? You feel a pain in your throat, as if you have returned to that night you died.

"That's not the true cause of her death." She takes out a new manga and looks through the illustrations. "Behind every death is another death."

"What exactly is that?"

"Death itself."

"Death . . . itself?"

"The 'original death,' or the 'ontological death.'" Summer Stream appears hesitant to reveal this secret. You can tell from her expression that she has never told anyone this before.

"The original death? The ontological death?" You feel like you can see that snake coming after you again. Besides the red cross, the other commonly used symbol for the hospital is a poisonous snake.

"Doctors are always trying to define death. Cessation of breathing, cessation of heartbeat, brain death . . . but there are those who believe there must be a more abstract, more decisive death. This is what you saw when that gate of flesh opened. Perhaps you were seeing that thing inside you that you felt so drawn to."

"At the time, I wasn't quite sure what I was seeing, and I didn't mean to look." You don't understand what Summer Stream means by "abstract death." "I didn't believe that a real doctor would ever say such things. I was scared." The image of that dead woman's thumbtack-shaped nipple suddenly appears before your eyes, and you can't help but stare at Summer Stream's body. The parts you are most interested in are blocked by the manga she is holding, a copy of *Millennium Actress*. The cover girl looks quite similar to Summer Stream.

"Perhaps the original death or the ontological death has some special meaning for this world," Summer Stream says. "Without it, life would not exist. This thing we call life functions solely as a means of resisting death." She raises her arms and gestures as if she is blocking the barrel of a machine gun. The very sight makes your blood pump.

You feel like you have returned to that moment in the hospital, your hands grasping the windowsill until the blood drips down like a vine. The fire inside your body is about to erupt. The fever raging within you is uncontrollable. You feel like it is about to split you apart. Your gate of flesh has opened.

It is difficult to breathe, and you lose consciousness. For the first time, you realize that you might have actually died that night. Your life has been lost. Its ability to resist death is so very weak. Once the battle has been lost, life must surrender to death, must bow to death, must become a slave to death. Is this what the exploratory team of monks was looking for on Mars? How to transcend death? Were the Pool of Dead Souls and the Cosmic Hospital created in order to engage in a dialogue with the original or ontological death?

The true aim of the hospital, you feel, is not to treat illness, but to provide patients with a proper identity and place in the world, so that everyone can have the rare opportunity to experience the entire process of death in accordance with medical science, making contact with this sublime original or ontological death. With the help of sophisticated machines, patients confirm that their bodies, each a dynamic and wanton system, will eventually disappear, despite advanced technology's efforts to save them. Beneath the skin of a typical human body, there are a "normal" number of organs, tissue, utilities, controls, feedback, reflections, rhythms, circulation, and other structures and functions, which are interconnected with each other and various systems outside the body, such as air, water, microorganisms, infections, families, morality, culture, and society, which form a massive thing, fundamentally a series of subparticles, invisible to the naked eye, which were released during the moment of the big bang. Nowadays, doctors use the syntax and semantics from the fields of linguistics and communication theory: information, programs, genetic coding, instructions, decoding . . . with that, such a shocking thing is effectively killed, decoded in a way that allows patients to witness the emptiness of existence personally—*this* is where the meaning of the hospital lies.

But were things arranged this way? Perhaps, when life in the universe evolves to a particular stage, it always invents medical science as a means of illuminating things that seem hidden in darkness? Perhaps this is precisely why the Buddhists began to explore outer space?

But are Einstein's actions an attempt to destroy this process . . . or perfect it?

You wonder what Summer Stream would look like if she were to die this very instant. If you strip away her upper garments, what would be exposed? Why is her life connected with yours? Who are her relatives? Does she, too, have a father like Einstein . . . ? You think about all kinds of things, but none are questions you would ever speak out loud. They are ridiculous. They would come off as much too contentious if you were to ask them. You fear what Summer Stream would say: *Your questions are really pathetic!* From a doctor's perspective, they would all be considered pseudo-questions.

"Who do you think those two men standing beside the dead woman were?" Summer Stream asks.

You think for a moment and realize this is truly the most mysterious part of that night. "Hmm, perhaps they weren't human?"

"Sometimes we refer to strange creatures that suddenly appear as apostles or soul stealers. But they are not aliens. After Drake's equation came the Fermi paradox. It is impossible for life-forms in the universe to traverse time and space to meet one other. Technological civilizations that advance to a certain point all end up destroyed. The hospital is nothing but a great filter. This is what it means when the universe is referred to as a 'hospital.'"

"Is this a manifestation of the original or ontological death?" you ask.

You shake your head in frustration, a cold chill overcomes your body, and you look like a corpse. You dread the thought of having to return to that most unforgettable moment from your childhood. You don't want to face death or experience it again. Yet you feel like Summer Stream wants to make the journey to the sea while she is still alive. Perhaps the answer lies on the other shore. You *must* accompany her on her journey.

Just then, she yanks you to your feet and leads you quickly out of the cafeteria and toward the crematorium exit. As you walk hurriedly, she says, "If you can't get your thoughts straight, don't bother thinking. It doesn't matter anyway, since what awaits us isn't death but change, a change of state, like an insect's metamorphosis. Little Wei, from now on you will have to learn how to adapt to these different stages. That's the only way to snap out of this depression."

"It's just a minor change, like water turning into ice?" you ask. "This is probably what reincarnation looks like. You can't expect everything to be perfect all the time . . ." You envision all of humankind's living and dead bodies piled together, completing a new series of sutures in the cycle of life.

The doctors and monkeys who ate first now grab the patients who are still eating, pushing them to the ground, slitting their throats, opening up their gates of flesh so that the alcohol and food in their stomachs come rushing out. Then they strip the dead of their white lab coats to make more flags. It is a good thing Summer Stream had the intuition to get you out in time. But where will you go next? No matter where you go, it seems, you cannot escape the Mars Hospital.

23

SONG OF THE DEAD SOULS

Summer Stream leads you into one of the sick wards to hide. Inside are patient corpses that the monkeys have murdered and defiled. Internal organs have been ripped out and gnawed away at until all that remain are bones. The two of you try to hide, lying down amid the corpses and playing dead. It is rare for you to connect in such an intimate manner, and you find yourselves embracing. You notice a series of wrinkles trickling down from her eyes, like small streams of water, and quickly look away in shame. Something about those wrinkles makes you feel even sadder, like you are holding that corpse you saw in the hospital as a child.

"Why did you insist on coming with me?" you ask. "Were you attracted to the scent of ontological death pulsing through my veins?"

"Probably," she replies. "Your life and death are all to be witnessed by women. Lacking in compassion, men are incapable of this witnessing."

"Ever since I first saw that drowned woman's body, a melody has run through my mind. I can't get it out of my head. I suspect it's the sound of what you described as the original or ontological death." You feign a self-mocking tone. "I returned to the hospital and, on my father's empty prescription pad, wrote lyrics to go with the melody. I wrote about the death scenes I had seen or experienced, incorporating the names of various medicines, diseases, and patients. Once I got into it, I became very inspired. I seemed to transform into another person, like I was possessed. My father was quite pleased. He must have thought that his dear son had finally discovered his passion for medicine and was at last ready to follow in his footsteps. He encouraged me to study hard so I could get into medical school, but I already had my own goal—I wanted to be a songwriter. I remember the pain when I was five years old and the police officer was choking me; I will never forget that feeling of being unable to breathe. I wanted to write songs so others could express the emotion I felt, through song. That's when I first came up with this idea. I later left home, and my father went looking for me. He continued to search for—"

"And now you are finally reunited!"

"No, I told you, he isn't my father. He doesn't even have the same name!"

"Isn't his name Einstein?"

"I forgot his original name. All I remember is 'Lonewalker.' That's also how others addressed him. I suppose it must have meant 'he who walks alone.' Everyone thought he was lonely, but that was show. He was just another self-consumed doctor, like all the rest. But on social media, he liked to use the name 'Sewer.'"

"Wow, that's different." Summer Stream looks a bit disappointed.

"I finally realize that after someone has died and been resurrected enough times, trying to figure out who he really is doesn't matter anymore. Whether he is Einstein or not is meaningless."

"So there's no reason to ask him where he's from or where he's going," she says with a forced smile.

"Many things in life are not absolute. Fate is just one of them." You are suddenly gripped by an almost voyeuristic desire. "Can you talk about your own experience? How did you first become a doctor?" After all this time, you feel like you are only now getting to know one another.

"Since you asked, let me tell you," she says calmly. "Right now, I'm more like a doctor and patient rolled into one. Our fates are different because our starting points were different. I also came from another world, somewhere likely not on Mars. I had an older brother. He was diagnosed at birth with congenital cretinism, and his mental growth was permanently stunted. When he was thirteen years old, he ran out into the street and, not knowing how to avoid the oncoming traffic, got hit by a car and severely injured. The hospital informed us of his critical injuries and predicted that he wouldn't last the night. My parents were shattered. Their hair practically turned white overnight, but they didn't believe their son would die, and they spent the entire night keeping vigil outside the operating room. In the end, my brother survived, but in a vegetative state. The doctors said there was a very small chance of recovery, but my parents didn't give up. They didn't have much medical knowledge, but they burned incense for him every day, and went to the temple to pray for him . . . and exactly three hundred days later, my brother suddenly awoke. But his brain had further atrophied. He couldn't take care of even the most basic daily tasks, he no longer recognized his own parents, and he would lash out and hit people without the slightest provocation. Their mammalian instincts drove my parents to continue caring for him, regardless of these challenges. He would occasionally turn to my parents and say, 'You are so good to me,' and everyone would be absolutely ecstatic. But my brother didn't seem to understand even what he had just said, and he immediately returned to his own sealed-off world. He was oblivious to the fact that he was incontinent, even though he seemed mentally aware of other things. He was thirty years old, and my parents were still stripping him naked and washing away all his filth each day. What was there to prove that he was still my parents' son? Was it the shell of flesh he wore? I'm not sure what my parents thought, but later they gave birth to me. The logic was simple: they knew they would die before my brother, and they needed someone they trusted to take care of him one day. They couldn't trust a nanny; it had to be a blood relative. That's why I was brought into this world. I had no choice."

"That's not fair to you," you say sympathetically.

"It's hard to say what's fair and what isn't. If they hadn't made that decision, I would have never been born. I would never have come here to save you. So I don't blame my parents. It is the imperfections of the medical system that provide the opportunity to live to people who should never have come into this world."

"This is what we call fate . . . So you took care of your brother?"

"According to the path set out for me by my parents, I studied medicine. All so I could better care for this amnesiac madman brother of mine. Let me tell you, amnesia is a horrific thing—he didn't know anything!"

"He was lucky to have you," you say enviously.

"He lived to the age of fifty. At the time, I had just completed my first year at the hospital and begun to fall in love with medicine. My parents were still living at the time, and they felt that I hadn't lived up to my responsibilities. They went so far as to say that they should never have given birth to me. In a fit of anger, I tried to hang myself . . . but I didn't succeed. So instead, I ran away, and for the next half of my life, I wandered. Until I met my husband."

So she *is* married. She maintained a *family* through all this. You never imagined, and you feel extremely dejected and deceived. You really don't want to continue talking, but you think about what brought you together. You share similar experiences: you were both forced to study medicine, both ran away from home, both have conflicted feelings about your families, and both "experienced death." Moreover, you both seem to have come to Mars from another world. You gain some consolation from all of that. Perhaps this sharing will yield some clue as to how to get to this place by the sea. But what if these are fake memories, created by the Pool of Dead Souls? That's probably why Summer Stream is really dead.

You notice a series of spider- and centipede-like creatures crawling up the wall. They march in a dense formation, crisscrossing one another. Not for eating, these functional organisms were created in a lab for research on how life adapts to outer space. Different biological communities do battle with one another. They, too, fight their world wars, experiencing pain, struggle, absurdity, and resistance. In your frustration, you pick up a blood-pressure monitor and throw it, killing some of the insect-like creatures. The entire wall is covered in blood. The war is over.

"What are you doing?" Summer Stream seems frustrated as she pulls you away.

"Preserving peace . . ." A vengeful smile lights up your face as you think of the lesson you learned from Winter Dew.

"I never imagined that you, too, would end up using violence in response to violence. You are indeed your father's son!"

"What else can I do? I die, and yet I live again. It's not easy."

"You need to stay alive. What other choice do you have?" She takes another look at the smooshed creatures on the wall.

"It's okay. From the looks of it, these creatures have yet to build their own hospital or Pool of Dead Souls. For them, one death is enough. They are in a much better situation than we are!"

"But this might lead to a butterfly effect that disrupts the entire history of the universe!"

"The history of the universe? Isn't that a bit of an exaggeration? Even if it does, it would only be the history of the Cosmic Hospital."

"The history of the hospital *is* the history of the cosmos."

"What do you mean?"

"You really don't know? Okay, let me explain it to you." She seems dissatisfied by your ignorance. "This unwieldy and pretentious universe is like a patient; ever since its birth it has been on the path toward death, from power to weakness, from vigor to decline. It, too, is governed by the laws of the original or ontological death. This is a one-way process that can never be reversed. Our deaths are merely small fragments of the universe's death. We are but insignificant bits that the universe sheds as it dies. This song of the Dead Souls plays continually; it can be heard everywhere you go.

You are a songwriter, so you should know something about this, a melody that you can't seem to get out of your head. The further down this road the universe goes, the more everyone adapts. The hospital is nothing more than a metaphor, showing us that everything is in need of repair. This is the job of treatment, which extends one's life to the point of avoiding death as its calling card to attract young people. All intelligent creatures have likely been projecting their energy into the great task of rejuvenating the hospital, externally described as 'the construction of the great harmonious society of the hospital universe.' This is the predicament we face today. It is not about optimization. The universe is unable even to maintain its current state, so optimization is an impossibility. If optimization is insisted upon, then it can only be some alternative, partial, temporary, or superficial phenomenon. Everything we do is in vain."

Her description leaves you with a deep sense of sadness, as if you have glimpsed a dark future that is soon to descend upon you. "So even you have betrayed the hospital. I suspect that the history of the universe has long been destroyed. But is that necessarily a bad thing? Tireless labor bears fruits, no?"

"From today forward, I have no idea what will happen . . . but from what I see, when people are alive, they love destroying stuff, probably thinking that this is their way of staying in sync with the death of the universe. It's like shining a flashlight in the dark to make yourself feel less afraid . . . but Little Wei, I'm afraid you'll go crazy, and I worry that one day you won't even remember me. So if what I say is a bit out of line, please excuse me. I hope we can both forgive one another. I'm sorry . . . I'm running out of meds, so I'm not speaking clearly."

"I won't go crazy, and I still remember quite a bit. I'm just in a lot of pain." You hum a few lines of a song, thinking that she might not really care about you. Summer Stream doesn't say a word. You both seem to be guessing what the other is really trying to say. Does this qualify as a form of mutual care? Has your relationship reached another level? You are too tired to think about it, so you fall asleep.

24

LIFE WITH FATHER

You awaken to discover that the universe seems to be intact. It hasn't broken or ended. The only difference is that Summer Stream is staring at you.

"Did you dream of me?" you ask. "Did any eggplants or wombs suddenly fall from the sky?"

She bursts out laughing. "Eggplants or wombs? Keep dreaming. Are those even listed in the Mars cookbook? I dreamed of my previous life as a frog . . ."

You feel like all your time together is one big dream. The Pool of Dead Souls is probably causing all this trouble. "I'm just afraid that one of us will wake up first." You want to engage in another mutual treatment session, but she isn't willing. The danger has yet to pass. "So were the doctors wiped out by some kind of bacteria or not? Perhaps Zifeiyu and his ragtag band of people and monkeys are also Dead Souls?"

"I'm not sure," she replies. "That's why we need to find the Hospital President. He is a crucial figure in all of this. If we can't make it to the sea, then we will have to get an answer out of him. The person who started this mess should be the one to clean it up!"

"That's right!" You are struck with a jolt that knocks you out of your depression: "I heard that the Hospital President is the only one who can help us find the Universal Treatment Machine."

You can't help but think about your old girlfriend, Bai Dai. She, too, once searched for the Hospital President. She even wrote a letter to him, and he actually responded! That's how you know how critical a figure the Hospital President is. But isn't he being held hostage by Zifeiyu? Just the thought of the old man's cold, stupid eyes makes you tremble in fear. "But there seems to be another problem: the danger factor. I'm afraid the Hospital President might be on his last legs. Like your brother, he probably doesn't even remember anything. Perhaps it is best if we just run away." The thought of running off with Summer Stream makes your heart race.

"Little Wei, have you ever heard the story about the old man who loved dragons, until the day that one descended upon his home? That's you! Where do you plan on running to? Did you forget we are on Mars? We don't even have enough oxygen to reach that place by the sea."

You wonder what the world beyond the Mars Hospital is like. You have absolutely no idea. You once looked up into space and learned that it is nothing but a massive, silent unknown, quite a disappointment. "You mentioned that place by the sea . . . have you actually been there? What did you see?" You feel like she is hiding something from you, that she hasn't shared the entire truth, but you are also scared that she might abandon you . . . or eat you up.

Summer Stream is indeed on the verge of losing her temper, but she restrains herself. "How many times do I have to tell you? I have never been to that place by the sea! I have never set foot outside of the Mars Hospital! Here we are, a couple, and you still don't believe me. Is it that hard for the living and the dead to establish mutual trust? No matter what, we have to find the Hospital President. He knows why the hospital ended up like this, what is actually happening in the world, and what comes next. All we can do is react to the situation as it unfolds. But this is extremely difficult, because you just destroyed the history of the universe! I'm really not sure what to do with a bad boy like you!" She seems stubborn, intent on going her own way. She turns to look at the spiders, centipedes, and human corpses surrounding you. She pats herself on the belly, having eaten so much to store up energy for the big task ahead. You feel your head, and it is completely bald, likely from the chemotherapy you have been undergoing. The good news is that you no longer have any gray hair, which makes you look even more like a child. You can now act cute to try and get what you want without worrying about misspeaking.

Summer Stream grows increasingly frustrated with you. "Little Wei, there's no reason for you to have such an inferiority complex. Did you forget that we slept together? I don't even sleep with my colleagues! Although you look like a child on the outside, deep down you are an old man. And I never look down upon the elderly. A lot of people don't start their own businesses until old age, yet they end up incredibly successful. Take Charles Darwin. He suffered from lactose intolerance, which had a torturous impact on his body. The poor man barely lived a comfortable day in his life. He was fifty years old when he published *On the Origin of Species*, which put forth the theory of evolution, effectively negating the view that humankind was the center of the universe. This book became the foundation of modern medicine. So in order to save the hospital—and the entire universe for that matter—we must rely on the elderly. If that bastard father of yours hadn't been so negligent in his duties, he might have succeeded. Is his name Einstein? This reminds me of another patient, also named Yang. He achieved great success in the field of science and was even awarded the Nobel Prize in Physics. Hmm, is it possible that *he* is your true father? I really don't like the name 'Lonewalker,' and I find 'Sewer' equally off-putting. Anyway, we should find the Hospital President. He's also an old man, but I'm not sure what his name is." The ups and downs in her speech reveal a hint of melancholy, but then her eyes light up, as if she's just thought of her husband. Even though she recently refused your advances, she now pulls you in, and you enter her.

Filled with a mix of excitement and frustration, you fondle and explore her structure, which is very different from your own, but even if she is merely a 3D printed body, your actions still have meaning: the hospital and the universe are both worth saving because, for the time being, they are the only islands upon which you can safely rest your mortal body. But you dare not take things too far, just in case she is actually a living being and you are not a police officer or forensic science technician. But you suddenly remember that she had intercourse with the AIDS patient Rousseau, and you are struck by a terrible fear. You want to pull out, but she has clamped down on you so tightly that you cannot move. You look like two frogs mating. You remember that the consequences for engaging in such behavior with a doctor are severe, and you are gripped by a mixture of depression, exhaustion, and regret. Moreover, you are unable to feel truly fulfilled. This can no longer be considered mutual therapy, or even mutual consolation. Perhaps leftover memories from a previous life have driven you to behave this way, like a gambling compulsion. You tell yourself it isn't a big deal; you just feel bad for the women. When it is over, they are nothing. Summer Stream is lucky to have lived this long without any special connections or family background. And that missing husband is unable to save her.

The mating process causes your blood flow to undergo changes, stimulating the amygdala cortex of your brain, activating a series of special proteins in your nerve cells, and ultimately allowing you to recover your lost memories, including more recollections of your father. Fearing you might forget them again, you start telling Summer Stream everything you remember.

Father often used to bring you to the hospital with him. You would sit on his lap, playing, while he saw patients. Sometimes he would have sex with his female patients in front of you, thinking you wouldn't understand what was happening. What you are doing right now, you learned from your father.

When you were four years old, he taught you how to dissect a frog, how to differentiate the circulatory system from the nervous system. With a tone of pity, he told you, "These frogs have sacrificed their bodies in the name of medicine, like those fervent believers who once sacrificed themselves in the name of God. We should learn from the frogs." He buried the frogs' bones in the empty plot of land outside your house, using bricks as their headstones. That was the first time you saw that look of solemn mercy on your father's face.

Whenever he dissected frogs with you, he always seemed to find ways to extend the process of death as long as possible. The state of concentrated observation he achieved while the frogs struggled during their final moments resembled an art connoisseur admiring ancient wall paintings in a Buddhist temple. The flesh of the dead frogs was given to your mother, who braised them with soy sauce for you to eat. She would place the bodies of both male and female frogs together in a large medicinal cauldron, and then place it before you and your father. The two of you would gnaw silently on the frog meat, like a pair of monsters. You were scared at first, but you learned to imitate the adults, using your bamboo chopsticks to pick up the frogs' white, humanlike thighs and put them into your mouth. As you carefully chewed, you could feel the mysteries of life breaking, and your entire body was filled with a sense of elation. You couldn't help but wonder, *Did this frog actually live? What does it look like when they mate?* Your father flashed you a smile of affirmation and began talking about various topics in the field of medicine, praising himself as the greatest doctor in the city. One day he would be the Hospital President and transform it into the most outstanding establishment in the entire city. Everyone would live in the hospital, spending their entire lives within its walls, from the cradle to the grave. That's when you quietly excused yourself to go to the bathroom and throw up. There you noticed an injured female frog hiding beside the urinal. Perhaps it had escaped from the kitchen? You caught it and placed it outside the window so it could enjoy its freedom. As the frog hopped away, it turned to look at you, raised its right arm, and waved.

Owing to advances in medical science, the terrestrial ecosystem began to undergo a series of changes. More and more frogs were used for experiments, bringing them to the brink of extinction. The few surviving frogs mutated, adapting to life in the ocean. Deep in their DNA, they still remembered that they were a crucial link between sea and land animals. Early fish evolved into amphibians before evolving further into human beings. So in some sense, frogs are our ancestors, though now they have returned to the sea in a process of reverse evolution.

After frogs had disappeared from the land, your father turned his attention to stray cats and dogs. Once they had been eliminated, he went after birds and insects. In the end, all the animals in the general vicinity of the hospital had been wiped out. Whatever descendants of these creatures survived returned to the sea. The environment has undergone radical changes, leaving many species unable to adapt, and this was one of the reasons the pioneers first decided to come to Mars. But where is this sea that is supposed to be brimming with so much life? The Pool of Dead Souls flashes through your mind.

You remember that back when you were still on land, there had been many types of animals. Your father sadly told you, "The animals are now gone, and humans are on the verge of disappearing. From today forward I will not receive any more patients. It is truly a sad affair. Perhaps I will have to seek out greener pastures on Mars."

Then one day when you were seven years old, your father pulled you into his bedroom to show you a large glass container beside his bed. Inside was a female corpse, preserved in formaldehyde. The skin from her face to her abdomen had been removed and was hanging off to one side, exposing eyeballs, muscles, blood vessels, the chest cavity, and internal organs, like a dissected frog suspended in a display jar. The body was different from the corpses you had seen in the hospital. You were afraid, but you tried not to let it show. You and your father sat shoulder to shoulder on the floor, patiently observing the body. You were so enraptured that you stayed up all night, neglecting sleep and forgetting to eat. Your father held a copy of *De humani corporis fabrica libri septem*. In sixteenth-century Europe, Andreas Vesalius would go out each night to dig up fresh corpses, secretly dissecting them the following day. His work revealed the secrets of the human body, and he wrote a series of classic books that would span the ages. That marked the beginning of the development of modern medicine. This was very different from the case of the Yellow Emperor. As your father read Vesalius's book to you, that look of benevolent mercy again appeared on his face. You had seen many corpses in the hospital, but this was the first time you'd seen the inner structures of the human body. It was a shocking sight. You'd never imagined that the fleshly body could be presented in such a manner, so different from that woman who'd drowned and all the other patients who'd died from various illnesses. This one looked more like a ritualistic art exhibition. The beautiful human body: nothing more than a bag of flesh filled with pus, blood, and rotten flesh—it was utterly horrific. Your father explained to you that observing the body through a microscope can reveal even more incredible things. The body's infinite layers of details are revealed, like looking at the Milky Way around Mars through a telescope. No wonder Vesalius is almost as famous as Copernicus. His work gave rise to new methodologies, new approaches to treatment. The history of medical science is a history of the human body, and the human body *is* the universe. Leonardo da Vinci also participated in the composition of the great book of medicine. As an artist he faced the risk of both moral censure and infectious disease to dissect more than thirty bodies of different ages and genders. The manuscript notes based on his dissections were later hidden in the Royal Library at Windsor Castle.

Your father went on at length about these dissections and his search for new clues to improve patient treatment, insisting that he was serving the best interests of the living. He was determined to find the criminal who had stolen life from his patients, but the horrific scene he'd created clearly demonstrated an addictive hobby, sustained for his own pleasure, a form of "private study," like Winston Churchill's obsession with oil painting at the height of World War II, or Leonardo da Vinci's entrance into that phase in which he was fully immersed in his art. As a doctor, your father used this religion or quasi-religion to escape from the suspicion and fear that he had actually committed a crime. Instead he played the role of the single most qualified expert on the art of death, showing off his accomplishments to his son. But you were all too clear about the fact that, compared to true philosophers and artists, your father had a lot of shortcomings. His natural abilities, his academic knowledge, the books he had read, and his practical experience all held back his progress. His passion for medicine—or rather, the undercurrent of hatred hidden beneath that passion—was actually quite superficial, and he was ultimately unable to win back his status at the hospital or his dignity in the eyes of his son.

That day you sat gazing, dumbfounded, your mouth gaping, at that female corpse. Something about her looked so familiar. But what most interested you were the parts of her organic structure that differed from men's, those parts normally hidden from view. Brimming with excitement and enthusiasm, your father explained, "Look, her ovaries have been attacked by malignant tumors, and some rather horrifying pathological changes are taking place around her cervix." Your muscles felt shocked, and your entire body began to tremble as your penis grew erect. Later your father left, but you lingered behind, staring at that body, imagining what it would be like to reach out and touch her. Being in the presence of dead bodies was the only time you felt so anxious, a feeling like what you now are experiencing inside Summer Stream's body.

After that incident with your father, you never again saw your mother. You asked your father where she went, and he responded casually, "Your mother went out of town. Perhaps she went off to the sea. I'm afraid she won't be coming back."

You missed you mother so much that you ran away from home. Later came the dawn of the Age of Medicine: the old hospital system collapsed, and "DNA sequencing," "genetic logic," "chromosomes," "stem cells," "cloning," "susceptibility," and "molecular imagination" all became popular medical terms. Overnight, medical science's dream of a technological revolution became reality. But as these advances unfolded, your father lagged behind. He became marginalized. The phenomenon of life ceased to be expressed through dissected cadavers or anatomical drawings, nor was it depicted with architectural or mechanical models. Treatment took place on the submicroscopic level, an area completely unfamiliar to your father. "Life is information" replaced "life is organic unity." Everything was reduced to an algorithm. The "Red Envelope Treatment Method," which your father had grown accustomed to for so many years, was replaced by "bioeconomics." Biocapitalism came to control the hospital, becoming the new method for productivity and production. One after another, physicians who had earned their doctorates while studying on the other shore returned with the support of angel investors and venture capitalists and began opening up immunology companies, gene technology companies, life-decoding companies, and genetic consulting companies, and the hospital grew dependent on them. As the medical revolution deepened, your father was labeled as a member of the conservative camp and was persecuted by those colleagues who had old grudges against him. His crimes were revealed during a public denunciation meeting. Not only was he attacked for multiple acts of malpractice due to his inferior medical skills, but he was also accused of malfeasance, sexually harassing patients, fraud, and bribery. It was revealed that he had killed multiple patients by injecting them with lethal doses of heroin, and there were more than three dozen cases like this. As to why he would have done such a thing, even he had no answer. He began to exhibit signs of schizophrenia, which saved him from being sent to death row. He was stripped of his white lab jacket and expelled from the ranks of the doctors, and he reentered the hospital as a patient. In the sick ward, he was subjected to insults and torture at the hands of his fellow patients, including several former patients who tried to bribe him with red envelopes on more than one occasion yet remained sick as ever. He became a vegetarian and started reading *The Yellow Emperor's Classic of Internal Medicine*, with which he became infatuated, and the book opened up an entirely new world for him.

One day amid your wanderings, you heard the news that your father had committed suicide by hurling himself from the hospital rooftop, and you heaved a sigh of relief. Now you had even more reason never to go to the hospital. The people who had purged your father also prohibited you from studying medicine. But at precisely that moment, you finally realized why your father had always insisted that you study medicine. It had been his way of expressing his love for you. He knew that one day, new medical science would change the future, that his son would never get ahead in life if he didn't study medicine, and that it was too late for him to catch up to this new era. So he used his death to rebel against it, a final act of defiance to maintain his vision of what a life with dignity should be.

After your father was resurrected—he is actually your father only in a probabilistic sense—he launched the insurrection. But was his motivation not born of the love and fear he felt for the field of medicine? He was unable to rest in peace and needed to return to fight for what had been taken from him. Love and fear alone transform into extreme behavior, and his vengeance was aimed at destroying the era that had destroyed him. So he took a 180-degree turn, employing a brand-new method and wielding the weapon known as *The Yellow Emperor's Classic of Internal Medicine*. By the time it came to you, you no longer understood love, only fear. You survived on medicine alone, and the desire for revenge gradually faded. This left you with a wretched and cowardly life, synonymous with failure, more pathetic than a frog.

Your father probably came looking for you because he believed there was still some kind of genuine blood tie that linked you together, the kind of connection that cannot be hidden or suppressed, even by going to Mars. Within the bloodline is contained life's code as it has evolved over the course of hundreds of millions of years. How could the original genetic network of relationships, gradually woven since time immemorial, change based on a doctor's sudden whim? There should be a natural way to restore the relationship between family members, but for this we must give ourselves over to the Yellow Emperor and allow him to possess our bodies. Your father has come to repay his son with the gift of love and teach you the skills and techniques to exact revenge. This is his way of making up for what he did when you were a child.

You can't help but think of the male peacock, which expended so much time and energy evolving such gorgeous feathers to attract the attention of females and carry on its lineage. But it is precisely the heavy burden of those plumes that makes it a meal for other carnivores. Is your father not such a peacock, unafraid of sacrificing himself? A magnificent power burns through him like a setting sun. You are reminded of your relationship with Zifeiyu, and you suspect some genetic or karmic connection between the two of you. Perhaps patients and doctors on Mars are one big family, and it is just difficult to untangle the tightly knit and sometimes messy relationships between everyone.

All of this started because of your father. But why not your mother? What if she set all of this in motion? You start to think about her, but she could not feel more distant.

25

DESOLATE SOUL

You and Summer Stream are only at it for a short while when she begins to grow bored, seemingly dissatisfied with the performance of her teammate. She makes a strange clicking sound with her mouth before flopping off your body like an amphibian, as if the whole thing was just a drill or a review. You don't cum, but you are used to that. It always seems to be the case when you are with doctors. The abrupt ending interrupts your recollections of the past, but you don't fall into another depression. Instead, you are inspired by a new set of expectations for the future.

Now that you and Summer Stream have concluded your mating ritual, she leads you out of this corpse-filled place in search of the Hospital President, but almost immediately you encounter Zifeiyu's brigade. With their white flags waving and green lights shining, the monkeys entertain themselves with various performances as they eradicate the last remaining patients, snatching them up, imprisoning them, punishing them, and providing them with "deep therapy." Those unable to be treated are summarily executed and their internal organs consumed. Order is gradually restored to the hospital amid a rush of blood, fire, and disinfectant. You're not sure if Einstein has already fallen into their net, but you can't worry about him now.

Taking advantage of the thick fog, you and Summer Stream quietly slip into the ranks of the Greenpeace Army. Once the Holy Warriors achieve victory, they begin to let their guard down. You're not sure if they don't see the two of you or simply don't care, but you notice that the stretcher that once carried the Hospital President is gone. Where could he have gone?

The monkeys waddle across to one of the rooms, and you follow them in. You see them turn on a typewriter, which spits out an endless stream of blank white paper. The typewriter's racket must be one of the most unpleasant and annoying sounds in the world. There seems to be no end to the roll of paper, which just keeps coming, like water pouring from the mouth of a well. This desolate scene is enough to make you shudder, reminding you of when you fell into that shapeless body of water and were struck by an acute feeling of helplessness. The monkeys spit in disgust at the paper and leave the room. You and Summer Stream take a moment to observe, but you can't figure out what is going on. You roll up some of the paper to take with you, and then you notice several large glass vats filled with a thick yellow liquid. Inside are human specimens, all of them skinned, exposing their inner organs and chest cavities. Some are in a sitting position, while others are upright. Some of the smaller jars don't even contain intact specimens, just random organs. You feel like you are back in a familiar place, but your father is no longer by your side.

You and Summer Stream sneak into another sick ward, where several dozen patients are hiding out like a pack of refugees. They gasp for breath and moan in pain. The second you enter the room, they retract in fear. A large insect-like creature squirms amid the patients. You take a closer look—it is the Hospital President! How could he be *here* of all places? Summer Stream is ecstatic and goes over to take a look. The Hospital President concealed himself by hiding out among the patients, but he seems to be injured, perhaps even on his last breath. He is no longer comatose, his eyes wide and staring blankly around the room. You feel bad for him. There is something pathetic about a Hospital President unable to save even himself, reduced to a desolate soul.

One of the patients stands up and announces, "It is we who saved the Hospital President! He is still the backbone of the hospital!

Everything from this day forward depends on him! Those damn monkeys can't stop us!" With those words, the patient falls to the ground and drops dead.

"Hurry," Summer Stream cries urgently. "We've got to get the Hospital President out of here!"

You are inspired with a new burst of energy. "Let's do it!"

With one of you on each side, you help the Hospital President up and lead him out of the sick ward, trying not to be seen by the doctors.

The Hospital President is covered in blood from some sort of injury, but it is unclear whether the doctors, patients, or monkeys were the culprits. You find a piece of cloth to tie around his wound. The Hospital President glances at Summer Stream, and a shimmer of gray lights up his eyes. He tries to speak, but no words come out.

"Do you know where to find the Universal Treatment Machine?" you ask him.

The Hospital President lowers his eyelids, and his entire body shakes like a mountain about to collapse. His face turns purple and swells, and the flaps of his nostrils pump in and out like the wings of a bat. His reaction makes Summer Stream reflect even more deeply. Meanwhile, you still wonder who her husband is. Here in the hospital, many unspeakable things occur.

You give the Hospital President some oxygen, and he starts to improve a bit. Thank goodness you and Summer Stream had the foresight to stockpile several oxygen tanks. Yet the crux of the problem has yet to be resolved, and you carry on toward the intensive care unit. There you use what equipment is left to carry out a more thorough examination of the Hospital President, discovering that both his wound and his overall condition are quite serious.

"We need to save him," says Summer Stream.

"Can we?" You feel it is a tall task.

"He is the only one who knows the hospital's secrets. Don't you still want to find the Universal Treatment Machine?"

You take another look at the Hospital President. "Huh, he actually resembles a peacock." You stand there, stupefied, as if in a daydream.

"A peacock?"

"That's right! A male peacock, the kind that displays its feathers in a fan." Your breathing quickens. Indeed, now that you notice this about the Hospital President, you realize that both he and Einstein look like peacocks. You immediately feel sad. They may both be peacocks, but your father still lags far behind the Hospital President. In the medical world, the Hospital President is the true lord of all winged creatures. With the exception of the battle that took place during the song-and-dance performance at the Pool of Dead Souls, the Yellow Emperor Program has not yet been proved through repeated experimentation. Many correlations have been observed, but causation has yet to be substantiated.

You feel self-conscious about what this says about your own family background. "Will he die?" you cry. "Hopefully after the peacock dies, it will achieve true immortality." You realize that if the Hospital President is not able to preside, then even if order should be restored to the hospital, it will all be in vain. Einstein is nothing but a pseudo–Hospital President, a traitor to the hospital.

"Then we must hurry," Summer Stream says anxiously. "It has now finally been proved that doctors can in fact die. Your father isn't going to make it, and what Zifeiyu has been doing won't continue much longer. But don't worry, I promise I won't mate with any of the monkeys."

The two of you set to work administering emergency care to save the Hospital President's life. Summer Stream has a lot more experience with this. She asks you to lend a hand, but before you can do anything, his breathing and his heart both stop completely. Summer Stream performs chest compressions, to no avail. The Hospital President's pupils are dilated and unresponsive, a pair of solid black marbles. Summer Stream knits her brow and bites her lip, racking her brain.

"He was perfectly fine before, and now he has died at your hands!" you say angrily.

"There is no way this could be considered malpractice," she says, clearly perturbed. "I did the best I could to save him!"

"I've got a bad feeling about this. I'm afraid we may have unleashed something terrible, setting in motion a new doomsday scenario." You gaze at the Hospital President, who resembles a massive ship about to be submerged, and you wonder, *Is this the face of death?*

"Cut the bullshit. Didn't you say you already destroyed the history of the universe?"

"Enough with the jokes. It feels like someone is using us, manipulating us in order to kill him."

"Little Wei, you're really fucking annoying! You're what we call a man of big words and little action!"

"Okay, then what do you think we should do?" You can't forget that moment when the Hospital President looked at Summer Stream with that strange, uncomfortable look, as if there were some sort of tacit agreement between them. It seems the Hospital President left some unfinished business here in this world, departing before he had time to say what it was.

Summer Stream suggests that you dissect the Hospital President in order to get to the bottom of the true cause of his death. She directs you to strip him naked. The Hospital President is nearly seventy years old and has a large frame. When he was alive, he could command respect without even raising his voice, and the average patient found it difficult even to approach him. His fat, bloated corpse is a pale white, like a beached sperm whale, swollen and heavy, his bones hidden deep within soft flesh. His chest is enormous and resembles the breasts of a woman. White patches of hair are scattered around his ears and the back of his head. His massive buttocks have collapsed. You wonder about the Hospital President's true gender. On the outside he resembles a man, but stripped of his clothes, it is difficult to be sure. The Hospital President does not have either male or female genitalia. So this is the person who has been controlling the hospital? Was he born like this?

Did he undergo some procedure? Your best guess is that the Hospital President is actually a reengineered human. You share your thoughts with Summer Stream, but she is noncommittal and just tilts her head. She examines the body from left to right, as if pondering an inflatable doll. It seems this organism is now completely unable to function.

The autopsy begins. The body is cut open from the chest down to the waist. Still warm, the Hospital President's blood sprays all over the floor. You think back to your experience as a child dissecting frogs. The first thing you want to find out is whether or not he has any reproductive organs, which might be internal. This is a crucial point, so you make an incision between his legs, but this quickly becomes a secondary matter, because you unexpectedly discover that the most shocking part of all this is not the thorough examination of the area where his genitals should be, or seeing the body divided into different sections, but the dismemberment process itself as your saw cuts across the natural structures of the human body. This is your very first time experiencing such a thing. You have seen the corpses of many doctors and patients, but handling the autopsy yourself brings about a different feeling altogether.

You carry out the autopsy with the utmost care, like a medical school intern. You cut into the body along the tissue planes, straight and firmly, slicing into the natural layers of human tissue in the most unnatural of ways. You spend the majority of time trying to peel away various external layers, discerning the boundaries of the body's natural shape, identifying tiny nerves, blood vessels, and lymph nodes. Once the body cavity has been fully opened, a quite unusual "interior" is revealed. By now, you couldn't care less whether he was once the Hospital President. Who he is and what he did no longer matter. The skin that once housed this body no longer carries the same meaning, like the skin of an orange once it has been peeled away. The thought that this is what your father used to do excites you. You feel like you are studying a foreign language, and everything leading up to this moment was just a warm-up. You envision a future in which you become a real doctor . . . again.

But soon you grow scared, your hands begin to tremble, and your movements are hard to control. Summer Stream keeps her cool and pushes you aside so she can complete the autopsy alone. She pulls open the Hospital President's chest cavity and takes a careful look inside. There is no evidence of mechanical devices. His is a pure and natural body that has not undergone any mechanical enhancements. His leathery lungs look like bloated, grayish-blue sponges after absorbing too much liquid. They have lost their ability to pump in and out like an accordion. This is the result of heart failure, in which blood flows back into the vena cava and pulmonary veins, causing them to dilate and tighten. You observe the enlarged heart behind the sternum, a soft and weak thing, unable to beat; a three-inch white scar runs along the muscles of the chest wall, surrounded by a series of smaller scars. Before the heart stopped beating, it underwent a severe spasm. The Hospital President must have suffered from heart disease, conclusively proving that doctors are also patients. You not only observe this process but also experience it, finally realizing that you have been wrongly blaming Summer Stream all this time, though you don't know how to apologize.

Next, you open the skull, where you discover that the gyrus of the brain has shrunk and split into two halves, shallower and flatter than normal brains, as if compressed, especially in the area of the frontal lobe. Some of the protrusions in the brain gyri have been squashed, others completely destroyed, leaving behind several holes filled with serum. Further examination under a microscope reveals several age plaques and fibrous tangles. Unlike in normal human specimens, several fluid sacs are attached to the hippocampus. Inside these black quail-egg-size sacs are clumps of brain-like matter shaped like pinkish-white mushrooms. They resemble implants, but they are not transistors. They are made from some unknown material in rough and primitive shapes, but they seem to have integrated well into the body and do not appear to have been transplanted through mechanical means, but instead appear to have been growing naturally and compensating for the Hospital

President's damaged neurons and axons. You are reminded of your "possessor," but these sacs are clearly different. Maybe they resulted from a surgical procedure, not to help the Hospital President achieve immortality but to create a series of backup brains to prevent accelerated aging and maintain basic brain function, and thereby, in a contradictory way, saving the hospital from its decline.

The Hospital President does not seem to have been using any form of artificial intelligence device. He clearly didn't want to be reduced to a machine or a cyborg. Could he have been embarrassed by the form he eventually took on, or its result? Perhaps he wanted to possess a traditional body that he could control? That would explain why he'd selected an accessory brain that approximated natural biological components. Perhaps this was the only thing he believed in? You suspect that the Hospital President might not be truly dead, but in a state *between* life and death, supported by this strange nervous system unknown to man.

Summer Stream agrees with your assessment. "This probably means that he is not yet brain dead. He tried his best to back up his neurons and arrange a temporary place for his desolate soul to come back to after wandering in the wilderness. So we can still make a copy of his memories. I'm sure they're preserved in these fluid sacs, which we don't see in the brains of ordinary creatures."

"Even though the peacock is dead," you respond, "its body has achieved immortality."

26

MEMORIES OF A CORPSE

You remove the fluid sacs from the Hospital President's brain in an attempt to retrieve the memories concealed within. You will need proper machine assistance to carry out this procedure, but most of the medical equipment has already been destroyed by the rioting patients. You finally find a barely usable three-phase disposal tank. You insert the fluid sacs into tubes for analysis and begin the procedure. A series of nanobots begins the work of extracting and reading the information contained within. As if coming alive, the fluid sacs begin to tremble gently. Is this his soul responding?

"Perhaps his consciousness is still intact, and he still knows what we are doing to him?" you offer with trepidation. "He is simply unable to communicate directly with us."

However, once the fluid sacs are removed from the body, the Hospital President begins to decline rapidly. Since the consciousness-detection machine was also destroyed by the patients, there is no way to check his current state, so you and Summer Stream insert another electrode to stimulate the sacs. As the electricity pulses through, a black liquid fills the sacs from the inside. You gather them together and use a display card to read the series of numbers appearing on the screen, but it is hard to interpret their meaning.

"There may be critical information contained within these numbers," Summer Stream mumbles.

"Is it possible that the algorithm is still running this system?" You're not entirely sure if you should support what she says.

Amid the remnants of broken medical equipment, you find an old computer. After carrying out some repairs, you use it to decode the data extracted from the brain. You see a partial representation of the Hospital President's thoughts, presented in numerical data. The fluid sacs serve as backup memory storage, likely prepared in the event of an accident. But you are uncertain whether the Hospital President arranged for these same memories to be uploaded to a computer somewhere too. Perhaps not. He probably decided not to pursue that route after predicting that the patients would destroy all the medical equipment. At the same time, he knew that the destruction of his physical body would be a tall order for most ordinary patients.

You think back to when you first arrived at the hospital. The patient Bai Dai took you up to the hospital rooftop, where you looked down upon the entire city and realized the whole thing was one massive hospital. You were within it, yet unable to interact with it. You finally realize that this is the Age of Medicine, but it won't be long before the Medicinal War breaks out, followed by the rise of the Medicinal Empire. But you have only fragmented memories of these events, and there is no way to understand how they relate to the situation unfolding. At the same time, you know that these are simply memories, and if you don't find a way to preserve them, they will have no real value.

From your splintered memories of the hospital, you remember that, starting three years ago, the hospital's senior executives, including the Hospital President, vice presidents, and the heads of various departments, began secretly augmenting their bodies in an attempt to achieve immortality. They linked their brains together, and into an advanced super-biocomputer, which was then connected to the brains of all the patients. This resulted in a new Doctor-Patient Unified Body, establishing a partial unification of the medical field. Over the course of this process, a new algorithm emerged. It was used to track the original or ontological death in order to achieve treatment once and for all. This was likely the origin of the Universal Treatment Machine.

The Doctor-Patient Unified Algorithm, also known as the Bio-Nature Algorithm, is a massive decision tree that breaks down life and death into a series of binary decisions. Under normal circumstances, all questions should be answered with "yes" or "no," generating tens of billions of nodal points for complex subjects such as those related to existence and extinction, obtaining answers through high-speed calculations. It then inputs these answers to obtain updated assessments, continuing the process over and over, adding layer upon layer of iterative deductions. This process is based on an idea first proposed by Gottfried Leibniz, who suggested that life can be broken down into a long series of linked binary decisions. The Hospital President's Bio-Nature Algorithm differed from Leibniz's theory in that, besides "yes" and "no" answers, there is also a hazy liminal space in the middle, where things do not fit into either category. The Hospital President believed that this was the only way to understand the true nature of illness and obtain a sufficiently advanced final answer, an ultimate response.

This is a top secret project. Senior doctors were all forced to sign contracts with the hospital and, through the process of transformation, were able to access the Hospital President's brain and share in his spirit. Later the project also covered various medical workers in the hospital. However, for some unknown reason, once the program was expanded to include patients, the results began to fall short of expectations. The bacteria probably took advantage of this gap to launch its attack on the doctors, possibly causing the entire system to collapse. It was later discovered that the bacteria were not even physical but digital. The Hospital President lost control of the situation, and his nervous system was taken over by lower-level physicians, who occupied his mind, exploited his soul, and hijacked his body. This led to the catastrophe that befell the hospital.

At this point you are shocked. The algorithm that the Hospital President created has the same goal as *The Yellow Emperor's Classic of Internal Medicine*. Could he have read this book and been inspired? But even this algorithm turned out to be a failure. Yet here you are, stuck in this Mars Hospital with a mysterious woman, peering into the secret realm of lost memories through the lens of the Hospital President's corpse.

"Can you see anything else?" you ask anxiously.

"Hmm, not much more," Summer Stream replies. "I still haven't discovered where the Universal Treatment Machine is hidden. It's difficult to stabilize the memories of the dead, but just as a preliminary observation, it's clear that the origin of the hospital was indeed problematic. We need to rethink a few things. It is not a simple process."

"That's right. The background of everyone here is a mystery, including you and me. But why was the Mars Hospital established?" You tug on Summer Stream's sleeve as if you are afraid she might leave you and run off to find her husband. She immediately swats your hand away.

The two of you conduct an exploration into the deeper recesses of the Hospital President's memories and find that there is an artificial cortex installed in the fluid sac on the subparticle level. But there you reach a dead end, as you are unable to read its contents.

27

CITY OF PUPPETS

Looking like she's feeling frustrated and helpless, Summer Stream suggests you go to the Museum of Hospital History, where you might discover something more. By comparing what you find there to the Hospital President's memories, you might fill in some blanks and get a more comprehensive picture of everything. Then you can decide your next move.

The Museum of Hospital History was originally the Museum of Modern Literature, before it was remodeled. A set of parallel vermilion buildings composed of two rows of rectangular shipping containers, it is not that large, and its overall layout and grandeur are comparable to the crematorium and the cafeteria, which together form a kind of holy trinity. The Museum of Hospital History was designed to resemble a temple, adorned with colorful signs emblematic of our era. The museum was still under construction when the hospital uprising put the project on hold because the workers ran away, so a few items remain on display, but they haven't been organized, so the historical relationship between the artifacts is chaotic, and the overall logic of the exhibition is unclear.

You enter the museum and look around. You don't see anything too special; again you find yourself pondering why a Mars Hospital was built in the first place. A man's head suddenly pokes out from the dust and fog. He is thin, with sharp features, his eyebrows like two city walls, his shoulders and wrists as thick as tree stumps. He is the Director of the Department of Nephrology. You turn to leave, but he stops you. "Leaving so soon? C'mon, that's insulting! Show me some respect!"

"Hey, what are you still doing here?" Summer Stream asks, pretending that this is really a big deal. "Why are you stockpiling oxygen tanks? Outside, everything is in chaos!"

"What?"

"The entire hospital is in chaos!" Summer Stream is a really good actress. She doesn't even mention the fact that the doctors have retaken the hospital.

"Chaos?" The Director of Nephrology laughs. "Where do I start? The hospital has always been in chaos. Since when was it not? On the outside, everything might look fine, but internally it is a fucking mess! The patients have never received proper treatment, and they lack faith! The relationship between doctors and patients is a ticking time bomb. But the Museum of Hospital History is the eye of the storm, the center of this chaos. Even in the most violent places, there must always be a site where one can find peace. The Hospital President established a Museum of Hospital History because he knew that a pure land needed to be preserved within the hospital, from which its former glory could one day be restored. He was truly a man of great vision who knows the importance of playing the long game."

"So are you trying to escape from the chaos?" you ask.

"Escape? What are you talking about? I'm the Guardian of the Museum. It's my job, my unshakable duty, to protect this place. Others might try to run away, but not me. I have faith, which is the single most important thing here in the hospital. 'Director of the Nephrology Department' is just a cover to protect my real identity." The man speaks with great solemnity. He unbuttons his white lab jacket to reveal a green army uniform underneath. "This project was spearheaded by the Hospital President himself! I will not think twice about shedding my blood or sacrificing my life to protect it! One day the Hospital President will return to observe our progress. I never imagined that our first visitors would be you. By the way, who are you?"

Summer Stream thinks carefully about how to respond. You silently groan. You want to tell the Guardian of the Museum that the Hospital President is dead and will never be coming back, but Summer Stream says, "We're not part of the patient insurrection. Just take us on a tour of the museum!" She neglects to tell him that she was once a doctor.

The Guardian of the Museum is only too happy to act as your tour guide, and he leads you off to browse the museum's collections. "No matter how chaotic things get, as long as the Museum of Hospital History is still standing, there is still hope for the hospital! The Museum of Hospital History is the source of our strength. Everyone here has received a strict orthodox medical education, so how come so many people have suddenly abandoned their faith in the hospital?"

After your experience with the instructor, you figure this doctor, too, still holds fast to his idealistic beliefs. You, on the other hand, feel empty. After touring the museum for a while, you come upon a yellowing, hand-drawn portrait. The subject of the portrait resembles a monkey. You think back to the Holy Warriors. Maybe they were designed with this portrait in mind?

"Who is this?" you ask.

"An apostle," the Guardian of the Museum responds.

"An apostle?" You remember several apostles being killed by the patients. They are now Dead Souls.

"He was the founder of the Mars Hospital," the Guardian of the Museum adds.

"Really?" You wonder, *Isn't he the leader of the advance forces, Dr. Linezolid?* The plot has taken an unexpected turn.

"He comes from the place by the sea," says the Guardian of the Museum.

"Oh, the place by the sea . . . and where exactly is that?" Summer Stream asks. Just hearing the name seems to trouble her deeply.

"I'm not sure. But the apostle traveled across an incomprehensible span of time and space in order to come here to Mars," says the Guardian of the Museum.

"Which apostle?" you ask.

"That's not important."

"How did he come here?"

"He came by ship."

"Who sent him?"

"Rockefeller."

You smile bitterly at that. It feels like everything is spiraling back to square one.

"Tell us about how the hospital was first established," Summer Stream says.

"The apostle—I'm really not sure which one—was shouldered with the mission to come to Mars and establish humankind's first outer-space hospital," the Guardian of the Museum begins. "He selected volunteers out by the sea. Everyone signed up to go. The requirements included a minimum degree of bachelor of science in medicine, with priority given to those with medical experience and candidates with distinction in terms of their intellectual background, moral standing, and overall character. The apostle informed everyone that carrying out this work would require a spirit of sacrifice—volunteering was essentially a one-way ticket. Once you left, there would be no coming home. After a strict selection process, the first team of volunteers was determined. The apostle created a simulation of a Martian environment in the desert to train the volunteers. After a series of repeated eliminations, the one hundred and eight members of the core team were decided. Then, after four hundred and twenty-four days and two hundred and fifty million kilometers of space travel, they arrived on Mars. At the time, this place was a wasteland, completely uninhabited. As pioneers, the apostle and his team had nothing—they started from zero. But he led them in laying out the material infrastructure, such as buildings and medical equipment. Under these most arduous conditions, they built the Mars Hospital, and his loyalty to Rockefeller pushed him to persevere. He endured great challenges and suffering to get the hospital started, and gradually turned it into a legendary place. The people he brought to Mars never cared about losses and rewards, instead selflessly giving everything they had to the hospital."

"Why did they want to establish the Mars Hospital?" you asked, confused. "I've heard all kinds of different explanations about this."

"One could turn things around and ask, 'Why *not* establish the Mars Hospital?'" the Guardian of the Museum responds.

"Okay, then why? Why should we all come here after death?"

"Let's take a look around the Museum of Hospital History," the Guardian of the Museum responds. "This is the only place where the truth is displayed."

You feel increasingly confused. You previously heard that a team of monks on an exploratory expedition were the first to discover Mars, searching for the Buddha, who was supposedly hiding in a crater. Dr. Linezolid told everyone how, during World War II, after being defeated by the Axis powers, the Allied forces lost their footing on both land and sea and decided to retreat to Mars, using outer space as a massive barrier behind which to construct field hospitals, treat the wounded, and plan for their counterattack. But the instructor told a different story. According to him, the Mars Hospital was established to create a new form of civilization and bring redemption to the entire universe. And the Editor in Chief claimed that the Mars Hospital was built by exiled prisoners, but how could such people possibly save the universe? And now, this legend of the apostle . . . all these different theories sound vaguely plausible but also suspicious, and they each contradict one another. The information provided by the hospital is always lacking, but of all the theories, those provided by the doctors are the most questionable.

The Guardian of the Museum is not interested in any further discussion about the background of the Mars Hospital and takes on an arrogant demeanor. "Things were extremely difficult when the hospital was first established. The crucial issue revolved around medicine. Just mentioning it is a rather painful experience for me. Mars once went through an era in which we suffered from an extreme shortage of medicine. We couldn't even produce our own penicillin! If things had carried on like that, the hospital would have been unable to function, so we started our own pharmaceutical plant while making contact with passing spaceships in order to set up an intergalactic drug-smuggling ring. But even that proved insufficient, given our needs, so for a while we had no choice but to turn to manufacturing fake medicine."

"You had the patients taking *fake* medicine?" Summer Stream responds with an exaggerated cry. Apparently she came to Mars only after all of this happened. You, on the other hand, are not a bit surprised. Back when you were still a child and your father was working at the hospital, you often saw pharmaceutical representatives selling all kinds of fake meds.

"They are called placebos, one of the hospital's trademarks." The Guardian of the Museum clearly has his own value system, but he does appear at least a bit embarrassed. "Of course, we also offered some medicine that wasn't fake, such as opium grown on the base farm. Because of the low gravity on Mars, the opium poppies grow quite tall!"

"That's how you get the patients to rely on the Mars Hospital," you say with some embarrassment. "You get them addicted so they won't want to run away."

"Actually, the greatest challenge wasn't the lack of medicine; it was the lack of patients. Since there was so little time, and the costs were so high, the apostle only brought medical workers with him to Mars. He didn't bring any patients."

"What?" Summer Stream is shocked. "So when the hospital was first established, there were no patients?" The whole story is becoming increasingly dramatic. Summer Stream is a doctor, but not even she knew this side of the story!

You assume that all of this must have been kept hidden for a reason. "So the Pool of Dead Souls was created to create new patients? To provide us with a sense of the world? So we would express our gratitude to the hospital?" You don't have the emotional space left even to express anger.

"I suppose that must have been the case," says the Guardian of the Museum. "What would have been the alternative?"

"Patients are nothing but puppets," says Summer Stream. "This is a city of puppets. No wonder everything here is so strange. I can't stand it anymore!"

"Without patients, the hospital would lose its purpose," you say. "This is something I understand quite well."

"It's a good thing we finally made it through that difficult period and arrived at the Medicinal Space Age," says the Guardian of the Museum.

"Don't you mean the Age of Medicine?"

"The history of the universe *is* the history of medicine. People in the universe are all in the process of undergoing treatment. That's why the hospital comes before everything else. Only after the hospital can we begin to talk about things like the search for life in outer space. Can you clearly explain just how fish turned into amphibians and began to walk on land? Or how reptiles grew wings and began to fly?"

"I'm sure we didn't evolve just so we could play mah-jongg one day!" Summer Stream seems annoyed.

"They must have been sick," you say, but that is just your assumption. You don't have any information or examples to prove your theory.

"So what happened later?" Summer Stream asks.

"Later, the Mars Hospital gradually began to function normally. The medical workers the apostle brought with him grew up. More doctors and volunteers began to arrive. The hospital expanded like a balloon, and the doctors began to have more confidence as the number of patients increased. It was a scene of prosperity and the entire hospital was thriving, until one day a certain doctor wondered, 'Why does the apostle get to control the hospital? Why don't we take turns?' Driven by his inflated lust for power, he banded together with other doctors and launched an insurrection. Over the course of the coup d'état, the apostle was assassinated, and his body was nailed to a cross. The new leader declared that the apostle had long abandoned his faith and betrayed the Rockefellers. He accused the apostle of having established the hospital not to heal the sick, but for his own secret ulterior motives. He said the apostle wanted to create an independent kingdom to compete with the empire by the sea. From that point forward, the hospital was transferred to the hands of ordinary doctors."

"So the first insurrection was actually led by the doctors!" you observe. "They showed no mercy when it came to murdering their own kind, so it is hard to say what befell the patients."

"Who was this doctor?" Summer Stream asks in an investigative tone. "Was it the current Hospital President?" You realize that even the Hospital President became a puppet.

"That's a hospital secret," the Guardian of the Museum says. "Since we lack the proper historical data, it's hard to verify his identity, which also attests to the importance of establishing a Museum of Hospital History. We need such a place to preserve the truth. This is even more important than maintaining the crematorium and the cafeteria. Forgetting the past is a form of betrayal. Whoever controls history shall stand at the apex of his era. The rejuvenation of the hospital depends on this. Anyway, after this big detour, you have finally come to the right place."

"Is this a question of historical nihilism?" you ask in confusion.

"Why don't we have a look around the museum first and come back to that question," Summer Stream suggests, curling her lips.

You are taken to the museum's main exhibition, which focuses on the hospital's glorious achievements and contributions to medical science, including the removal of giant tumors, limb transplants, synthesis of insulin, etc. The exhibition also highlights medical advances related to interstellar travel, such as preventing the human brain from warping after extended exposure to zero gravity, testing new microbial variants under strong radiation, and cultivating protein crystals in space. A rich collection of material documents these achievements, but the great medical catastrophe that befell the hospital is conveniently omitted without so much as a single mention. There is no documentation concerning the Dead Souls. The focus is the development of military medical technology: after the death of the apostle, 301 Base and the Rockefeller Foundation by the sea found themselves in a state of conflict, and in order to suppress the insurrections on Mars, Rockefeller sent a fleet of starships on at least two separate punitive expeditions, resulting in two wars. These were World War I and World War II, the Intergalactic Drug Wars.

"No matter what, the hospital now functions as usual," the Guardian of the Museum continues. "It is once again the tower of strength that it once was, a pillar representing the correct path for humankind to follow. If it had not been for 301 Base, we would not be where we are today. All of human history would have to be rewritten!" He gazes at you and Summer Stream with a look of anticipation, hoping that his words might sway you.

"All of the hospital's files are housed here?" Summer Stream asks, looking around as she takes notes as if hoping to sort out all the messy clues before her. You suddenly mistake her for Winter Dew.

"That's right," the Guardian of the Museum says proudly. "Every single file is contained here! These documents are the most authentic and moving portrait of how the hospital forged its own path!"

Yet you feel as though something is missing. What you see before you is too clean, too sanitized. You don't see any signs of the bloody side of the hospital's history. After all, as soon as you step foot in the hospital, there is blood . . . not to mention war. Puppets must rely on blood to survive. This is what you most want to see, yet are afraid to see. Perhaps after the Dead Souls are resurrected, any trace of them is purged from all formal settings. They are all a bunch of soulless hypocrites.

The final section of the exhibition hall is devoted to the future of the hospital, presented in comic book–style illustrations that look like they were rendered by children. The image depicts the entire universe. All the major galaxies are connected in a massive network, twinkling like festive lights. Billions of little red crosses mark celestial bodies, which are all connected by a massive red cross at the center. The entire universe is a hospital. Mars is but a speck of dust, but it is where everything begins. Absent are any details about the great, harmonious medical society, nor are there any traces of the Universal Treatment Machine.

28

A TEMPORARY PEACE

Two heads peek into the exhibition room—Spring Tide and Autumn Rain! You have no idea how they found the Museum of Hospital History. You remember them resembling Sister Jiang and Ah Bi, the people who first brought you to the hospital, triggering all the various troubles that followed. But all of that took place within the Pool of Dead Souls, so there is no way for you to know what really happened. As soon as she sees the girls arrive, Summer Stream unconsciously knits her brow, but she isn't in a position to say anything. She knows them quite well—they are colleagues of sorts—but at this moment, she does not seem to want them involved. But there is no one around deciding who is and isn't allowed into the museum.

"You're here too! That's just wonderful!" The Guardian of the Museum welcomes Spring Tide and Autumn Rain.

With sweet smiles, the girls respond together, "Yes, and this is such a wonderful place! It's so good to find a safe haven away from all the chaos raging outside! It is so serene. Somehow you have managed to preserve such a peaceful environment here. It feels like the kind of place where you never have to worry about raging fires, fights, and murders. You probably don't even need oxygen tanks here."

The appearance of Spring Tide and Autumn Rain brings you some comfort. You feel they will bring a kind of balance to things. Yet their identities and actions remain strange. They aren't with the doctors, but they also seem to maintain a certain distance from the patients. This is also the case with Summer Stream, but she is even more extreme. Amid all the twists and turns that history has been taking, some people have ended up pushed in different directions.

Without getting permission from the Guardian of the Museum, Spring Tide and Autumn Rain strut over to the massive garbage-heap-like pile of exhibition pieces and start searching for your medical records. This surprises you. You are also moved that such documents have even made it into the museum. Then again, the Museum of Hospital History was originally the Museum of Modern Literature before its remodel, so it is only natural for your medical files to be here, preserved with all the other ancient classics. But then you begin to get nervous. You don't want your medical files and treatment history to be exposed. Those records contain many shameful stains from your past that you would like to keep secret. For some time now, you have been known as the Team Leader of the Red Label Commando Unit, a title given to you by the late Professor Eternal. And even though you participated in Einstein's insurrection as the leader of the "puppet-government," your original title was never revoked.

"That's okay, things like titles don't mean much here, and they can be revised at any time," Spring Tide confidently explains, seemingly revealing all the Museum of Hospital History's secrets with one simple sentence. She turns to you with a playful gaze. "Whether you're a doctor or a patient, none of that even matters. Those titles can be changed at any moment. Medical records are historical documents, but they have no practical use or significance. All they record are lists of symptoms that should never be shared with others, diseases that should never be spoken of, and descriptions of death that should never be witnessed. Feel free to get rid of whatever records you want to. The Museum of Hospital History was established specifically to avoid conflicts between doctors and patients. Going forward, no one will dare make irresponsible comments about the treatment process. As for your father's identity . . . Was he a doctor or a patient? Did he help construct the hospital or destroy it? Does any of that even matter? Those responsible for cases of malpractice, and the souls of those wrongly killed, all their names are recorded in the history books. We are standing at the starting point of a new page in history. Do you agree?"

"We have been away from the hospital for so long that we don't know what's been going on," Autumn Rain chimes in. "That's the job of the Museum of Hospital History. We may be women, but we are well connected. How else do you think we endure such hardships and persevere? And how do you think we continue selflessly serving others?" She casts a cutting glare at the Guardian of the Museum. The old man appears hesitant, but he nevertheless leads the group forward into a dark room. Here you see a manual modification machine with old-fashioned gears. The Guardian of the Museum explains that, if you are willing to pay some money, you can have your records changed on the spot.

"Do you have any idea what's going on right now?" Spring Tide cries with disdain. "You want us to pay money? Who the fuck do you think you are?"

The Guardian of the Museum blushes.

"You think blushing somehow proves you are a decent person?" asks Autumn Rain. "We should thank him for preserving the hospital's history. What a tough job! Especially when everyone else has run away!"

The Guardian of the Museum flashes her a smile of gratitude.

Summer Stream addresses the two girls. "You two are the ones with all the money."

You remember that they were cashiers. They probably embezzled a lot of money. You are inclined to tell them that none of this is of any use, because so far no historical information of any value has been discovered. But on the other hand, you would really like to change things up a bit and see what happens. Perhaps everything will be okay after all, and the peace can be preserved? All the chaos and unrest came from these medical files. Spring Tide and Autumn Rain must have some money on them, so you ask them for help. Out of consideration for you, they agree. But this angers Summer Stream. The Guardian of the

Museum acts like he has no choice and begins the process, working with the smoothness and proficiency of a skilled soy sauce maker.

But Summer Stream suddenly changes her mind and stops him from going forward. She says what they are doing will destroy the original documents, thrusting the truth about the hospital into the fog and inciting a new wave of riots and unrest. You assume she just doesn't want the secrets to be shared with others. There is something sneaky about her. She wants to keep the hospital's information for herself. Spring Tide and Autumn Rain try to stop her, but Summer Stream is much older than the other two girls, though she appears much weaker. She is instantly pushed aside. You're not sure who to help and end up retreating to one side. Summer Stream stamps off to the corner in anger and sits down, her bulging eyes boring into Spring Tide and Autumn Rain, and takes out some alcohol and a few snacks to munch on.

It doesn't take long for your medical records to be corrected. Your identity in the hospital is changed to that of a janitor. You are no longer labeled a patient. Spring Tide and Autumn Rain are assigned the roles of Director of Medical Affairs and Chair of the Pharmaceutical Management Commission. Everyone excitedly passes around their new medical files, which they peruse with great pleasure. The atmosphere turns happy and relaxed. The Guardian of the Museum is complimentary about the new files, but you immediately regret that you neglected to read your original medical history before it was altered. Was the original file your new medical history, or the old one that had been stored in the Museum of Modern Literature? Perhaps one of the hospital administrators left a detailed account of your history, including how you died, but now all of that will remain a mystery. You now have no way of knowing Spring Tide and Autumn Rain's true identities. You are wary of them, yet you hope they will stay. But who cares? No file can explain the true problem lurking behind everything, not even *Principles of Hospital Engineering*, which has been revised countless times, each revision bringing a new period of peace.

29

SEASON OF BETRAYAL

Something is again stirring in the hospital. You are shocked to see Einstein and Winter Dew marching into the Museum of Hospital History carrying the corpse of the Hospital President. Einstein holds his head, Winter Dew holds his feet, and they sing in unison—"Heigh-ho, heigh-ho!"—like a song-and-dance routine. The corpse is massive and resembles a slaughtered pig carcass. The chest cavity is empty, and black clumps of blood drip to the floor as they move through the museum. You are in utter shock: Why hasn't Einstein been arrested by the doctors? And how did he get his hands on the Hospital President's body? Has he been following you all this time? Your eyes meet Winter Dew's before you quickly avert your gaze.

Everyone who just arrived exchanges looks. After a fit of coughs and gasps, Einstein sprays some medicine into his mouth.

"Ah, how peaceful," Einstein declares. "We've come to the right place! Here we will regain our strength. But the most gratifying part is that I can finally see my son again! Brother Yang Wei, I trust you have been well since we last met?"

They place the Hospital President's corpse in the corner as if they have done this a thousand times. Based on the extreme professionalism they exhibit, you would think they were both trained as corpse movers, especially Winter Dew. She is particularly strong, fluid in her movements, and efficient in handling the body. She is not to be underestimated. The Guardian of the Museum takes one look and rushes over to embrace the corpse in a fit of mournful crying.

"What happened to you? Did you promise to come and tour the Museum of Hospital History?" the Guardian of the Museum bellows. "We are patiently waiting for you to direct our efforts so we can all work together to rejuvenate the hospital!"

Einstein bursts out in a fit of laughter, releasing an atrocious stench from his mouth as he points to the Guardian of the Museum. "Did you know that he is the Hospital President's son?"

"He looks too old to be the President's son," says Autumn Rain.

"It has nothing to do with age. Come to think of it, the Hospital President's age is not what most people think it is. He has been alive for more than a century, and for all that time, he has been running the hospital. There has never been another Hospital President. But every thirty years he replaces his body, implanting his consciousness into a new flesh-and-blood shell."

"C'mon, that's impossible!" exclaims Spring Tide. "You must be imagining all of this! How could none of us have known?"

Einstein points at you. "My son is right here. He is an amazing person, and he can attest to what happened. How could he have imagined this? You really think I ran away in the middle of a battle? Never! I've been secretly assessing all the sick wards and clinics in order to get to the bottom of what's happening inside the hospital as quickly as possible. Brother Yang Wei, you've seen what's happened. Am I correct? All I've ever done is use what meager strength I have to serve the higher good of truth and justice. And if people don't like it, there's nothing I can do about it. You already know all this. You boldly took it upon yourself to dissect the Hospital President and extract his memories. What did you discover? Do you know where the Universal Treatment Machine is?"

Einstein's words leave you particularly uncomfortable. Summer Stream doesn't say a word. She just stands there, observing everything with a cool gaze.

Einstein clasps his hands behind his back and strolls through the exhibition hall to take in the various displays, looking like he is the true master of this place. He never actually gave up his title as "Hospital President," so technically speaking, he is still the "King." No one can take that away from him, but after this recent change, he is no longer possessed by the Yellow Emperor and has returned to his old self. Taking interest in some of the illustrations on the wall, he says, "Winter Dew, it's your turn to play the role of tour guide! Tell us about the hospital's actual history, and let's see if it matches with what the museum says."

"With pleasure," responds Winter Dew.

You knew she was no simple woman. She has two master's degrees in medicine; she's also not only Einstein's lover but a senior researcher of hospital-related affairs. Perhaps one day she might win a Nobel Prize in Physiology and Medicine, or even a Nobel Peace Prize. Between Winter Dew and Summer Stream, you have to be especially careful not to take any improper actions.

Winter Dew speaks: "During our inspection tour, we discovered that the hospital has been failing for a long time. Those warning signs have been present for quite a while. The hospital was not brought down by the patient insurrectionists or Rockefeller's expeditionary forces. Our investigation has revealed the true cause of the problem: everything was the result of an internal crisis. After the apostle was murdered, the good days were numbered. Things quickly went into a sharp decline. The Pool of Dead Souls couldn't be sustained. It proved unable to produce new patients. In this Martian environment, every effort was taken to achieve the best results in the shortest amount of time, but the rate of decline outpaced everyone's imagination.

"Naturally, the Hospital President knew all this. After all, he worked his way up from the bottom and has a deep understanding of where the hospital's disorders lie. But he was not willing to give up, and he decided to take steps to eliminate the institution's shortcomings and revitalize the hospital. He designed a set of reform policies that would breathe new life into the hospital. The invention of the Universal Treatment Machine was but one such example. It was designed as a means to treat both patients and doctors. But the first step involved the creation of an environment in which doctors and patients could peacefully coexist— only then would the hospital be in a position to carry on.

"But his policies proved impossible to implement across the board. After the assassination of the apostle, the hospital fell into an era of betrayal. Everyone abandoned their former ideals. There were too many doctors, and while they superficially agreed with one another, they were secretly scheming behind each other's backs. Each department became its own vested interest group. Medical personnel began to oppose the development of the Universal Treatment Machine because of the ramifications it would have on their employment and ability to extort extra money from patients. Even more critically, they did not even admit that they were sick, nor did they believe that doctors and patients could ever truly unite. No matter what planet you're from, the logic behind this proposal just doesn't make sense.

"But do you know what they were most concerned with? Here in this Martian environment, where families have been eradicated, how could they carry on their genetic lines? This became their top priority. For quite some time, male doctors had been carrying out illicit sexual relationships with female doctors and nurses, in direct violation of the oath they took when they first arrived on Mars. They banded together to subvert the Hospital President's power, both covertly and openly. With the instructor as their leader, they usurped the Hospital President, even formulating a plan to assassinate him, just as he had assassinated the apostle.

"The Hospital President was beside himself. He didn't know what to do with these people. Being isolated in space, no reinforcements could be sent to the Mars Hospital, and the President was already dealing with the threat of war, so he needed these people to maintain things at the hospital. For a period of time, the hospital slipped into a state in which no one trusted one another. It was pure anarchy. Those with power and influence made money any way they could, while those without power and influence took to bullying the patients. The hospital had deviated from the original principles upon which it was founded, and it was brought to the brink of collapse. There was no way for the reforms to continue.

"Yet the Hospital President persevered. He thought that as long as he could hang in there, the hospital would survive. So he gritted his teeth and tried to hold on until they could get past this calamity. The turning point came when he began to upgrade his own brain and body. He made all the other doctors participate in their own series of upgrades in order to link everyone's nervous systems to his own brain so that they could follow his unified commands. The Hospital President staked everything on this. He knew that if he was able to remold all the doctors physically, using this method, he would turn things around.

"But he overlooked one fatal question: The hospital was already broken as a system, so what was the point of remolding the doctors? Medical science itself was on the road to destruction. Someone discovered that even mathematics was disappearing. No one could have anticipated this when they first came to Mars. People just thought that going into outer space would allow them to develop more advanced forms of medical technology. But as medical science advanced, it became more unreliable. This is the kind of philosophical question that no one was prepared for. No one understood why medical science was heading toward its own destruction. There seemed to be some strange law of the universe that defied comprehension. The fundamental thing that has always supported us was gone. This was an even more extreme form of betrayal, one that came from the deepest place.

"The Hospital President finally came to the realization that everything had been decided long before the birth of the hospital. Whatever action he took would be too late. The doctors saw through his charade and refused to participate in the remolding program. Instead, they banded together and decided on their own to extend the life of the hospital. The Hospital President was left with no choice but to take drastic measures, so he released the patients from the Pool of Dead Souls and mobilized them to save the hospital. That marked the beginning of the uprising. But in the end, this transformed into another form of betrayal. The Hospital President was unable to control the patients, which only hastened the hospital's demise."

"That part's not right!" Einstein interrupts, clearly dissatisfied with Winter Dew's version of the story. "Why can't the patients save the hospital? They are the only ones we can rely on! Even if the Hospital President hadn't called on us to rise up, we would have busted out of the sick wards on our own! How can you describe that as a form of betrayal? This is what the Yellow Emperor asked us to do. Isn't that right, brother Yang Wei? There is no reason to pity the Hospital President. He made his own bed, and now he can sleep in it!"

"That's right," Winter Dew adds anxiously. "That's also what I was trying to say. The patients are amazing, and their betrayal was carried out in the name of justice! But look now, what the hell is going on?"

You suspect that the patients must have been defeated by the Greenpeace Army, which would explain why Winter Dew seems to have changed her tune. Now quite dejected, she doesn't say anything else, instead just turning and walking away. Einstein looks to you, as if hoping you will say something to support him. Never in your wildest dreams could you have imagined that the Hospital President was orchestrating the insurrection from behind the scenes. You used to think that the more serious the illness, the better the chance of survival. You turn to Summer Stream and flash her a look that implores, *Did you know about all this?* She doesn't look good. She hugs her arms; her face is a pale metallic color, and she stares at Winter Dew. Spring Tide and Autumn Rain stand on opposite sides of the room, appearing very interested in how all this plays out. The Guardian of the Museum leans over the Hospital President's corpse in an awkward position, trying his best to remain loyal, responsible, and filial to the dear dead president. He occasionally glances up at Einstein with a look of hatred and disdain, probably thinking that Einstein is responsible for the Hospital President's death. He dresses the corpse in a set of fresh clothing. You thought the crematorium was the only part of the hospital where the mourning services were performed, but somehow the Museum of Hospital History has several sets of mourning gowns on hand. They've really planned for everything.

You turn to Winter Dew. "Hey, what were you just saying?" Feeling increasingly bold, you want to blame her for being an alarmist, hoping this might break the spell that Einstein has over her.

Dissatisfied with your attitude, Einstein points at you and scolds, "My son, behave yourself!" You immediately shut up.

Emboldened by your encouragement, Winter Dew perks up and prepares to continue her speech. But she is part of Einstein's clique, and you're not in the mood to listen. You realize that this might hurt Summer Stream but dare not do anything too rash. Einstein says that everything he has done has been to save his son, save the hospital, and save the world, all things the Hospital President was incapable of. Einstein is willing to do anything to achieve these goals, including feigning illness, actually getting sick, abandoning his credentials as a doctor, launching a patient insurrection, putting his life at risk to do battle with the doctors, stripping white lab jackets off the bodies of the dead, searching for the Universal Treatment Machine, destroying it, obliterating the old hospital, establishing a new hospital, founding the Medicinal Empire, personally assuming the role of Hospital President and King, hailing the Yellow Emperor's call to spread traditional Chinese medicine throughout the universe, altering the very structure of space and time . . .

This is the only correct path forward, the only way to prevent the field of medicine from coming to an end. You feel like Einstein is struggling, on his last leg. He is now alone in the world. You feel a sense of relief and heave a deep sigh. You take another look at the Hospital President's son and feel like you are now in the same boat. Why didn't the old man just stick to being a doctor? How did he become the one to narrate history and serve as its caretaker? Is this the kind of illicit transfer now popular at the hospital? You feel a chill running through your body and an urge to embrace any one of the four women.

"It is such a rare opportunity to have all of you gathered here together to view the top secret files that have never before been made public," says Einstein. "Only those core secrets can prove that what I'm saying is true. Winter Dew, you need to keep going! People who truly love what they do, all the way until the very end, are lucky. Brother Yang Wei, what do you think?"

Winter Dew doesn't respond to any of this.

You lower your head.

The Guardian of the Museum anxiously tries to stop him, but Einstein pushes him aside. Everyone follows Einstein. The Guardian of the Museum struggles to keep up. When you reach a secret chamber with a seal on the door, Einstein tears off the seal and breaks down the door. Inside is a safe. Einstein demands that the Guardian of the Museum tell him the code, but the Guardian of the Museum refuses, claiming that, according to the rules, the safe can only be unlocked when both he and the Hospital President simultaneously enter their codes.

After thinking for a moment, Summer Stream says, "I've got it!" She takes out the roll of white paper printed out earlier and applies the substance extracted from the fluid sac inside the Hospital President's brain. A set of numbers immediately appears on the paper.

"That's not the correct code," the Guardian of the Museum says.

Einstein orders Winter Dew to beat him. After several of his teeth have been knocked out, he finally spits out the code. This code and the one extracted from the President's brain are combined, forming the complete sequence to open the safe. Once it is unlocked, you see a machine inside, but it is broken. Einstein removes the hard drive and finds a decoding machine to access the contents. Inside is a record of the original hospital files.

30

AN UNINVITED GUEST

The files are in video format. You see the hospital: it resembles a diving bell, sinking into an ocean of dark-green smoke. The hospital is surrounded by an army of superbacteria. They coagulate into a thick, opaque mass. They enter the bloodstreams of doctors and patients, triggering flu-like symptoms, but they very soon begin eating away the lungs and esophagus, then the brain, rerouting neural pathways and reprogramming enzyme activity, controlling the subjects' emotions, desires, and ability to reason, reconfiguring the organs, fundamentally altering biological characteristics, stripping them of their essence, reducing them to a terrifying, zombielike state. Antibiotics have absolutely no effect.

No one knew the origin of this uninvited guest, which led to all kinds of hypotheses. Some claimed it came from the deepest depths of the universe and could travel long distances instantaneously. Another explanation claimed that it had used quantum teleportation to split itself into two. One analysis suggested that the bacteria's place of origin must have been rich in energy, explaining why it preferred to accumulate in hot areas and could even survive inside stars. But others pointed out its artificial characteristics, indicating that it was controlled by some form of intelligent life. However, there is no way to know who created the bacteria. The Rockefeller Foundation never claimed responsibility, so it is likely that an even greater and more powerful enemy was hiding behind the scenes, intending not just the destruction of the Mars Hospital—that is just the beginning—but hoping to infect every galaxy, occupy or replace all existing biospheres, and allow bacteria to rule the universe.

Perhaps this was all a form of retribution, but there is no way to know what original sin it related to. The universe is simply too complex. Various methods were attempted, but there was no effective way to combat the bacteria. Professor Eternal pointed out that in order to eradicate this superbacteria, the energy supplying the entire system would need to be dramatically reduced. "This is a new form of warfare that requires extreme measures to be taken."

The Hospital President agreed. "In the face of an unknown threat never before encountered in the history of medicine, we have no choice but to take the most drastic measures. All other matters will have to be put aside."

From that point forward, the Departments of Interventional Radiology and Nuclear Medicine began implementing energy-reduction plans to cut off the chain of infection. The price they paid was that a group of doctors and patients died almost immediately, due to a lack of energy. After this heavy sacrifice, the bacterial threat was eradicated, but it wasn't long before the disease appeared in new areas, rampantly spreading. The bacteria began to target the sick wards, the second-highest source of energy consumption, as a new primary site to occupy and multiply. The energy levels of these sick wards were then reduced, but then the bacteria targeted wards with even lower energy-consumption levels, and so the vicious cycle continued. Without any alternative plan, the only option was to continue cutting energy supplies. As things continued, the energy-reduction plan would soon reach its lowest levels, and the entire hospital would be reduced to a lifeless place.

"And this just keeps going on!" the Hospital President exclaims in the video. "Didn't the whole thing start out with simple flu symptoms? How could it end up like this?" He flashes an anxious gaze at Professor Eternal, suspicious that the professor might be working in tandem with the enemy.

"No, this just shows that we are closer than ever to achieving our goal," Professor Eternal insists firmly. "This bacteria is extremely stubborn, but if we stick to our guns and continue reducing energy consumption, we will eventually eradicate the threat."

The camera pans to the intensive care unit, where the energy channels have also been blocked off. Intubation lines and artificial lungs have stopped working, cutting off the entire biochemical reaction chain and leading to the deaths of even more patients. But the bacteria survives, spreading to the morgue, where even less energy is consumed.

"What should we do?" the Hospital President cries.

"Cut off the energy supply to every doctor, nurse, and patient! Not even babies should be spared!" Professor Eternal shouts.

"You want them all to die?" the Hospital President retorts.

"Under this bacterial assault, their minds and bodies have undergone mutations. They aren't even human anymore. So what's the difference if they die or not? At least we will save the hospital," explains Professor Eternal.

"Okay then, we will do what we can to save the hospital," the Hospital President says decisively, "for where there is a hospital, there is hope. Everything else can be sacrificed."

The following day he wakes to find the hospital still standing and feels a great sense of relief. The buildings that make up the hospital structure remain dense, but they are now filled with a sense of emptiness. Not a single doctor, nurse, or patient can be seen.

"Where is everybody?" he yells. "Come out!"

But there is no response.

The Hospital President patrols the hospital grounds, but the entire area is completely deserted, with no sign of Professor Eternal or the patients whom the bacteria transformed into zombified corpses. The Hospital President climbs to the crematorium to discover its furnace fires extinguished. He steps outside the main gate of the hospital and, for the very first time, sees the world outside. Its strangeness welcomes him. Everywhere he goes, energy consumption has dropped to zero, leaving everything enshrouded in a deathlike silence. Life has disappeared. All activity has ceased. Everything is covered in a pure frost-like snow.

"Is anyone here?" the Hospital President cries.

There is no response.

The hospital begins to disappear gradually, until the only thing left in the universe is the Hospital President. He walks aimlessly until he can no longer lift his feet. His body grows cold. He gazes up to a sky devoid of stars, unable to figure out what happened. The Hospital President wonders: *Everything was fine. How could it all turn into this? Why am I still alive? Who am I?*

31

THE NIGHTMARE

The video ends. Einstein checks the reactions of everyone in the room. He seems to want to know if anyone has anything to say, but everyone just lowers their heads, seemingly unwilling to express what they are feeling. The video had a very powerful sense of the ritualistic, like an excerpt from an anime. You wonder which doctor or patient created its extremely unique perspective to tell the story of how the field of medicine came to an end. These bacteria of unknown origin proved to be the fatal blow to medical science. Is this why the Hospital President's brain is unable to recover its memory? Is this the true face of the catastrophe that befell the hospital?

You think back to the knowledge you acquired as a child. Energy is the quantitative conversion of physical movement. It never disappears; it just transfers to other places. Energy that cannot be released is entropy. As an isolated system, the entropy in the universe increases with the passage of time and, in the process, turns from order to disorder. When the entropy of the universe reaches its peak, all effective energy will be converted into heat, and the temperature of all things will reach a thermal equilibrium, a state referred to as "heat death." A universe that reaches this state can no longer support motion or sustain life. This sealed the hospital's fate forever. At least, that is what the video seems to indicate. The hospital—along with all the doctors, patients, and diseases—is finished, as is the universe it created. The enemy hiding in the shadows has finally succeeded. If this is true, then all of us are nothing but Dead Souls.

"This core concept of the video is all about 'heat death,'" says Spring Tide. "But there's nothing new about that idea."

"Anyway, the main point is that no matter who you are, or how amazing you might be, we all die in the end," says Autumn Rain. "At the end of the day, all that's left of us is a cold, indistinguishable mass of flesh."

Summer Stream doesn't say a word, but she has a depressed look on her face. She is probably thinking about ontological death again, and that is probably what that video was really about.

"This time microorganisms were used to achieve their goal," says Winter Dew, "but I still haven't seen anyone using superbacteria in their actual medical practice. Can such things really be produced?"

"What we just saw was a movie," says the Guardian of the Museum. "I've never seen it before. Anyone can make a movie. I'll bet they were just using it to distract our attention. Where is the real evidence?"

Einstein violently mashes his finger into the Hospital President's body. "How can you say there is no evidence? *This* is all the evidence you need! From the cultural perspective, this dead body is as amazing as any priceless historical relic! A treasure like this should be put on display at the Museum of Hospital History!"

Hearing that, the Guardian of the Museum breaks into a fit of tears.

"It's okay," you say, doing your best to console him. "It seems that Dead Souls can now be reborn. Even superbacteria can't hurt us. We are all here and doing just fine." Now you, too, want to cry.

Another video begins to play, but this time you appear on-screen, naked and lying on a surgery table, wearing an oxygen mask. A man and a woman in white medical jackets stand beside your bed. A caption appears on-screen: ORIGINAL TREATMENT. The voice of a female narrator says, "*. . . the operation was successful. We were able to implant the Pool of Dead Souls into the patient's brain. With this as our foundation, we will rebuild the hospital, medical workers, patients, as well as . . . the lost world.*"

You are utterly shocked. *The Pool of Dead Souls exists within your brain?* Could your brain fluid be that restless pool of crimson water? From the looks of things, it seems that the hospital was indeed rebuilt according to your consciousness, the dead resurrected based on your memories. Even that lost world was re-created according to your nervous system . . . this realization comes so suddenly that you shudder in disbelief. But some things are easier to explain. Under your spiritual guidance, it was decided that all patients should be old men and all nurses young women, based on your imagination, your own subjective decision. You directed the killing of the doctors and patients, as well as the implementation of vengeance-based treatment. After allowing the patients to achieve a temporary victory, you were defeated by the returning doctors. This is all part of the uncertainty of the human condition, the game of life that you are playing. You have created wonderous feelings, thoughts, actions, and consciousness, placing all sentient beings in a state of suffering. But at what cost? And who foots the bill . . . ? You are terrified to discover that everyone is staring at you with strange looks, as if you have just transformed into a real zombie.

Einstein points at you with a trembling hand. "I always knew my son was amazing! The Yellow Emperor has issued his latest decree: if we are to be saved, we must rely upon brother Yang Wei to bring us salvation! The title of Hospital President and King of the Medicinal Empire shall be bestowed upon Yang Wei!"

Spring Tide steps back in fear. "So we are all products of this man's memories? And the information he provided has restored entropy?"

"He is the Dead Soul to end all Dead Souls," says Autumn Rain. "His brain sac is filled with the ontological soup. We shall be reborn like bacteria!"

"Didn't everyone die already?" asks Summer Stream. "Who will perform this therapy on him? And who are the doctors and women in the video?"

"Let's keep watching," says Winter Dew.

But everyone is too terrified, as if encountering the devil himself while sleepwalking.

32

EVE OF THE REBIRTH

The third video clip plays. A boy and girl in green army fatigues sit in a helicopter, holding syringes filled with potassium cyanide as if they are toys, their faces solemn and suspicious. They seem to be discussing an issue of military strategy that will affect the survival of the entire human race. Caught in a protracted war, it seems to them impossible to find a way out of the current deadlock. In order to deal with the superbacteria, the hospital has established a defense system utilizing chemical enzymes and genomes as weapons, an all-new form of Medicinal Star Wars.

"Will we win?" the girl asks.

"According to the Supreme Commander, we won't suffer any casualties, and the enemies will be eliminated by our pharmaceuticals," says the boy. "But that is just a lie the Commander tells the patients . . . the enemy is much more powerful than we imagined. Victory clearly cannot come by engaging the enemy head-on. In the face of this new strain of superbacteria, traditional weapons are useless scrap iron."

The girl gently curls up close him. "Can't Professor Eternal's energy-reduction strategy turn things around?"

"No, that's an idiotic plan," the boy says resolutely. "Following the professor's plan is basically suicide. Professor Eternal is a traitor. He's had his sights set on destroying the hospital for a long time."

"Does that mean we're all going to die?" the girl asks hesitantly. "What should we do?"

"There is only one strategy left . . . ," the boy says. "True victory is not about destroying the enemy so you can survive; it is about becoming one with your enemy. The enemy resides within me, and I reside within the enemy. You must give yourself over to the enemy's rules. This is not surrendering . . . rules, after all, are constantly changing. There's no point in making them into some sort of doctrine. Historical experience has proven that the enemy's rules will one day become our own. We all share a common origin. This conclusion comes from the long-term practice of medical struggle. The original face of the enemy is bacteria, the most primitive life-form in the universe. Even human beings evolved from bacteria. I have been researching the laws that dictate the survival of bacteria. My dear, just take a look: they live with zombies, absorbing nutrients from their flesh while maintaining their own physical functions and unique characteristics. They magnify their own weaknesses, including their diminutive nature, poor intelligence, and lack of mobility. These become advantages, mutating to adapt to their environment and coexisting with their hosts. This is the ideal war strategy, so the smart approach is not to transform into a complex and powerful animal like the wolverine, but to go back to the most simple bacterial form and live like a parasite within the enemy's body and merging with it. *This* is the highest strategy: a new form of endless, symbiotic warfare, which is also the ultimate peace."

"Peace! Do you have any idea how many years people have been talking about peace?" The girl casts a look of ardent hope at the boy. "Do we really want to transform ourselves into bacteria? To give up who we are and live the rest of our existence as mere parasites?"

"Why not? Bacteria are amazing!" The boy raises his eyebrows and affectionately gazes at his partner. "They are the most successful of all life-forms, most adored by the Creator. Humans and aliens all evolved from bacteria, though now that we have evolved into complex organisms, our tenacity to survive is far weaker than our ancestors' was. My dear, just look at subcellular or single-celled bacteria and algae, which have survived and flourished on this planet for over 3.8 billion years. Meanwhile, multicellular animals have died off, one by one. Reptilian creatures like dinosaurs went extinct in less than one hundred and eighty million years. Mammals have only been around for less than ninety million years, and most of them have also gone extinct. *Homo erectus* walked the earth a mere three million years before dying out. According to the Mitochondrial Eve theory, modern *Homo sapiens* arose two hundred and fifty thousand years ago and are already on the verge of extinction. We have become the most advanced life-form in the universe, the ultimate creature—but also a species on the eve of extinction. The more advanced a species on the evolutionary ladder, the higher the probability of deforming mutations, which in turn hasten its extinction. No wonder the hospital is thriving so robustly! This is a simple case of 'improving social dependence and intelligent attributes,' no different from drinking poison to quench one's thirst. So when the day finally comes that the hospital is under attack, it will be helpless to defend itself. The Achilles' heel of the most advanced life-form in the universe is actually the most primitive life-form."

"Brother Zifeiyu, you are truly a genius!" the girl exclaims admiringly. "But how can we transform into bacteria?"

"Technically, nothing stood in our way, but many opposed it on the basis of ethical arguments, including conservative doctors, patients and their families, civil identity planning organizations, the Alliance for Traditional Genetics, and various feminist groups. None of them would stand for humankind's being reborn as bacteria . . ." The boy called Zifeiyu appears consumed with a combination of regret and anger.

"So what happened?" the concerned girl asks.

"Under the leadership of the ruling party, the hospital turned to its former enemy, the Rockefeller Foundation, and formed an alliance. With the support of the Rockefellers, they sent the apostle to Mars to rebuild the hospital in the crater, to create the Pool of Dead Souls, and, after the destruction of the world, to use artificial memories to resurrect the dead. That is how we're sitting here together today."

"So we're already dead? This is all a reconstruction created from artificial memories?" The girl punches the helicopter's control panel in a fit of shock and anger. She knits her brow, as if her brain is not functioning properly. The entire timeline seems to have been upset suddenly, twisted like a snake biting its own tail. Cause and effect, beginning and end, all seem to collapse into one another.

"It is a hopeless situation," the boy says. "The only way to avoid the coming cataclysm is to create a new, even greater cataclysm! Rockefeller said we can leave that new crisis to the next generation. Once reborn, they will certainly be smarter than we who are already dead. Right now, we need to focus on surviving the current crisis playing out before our eyes."

"But isn't that kind of irresponsible?" Dejected, the girl shakes her head. "We need to take care of where we'll go after we die. But why Mars?"

"Because, as the closest planet to us, it is the most convenient."

"But what I really want to know is, is it heaven, or is it hell?"

"According to the findings of the interstellar census, there is no such place as heaven or hell in the known universe." Zifeiyu speaks slowly, with a somber tone. "There is only the hospital."

"Then what should we do?"

"I can't stand by and watch this happen. I will lead the doctors, and we will fight our way back to the hospital. We'll give those patients what they really deserve and get the hospital back on its proper path!"

"But if we can't transform into bacteria, will we still . . ." The girl bashfully reaches out and pulls the boy close to her.

The video ends with the two of them beginning to mate.

Everyone watches with bated breath.

"That was weird," Spring Tide comments with a serious tone, "and that part at the end was kind of disgusting. But I guess we never turned into bacteria; otherwise we wouldn't be here right now. We wouldn't even know each other."

"The logic is all messed up," says Autumn Rain. "Someone is playing some kind of trick on us. You have to accept reality as it is . . . but
I still want to know what kind of trick they played. Did they really
create a Pool of Dead Souls inside this guy's brain?" She flashes you a
suspicious look.

"This has nothing to do with me," you say defensively. You feel like
a prisoner being interrogated. You are interested in Zifeiyu's strategy
of human rebirth as bacteria, which feels somehow connected to the
philosophical ideas presented in *The Yellow Emperor's Classic of Internal
Medicine*. It also reminds you of doctors transforming into patients and
patients transforming into doctors, but by this point, you are already in
a rather perilous position. All attention is now on you.

"According to my analysis of the information relayed in the video,"
says Winter Dew, speaking with an authoritative tone, "the Pool of
Dead Souls and the Mars Hospital are two sides of the same coin. Both
were created within the artificial memories contained within Brother
Wei's body. From a technical perspective, this is a truly incredible feat of
engineering! I suspect that probabilistic medical technology was likely
used to take advantage of the patient's consciousness, collapsing the
wave function and bringing the dead universe back to its diseased and
'uncomfortable' state. That's why it's referred to as 'ontological treatment.' The true objective of resurrecting Dead Souls is to enable the
hospital's rebirth. This is the best policy to save the hospital. Therefore,
there's no real necessity to transform into bacteria. Thank goodness we
have the hospital back. Now our diseases can finally return! Both doctors and patients have a reason to exist. Laboratories and pharmaceutical
companies will enjoy a great renaissance! This is why all of us have been
brought together. The problem, though, is that even this new, artificial
world is broken." She casts her gaze at you.

Finding all this difficult to believe, the Guardian of the Museum
exclaims, "This is much too complicated! How could any ordinary person be expected to follow it? Even I never imagined that such files

existed here in the Museum of Hospital History . . . But why would they choose a man like this?" He looks at you disapprovingly, as if everything went to shit just when you showed up.

Winter Dew continues: "I noticed one detail in the video about him once being a cannibal and ending up infected by contaminated food. The prion proteins accumulated in his brain, forming insoluble fiber and ultimately turning his brain into a sponge. The patient died, and his corpse was almost discarded. But Professor Eternal implanted his dead brain cells into his skin cells and reengineered him into a mathematical genius. The creation of the Pool of Dead Souls required mathematical tools, and only then could a reawakened consciousness freely roam the universe after it ends . . ." She seems intent on gaining the upper hand in this conversation, but she fails to apply the system of discourse provided by *The Yellow Emperor's Classic of Internal Medicine*. You think about how sad it is to have given up so quickly.

Einstein is furious. "Winter Dew, everything you just said is completely wrong!" he barks. "It has long been proved that no such thing as mathematics exists in the universe! How could there possibly be a probabilistic medical treatment technology? And how could there be a mathematical genius? This was all arranged by the Yellow Emperor, an ongoing reverberation of his battle with Chiyou, which resonates throughout space and time."

Summer Stream has been carefully following the conversation, and she finally jumps in. "Humph! I think you're all wrong! These things you say are clearly adapted from some old screenplay! None of it's true. The only way to retore history is through visual data. It's just not clear which manga was used as the script. Besides, the director clearly has both good and bad points." She seems to be trying to help you out of your predicament.

The images you've just witnessed on-screen leave you enraptured, but you feel trapped inside, unable to escape. You suspect that the doctor who stood over you during your surgery was the apostle, sent by

Rockefeller from that place by the sea. But then who was that woman? You feel like you have seen her somewhere, but you can't remember where. Was she the person in the helicopter with Zifeiyu? More and more confused, you feel terrible that humankind was unable to return to its bacterial state, and that you are somehow connected to it, leading to the current circumstances you find yourself embroiled in, riddled with strife, discord, and pain. You can't help but believe that the doctors and patients before you were all created from your brain. Everyone and everything lives within your mind. No wonder everything that everyone says doesn't feel real—it isn't real! How awkward and fortunate!

Jesus resurrected someone who had been dead for four days, but you re-created an entire hospital, an entire world! This feat required an incredibly large processing capacity and a super-long-term memory— how could your own pathetic little brain cells be enough? Where could all that extra memory have come from? This isn't a project the Yellow Emperor can control . . . and yet, if you are merely a cloud of emptiness, a void without substance, why can't you just do anything you want? "Ontological treatment" is a minimalist form of treatment, not deep and complex, as Winter Dew would have you believe. You can't figure out why you are the chosen one. Would it have been any different if someone else had been chosen? After all, who isn't living in a world of their own making?

You have seen too many people stubbornly hold on to their own beliefs. Everyone believes that what they think, feel, and see is the correct reality, and they try to impose that on others. They want everyone to exist within the framework of their own perceptions and opinions. Even if medical methods are not being employed, this remains the reality of our normal environment. But isn't the entire environment a creation of your mind? You figure that those who launched the attack should also be among the doctors and patients you resurrected, so you and your enemies will die together, and through this deathly exchange, a new life will be born. Eventually it will be impossible to distinguish the enemy from yourself. At that point, all will live in a world of great bliss, and through this alternate path, Zifeiyu's dream of harmonious coexistence will be realized, though everyone will be a stranger.

"Contained here, within my body, is an assortment of Dead Souls from all over the world," you mutter.

It's not a very good feeling, but you don't dare ask Summer Stream what is really happening.

33

CYCLE OF SUICIDE

Growing increasingly excited, Winter Dew carries on with her speech: ". . . it actually doesn't require such a large amount of storage or energy; it is simply a lab-based micro-nervous system. Copy a small group of doctors and patients, and that's more than enough. They can die and be reborn, again and again, continually recycled like puppets in a play. Isn't that right? But what Zifeiyu said also makes sense. The calamity will repeat, just as predicted. Today the hospital enters a new cycle of birth and death. The patients and their consciousnesses have decayed yet again, and a new moral crisis has reappeared, bringing about a bloody revolt and a period of turmoil—the hospital finds itself again on the brink of destruction. The Pool of Dead Souls is broken, throwing the world into instability. This is why the Hospital President decided to use the Universal Treatment Machine, undoubtedly the ultimate life-saving tool that will allow the hospital and universe to carry on. This may be a case of cutting out a chunk of flesh in order to remove the sores, but it will allow us the opportunity to rewrite military medical history! We shall fill in the gaps of time, end this period of war and conflict, and be awarded the Nobel Peace Prize!"

Einstein flashes Winter Dew a disappointed look, probably feeling like she has betrayed him. Anyway, she has a tendency to be fickle. Unable to accept this strange reality, you feel a tremendous burden and are extremely concerned about what other people might think. But the others wear a mask of indifference, as if nothing has happened.

You are unwilling to face what is happening and even wonder, What if you just let it all go? Everything feels like a dream. The brain can create dreamscapes, and in the world of our dreams, there are scenes, atmospheres, characters, plots, a kaleidoscope of colors where truth and fiction are difficult to differentiate. These dreamscapes can inspire a broad spectrum of emotions including excitement, joy, comfort, love, uneasiness, loss, loathing, fear, despair, jealousy, hatred, and loneliness. One can even reach sexual climax. Are dreams not simply another form of artificial memory? You could even say that sleep is equivalent to death. When you expand that to the entirety of history, you see what Arthur Schopenhauer referred to as "the long, difficult, and confused dream of Mankind." But as long as one prevents oneself from waking up from a dream in laughter or tears, everything should be okay. Doctors can already achieve this using technical means. The hospital is, after all, the ultimate dream factory. But it does not create dreams for a specific person; rather, it creates a series of super-sensory experiences with you at the center, allowing the Dead Souls to share in your dream while being manipulated like puppets. Perhaps some will claim that the world created in these dreams is not of the highest quality, but the quality of the real world isn't so great either. It is more than simply a question of what we are accustomed to. Most people living today have never had any actual contact with the real world. You feel a sense of relief, even though you are still upset because none of them are prostrating themselves before you.

As you continue your tour of the museum, you become increasingly cautious, though you cherish the rare opportunity to live again. You feel like you are visiting the extraordinary ruins of an ancient Egyptian temple. Before you are artifacts that have withstood the vicissitudes of thousands of years yet remain full of life. The Guardian of the Museum is silent, but he says everything he needs to say by saying nothing. At least one thing is correct: the audience's existence was determined in advance by the Museum of Hospital History, a massive project unlike anything witnessed in history, not unlike the majestic royal tombs of old. As the tour proceeds, the visitors are left in a state of amazement. The Guardian of the Museum takes you to see some additional archival materials, which are both a faithful record of the past and incredibly inspiring. It took many rounds of discussion and an open bidding process before the Department of Infrastructure won the contract to build the Museum of Hospital History. The workers assigned to the project were all critically ill patients, but they chose to sacrifice their lives to the project so that after death, their names might be recorded in the annals of the Museum of Hospital History. Many patients who died during the construction process were posthumously given the title of "doctor" or "physician's assistant," a great honor for them.

"Weren't you looking for the Universal Treatment Machine?" The Guardian of the Museum unexpectedly starts kissing up to the visitors in an attempt to secure his position, taking the initiative in leading the group into a special room not open to the public. He opens a safe and removes a metal box. Inside is a scroll, which he removes and unfolds to reveal a set of blueprints for something that resembles a urinal.

"Behold! *This* is the Universal Treatment Machine!" The Guardian of the Museum waves the blueprints in Einstein's face.

"After searching so long, can it be that it has finally appeared?" Einstein snorts in disbelief. Winter Dew rushes forward to get a closer look, while Summer Stream's expression undergoes a slight change.

"That's right, this is it," declares the Guardian of the Museum. "It's different than you imagined. But in reality, this is just a set of blueprints. The actual machine has yet to be created."

"If that's true, then we are truly doomed," announces Spring Tide.

"Thank heavens it hasn't been created!" says Autumn Rain. "Otherwise, it would have cured everyone! In a world devoid of disease, there would be no need for the hospital. That would be the greatest calamity of them all! Where would we all live? Without disease, doctors and patients would have no opportunity to meet and form the happy family we have!"

"And here we are presented with a sparkling paradox," Einstein says, gazing at the blueprints with a strange expression.

"Who invented this?" you ask, your voice brimming with hope. "Whoever he is, he must be a true genius of his age! He is the one to bring salvation to us all!"

"You have no right to speak here!" the Guardian of the Museum barks. "The Universal Treatment Machine was designed according to the Hospital President's orders. He saw that the resurrected hospital had again fallen into difficult circumstances, and he put forth a plan that would require artificial interference to relieve the Dead Souls from their suffering."

"I've heard that disease is actually an alternate form of life," says Autumn Rain. "To eradicate disease is to eradicate life itself. That would be a terrifying prospect."

"The whole thing is much too twisted," says Einstein. "But I like it."

"Our understanding of what eradication and survival mean are quite different," exclaims Winter Dew. "We need to conduct in-depth research and repeated lab experiments to get to the bottom of this. Maybe in the eyes of the Hospital President, death is a form of rebirth? We must be sure not to approach this problem in a narrow, mechanical way, or all advancements in medical science will come to a screeching halt!"

"Stop saying such crazy things!" Einstein admonishes her. "Do you have any idea just how late in the game we already are?"

But Winter Dew stubbornly carries on. "I'm speaking the truth. Not a word I say is false! While I promise to not say one word that isn't true, I can't guarantee that I will tell you everything that is true."

Einstein has lost control. He can't even rein in Winter Dew anymore.

You are very curious: How does she really know what is true and what is false? Not even you know how to tell those things apart.

The Guardian of the Museum flashes an anxious look at Einstein. "Bioevolution is inextricably linked to disease. Disease is a necessary price we pay for life to evolve. Over the course of human evolution, disease has continually improved the quality of life. The ultimate value of disease is the role it plays in stimulating evolution and manifesting the autonomy of life. This is what one refers to as 'survival of the sickest.' It would be impossible for human beings to realize their ideal of a healthy world devoid of disease. That's why we have the hospital. So the patient insurrection is not because they weren't sick; it is because they want to evolve with their illnesses. Under these circumstances, how could we possibly allow for the emergence of the Universal Treatment Machine?"

You can't help but think about something Erich Fromm once said: "The most normal are the sickest, and the sick are the healthiest."

"The big question is, What does the Universal Treatment Machine actually do?" Spring Tide and Autumn Rain ask in unison.

"Let me explain!" the Guardian of the Museum interjects. "The Universal Treatment Machine is much more advanced than all other machines. It is of critical importance. Sometimes the machine exhibits a human side, and other times it appears most inhuman. Sometimes the machine exhibits a superhuman side—that is, its capabilities surpass every form of simple artificial intelligence. This is the most determinative factor. From its original design, the machine is clearly the ultimate savior, sent here to atone for the Pool of Dead Souls' inherent deficiencies. From the Hospital President's perspective, evolution brought about our downfall, a trap akin to the Möbius strip. If we don't bring an end to evolution, humankind will be doomed. Do you understand the profound meaning of all this? It is a deep philosophical proposition."

Everyone shakes their heads in confusion over this profound topic, more mystifying even than *The Yellow Emperor's Classic of Internal Medicine*.

"But there is a problem here," the Guardian of the Museum continues, "a very grave problem. Please take another look at the blueprint. According to this, under most circumstances the Universal Treatment Machine is not carrying out actual work but instead directing other work. To be more specific, it's a form of technology that implements commands and control. If there are no commands being issued to it, it will feel uncomfortable and quickly come to the conclusion that its existence has no value. What does this illustrate? It shows us that, over the course of its evolution, the hospital has already transformed into a bureaucratic machine.

"And what is a bureaucratic machine, you ask? It's the kind of monster that wants to live forever but ends up destroying itself, and the more it destroys itself, the more it desires to go on living. And the cycle continues, on and on, over and over. In the end, it has no choice but to kill itself. You may eliminate corruption, but you can never do away with bureaucracy. The purpose of the Universal Treatment Machine has changed, from initially attempting to bring an end to evolution to adapting to the existing ecology of the bureaucratic system. Since it is universal, it can make bureaucrats ignore reality and neglect their responsibilities. On the surface, they appear quite keen about strategies concerning the existence of the enemy—whether to fight or attempt to coexist—but in reality, they have no interest in any of this. When it comes to topics like the definition of the hospital's lofty mission, the concrete tasks various doctors are responsible for, or what direction medical science should take, the machine has no passion or drive. Whether it be evolution or devolution, it is devoid of feeling. This is the rhythm that leads us to death. Do you know what death means? Bureaucrats are addicted to technology because it creates the illusion that everything is under their control. The machine is like the devil, drawing the bureaucrats' attention to itself, leading the angels in white to grow lazy and waste their time playing golf. If this situation continues, one day we will witness the following result. If Adolf Eichmann had claimed that he wasn't the one who sent the Jews to be exterminated, and instead had blamed the machines, he could have evaded moral responsibility for his actions.

"So now you know what death is. Doctors can stare unflinchingly as humankind walks straight toward death, without feeling an ounce of guilt or remorse. It is a disaster. The Hospital President, your father, he is the biggest bureaucrat of them all! Everything he's ever done has been contrary to what he promised, and he never even realized it! I hate him. From this perspective, the Universal Treatment Machine will help the evildoers inflict greater harm. That's why I am so sympathetic to the patients. But now that the Hospital President is dead, my hatred has dissipated. Besides those of you here, no one else would use the Universal Treatment Machine. The doctors have no interest in it. You should stop now, before you take things too far."

"According to what you're saying, the more we try to destroy the hospital, the more it will thrive," Summer Stream says coldly, "and the more it thrives, the more it will be destroyed. Humph, I guess the patient uprising was totally unnecessary."

"That's because the Universal Treatment Machine has been stuck at the blueprint stage," Spring Tide mutters.

"All the more reason not to take any of this so seriously, like the emperor's new clothes," Autumn Rain says, showing off her wit.

"That thing depicted in the blueprints is truly magical," Winter Dew says confidently. "One glance and you can see that the wisdom of multiple academic fields is concentrated within its brilliant design. The belief in clinical technology really is no joke."

You are now in a desperate situation, but you remind yourself that all of this is simply an extension of your imagination. You are the director of this play. No wonder you cannot die. You created this world, and these patients, and even yourself, all in your mind. It is not your head that you carry on your shoulders; it is someone else's. Like Professor Eternal's brain, suspended in a jar in the cabin of a helicopter, it is hidden away in some corner of the hospital, where it continually spouts images, like a film projector. Among those images is this version of "you." These muddled thoughts are not under your control. They play automatically, transforming into reality. If you want to end your pain and suffering, you must destroy this thing. Searching for help from the Universal Treatment Machine will not save you. But an internal contradiction prohibits you from taking action. Action will result in your complete destruction, like a cycle of suicide. So your only choice is to continue your search for the Universal Treatment Machine, hoping it can do magic. Trying to save the day with limited resources is still better than nothing, right?

You are reminded of something Zifeiyu once said: disasters are never singular events; they are bound to strike again. That's what makes this problem so serious. You want to discuss this with everyone, but Summer Stream flashes you a look to keep quiet. You stay silent, but you realize that everything that has occurred today stems from that night as a child when you saw the corpse of that drowned woman. That was the moment the program started running. This flash of sentimental self-indulgence, triggered by the original or ontological death, would go on to become a pattern of repeated and relentless suffering.

"Disgusting! Under no circumstances can we allow it to exist!" Einstein snatches the blueprint and tears it up, an act that might avoid, or might hasten, the second destruction of the world. Evolution can now carry on, perpetuating the cycle of life, death, and rebirth. In this way, life shall persist in the face of illness, and death shall persist in the face of life. Einstein takes out a medicinal inhaler and frantically sprays several shots into his nose.

Whether out of sympathy or delight, the Guardian of the Museum exclaims, "Ah!"

You have the urge to spring forward and snatch the torn blueprints from Einstein's hands, but you are paralyzed. You wonder what all the fuss is about. After all, didn't they say it would be impossible to create the Universal Treatment Machine? It is forever destined to remain a blueprint. Even if someone were to succeed in producing it, it would be pointless to keep it, because with the Hospital President dead, there would be no one to issue the order to use it. However, you still desperately yearn for it, the only thing that can cure your illness and free you from the physical and mental prison imposed upon you (which, perhaps, you willingly accepted). You are now starting to believe that the machine might be the toll for confronting the impending disaster, even if that means facing extermination again.

34

REBIRTH OF
THE KINGDOM OF DEMONS

Everyone goes back to wandering aimlessly around the Museum of Hospital History, lost and disoriented. History may indeed be reality, but reality does not necessarily lead us to the future. The truth about the hospital is proving to be even more unsettling. The ground begins to shake as the Greenpeace Army engages in a final battle with the remaining patients. The cries and screams of the monkeys become even more intense. It is possible that the entire dome will collapse, exposing everything inside the hospital to the radiation and dust. The patients and doctors will be killed, their bodies scattered without a final resting place. When that happens, what use will the Pool of Dead Souls or the Universal Treatment Machine be? From the looks of things, all roads to salvation have been cut off.

"The time for the memorial service is upon us!" the Guardian of the Museum announces with a raspy voice. "According to what you have all said, the Hospital President—my father—may have made some mistakes, but he remains a hero to our people. He died before achieving the final victory, selflessly sacrificing himself for the cause. He had good intentions, dedicating himself wholeheartedly to the hospital."

"We are holding the memorial service right now?" Spring Tide and Autumn Rain ask.

"If not now, when?" says Winter Dew.

"That's right," says the Guardian of the Museum. "There are exactly seven of us, an auspicious number. Didn't the Hospital Affairs

Committee have seven members as well? We could each play the role of the committee members!"

Summer Stream observes with a hint of mockery and visible fatigue. You have trouble making heads or tails of her reaction, but given your current status, it is best just to keep your mouth shut. The Guardian of the Museum takes out a bottle of liquor and starts pouring glasses for everyone. The color and texture of the liquor ignite the fire in your heart. You're not sure when you became so enamored by the taste of alcohol, but once the urge takes hold, you are unable to control it. A ravenous look appears on Summer Stream's face when she sees the alcohol—she's already finished what she brought with her. The Guardian of the Museum pours a smattering on the ground, likely as some kind of ceremonial tribute. He then leads the seven in a prostration before the corpse of the Hospital President. Einstein and Summer Stream refuse to kneel.

The Guardian of the Museum cries mournfully, unleashing a river of tears. "You were a good man," he sobs, "but you were misunderstood. Everything you ever did was to save the hospital and its people. Tragically, you not only became a bureaucrat, but the biggest bureaucrat of them all! No one can blame you, though, as this resulted from the Martian environment in which you lived. The people you surrounded yourself with took advantage of you. They all harbored ulterior motives, and in the service of their own selfish goals, they stole oxygen tanks from the sick wards and hid all the scalpels. They were all intent on toying with you! Playing tricks on you! You somehow believed their bewitching lies and flowery promises. They hijacked you, but the true tragedy was that you never saw through their deceit. Even if you had, there was nothing you could do . . . once the bacteria in areas of high energy consumption were eradicated, they moved on to gather and multiply in the low energy consumption areas, and there was no end to the cycle. If someone else had been Hospital President, he, too, would have been helpless to reverse this tide . . ."

Summer Stream sneers watching this performance. She finds something amusing about this pathetic show, a tragedy devoid of genuine sympathy. Occasionally, this middle-aged military doctor really resembles a child. She steals the bottle of spirits from the Guardian of the Museum and, right in front of his face, throws her head back and finishes it. It is an exaggerated open challenge to the Guardian of the Museum. You worry about her, but the Guardian of the Museum doesn't do anything to stop her. He just kneels there, burning paper money, paper clothing, paper medicine, and paper medical equipment for the Hospital Director to use in the afterlife.

Wiping away his tears, he continues, "My dear father, you are the true Hospital President! As the hospital's highest-level leader, you tirelessly devoted yourself to the public, day and night, sacrificing everything to ensure the hospital's survival and everlasting prosperity. With this memorial ceremony, we vow to carry on your indomitable spirit and fulfill your mission. We shall complete the work that you left unfinished!" He scans the faces of the seven present as if keen to gauge their reactions to his words. "Hey, didn't you all want to know how the doctors died? Well, now you have seen the process firsthand! Is that what you wanted? Are you happy now? Take a good close look! Etch this scene into your minds, and don't ever forget it! Ah, may he rest in peace!"

Einstein turns his head and spits in disgust. "I'm the real Hospital President, and I have children too!" He flashes you a dissatisfied glare, as if blaming you for not being more useful during this critical historical moment. Spring Tide, Autumn Rain, Winter Dew, and you are the only ones kneeling. Suddenly, everyone's arms are lifted, as if pulled by something invisible. Your bodies draw circles, lines, and peculiar glyph-like shapes in the air. Dark shadowy shapes resembling flies or mosquitoes appear before your eyes, like negatives of a starry sky. Your hair stands on end, and your thoughts go back to the crematorium.

After the ceremony, the scent of ashes mingles with the intoxicating air, forming a new atmosphere for the Dead Souls. Utterly exhausted, the group decides to spend the night in the Museum of Hospital History. The Guardian of the Museum lets Summer Stream take the sole wooden bed, while everyone else sleeps on the floor. Dissatisfied with the arrangements, Einstein kicks Summer Stream out of the bed so he can sleep there himself. Summer Stream doesn't utter a word of protest and settles down on the floor. After all, she isn't a child. As an experienced doctor, she is well read and has had a rich life.

"I can't sleep," you utter with concern, curling up against Summer Stream's body. You still feel like you need to protect yourself from those around you. "I'm worried that the Holy Warriors might attack again."

"Don't worry," Summer Stream comforts you. "I'm sure those animals are also asleep. The entire world may be upside down, but from a standard psychological perspective, all animals usually maintain their standard sleep functions. Besides, this is the Museum of Hospital History—who would dare intrude upon this sacred ground?"

Full of gratitude, you extend your hand toward her, tightly grasping hers as a sign of trust. Your other hand tentatively explores around her rib cage. She feels so real, so tangible. Even after so many difficulties, her muscles remain tight, supported by her well-defined bone structure, and you can see the blood pulsating beneath her skin. This gives you back a sense of security. You want to enter her, but you retract back into your shell when you remember that there are so many people around.

"But this isn't the same hospital as before," you say, trying to make her understand that it's not your fault things have turned out this way. You are also a victim of circumstance. "No one really knows what this place is."

"Now that I think about it," she responds, "perhaps what your father said was right. Maybe the patients really should establish a brand-new hospital of their own, a homey, down-to-earth hospital. That would change up our lifestyle and end our living according to what you created for us in your mind. Then everything would be okay. Is that what you meant?" She yawns, which makes her look a bit old, but it also turns you on. Unfortunately, she has no interest in doing anything sexual with you right now.

You still can't figure out what this woman is thinking. "I still refuse to accept him as my father," you mutter.

"The Hospital President destroyed the hospital with his own two hands, while your father helped the hospital be reborn as the Dead Souls are resurrected. While there is nothing very novel about this concept, it's still better than the ideas the young people have come up with. That's what makes it so divisive and hateful."

"It all comes down to a lack of manpower."

"Speaking of manpower, there are seven of us. That's more than enough. When the apostle first arrived, he was all alone. You, too, are but one man."

"C'mon, I'm not the hero you and my father have been hoping for. I'm useless. No one can change the plan that our predecessors laid out for us. What's more, their special skills have been lost to time, and no one today understands how they created the things they did. Later generations have tried to replicate it, but the results are always extremely crude. The old man brought the Yellow Emperor back in an attempt to fight fire with fire, staging a kamikaze counterattack, but the end result was just a crude imitation that only succeeded in making him look ridiculous . . . the best option is to continue our search for the Universal Treatment Machine. It should be a real thing, of this world, and not just some blueprint. My intuition tells me that it has indeed been created, and it certainly isn't just some cheap replica of an old antique. Whether this qualifies as 'bureaucratic' is just a word game with no real meaning. What matters is who's in control. If we're lucky, even the most ridiculous object can unleash primordial power."

"That's all bullshit! I think the most important thing is to find your real brain. It's certainly not the thing bouncing around inside your head.

It's probably hidden away in some dark corner of the hospital. Strictly speaking, even you are but a figment of its imagination."

"You're killing my self-confidence with that kind of talk." You sigh. "But what's the point? Everything has changed. Even if the Dead Souls are living in an illusory world, they still have their own ideas. Once resurrected, they remember what they should remember, and they have their own interests, which they can pursue as they please. They no longer need to rely upon me. I simply set them on their path. It's like witnessing the rebirth of the kingdom of demons. The subsequent phase of evolution will follow the chaos equation and be nonlinear, understand? It will be random, unpredictable, and unrestrained, so what does any of that have to do with me?" You try to defend yourself in an effort to clear your good name, but you are suddenly assaulted by an overpowering sense of exhaustion. You lean against Summer Stream and drift off to sleep.

You awaken suddenly, in the middle of the night, to discover the Guardian of the Museum standing over Summer Stream, who is still asleep beside you. He stares down at her with a rapacious gaze. He lowers his head, presses his nose and mouth against her, and begins to sniff her chest. You prop yourself up and stare at them in disbelief, but the scene unexpectedly reminds you of something. You push the old man aside, and Summer Stream wakes up. Nothing about what just happened seems to faze her, and she nonchalantly fixes her hair.

Flustered, the Guardian of the Museum pleads, "This is all a misunderstanding, just a misunderstanding . . ." As he speaks, he indicates that he has a new secret he wants to share with the two of you. Taking out a pile of files, he hesitates before telling Summer Stream, "You are the Hospital President's daughter. I recognized you a long time ago, but I wanted to wait until we were alone to share this with you."

You feel like you have just seen a ghost. This means that the same blood runs through the veins of both the Guardian of the Museum and Summer Stream. Could they really be siblings? You remember Summer

Stream once telling you that she was brought into this would to care for her older brother, who had some kind of mental issue. Could the Guardian of the Museum be this madman? Or has he already been reincarnated? You look at Summer Stream like your daughter; and in her eyes, you are her little brother. And yet you have engaged in mating activities with her. All of this indicates that the family structure, which you thought had been completely eradicated, has in reality been reborn, growing new branches, ever more complex and intricate. Exposing these family secrets serves as a fatal blow. Summer Stream now appears embarrassed by this revelation. She seems to have known nothing about it, yet she quickly calms herself. She walks over to the Hospital President's body to find some alcohol, paying no heed to the Guardian of the Museum.

35

THE CURSE

The Guardian of the Museum says that although the Hospital President remained unmarried throughout his life and never had children, he used a gene-synthesis process to create a synthetic person. Utilizing an artificial uterus, he developed this child. Once she was born, he adjusted her brain-processing abilities by enhancing the density of her gray matter to surpass any male in terms of intelligence, but he also erased all her original memories. She was trained as a clinical doctor. Later the Hospital President treated her as his closest confidante and eventually sent her to that place by the sea to search for Rockefeller. Based on his understanding of things, the Hospital President knew there was no way to save the hospital from the coming calamity, so he secretly sent a special envoy to seek help from his enemy and discuss strategies for moving forward.

"But why her and not you?" you ask the Guardian of the Museum, addressing the man competing with you for the same girl.

"Because Rockefeller is our common enemy, of course," the Guardian of the Museum explains. "He was responsible for the previous two world wars. But when it comes down to basic issues of survival, he lets those other issues fall by the wayside."

Spring Tide blearily opens her eyes. "Does the enemy have a preference for women?" she asks.

Autumn Rain also wakes up. "That is all part of a marriage alliance strategy," she mumbles with a smile. "This approach has been tried many times before."

"That's not it," the Guardian of the Museum counters. "It is all a manifestation of the Hospital Director's selfless sacrifice. He would never allow his doctors or patients to be sent. He sent his own flesh-and-blood daughter instead, because there were many uncertainties and risks involved. Although the war had been raging for a long time, very little was known about the enemy. The enemy was, after all, Rockefeller. He thought sending anyone else would be immoral, and he could never rest easy. This concerned the very survival of the hospital itself! I increasingly realize just how great a man my father was." Yet why didn't his father send him? Was he not the legitimate son of the Hospital President?

"That's just how the world works," Summer Stream utters disdainfully. "Any attempt to figure out who any given person used to be is pointless. It's not like I'm the Hospital President's illegitimate daughter. I have no such father. How could he have created me? Did you forget that I'm the one who performed an autopsy on him? What *don't* I know about him?"

"Well, he never publicly said anything about having children, nor did he save the memories related to this," the Guardian of the Museum stubbornly argues. "People produced with synthetic genes should be considered as not having any real parents. To hide your identity, he told people that you were just the child of an impoverished family that brought you into this world to care for your crazy older brother. But in reality, you were indeed his creation, entering the world after a full ten months of gestation, just like when Super Patient gave birth to Zifeiyu. Your birth also attests to the deep links that bind doctors and patients; therefore how could anyone claim that you're not his child? If you complete your mission, you shall be a true goddess!"

"A goddess? What the hell does that even mean?" Summer Stream bursts out in a strange fit of laughter. She looks at you as if reevaluating your relationship.

You quietly say to yourself, "Hey, Goddess of the Storm! Stand up!" You feel like you can see her frolicking with Zifeiyu. They are, after all, both synthetic humans. They are inside the helicopter mating . . . your mind is in a state of turmoil.

"Once we find Rockefeller, will we be able to create the Pool of Dead Souls?" Spring Tide and Autumn Rain interject. "How can the Hospital President know the situation by the sea?"

"That is the result of their analysis after watching the enemy's films," says the Guardian of the Museum. "They collected prints of seven hundred and twenty thousand Hollywood films. He rarely left the house in his later years, spending every day in his home office watching movies. Through those films, not medical records, he gradually unraveled the secrets of what was happening by the sea. Through those movies he was able to see traces of heroism and patriotism in the enemies as well." The more he speaks, the more chaotic his words become.

Winter Dew awakens, and her disgust is evident. "Are those the same films we were just watching? This is just too absurd! I don't see the relevance of those films to medical research!"

Only Einstein still enjoys his beauty sleep, or maybe he is just pretending.

"The hospital places the utmost importance on images," the Guardian of the Museum continues confidently. "Diagnosis and treatment would be meaningless without images! Ever since the time of Aristotle, we have seen how great ideas always transition from images to religion, and then from religion to science. Later, they transition from science back to religion and eventually return to images. That's simply how it goes. The structure of the retina determines the appearance of the world."

"You mentioned that place by the sea," Summer Stream interjects disdainfully. "Since I've never been there, I was wondering if it might simply be an image? According to the video we just watched, all the enemies should also be living within Little Wei's memories. That would mean that everything is fabricated. Little Wei's memories are so muddled and distorted that they just keep building one layer of chaos on top of another."

"Indeed, that's why there's nothing we can believe besides what we see in movies," Spring Tide and Autumn Rain declare in unison. They wink comically at Summer Stream. "That's why she is our true savior—our goddess!"

You look back at Summer Stream, who appears sulky and dejected. You think back to that moment when she first fished you out of the water, freeing you from the Pool of Dead Souls. Did she also help you step outside your own mind? That is hard to say, but she did seek out Rockefeller. You long sensed that she had been to that place by the sea, and it turns out that your intuition was correct. Hmm, is it possible that she was the woman standing beside the apostle during the "original treatment"? Did she participate in your creation and that of the Pool of Dead Souls? These things were all her doing. So who is the true enemy?

"No, according to what's recorded in this file, she went to that place by the sea but ran away shortly after arriving!" Finally finding some much-needed leverage, the Guardian of the Museum waves the file in the air. "She returned much sooner than expected and doesn't even remember what she saw or did there. Yet another mystery! And because of this, the Hospital President lost everyone's trust in the hospital, along with his control of the situation. The patients took the opportunity to launch their insurrection. And this woman let her father down. Therefore, she is not our savior. She is the true reason for the catastrophe that has befallen us! She has defiled the very title of 'goddess'!" He casts an ambiguous glance at his sister—they don't really look anything alike.

"Humph, so you're saying she is the real mastermind behind all of this," says Winter Dew. "If that's true, it will rewrite all of hospital history! Why is it always that specific individuals are deciding the fate of history?" From behind her glasses, a chill emanates from her eyes.

Summer Stream's face lights up with a look of hatred. "Stop playing games with me! I don't remember any of this! The Hospital President couldn't possibly be my father! The whole thing is ridiculous. I've never been to that place by the sea. I once thought about going, but my application was rejected by the hospital's Personnel Department. Little Wei, didn't I tell you all this?"

The Guardian of the Museum stubbornly raises his voice. "This is not a setup or a disruption, and it's certainly not the result of an older brother's jealousy of his sister. Every piece of evidence the Museum of Hospital History has in its archive proves that you went there. We even have the letter you sent from there to the Hospital President. Who besides you would dare to write to the Hospital President? Not even *I* had the courage to do such a thing! You never completed your mission. Instead, your mind wandered, and you became distracted by other tasks. This proved to be a great embarrassment for the hospital. The information we have reveals that you even had a child with the enemy while you were there! And you dare claim to have forgotten all this? You need to be awakened, like all the other patients! By the way, was your husband . . . one of our enemies?"

The color drains from your face. Your thoughts are in disarray. The situation is becoming increasingly entangled. You have already come to the realization that there is some kind of important connection between you and Summer Stream. She is likely your creator; and then you went on to create the world, including everyone present. So what then is your actual relationship? It is like a Möbius strip. Since you don't really understand it, you can't explain it to the others.

But now you have learned something else: Summer Stream may have had a child with the enemy. This is utterly outrageous! Who is her husband? Could it be Zifeiyu? Or the apostle? If they created the Pool of Dead Souls, which gave life to you, then you are their child! Just thinking about it makes you sick, breaking the natural boundaries of the human brain while also injecting the pleasure one gets after seeking revenge.

Summer Stream smiles with a mixture of ferocity and defiance. "You're accusing me of colluding with the enemy? That's a serious allegation. Why don't you just go ahead and execute me as a spy then? But let me ask you, How reliable is the Museum of Hospital History's archive? How many of those files have not been tampered with?"

You think back to another woman you once had relations with— Zhu Lin. You were on a ship together headed for that place by the sea. And now, in this very moment, the images of Summer Stream and of Zhu Lin standing against the ship's railing suddenly overlap, both so close and yet so distant. Everything began back with that question Bai Dai asked: *How do doctors die?* And even today, that question still remains shrouded in mystery. Many were murdered by the patients, but that is just a superficial phenomenon. You saw the Hospital President's corpse with its internal organs removed, transforming him into a strange object.

"Let's freeze him now, while there's still time," you suggest with a mixture of fear and jealousy, though it is actually just an attempt to distract everyone's attention. The pressure is building, and you can barely take it anymore.

"The power has been cut; there is no way to freeze him," Winter Dew replies matter-of-factly. "Perhaps we should mummify him? Then we could really take our time researching him."

You hear the thunderous sound of Einstein snoring. Even as things are coming to a critical head, he is astonishingly able to go on sleeping like a baby. Somehow this feels like a prelude to death. It is hard to predict what the old man would look like as a mummy. He turned what began as hospital reform into an all-out revolution, a war that would claim countless lives and destroy the hospital. How will all of this end? Father's blood runs through your veins. That blood came from your grandfather, and great-grandfather . . . all the way back to the Yellow

Emperor. Then again, perhaps your blood comes from Rockefeller's family line . . .

Either way, does it make any difference? In the end, everything can be traced back billions of years to some single-celled organism floating in the vast ocean. The path that evolution takes is so treacherous that one tiny misstep could have prevented our arriving here today, which is why it is more likely to have been the result of a clever plan, each and every step meticulously arranged. You thought you had escaped, but you are still caught in the middle. Everything is utter chaos, forever stuck in a never-ending cycle. Behind every living being are billions of ghosts casting a curse from which none can escape. What determined that you appear at this place, at this time? Why does Einstein always insist on finding you? You still cling to the hope of finding the Universal Treatment Machine, using its power to wash all this putrid blood away. You want to eliminate all falsehoods and bid farewell to all impurities. Perhaps then you and your father could reconcile and establish an authentic family together. You finally realize that "family" is the most effective weapon against this chaotic world.

Throughout this exchange, you stand there, frozen like a withered tree. There are four women present, and you feel like you will lose control if you look any one of them in the eye. You still can't be sure of your actual relationship to them, but for now it seems necessary to cooperate with them in order to get through the current crisis. You desperately hope that Einstein might awaken from his slumber and say to you, *I've been looking for you, my child. I recognized you as my son a long time ago. This is something you cannot deny. You must not betray your ancestors and forget your roots.* How you long for him to speak those words, though they would terrify you.

36

PANDORA

Summer Stream is now completely ignoring the Guardian of the Museum and her brother, but she doesn't seem openly upset. She approaches you like an ally, adopting an intimate tone. "Hey, Little Wei, we both refuse to accept that we could possibly have a father like him, right?"

"That's right. I definitely don't accept him as my father. At the very least, they raised us without ever seeking our permission!" You nod your head as if welcoming backup forces.

"And the result of what's been happening is your fault, right?"

"Of course."

"In that case, I have an idea."

"What's that?"

She gestures toward the sleeping Einstein with her chin. "I hope the old man stops following us. He's the real troublemaker. If he hadn't shown up, there wouldn't have been those videos. He has forgotten his original aim and has achieved nothing in his old age, instead becoming an obstacle preventing us from completing our work. He will continue to bring us more trouble in the future, which is the true source of the catastrophe we're facing. Didn't you say you still wanted to find the Universal Treatment Machine? We can never let it fall into his hands. And what if he tries to steal your girlfriend?" She doesn't seem to be referring to herself, which you find disappointing.

"That's right, he's much too conspicuous," you say. "The hospital has already sent out a warrant for his arrest."

"Isn't he the mastermind behind the hospital insurrection? If this keeps up, we'll all be captured by the doctors, and that will be our end!"

"But he will never leave on his own. I know all about his background." You feel torn, like Summer Stream is trying to deflect attention from herself. She has taken your place as the new focal point of the situation. Everyone now believes it was her betrayal that led to the current crisis. You have been exonerated, yet you can't help but feel jealous of her for being the center of attention.

"We don't necessarily need to make him leave. We could just make him disappear completely!" Summer Stream waves her fist in front of you. She seems to be thinking clearly, her actions revealing the cold, calculating approach inherent in most doctors. She takes out a box and hands it to you.

You never imagined she would advocate such an approach. Wasn't she always against retributive violence? Although you despise Einstein, the thought of him dying is not something you are ready to tolerate. But a woman's heart can be more venomous than a snake or scorpion. Her words are not to be trusted. Perhaps the HIV virus that Rousseau injected into her is beginning to affect her behavior? Now she, too, is seeking revenge. You are again reminded of that time when she had you remove the oxygen tubes from a patient. You continue to refuse to accept Einstein as your father, but now that they are about to kill him, you are suddenly gripped by apprehension. The old man still wears his bloodstained lab jacket. Besides being Einstein, he is also Guevara. Summer Stream once told you that his original aim was to make a more significant contribution to humanity, but thinking about that now seems pointless . . . and time has run out. The more important matter to consider is your relationship with Summer Stream and where it is going, so you decide to block those other crazy thoughts and just listen to her.

"This is Mars," she says, "so you don't need to have any scruples about what we're about to do."

The red planet inspires you. You can do anything you want here, without having to worry about the repercussions. Even when blood is spilled, the color of Mars conceals its hue. You open the box that Summer Stream gave you and see pills disguised as candy. You hold up one of the pills to entice Winter Dew. At first, she appears indifferent, seemingly intent on maintaining her loyalty to Einstein—an idiotic decision, you think, but perhaps she is just pretending. Winter Dew is a woman with grand ambitions and a strong sense of purpose. She will probably win the Nobel Prize one day and take over as Hospital President. She never believed that Einstein would provide her with sweets for her entire life. This woman who researches the history of military medicine knew the old man was done for a long time ago. The two of them have had their disagreements before, and now it is time for them to part ways. He engaged in warfare in the name of peace, while she used the methods of war to sacrifice herself for peace. You don't hate Winter Dew, but the pity and loathing you feel for Einstein have grown stronger. You continue tempting the woman with candy-coated medicine, and soon she picks up the scent like a mother bear. She comes over, extends her tongue, and swallows it down with a gurgling sound. Einstein probably neglected to feed her any candy these past few days, while they were on the run.

"That's a good girl. Is it tasty?" You gaze at her with mixed feelings. She reverts back to her animal nature as she eats, which improves your impression of her. She asks for more, and you immediately oblige, stealing a glance at Summer Stream, who stares blankly back at you.

"Just what kind of game are you playing?" Einstein suddenly asks, midstretch, having just awakened. You awkwardly turn away. Spring Tide and Autumn Rain are quietly discussing something. Summer Stream keeps a close eye on your every move, occasionally signaling you with her eyes.

"If you want some more candy, you're going to have to offer something in exchange," you tell Winter Dew. Experience tells you that all the women in the hospital are gluttons, their good and bad qualities related to this gluttony.

"What do you want me to do?" she asks, her eyes locked on the candy.

You pout your lips in the direction of Einstein. She adjusts her glasses and immediately understands, though she seems disinterested. You try to encourage her. "It's not a difficult task. In fact, it's quite simple. If you want to be the Hospital President one day, you will have to do as I say. Don't you still need to complete your doctoral dissertation and win a Nobel Prize? This is an essential step to attaining lasting peace."

"I know," she replies.

She stands up, strips naked, and spreads her legs. Einstein's dead eyes immediately light up. He takes her in his arms and pushes her to the floor. They probably haven't been intimate for quite some time. Her actions look like a cross between a performance and an internship. As they engage in their mating activity, she takes out a roll of tape and wraps it around his neck in an attempt to cut off his oxygen supply. You are left dangling in suspense, as if your entire body has been thrust underwater. Einstein doesn't utter a sound, as if he knew this moment was coming. He slowly turns his head to fix his gaze on you. There is no hatred or fear in his eyes, just a look of kindness and affection. You witness what it means to "part with what one loves most" and can't help but feel astonished.

Einstein starts coughing up phlegm, and the coughing grows increasingly violent, accompanied by the sound of metal cracking. His facial muscles twitch, and a thick green fluid dribbles out of his mouth. He struggles to reach for his inhaler, but Winter Dew slaps his hand aside. Spring Tide and Autumn Rain clench their fists, silently observing, though they're more concerned with Winter Dew. Summer Stream casts the Guardian of the Museum a sidelong glance, seemingly a warning that he'd better start behaving himself. This is where her true intention lies. You are on the verge of prying Winter Dew's hands away, but you don't move a muscle. Winter Dew becomes increasingly excited, her broad forehead turning a bright red as if actually mating. Einstein's shoulders and chest tremble; then he collapses to the ground like a sack of straw. A sound escapes his throat, and after carefully listening, you hear him utter, "Guevara, Guevara . . ."

No one dares say a word as they await the final result. Einstein's face turns pale, and his living body inexplicably transforms into a pile of human remains. Even those who have never seen a dead body can recognize that he has suddenly lost that quality that made him human. Only now does Winter Dew pull herself out from under the old man's body. A faint, dark light projects down upon the corpse's face. Such is the type of crime that can be committed only on Mars. Einstein must have known the end was coming and allowed Winter Dew to kill him. He didn't offer even the least resistance—it was essentially a form of suicide, wholly unexpected. You think back to something he once said: *They are no different than dreams, shadows, dew, and electricity!* Only now do you realize that you never really understood him.

You are a bit sad, but you do your best to calm yourself down, as if repenting of your original sin. You suddenly see a shadowy figure, suspended in midair, right before your eyes—it is the Yellow Emperor! He takes the form of a listless elder with a bloodred halo . . . but he quickly disappears into thin air. You think, *Einstein has toiled tirelessly his entire life, and now he can finally rest.* You no longer need to worry about whether to acknowledge your father-son relationship.

You suddenly remember that your true birth father died a long time ago. You were still a child when he was murdered by a patient's family after a medical dispute. A woman who claimed to be your mother appeared, rushing to the morgue to say a final goodbye. Leaning over your father's body, she whispered, ". . . root of evil." Then she walked over to hold you in her arms. So close to her, you could smell the musty odor of her body and see the reddish-brown cross-shaped scar emblazoned across her throat. The memory of your mother's appearance during that final moment almost makes you faint. It feels like this ending has played out before, countless times, but each time the details are somewhat different. You wonder if all of this might be a figment of your imagination, which leaves you even more depressed.

You ask the Guardian of the Museum to look into Einstein's hospital files for you. You remind him that Einstein was not originally a patient, but a doctor. He was once the hospital's most devout disciple, though he used a rather extreme method to express his devotion. His files shouldn't be with the other patient medical files. The Guardian of the Museum examines Einstein's corpse and glances at Summer Stream before saying it should be no problem. Perhaps he agreed, thinking that you and he are indeed relatives. "We will resurrect him once we find his files," he says. He slips away into another room and doesn't return for quite some time.

The group goes to check on him and discovers that he has committed suicide by bashing his head into a wall. His brains are splattered all over the wall and floor. Summer Stream lets out a cynical laugh. You are assaulted by an added layer of guilt. With the death of the Guardian of the Museum, the hospital's history is now finished. Just like that, the most important hospital elders—the Hospital President, Einstein, and the Guardian of the Museum—have all taken their leave.

Only you and the four women remain. Summer Stream is the oldest, then Spring Tide and Autumn Rain, and Winter Dew is the youngest. Until now, you have yet to form a family with any of them, but now that the other men are dead, perhaps you have a better chance? You hear the cry of the monkeys getting closer, so you and the women quickly find a place to hide.

THE FATE OF WOMEN

37

MOTHER

Zifeiyu leads Dr. Daptomycin, the Editor in Chief, and the monkeys on the charge into the Museum of Hospital History. They look everywhere, sniffing around every corner of the museum, but they can't find you and the women, so they steal all the medical files they can get their hands on. It takes a long time before the Greenpeace Army finally leaves.

"What should we do now?" you ask Summer Stream. If an even greater calamity should befall the hospital, you are worried that four women and one man will be unable to protect yourselves.

"First let's find something to eat and get some rest," she replies. "We'll worry about the rest later."

Everyone seems to agree, so you find some food before curling up next to the corpses of the three old men to get some rest. It's actually quite comfortable. You have had far too little rest lately and are devoid of energy.

Once you wake up, you work up the courage to ask, "Shall we look for the Universal Treatment Machine?"

Summer Stream hesitates before nodding. The other three women don't seem to object.

Now that you have regained your strength, you can set out. "Thanks for taking care of me." Your words come from the heart, an attempt to show how thankful you are to be alive and to ingratiate yourself with the women. You are in a perilous situation, and you can't survive without them. They surround you like a pack of female animals protecting their offspring, and you begin to develop the kind of attachment a son has for his mother, a new feeling that you are only now beginning to experience, having partaken in the murder of your father. The women also seem to need you. At least according to the film you watched, everyone is a product of your mind, which means that you are also their father, a rather strange relationship. The three other women also don't want Summer Stream to dominate them.

The five of you—one man and four women—leave the corpses behind and set out on foot, marching off together like a ten-legged insect. It feels almost as if you are playing a game, not a grand game of survival. But where exactly are you heading?

Summer Stream tries to be considerate. "Let's let Little Wei lead the way. He is, after all, the creator of the hospital, isn't he?" She speaks as if your responsibility has nothing to do with any of them. She links her arm with yours to display her special connection with you, a relationship unlike any other.

You anxiously respond, "No, that's not me . . . it was you that . . ."

The other women flash you a cold gaze.

"As Little Wei suggested, let's go find the Universal Treatment Machine!" Summer Stream continues. "It's got to be more than just a blueprint. Let's go find out just what wonders it holds! And if it turns out to be a bomb, so be it! Sometimes, people need a good letdown, right? Otherwise, this kid will be too arrogant and won't listen to anything we say. Regardless of his background, he is, after all, still a patient. It's our responsibility to look after him. But this will be a difficult journey, and we must be prepared for the sacrifices ahead. Hey, do you think you'll be able to handle that?"

The three other women respond in unison: "We are not afraid of death, but we will not sacrifice ourselves in vain. If we locate the Universal Treatment Machine, we should all reap the rewards." The women approach and lift you.

"Okay then!" you shout. "If the hospital is rebuilt one day, I will be sure to appoint all of you to leadership positions!" It is a haphazard promise, and you know you need to consider a more unified strategy.

"Then who will be the Hospital President?" ask Spring Tide, Autumn Rain, and Winter Dew. They flash Summer Stream a look that could be jealousy or animosity, but it is hard to tell.

"Hospital President? You think *I* want to be the new president?" she protests. "I have no interest in the position. It's fine if we decide to just leave that post vacant. Who cares, anyway? Didn't you see what happened to those three old men? I don't think Little Wei minds either." She is unyielding, much bolder and more visionary than the others, even going so far as to challenge Winter Dew—your father's woman.

"I don't think any of us believes a word you just said," pouts Autumn Rain.

"We need to find some men for ourselves," Spring Tide responds unscrupulously. "It's high time we got married. None of us is getting any younger." She flashes you a sidelong glance.

Having lost the upper hand, Winter Dew now seems beside herself. She is the youngest of the four women and has just lost the man who had protected her. Filled with regret, she removes her glasses and wipes them compulsively. You are the only one she can rely on. Now more than ever, she feels like you belong to her. She once possessed your father and even had contact with you.

The women finally place you back down on the ground.

"Do you think you have what it takes?" Summer Stream asks the other three women disdainfully.

That's when the thick mist rolls back in and the ground begins to emit a hissing sound.

Spring Tide slaps her chest. "Don't worry about getting lost. I'm here, and I've got money!" She leaps to your side and winks at you.

Undaunted, Autumn Rain approaches you. "I also have money!"

Growing flustered, Winter Dew joins in. She never got anything from her time with Einstein. She was unable to continue her research on war and peace, and now she's not even sure if she will finish her dissertation and earn her doctorate. "With the fog this thick, we won't be able to see the road," she says. "I'm afraid money won't do us any good."

"No matter how twisted the road might be, it's just a matter of putting one foot in front of the other," says Spring Tide. "I've walked that road a hundred times. I can do it with my eyes closed. What do you say, Little Yang? There's nothing to worry about."

"Nothing to worry about?" counters Autumn Rain. "Humph! If that's the case, then why did we run off to the Museum of Hospital History in the first place?"

"Let's not scare Brother Wei," Winter Dew says cautiously. She casts you a pleading look. You obediently return her gaze.

Summer Stream rolls up her sleeves. "What the hell are you trying to do?" She is acting like everyone's big sister. She is the only one here who's had a physical relationship with you.

The women break into a full-fledged argument, each trying to pull you to her side. The foul language grows heated—they will say *anything*. Isn't that how all shrill women behave? Is there really any fundamental difference between cultured women and lower-class women? Well, the same goes for things here on Mars. As the saying goes, scoundrels and women are always difficult to deal with—you feel frustrated and scared; none of them has the qualities one looks for in a mother.

You break free from their grip and, mustering up your courage, try to play the role of peacemaker. "C'mon, you all need to let this go. We still have a long road ahead of us, and things are bound to get difficult. Arguing back and forth like this is only going to exhaust us, and we'll never get anywhere." Your words come out sounding awkward, and you try to appease them all, but by taking the high road, you appear like the only adult in the room.

Seeing your look of sincerity, the women stop their bickering, but they remain angry. You still feel frustrated, but at least you've swayed them a bit. As the sole remaining male, you are now a precious commodity. This is what it's going to be like, you figure. They remain petty and shortsighted, even after having been transformed into Dead Souls. Yet you are also moved by their actions. You have regained your confidence, but you're still not sure which of the four women you fancy most. Too much choice can be a problem. You have been with Summer Stream throughout this journey, but the younger Winter Dew is quite cute, and there is something charming about Spring Tide and Autumn Rain. Having exhausted their argument, the women go right back to being close friends, chatting and laughing together, even linking arms as they continue on their way. Yet you can sense that even amid their jovial reconciliation, Summer Stream retains her somewhat dominant presence.

38
SEMIHUMAN CREATURES

The first stop is the nurses' station, where the women search for lipstick and facial cream. It feels like everything leading up to this was just preparation, and that things haven't really gotten started. Armed with beauty supplies, the women usher you on. They talk as they walk, discussing the Universal Treatment Machine. Autumn Rain says it is a sponge infused with toxins extracted from dead bodies. Spring Tide claims it is love. Summer Stream suggests that it might not even exist and is simply made up. You believe it was developed from narrative implant therapy and can connect all living things using sensory therapy.

"You're all wrong!" Winter Dew interjects. "According to my research, it is humanity itself! The appearance of the Universal Treatment Machine is destined to wipe hospitals, including the very word 'hospital,' from the face of the universe. Humankind will return to an age without hospitals, like every other living creature in nature. If animals can exist without hospitals, shots, and medications, why can't humans do the same? Haven't you seen how animals in the wild survive and protect themselves? A crocodile in a dirty swamp could have its leg bitten off and, without any medicine, somehow avoids infection and heals on its own. Humans have this same inherent ability to heal themselves, but it has been taken away from us by the very civilization we created, making us reliant upon drugs and medicine. Humans have fallen behind other animals in survival skills, fueling the vicious cycle that makes us even more reliant upon hospitals. What does the Universal

Treatment Machine actually do? It allows humankind to return to its natural state—it is the art of self-healing!"

Winter Dew's complex ideas, which were likely drawn from her doctoral dissertation, were intended to both please and subdue you. At least she didn't mention the Yellow Emperor.

"Humph," Summer Stream snorts, expressing just how childish she thinks this theory is.

Spring Tide and Autumn Rain scoff in unison: "Return to nature? Take a look around; where the hell is nature? Stop trying to deceive Little Yang; he is still a child."

Soon you see more and more corpses littering the road, though you can't tell if they belong to doctors or patients. You all proceed with caution, tiptoeing around the bodies.

"We better not go any farther," Winter Dew suggests timidly.

"Humph, lacking determination, are we?" Summer Stream sneers. "Yet you had no problem letting a man get so close to you—what a joke!"

A pack of strange creatures with long necks and protruding horns feeds on the dead, occasionally looking up at your group. They are humanoid, but certainly not monkeys; in some ways, their features resemble rats. But it is an artificial species—originally created in the hospital's lab with implanted brains and special genetically modified bacteria—that has since mutated.

"At a critical moment like this, we should let the man decide what to do," Spring Tide says, seeming hesitant about what to do next.

"He's our guiding force, right?" says Autumn Rain.

"I . . . I . . ." They want you to take the lead, to make a decision, but you can't do it. You hide behind Summer Stream.

Autumn Rain and Spring Tide sigh and rush over to pat your shoulders. "He may appear young, but deep down he's still an old man. Just look at his bald head and hunched back. Poor thing."

Winter Dew anxiously nudges them. "Don't do that. You might hurt him."

The women seem like they can't live without you.

"Nonsense!" cries Summer Stream. Finally, she makes the decision to continue on through the corpses and monsters.

The women walk with a certain choreography, as if part of a song-and-dance performance. They remind you of your old buddies, Fistula, Wart, Buboxine, and Spasm; aboard the Hospital Ship, you once wandered freely together, exploring all kinds of beautiful scenery. But this is Mars, and everything here is different. You manage to avoid the humanoid creatures, but eventually your path forward is blocked by a series of collapsed floorboards. The entire hospital has been reduced to ruins. Your legs grow weak. The four women get under you and, with a collective heave-ho, lift you up. It takes a lot of effort to get through the perilous pass, and you notice bloodstains scattered all over the debris.

"Something is wrong," warns Summer Stream.

"How do you know?" asks Spring Tide.

"Don't you have eyes?" Summer Stream says dismissively.

"Who are you trying to scare?" Autumn Rain grows annoyed. "We've all spent time in the hospital."

They start to argue again, but Winter Dew waves her hands to break up the fight. "Sisters, please stop. Let's not do this again. Why don't we have Brother Wei walk between us?"

Spring Tide and Autumn Rain agree. "That's a good idea. Little Wei, we will protect you. You're our little treasure; we'll be your bodyguards."

"Will you all protect me at the same time, or take turns?" you ask.

Summer Stream seems offended by your question and makes a strange sound. The other three women just stare blankly at you.

"Just listen to how he talks, pretty cute, huh?" says Summer Stream. "He still sounds like he used to. He's one of us now, so let's not fight."

Spring Tide and Autumn Rain both look pleased. Winter Dew keeps staring at you. She seems afraid of something.

You continue on, walking between them like filling in a sandwich, back to the hospital farm. There you discover more dead animals, their guts hanging out. You see stragglers from the battle, but you can't tell if they are doctors or patients. Some are human, others look more like ghosts, but they are all male and zombielike, wandering aimlessly through the dense forest carrying golf clubs and sacred talismans. They look like they are starving and occasionally stop to consume the corpses littering the ground.

You and the women hide behind the tall trees so you aren't discovered, but it isn't long before another group of semihuman creatures appears, mostly naked, covered in blood, some missing limbs. Through the trees, they catch sight of you and begin limping toward you like a pack of lions surrounding a family of mules. More and more of these strange, putrid creatures converge around you with twisted necks, gaping mouths, and lewd sinister grins that emit a continuous whistle-like hissing. They have their sights set on the women and don't even seem to notice you, which makes you feel a bit insulted.

"Hey, maybe it's time for you to protect us for a while?" Spring Tide suggests.

"You're the ones who told me to stay in the middle," you complain, like a little boy who has been wronged. You tremble with fear at the monstrous creatures, which have pulled their tattered sleeves over their shoulders, revealing explosive biceps. Their dark-green bodies are covered in scales and littered with oozing wounds.

"Okay then, have it your way." Autumn Rain grits her teeth. "We big sisters will continue to take care of you, you little freeloader."

"What the hell are those things?" Winter Dew asks Summer Stream.

"Calm down," says Summer Stream impatiently. "What are you afraid of? Haven't you seen them before?"

The hospital is being taken over by these mutated creatures, which are no longer even close to human. They suddenly begin to speak, and you have to strain your ears to make out the garbled words that spill out of their mouths: "It's been a long time since we have touched a woman . . . so long since we have touched a woman . . . let us have a little taste . . ."

The four women quicken their pace, but the bizarre creatures are faster. Some of them leap into the air and cut the five of you off. With a call to battle, Summer Stream leads the women forward, striking down the monsters with a large red cross. The women keep you behind them, protecting you, but they are outnumbered by the monsters, which continue to surge forward, whistling and howling. A pair of large hairy hands grabs Summer Stream's collar, and she roars like a lioness.

"Quick, help her!" you yell.

Spring Tide and Autumn Rain hesitate before leaping into action. Waving their red crosses in the air, they drive the monster off and save Summer Stream. Winter Dew appears frozen, perhaps in shock, or pondering some obtuse academic question. More creatures appear, ferocious, streaming saliva from their mouths, and heading straight toward you. Summer Stream grunts an order, and the four women form a circle, with you protected in the middle. They wave their weapons like windmills, preventing the monsters from getting too close. But the creatures seem to multiply, layer after layer of them descending upon you like a pack of snarling wolves. Twisting and turning, the creatures pile up. Winter Dew is on the verge of being torn apart.

"We can't go on like this," Summer Stream says, glancing at Winter Dew.

Realizing the grave danger she is in, a look of terror appears on Winter Dew's face.

You scream, "No . . . no . . ."

Luckily, Summer Stream, Spring Tide, and Autumn Rain react quickly. Extending their hands, they pull Winter Dew up and catapult her toward the creatures. Winter Dew tumbles through the air, knocking her glasses off, and falls directly into the clutches of the roaring monsters. Winter Dew silently turns pale and shuts her eyes tightly. With the monsters distracted, the three remaining women help you up, and the four of you sneak away.

You look back, your heart in a state of turmoil. "You aren't going to save her?"

Summer Stream pats you on the head. "Winter Dew will be just fine. She knows how to take care of herself. Moreover, it's high time she made a little sacrifice. She's the toughest one of us, as well as the youngest and smartest. She's a medical genius and knows how to speak the language of those perverted monsters. If you can't see this, then we won't play with you anymore." Spring Tide and Autumn Rain take you by the hand, dragging you away. You look to Summer Stream for help, but she is pulling too.

39

THE ANGELIC TRANCE

Like your very first trip to the hospital, women support you as you move forward. They seem to remember that they were the original masters here, and you are merely a guest. Summer Stream walks the fastest, filled with indignation and distrust for the other two women. The hospital farm seems to go on forever, with new plants growing everywhere, a chaotic and clamoring scene. You find it difficult to discern whether you are hearing the melody of birth . . . or death. Physically and mentally exhausted, you are also despondent, having just lost Winter Dew. Once you find the Universal Treatment Machine, you wonder what will happen if the remaining women fight over it. Whose side will you take?

"Hey, what's wrong with you?" Autumn Rain scolds you with a kick. "Just look at the gloomy expression on your face! We almost died trying to save you!"

Not wanting to be left out, Spring Tide bops you on the forehead and boasts, "Don't you realize that we care about you?"

"I'm old and tired," you mutter, utterly dejected. "I can't go on anymore. Why don't you go find the Universal Treatment Machine without me."

"What?" Summer Stream stops Spring Tide and Autumn Rain from beating you. "We can't stop here, it's not safe. Even if you feel like you can't go on, you must push yourself."

"Why do you insist on taking me with you?" you ask.

"Aren't you the one who created this mess we call the hospital?" says Autumn Rain. "Don't think you can scare people with that! We

are angels sent here to save you. No matter what happens, we need
to rely on you to carry on our family line. We will use the Universal
Treatment Machine to fix you up like normal." She flashes a look at
Summer Stream.

Not wanting to appear weak, Summer Stream shoots back a fierce
gaze. You wonder, *Is the family unit really coming back?* You both crave
and fear it.

Spring Tide rolls her eyes. "Why don't I tell you a little story to help
you relax? You are a big bundle of anxiety!"

"Okay, my angel," you agree reluctantly, thinking that all creatures
traveling between the divine realm and the mortal realm probably possess a greater degree of maternal love.

And so, she tells her story . . . "There once was a patient who created a doomsday escape ball, which could roll down mountains and
float in the sea. On the day of the apocalypse, which happened to be a
Sunday, he hid himself inside the ball. But he accidently locked himself
in and couldn't get out. While everyone else was enjoying their Sunday
vacation, he was experiencing the apocalypse. This is a true story. His
problem was that he had faith in himself, but not the angels." Spring
Tide lets out a hearty laugh, but you don't find it funny. You suspect
she is trying to mock you, comparing you to the patient in the story. In
exchange for listening to her story, you edge closer to her. The strong
avian smell coming off her body makes you dizzy.

Taking note of what is unfolding, Autumn Rain interrupts. "We
have just gotten a glimpse of the hospital's secrets. We need to leave
now. If we don't go, we will be eaten alive by those zombified monsters. The true apocalypse is upon us, right now! Little Yang, aren't you
terrified?"

You are well aware that the women have taken over and you are
losing your autonomy. But you still don't understand just what special
value you have. The world you created has already died many times
over. You don't know who you were before its creation. All this played

on-screen for just a few moments, yet the women immediately believed it to be true. That is what it means when we say that the world is dominated by images. But why should you be given the title of Creator? Who cares whether they save you? Now that you are together, you don't want them to leave, and you fear they will grow tired of you and leave you behind.

"Is Winter Dew dead?" you ask.

Summer Stream shoots you a glance. "Still thinking of her?"

This is when another group of gray shadows appears ahead. Each is about half the size of a human child, with a soft jellyfish-like consistency. They extend their webbed arms, gatekeepers blocking the path forward. This time, you fear you are done for.

"Hey, what do these creatures want? Sex or money?" Spring Tide mutters with a strange expression.

"They probably want money," Autumn Rain grumbles. "Just look at their miserable appearance. They must be running low on energy. I'm sure they have no interest in our bodies. We've known for a long time that, here in the hospital, it's money that makes things happen."

"Are the two of you in charge of the hospital's finances?" Summer Stream asks stonily. "Didn't you say you had money? Quick, hand some over to these pathetic creatures!"

"No way," argues Spring Tide. "In case we end up not being appointed leaders of the new hospital, we'll need that money for our retirement."

"Perhaps we can just use some of it." Autumn Rain looks at you with concern. "This is an emergency situation. We are angels, after all!"

"If I agree . . . how will you repay me?" asks Spring Tide.

"I'll promise to take care of you when you get old," proposes Summer Stream. "How's that?"

"I also want a man," Spring Tide demands.

"Then you better get in line, because I want one too," Autumn Rain jokes.

"Okay, whatever you want!" Summer Stream agrees, but she flashes you a challenging look. You awkwardly nod your head.

Spring Tide and Autumn Rain laugh. "You're always making promises you can't keep. We've seen so many things in this world. This hospital is nothing but a huge scam. We don't have any faith in it." Despite this, they reach into their pockets, take out some money, and divide it among the creatures. As they hand the money out, they say, "Here you go, kids! Here's a fun game for you: see if you can count how much there is!"

The creatures take the money and start counting. The women looked stunned, like they might be hallucinating.

"Their brains are like machines that have been conditioned by the Red Envelope Program," Spring Tide says. "No surgery unless you pay!" You have never seen a creature like that counting money; it is a truly ridiculous sight. They are more intelligent than humans, and more diligent too. A look of amusement and horror appears on Summer Stream's face as she watches.

After counting all the money, the creatures stand aside to let you pass. The four of you continue on. But soon you encounter other mutated life-forms, a fringe species born in the garbage dump after the fall of the hospital. These creatures were not consciously designed. Some have fat human bodies with piglike heads. Others look like long, spiky meat sticks. You dodge various monsters as they attempt to catch you, and then you come upon a conveyer belt used to transport corpses.

"Do we need to follow this conveyer belt?" asks Autumn Rain.

"Is this the right way?" Spring Tide asks Summer Stream.

Summer Stream silently waves them forward, so you all lie on the conveyer belt. As it moves you along, you are assaulted by a bout of motion sickness. You catch a glimpse of the women applying makeup.

"Good luck!" Summer Stream says. "After making the required sacrifice, we will reach our goal." She seems to be egging the other women on, but maybe she is deceiving them? Perhaps in situations like this, even angels can lose their way.

"Winter Dew checked out at just the right moment. Now we shall prepare for our victory!" cheers Autumn Rain.

"But what about our money?" Spring Tide seems pained about giving so much to the monsters.

The two of them extend their arms out from the conveyer belt, attempting to lock them with Summer Stream's. They can reach her, but Summer Stream looks reluctant to take their hands. You feel both angry and amused, thinking how pretentious the women look. Deep down, they are probably cursing each other.

Autumn Rain groans and says to Spring Tide, "We look like a bunch of patients on the brink of death. The men will surely pity us."

"Not necessarily," says Spring Tide. "We are the healthy ones. What men really want are angels who are robust, powerful, and free from illness."

They turn to you and say in tandem, "Team Leader of the Red Label Commando Unit, no need for such a long face. Don't forget that you are our guiding light!"

After linking arms with Summer Stream, Spring Tide and Autumn Rain sit up on the conveyer belt and lean over to give you a little kiss. Summer Stream pretends she doesn't see.

"That's right, everything we do is for you." The two women giggle. "We can't let you die. It feels like we are on our way toward a happy ending, a place where light from the divine realm is scattered everywhere. Hey, do you know what a woman's definition of happiness is?"

You shake your head in despair. You're not sure when, but you realize the women have changed into different outfits, exchanging their white lab jackets and military uniforms for black skintight outfits that resemble lingerie. You assume they did this to please you, and now they look even more like angels.

"We worship heroes, heroes among men," Spring Tide and Autumn Rain say seriously, exchanging a mysterious look. "But the old Hospital President is useless. Let's hope you don't leave us disappointed like him."

You feel like you are about to throw up, but you worry that the women might be upset with you. You think about how wonderfully unique it would be to explore the flesh of an angel. They are like creatures from a parallel universe, and yet you are still unable to enter their world. You are full of anxiety and regret. But then you notice a strand of red liquid hanging from Spring Tide's lower body. Perhaps she is having her period. That would prove she is not a machine. Shaking with fear, you assume this means she will be even more jealous.

Finally, unable to bear it any longer, Summer Stream steps in and orders Spring Tide and Autumn Rain to stop teasing you. "Do you think this is some movie like *If You Are the One?*" she admonishes. "Little Wei isn't the kind of man you think he is! He's still a boy!"

Spring Tide and Autumn Rain stick out their tongues and glare at Summer Stream, but they don't dare talk back. They know she means business. Although she didn't complete her mission, she did make it to that place by the sea, and apparently even left a child behind. She was also the first among them to bag herself a man.

As the conveyer belt takes you farther away, they are no longer molested by those strange monsters. The remaining stragglers see you going by and probably think you are already dead. As you ascend, the smoke thickens, and the stacked sick wards gradually retreat into the distance. Gazing out beyond the dome, you see an expansive chaos shrouded in a veil of green smoke, but you still can't see that place by the sea. As the smoke thickens, you can't even see the women clearly, and eventually they entirely disappear from your field of vision. Finally, after passing through the dangerous and expansive hospital farmland and traversing a series of golf courses, you reach a partially collapsed building that resembles a birdcage. You and the women hop off the conveyer belt and climb upward.

This seems to be the center of the hospital. After walking for a while, you unexpectedly arrive at the Pool of Dead Souls, but you can't tell if it is the same pool from which you came. There is movement in the pool: a new artificial life-form, a grayish gelatinous substance resembling porridge, its face and limbs yet to stabilize into a concrete form. Though extremely dark and gloomy, it somehow conceals a hidden brilliance. Seeing this strange creature suddenly inspires you to write a song. For the first time in a long time, you feel that sense of mission that you felt when you first checked into the hospital. As if completely attuned to your thoughts, Summer Stream begins to sing softly:

> One day humanity will live only in the present,
> Abandoning their longing for an illusory future.
> No dark hell awaits us,
> No bright heaven for us to escape to.

You never knew Summer Stream could sing, let alone a classic by one of your favorite singers. Now this gorgeous military doctor looks just like Whitney Houston. Whose Dead Soul is she, really? You feel guilty, and the sound of her voice makes the other two women feel ashamed, too, and they put aside their arrogance.

You would like to write a new song dedicated to the heroic spirit of your companion, who faced the threat of death with such bravery and grace, but alas, your talent has been exhausted. You can still recite a few lyrics, but you can no longer compose anything new, and there is no way to use song to express your affection for her. This may very well be the most humbling moment of your life.

40

THE FINAL ACT OF BRUTALITY

Beside the Pool of Dead Souls lies a brass control device shaped like a rotating wheel, adorned with the image of a naked Buddhist sitting cross-legged on a lotus throne. It is impossible to determine the figure's gender, and it doesn't seem to be the Universal Treatment Machine. You all suddenly stop in your tracks when you realize that Zifeiyu, Dr. Daptomycin, the Editor in Chief, and the monkeys are there, anticipating your arrival. They emerge from the shadows with sinister grins, clearly waiting for you to fall into their trap, and you realize you have delivered yourself right to their doorstep. The three women tighten their lips in an attempt to maintain their composure. Having weathered many storms and survived all kinds of difficult situations, they are mentally prepared to deal with unforeseen events like this. Perhaps women have a fundamentally different emotional foundation than men, allowing them to push life-and-death matters aside. However, you have no way of anticipating what they might do, and you are gripped with panic.

"Don't you dare think that what you are seeing lies beyond the scope of real life," says Dr. Daptomycin, waving a white flag and pointing at the porridge-like creatures squirming around in the pool. "These creatures may be the product of design, yet they remain independent life-forms. The initial synthesis of artificial genomes involved over ten million nucleotides and approximately ten thousand genes. This is the kind of work that only an almighty Creator could undertake . . . and look over there; you shall see an even more miraculous species! They have their own metabolic system and respiratory functions, but they lack proteins, carbohydrates, and DNA. Their lifespan is even shorter than that of humans, yet they are full of imagination and certain to dominate the future . . . throwing in with them will be the only way to overcome future calamities. These are the true angels, the creatures that helped the doctors defeat the superbacteria. It is only because of their contributions that we are standing here today."

"How did they come about?" Autumn Rain asks preemptively, attempting to overwhelm the medical staff. "Are they here to replace the patients?"

"Oh, they are newborn warriors," explains the Editor in Chief. "This place is the launching ground for the future space war. The enemies are coming from the other shore. The Pool of Dead Souls has already transitioned into the Pool of Life, which signifies the creation of a new, stronger breed of Dead Souls. This new species will have its own brand-new belief system, providing the necessary tools to combat any disaster that might come their way. The construction of the Cosmic Hospital is about to begin!" He dusts off his green outfit and glances at Zifeiyu, seemingly in the hope of getting his approval. Carried by a team of monkeys, the overgrown child Zifeiyu maintains a restrained smile, appearing both pleased and saddened at the same time. He casts a strange gaze at the Forbes logo adorning the white flag. It is as if everything is playing out exactly as he had anticipated, and saying anything else would be superfluous.

You think back to the frog under your father's scalpel, and the image of your old man's shameless face appears before your eyes. Einstein is just one step away from victory, yet he now has no choice but to face his death. If he were still alive, how would he have faced this situation? As one of the masterminds who took part in patricide, what responsibility should you bear?

Your suspicions get the best of you, and you ask Autumn Rain, "Did you lead them here? Was it you who betrayed us? I never imagined you would turn out to be the ultimate spy!"

Summer Stream steps in front of you protectively. Spring Tide and Autumn Rain gradually wade into the pool of water, slowly approaching the strange creature. Two monkey soldiers link their arms, creating a palanquin for Dr. Daptomycin. Raised above everyone's heads, the good doctor swoops down with a pair of crescent-shaped forceps. He stabs Summer Stream in the abdomen, causing her intestines to gush out. Summer Stream slightly knits her brow but manages not to utter a sound.

Before Dr. Daptomycin even has a chance to remove his weapon from her body, Spring Tide has already leaped onto his shoulders. She straddles his neck and wraps her legs tightly around his chest before taking the red cross from her mouth and stabbing it into his head, killing him instantly. Autumn Rain stands off to one side, quietly watching. Just before Dr. Daptomycin dies, his eyes widen in disbelief. In her shock, Summer Stream extends her arms as if to hold his corpse close to her, but instead she just squats down on the floor. Doing her best to withstand the pain, she smooshes her intestines back into her stomach. Autumn Rain takes Summer Stream's place in front of you in an effort to keep you safe.

The Editor in Chief struts over and lashes a steel-wire whip at Autumn Rain, which she unsuccessfully tries to dodge. The noose of the wire tightens around her neck, quickly constricting her breath. You clearly hear her flesh and bones tearing, like the sound of mercury exploding. With one additional flick of his wrist, the Editor in Chief whips Autumn Rain into the air and directly into the Pool of Life. Her splash resembles a red flower blooming. All the humans and beasts immediately stop what they are doing and gaze into the water in astonishment. Autumn Rain's body splashes around, her fair thighs scissoring like synchronized swimmers' during competition. But that only lasts a moment, and then she is quickly torn apart, her body disintegrating before everyone's eyes. The creature in the pool converges for a moment before dispersing and descending upon the remains, devouring what is left of the pulpy substance that was once Autumn Rain's flesh and bones. Having replenished its nutrients, the creature darts through the water, swiftly merging back into a single form. The humans and monkeys standing around the pool feel a sudden rush of excitement as the creature in the pool emits a strange hissing sound, a cry of exhilaration after a most satisfying feast. You are reminded of Pavlov's theory of conditioned reflexes, and only now do you finally see that Dr. Daptomycin was right: this thing before you is indeed the ultimate life-form. But when the final moment comes, even this creature shall be doomed. Soon it will run out of food. It consumed every last bit of Autumn Rain, but it is still hungry. Confined to the pool, it laments its limited living space.

Zifeiyu is grinning from ear to ear. Saliva drips from the corners of his mouth. The two remaining women stand dumbfounded. The resemblance between you and Zifeiyu is stunning. The monkeys take advantage of the situation to attack. You figure that this time, it is truly the end of the road. At this critical moment, you feel a wave of heat approaching from the side. You turn to see Funeral Artist, a.k.a. the Fire Chief, a.k.a. Weber, a.k.a. Malnutrizole, his face a burning red. He holds a metal pipe and carries a row of oval-shaped steel tanks on his back, resembling the Chinese god Nezha.

Weber addresses those present. "Do you still have those pieces of art I sold you? They are one-of-a-kind handmade works!"

You urgently cry, "Hurry, save us!" You remember, back during the days of medical tourism, when Malnutrizole told you that in the end, only the crematorium could save you.

Weber nods solemnly. "Whether in thought or action, under no circumstances should we commit to a fool's idea of paradise. And we certainly shouldn't try to take any kind of shortcut to get there!"

Noticing how much he has prematurely aged, Zifeiyu grows anxious and quickly orders the monkey soldiers to advance. Funeral Artist presses a button, which releases flames from a series of pipes like a fire-breathing dragon. Holy Warriors in the front line catch fire and curl up on the ground, screaming in agony as their flesh burns. You wonder if these flames could be coming directly from the crematorium. It seems the brilliant Funeral Artist has created a brand-new artwork. The flames reveal a hungry countenance as they surge forward, burning more of the simian soldiers alive. The Editor in Chief is also touched by the flames, and his body ignites in a dance of radiant color. His contorting physical form morphs into a charcoal-like stick, but you can still make out his explosive grin.

Zifeiyu releases an exasperated sigh and climbs down from his monkey throne, attempting to escape on foot. But due to his massive infant-like body, his movements are clumsy and slow, and it takes only a moment for the flames to catch up to him. Weber breaks into a fit of hysterical laughter, savoring every moment of this ritual. He arrived at just the right moment. With this show of artistic prowess, Funeral Artist has taken his artistry to another level. Amid this cycle of continual destruction, his final act of brutality has created something completely new and of unparalleled beauty. As the flames approach the Pool of Life, they seem to tame what lies within. The entire ground transforms into an expanse of steam, which swirls into the air like multicolored mushroom clouds. A kaleidoscope of bright purple, pink, greenish black, and dazzling yellow floats over the ruins. One look at the expression on Funeral Artist's face and you can tell that this wanton and unbridled release has finally reached its explosive climax.

You sense that this is exactly what you have been craving. The hospital never provided this type of service before. But as Zifeiyu burns, you are struck with an intense pain, as if you are the one being immolated. A profound sense of sadness fills your heart as you realize that even the Greenpeace Army was but a fleeting presence, and now it, too, is gone. The two women quickly pull you away. Reluctant to part with Weber, you bid him farewell with the words, "Until we meet again . . ."

On the road you encounter more corpses. They seem to have killed each other while fighting over something. You can't tell if they are humans or monsters because their faces have been ripped apart. Spring Tide squats to take a closer look.

"Hey, what are you doing?" Summer Stream admonishes her impatiently. "Are you looking in the mirror? This is no time to be putting on makeup!"

Thanks to Summer Stream's reminder, Spring Tide takes out her lipstick and begins to apply it.

"Enough of that, we've got to go!" you say. But Spring Tide is still reluctant to leave; she seems transfixed.

"What exactly did you see?" Summer Stream asks.

"I saw a young version of myself," Spring Tide replies. "I was like a flower in full bloom, strolling through a sea of patients, attracting all their attention." She looks up, gazing at you like some sort of delicacy.

Summer Stream quickly pulls you away.

Spring Tide reluctantly stands up. "What are you doing?"

"We need you to lead the way," you say, with a mix of sincerity and fear. "You know this place better than anyone, right?"

"We can make it without her if we have to," says Summer Stream.

"Of course I'll guide you!" says Spring Tide. "Don't we still need to find the Universal Treatment Machine? But you better not go back on your promise! You still have to let me take a leadership position in the new hospital! And I want a man too!"

You hear the gurgling sound of plants singing, an ominous sign. "We must leave this place right away!" you urge them.

41

VIOLENCE AND ECSTASY

On a ridge overlooking the hospital farm, you finally see an abandoned machine shaped like a metal rod with a handle, though the various holes and bumps differ from what you saw depicted in the blueprints in the Museum of Hospital History. Nevertheless, you are utterly ecstatic. "Is this the Universal Treatment Machine?"

You take a closer look at the inscription beneath the machine: UNIVERSAL DISEASE MACHINE.

"A machine that induces disease? This must be wrong." You feel extremely disappointed. Spring Tide looks dumbfounded.

Summer Stream mocks her. "Did you lead us the wrong way on purpose? Little Wei will never forgive you for this."

"How could I?" Spring Tide stammers. "I would never do such a thing . . ."

Feeling like Summer Stream is mocking you, too, you awkwardly respond, "So the Universal Treatment Machine is actually a Universal Disease Machine? How could this have happened?" You heave a sorrowful sigh, realizing deep down that this is a case of "suffering due to unattainable desires." But this actually might be for the best. After all, weren't you trying to regain that lost pain from your past? In order to do so, your illness must worsen, or else you must come down with a new illness. In short, you must completely give up on all forms of treatment. That is the only way to evolve to the next level. You think back to that first visit to the hospital after drinking a bottle of mineral water in C

City. Such a distant memory . . . and yet it feels like just yesterday. All the circumstances that have befallen you began in that moment.

Confused, Spring Tide looks to you, hoping you can her help decide what to do, but you maintain a stern expression and remain silent. She cries and runs away.

"Don't go . . ." You want to go after her.

She screams in terror. "I think I just saw that damn husband of mine. He's looking for me!" She runs faster and faster.

You try to follow her, but Summer Stream stops you. "What do you think you're doing?"

"She's not a bad woman . . . ," you respond.

"And how do you know that?"

In the blink of an eye, only the two of you are left—one man and one woman—but a strange distance hangs between you. You go over to fiddle with the Universal Disease Machine, but you have no idea how it works. You are tempted to seek Summer Stream's help but are too embarrassed to ask. Summer Stream stops short of volunteering.

"We should go back and look for Spring Tide," you say. "She still has some money on her."

Summer Stream looks at you with an expression of annoyance and pity. "And what would you like to see happen?"

"I'm no longer interested in being a Dead Soul again. Living means getting sick, which leads to pain."

"It is only when we feel pain that we truly live," she counters. "Little Wei, you always get things confused. You seem to indeed be suffering from premature aging. You don't even remember whether you are alive. What's the use of a kid like you? Hey, haven't I always been good to you? Anyone else would have abandoned you by now! Anyway, forget it. I'll lead the way from here on out. Perhaps there are other strange, rare objects here in the hospital. Let's find them! If not to satisfy your ego . . ."

You think about your unusual relationship with her, especially the fact that you conspired together to commit murder, and decide to follow her anyway. You unexpectedly encounter Spring Tide, but she is already dead. Her lifeless body hangs upside down, suspended in midair. One of her ankles is tied with an electric wire, and one of her thighs has been torn off at the hip. Her body has already turned a charcoal black, but her protruding genitals are red and swollen, more alluring than ever before. You are reminded of that very first time you saw a female corpse, and a bolt of excitement surges through your heart.

"I had nothing to do with this," attests Summer Stream.

"Then who did?" Spring Tide and Autumn Rain looked identical to those women who once went by the names Sister Jiang and Ah Bi, who first brought you to the hospital, leading to all kinds of strange complications. But they died. It seems like throughout your life, you have always been destined to encounter women who are dead. They spent time with you, allowing you to live, and with them you first experienced the warmth of a woman.

Summer Stream bluntly tells you, "What's all this nonsense you keep thinking about? I can't believe that you would entertain obscene thoughts at a time like this!"

Suppressing the chaos raging through your heart, you go back to look at the Universal Disease Machine and wonder why the hospital would ever develop such a thing. When discussed in public, it was always referred to as the Universal Treatment Machine, but you are left with the impression that it is just a crude and primitive machine.

This is when the massive flames begin to approach you from behind. Funeral Artist is still reveling enthusiastically in the excitement. "You took away my toys," he shouts, "so I shall use my flames to set you ablaze!" His seems to want to burn everything to the ground—that means the hospital or the entire universe. The act of cremation is the essence of the world, a way for him to forge new works of art to sell to collectors.

Not wanting to see you consumed by the flames, Summer Stream pulls you away. After running for a while, she curses the Universal Disease Machine as a useless, clunky piece of junk to be abandoned.

"Huh, what are you doing?" you plead. "Please pick it back up."

"I told you a long time ago," she says, "this thing is utterly useless. It has nothing to do with evolution. Everyone is already sick, so what the hell does anyone need a Universal Disease Machine for? This entire hospital is one big sham!"

"But just think of how many people sacrificed themselves for that machine. Spring Tide, Autumn Rain, and Winter Dew all paid the ultimate price . . ." You worry that Summer Stream might be next.

Summer Stream spits twice. "All you think about is them . . ."

"No, I also think about my father, the Guardian of the Museum, the Hospital President, and your father . . . they all died for this hospital. We have been so consumed by what's been unfolding, we should really see something come of all this. Who cares if it's even real?" You pick up the Universal Disease Machine.

Realizing she cannot convince you otherwise, Summer Stream relents. "Okay then. Why don't you just bring it along as a good luck charm or a toy to play with. But let's go—it's really heating up in here! Even the thermometer is about to break." At that moment, the mercury thermometer mounted on the top of the red cross shatters. Things are getting serious.

But now you don't know where else you can go. As you continue, the Universal Disease Machine seems to grow heavier. Perhaps it is not actually increasing in weight, but some other change is taking place in the hospital. The very structure of space and time, embroiled in a tug-of-war between various forces, is warping before your eyes. Or perhaps the mass of the instrument is undergoing some kind of transformation? It is no ordinary instrument, but composed of special materials from another world. Or maybe the early apostles brought it when they first came here from the other side of the sea. No one can say for sure whether it serves a purpose. You and Summer Stream get into another argument over it. If you aren't careful, the Ultimate Disease Machine will again be lost.

"I never imagined the two of us would argue," you mutter listlessly.

"That's how we always are. On the surface we appear to get along great, but there has always been a big gap between us. What do you expect from doctors and patients? This is one of the tragedies of life, but it is also a comedy." Summer Stream's eyes gleam with tears.

"I'd like to suggest that we split up." You start to stomp off.

Summer Stream grabs you. "You can't go, Little Wei. I can't let you go it alone. You'll never make it without me." She bends over to pick up the Universal Disease Machine, but as she squats, her intestines pop out again. You look at her bloody hands as she stuffs them back in and can't help but think about the high probability that she is about to die.

That's when you hear a burst of commotion. A human form emerges from the flames—it is Zifeiyu. He has been reduced to a blackened skeleton, waving his arms wildly like a ferocious beast, his bones grinding the ground with a crunching sound. His belly drags like a piece of luggage, dripping yellow oil. With great difficulty he extends his hands, which grasp Spring Tide's burnt thigh. Somehow, without the help of his army of monkeys, this massive infant makes his way to Summer Stream, swinging the thigh at her. Summer Stream instinctively raises the Universal Disease Machine, which emits a cracking sound before spitting out a bolt of lightning that pierces a hole in Zifeiyu's chest. Black blood sprays from his body as he collapses to the ground. You feel a jolt of pain run through your own body, and you scurry off as if you've just been attacked. Your cry startles Summer Stream, who throws the machine aside and leads you off. But your pain only increases, and you are struck by a feeling of great sadness as you realize that the dead boy could have been you. You want to go back and retrieve the Universal Disease Machine, but Summer Stream stops you. Realizing that the situation is hopeless, you break into a fit of uncontrollable tears. You are still crying when the sounds of roaring flames and Weber's laughter descend upon you.

Summer Stream looks back. "Setting fires is no different from putting them out," she says.

42

THE SEA WITH NO EXIT

You enter a tunnel where, for the time being at least, the fire dragon is still unable to penetrate. Soon you arrive in a basement storage room decorated with a dampening device that resembles a demonic talisman. This place couldn't be more different than the sick ward, a vast open space filled with all kinds of strange devices and peculiarly shaped machines, most of which are no longer in working order.

"It looks like a multifunctional workstation," says Summer Stream.

Some of the machines are futuristic, while others still run on steam power, as if from the premodern era. Some machines are inscribed with Arabic words, while other are branded with English letters. Metal signs emblazoned with **TOP SECRET** or **DANGER** can be seen all over the room, along with several rows of short factory structures with chimneys, some of which spew weak strains of black smoke, another source of the thick smog perennially enveloping the hospital. You never imagined that such a structure might exist here, beneath the Mars Hospital. You take a deep breath of oxygen from your tank.

Summer Stream hobbles around the room, taking everything in. "Now I understand. The hospital is not just a place to deal with patients, but also a comprehensive production facility. Just look, they are manufacturing MIRV-style exoatmospheric ballistic smart missiles, nuclear explosion devices, quantum computers, artificial life-forms, superbacteria, extraterrestrial life-detection devices, big data–collection hubs, the internet, navigation satellites, surrogacy devices, high-value-added products, spaceship components, nanospheres, ion engines . . . just about anything you can think of!"

"Is this the true face of the hospital?" you exclaim in wonder. "This place that can do anything!"

"The hospital is where the ten thousand things can all be created. Perhaps, according to the logic of the hospital, all is medicine, and all this manufacturing is in preparation for the next calamity."

"Is it all being done to prepare for disaster?"

"Actually, I'm not sure."

"So what exactly is the hospital?"

"It is life."

"Life?"

"Now you see clearly . . . all complex physical systems eventually develop consciousness. Look, it has its own metabolism, cognitive abilities, a lust for life, and a fear of death. It can evolve, even replicating itself on Mars, where it can absorb energy and knowledge. It is no longer limited by the traditional constraints of time and space. Humankind can no longer support its endless appetite. Using the Mars Hospital as a springboard, it wants to replicate itself further, creating more hospitals throughout the solar system, the Milky Way, beyond the galaxy, eventually covering the entire universe . . ."

You realize that when this is accomplished, it will become a true Cosmic Hospital. Only through this process of continual replication can the hospital challenge calamity and death, preparing for something even more mysterious that one day might befall us. But has it transcended the Pool of Dead Souls? Or is all of this taking place within the Pool of Life? Is any of it related to you? Can one still claim that this is all a product of your imagination? Or does it exist independently of you? Or are you merely a figment of the hospital's imagination, a dream within a dream . . .

"The scope of all this is simply too large." You sigh. "It's far beyond anything I can imagine or comprehend."

"That's right, the energy supply alone is not enough to sustain it. I think the situation is extremely precarious."

"It's so complicated that it only takes one component to fail for the entire system to come toppling down."

"Such is the hospital's destiny. Calamities cannot be avoided, for it will always unleash more calamities of its own making."

"And what is the place of the Universal Disease Machine in all this?"

"I don't think it is anything special; it is simply one of many accessories here. From the looks of things, in order to prevent its own destruction, the hospital tried everything, even attempting all kinds of horrific things no one else would ever have attempted."

"So why did the hospital insist on imbuing itself with life? It's so much damn trouble!"

You both realize the extraordinary effort the hospital has put into achieving its goals, not unlike Sisyphus, who once kidnapped Death himself in order to eliminate death from the world, though his efforts resulted in the greatest tragedy of all. This effort goes far beyond anything that typical doctors or patients are capable of understanding or even imagining. But isn't that precisely why the moment of the hospital's collapse will also signal the destruction of the entire universe? Once the neural network constituting the hospital breaks, the massive cache of medical data will be lost.

The equipment laid out before you represents the hospital's legacy. Any other man in your position, seeing such a startling array of equipment, would want to possess these marvelous things for himself, but you are different. Not only do you not entertain such thoughts, but you feel as if those things are already yours, as if all the various interlinked mechanisms and facilities were yours from the moment of your birth. You are their master—you just don't understand how they function. They have broken free from your control, evolving to the point that each piece of technology is like a wild horse running free. But even a tiny flaw in this long, interconnected chain can trigger a catastrophic event on a global scale. Neither humans nor technology can eliminate all these flaws. And so, the medicine designed to save lives ends up being used to commit suicide.

Summer Stream's eyes light up as she gazes at the machines with a look of lust and greed. Only now do you feel fear, terrified that she might fight you for control of them. Static electricity gathers, making her hair stand on end, and she suddenly transforms into a fairy demon, her veins shining and pulsating beneath her skin.

You notice a sign with black letters and yellow trim that reads CONTROLLED NUCLEAR FUSION CHAMBER. As the two of you approach, you see a large black stone about the height of a person. "A meteorite?" you ask.

"But there is just this one piece, so why would it land here?" Summer Stream wonders.

"Perhaps it was seized by the hospital?"

"No, it is more like a time bomb disguised to look like a meteorite."

You notice faint remnants of some strange writing inscribed all over the rock. The squiggly, tadpole-like lines make up a book entitled *Hospital*, which records the hospital's history. But the history contained in this stone carving is very different from the archival documents preserved in the Museum of Hospital History. According to this chronicle, the hospital has existed for more than thirty thousand years. Over the course of its long history, it has been destroyed and rebuilt a total of thirty-eight hundred times, but it doesn't reveal when the Buddhist exploratory team first arrived here.

"The fuel used for nuclear fusion is deuterium, an isotope of hydrogen vastly abundant in seawater," Summer Stream explains. "Whoever controls this resource will dominate the world. The funny thing is, if we start from the Stone Age, deuterium should be considered the very first tool of self-destruction ever invented by humankind, later followed by nanoweapons, artificial intelligence, and superbacteria. After several million years of evolution, it took humanity only a few decades to master the power to exterminate entire races. Now that power is all concentrated here in the hospital. Isn't that a coincidence? Our previous understanding of the Age of Medicine was far too superficial. There are many ways to die, and only with the true diversity of death can a hundred flowers bloom!"

"What are your thoughts? Is the Buddha now hiding within the doomsday machine?"

"Just think of the sea: the true nature of the sea is predicated on the elimination of all forms of fire, including Buddha-nature."

"So it is. That means that the Buddhist exhibition team is nothing but a legend."

"By the way, didn't you once take a trip on the sea?"

"But that happened within the Pool of Dead Souls. It was a sea with no exit."

"Oh, even though it was fabricated based on your memories, to everyone involved it was just as authentic as the real world. Sometimes a single word can transform into an entire world. A simple thought can create a vast 'ocean' out of nothingness, its every wave causing immense physical pain and mental suffering. It's amazing that you can sense this! But regardless of how tenacious you may be, you still can't save us. Recognizing that there is no exit is, in itself, the only way out." Mournful and contemplative, Summer Stream takes out a manga entitled *Gyo*, or "fish." She holds it in a way that seems to demonstrate that it has been her sole companion throughout her life.

"Really . . . ?" Somewhat embarrassed, you begin to thumb through the manga. A school of fish swims aimlessly through the sea. Drawing is an art that involves remembering things that never existed, yet the sea is portrayed so clearly and vividly in these pages. In the past, you personally witnessed how the sea devours life. You saw the pain, fear, shame, and regret that people experience right before death. You can still feel the suffocating sensation of burning underwater and the agonizing pain of being entangled in fishing nets. Yet you can never transform yourself into a fish and swim away; at best, perhaps you can play the role of an amphibian, imagining that the exit lies somewhere on land.

Summer Stream explains that the sea contains an endless supply of deuterium, an incredible power source. With nuclear fusion, energy can flow endlessly, providing the necessary power to sustain the hospital forever. Under the current circumstances, relying upon this power source is the only way patients can be transported out of the hospital to that place by the sea. However, most people are usually only interested in how much fuel is needed to burn corpses, and they often neglect this issue, as if it were outdated, forgotten, or sealed away like some taboo topic never again to be discussed. So perhaps nuclear fusion is the only way to access the walled-off sea? But, then again, perhaps you are too late . . .

A foam statue has been erected on a discarded tire. It depicts a diseased old lady wearing a white gown and a bulletproof vest, her breasts partially exposed. She holds a small glass vase with an unknown red flower twisted into the shape of a cross. She holds the flower close to her mouth, as if she can taste it. A strange look on her face faintly resembles a smile.

The statue doesn't look anything like the Yellow Emperor, nor does it resemble Rockefeller. You look at Summer Stream and can't help but notice a similarity. You let out an uncontrollable belch and sit down under the statue's hips. You catch a whiff of an atrocious stench coming from above you, and it gives you goose bumps.

Summer Stream sits beside you. You both seem to be waiting for something. You glance down at the wound on her abdomen, where you can barely make out what looks like a nest of coiling, dark-red snakes. You wonder if you should offer to bandage her up, but you hesitate. After all, she has always been the one to save you, and not the other way around. After a while, you slip into a partial embrace, quite formal, as if you are feeling each other out, but neither of you takes things further. Besides being exhausted and wounded, you are also bored and apathetic, with no sense of what the future will bring, only an overcoming sense of indifference. You are different people than you were before, and you see those changes in each other's eyes. You are also jealous of her, but right now, in this moment, the most powerful sense you get from her is of loneliness. The two of you together are a thousand times lonelier than you were by yourself.

The loss of the Universal Treatment Machine—or rather, the Universal Disease Machine—signals the ultimate loss of all your dreams. Sometimes, you feel like the woman beside you is someone else entirely, like she has long been dead in reality, as she has in your heart. You are her tomb in the sea, where the water sweeps everything away, never to return. Thirty thousand years of must and mold emanate from her body, and from yours. Something repels you from one another, so close yet so far, destined never to be truly together. So what is the point of embracing? You feel so very uncomfortable. Who allows you to exist, and who has the power to destroy you? Your last ounce of confidence is gone.

43

HALL OF CORPSES

You see a gigantic barrel-shaped container, the outer shell made from a zirconium alloy. The interior is equipped with a coating of neutron shielding, like a boron water pool. The walls are covered with lead shielding. It is extremely dry, but all the helium in the air has dissipated. Will the radiation leak? Beside the Controlled Nuclear Fusion Chamber, you discover the cover to a well, sealed with a sign that reads No Entry.

"It looks like a strategic missile launch well," says Summer Stream. "There might be nuclear weapons inside. It seems to be located in the most central part of the hospital, so it must be here to prevent against enemy attacks. Let's open it up and take a look."

You dare not follow her advice. It's not that you are afraid of a missile launching out, but you worry that boiling seawater might come rushing in, transforming the hospital into a massive marshland. That would not only cause a short circuit in the electrical grid, but it would likely also give rise to a new set of myths about how the hospital was built on a wasteland after a massive flood, how a massive ark arrived to save everyone, and all the rest of it . . . these stories might be developed into a religion, and on that basis the hospital would be founded. You are again struck by a strong feeling that this place called the sea really does exist. Seeing you standing there without taking action, Summer Stream starts looking for the control panel to open the well cover.

"Hey, don't open it!" you say urgently. "There are monsters underground." You tell her the story from the classic novel *The Water Margin*, about how General Hong accidently opened a portal to the demon realm, unleashing chaos in the world. This place is very different from the Pharmaceutical Mine beneath the hospital.

"But opening the well is our only hope," pleads Summer Stream. "We have been at a dead end ever since you conspired with the hospital to construct a world of your own making. We need to try something new, even if that means going back to the old system. Moreover, you talk about unleashing chaos upon the world, but isn't the hospital already in chaos? So what's the harm if we unleash a bit more? There's a fine line between ultimate chaos and ultimate order. Perhaps your true brain is hidden down in this well. Maybe it contains untapped potential we can harness to save ourselves."

"How could you accuse me of conspiring with the hospital? You're the main player here!"

She gives you the cold shoulder and rips the seal off the well. There is nothing you can do to stop her. She removes the seal, and you notice thousands of red names carved into the cover, written in tiny characters that resemble "oracle bone" script, but you can't understand a single word.

"This must be a list of dead patients," she says after studying the names.

"Or maybe they are the names of dead doctors?"

After additional scrutiny, the two of you finally identify some of the names. Besides various doctors and patients, you figure out the names of all the hospital presidents who have served over the course of the last thirty thousand years, but you can't find the names of the Yellow Emperor or Rockefeller.

"The Hall of Classics?" you ask, pointing to a distorted cross.

"No, the Hall of Corpses."

"The Land of Skulls . . ."

"Well, they are dead, after all . . . this one actually looks like you." She points to one of the names.

You are shocked to discover that she is right. Squinting your eyes, you read the name aloud: "Yang—Wei—" You pronounce the name as if you've never heard it before.

Summer Stream tilts her head quizzically, as if this name has emerged from a black hole to upset her state of mind and destroy her expectations. She finds something about it difficult to accept. "I think this is the name of the apostle," she says with a stilted tone.

"Or maybe a monk?" You reach up to touch your bald head.

"How long have we known each other?"

"How should I remember?"

"Shall we continue?"

"Whatever you want; it's up to you."

"Are you still worried that we might destroy the hospital?"

"Hasn't it already been destroyed?"

Your conversations are becoming increasingly incoherent, as if the hands of fate that once brought you together are now tearing you apart. It is terrifying how short and limited is our contact with other people through the endless cycle of permutations we undergo along the river of life, which have nothing to do with who we are and what our names are. A wave of cold, clammy air descends upon you. You look closer at the names of the deceased hospital presidents and realize that this Hall of Corpses is also the "Mausoleum," containing the remains of brave heroes who sacrificed their lives to protect or seize the hospital. These people attempted the systematic construction of a circuit to run through space and time and have lasting military significance, like the Great Wall. Catastrophes have befallen the hospital many times in the past, and in order to prevent them, people continue to sacrifice themselves like moths to the flame. But in the end, doesn't everything end in war? Don't we always resort to war to win the peace? War is never condemned, never prohibited. At most, some people try to smooth out the edges, to make it more acceptable. Winter Dew was right. The hospital is not a place that prevents its own destruction through war;

instead, it is here to escalate conflict. Only war can pave the path for all deaths to the resurrection. When will the next cycle begin? How many more will die and be reborn?

You notice a passage that explains the motivation behind the creation of the hospital, which turns out to have been established to welcome the monks arriving on their exploratory mission! The text reads:

> The enlightened ones indeed exist, sometimes referred to as "the miraculous existence." Once they attain Buddhahood, they transcend all tangible, living phenomena, even the very state of material form. The nature of Buddhahood is "emptiness" and "nothingness."
>
> However, as far as ordinary practitioners are concerned, life is essential. Take, for example, the flesh-and-blood bodily forms of human beings. No matter how short their existence, they still try to live to the fullest. This is what is meant by two sayings: *The human body is precious as a night-blooming cereus flower* and *Once you lose your body, you shall never escape from the cycle of eternal damnation.* And this is precisely why humans welcomed the Age of Longevity, the importance of which should never be overlooked and which gave new meaning to the value of medicine.
>
> But isn't the practice of medicine imbued with boundless compassion and thus completely aligned with the spirit and precepts of Buddhism?
>
> The Buddha had appeared only once on Earth, 2,500 years before, and he had not appeared since. After the living hell of the most recent world war, all of humanity

had been longing for the Buddha's return, but it seemed unlikely that he would appear again on Earth.

The deep space quantum entanglement detector, jointly developed by the Indian Space Research Organisation and the Indian Institute of Technology Kanpur, had discovered "species suspected of having godlike qualities actively spreading an information flow consistent with an advanced living being" in the high-dimensional space beyond Earth. This may have provided a hint at the Buddha's existence.

As a terrestrial planet that had given birth to life, Mars had been identified as one of the most promising targets for exploration.

You feel like you have encountered this text before, but you still cannot understand what it means. Was the Buddhist monks' exploratory team here? Or has it yet to arrive? You find the strange place called "Earth" bewildering. It seems to have a corresponding relationship to Mars, much like your relationship with Summer Stream. Feeling utterly flustered, you collapse atop the well cover and break out in tears.

Ignoring your emotional fit, Summer Stream finds the control panel and opens the well cover, revealing a perfectly silent, pitch-black abyss. Looking down it, you see no sign of fire or water, just a bottomless pit, like a vast expanse of space after all the billions of stars have been extinguished, very different from the naked universe you saw hanging over the crematorium.

"This . . . must be your original brain, hidden here among the bodies of the dead," Summer Stream says with a sense of wonder, as if discovering a priceless treasure.

"Nothing . . ." You feel completely lost, as if your soul has slipped from your body and fallen down the abyss.

"Nothing? Nothing what?"

"There is nothing there . . . pure nothingness." You glance at her body, which has gone translucent.

At first she hesitates, but the moment the abyss meets her gaze, this place of nothingness suddenly begins to stir, as if, after billions of years of waiting, it has finally been acknowledged by a conscious being and is now ready to be reborn, and to re-create the world. You both sense something stirring at the bottom of the abyss, expanding as if something is growing inside. A rush of cold air surges from the hole before gradually turning warm. Looking down, you just barely make out a dark-crimson shape moving, slowly revealing itself in the shape of a peacock. Seemingly born from nothing, at first there is just one, but soon there are many, varying in size, the entire muster soaring in circles around the well as they ascend. Is it a band of demons unleashed?

Summer Stream guards the mouth of the well. Armed with an electric net, she captures one of the flying beasts. She immediately kills the bird and extracts a crystalline polymer substance from its brain. The structure of the brain is orderly, taking the form of a cross engraved with several ornate words. It seems to be what you have been look-ing for: "Einstein's brain." The formula that determines the nature of the universe is contained within, the memories of all deceased patients collected and backed up before being digitized (a merely formal step) and implanted in artificially synthesized polymer chains capable of storing information (an approximate expression referring to something else). It does not appear terribly complicated, just a rough simulation of DNA and RNA, but its storage density is a trillion times that of biochemical components or an average human brain. Numerous molecule-shaped "tweezers" are arranged on the chain to read and translate the "information," guiding the process by which life is reprocessed. The structure appears extremely primitive, but surprisingly it surpasses binary processes, creating a fusion zone between "yes" and "no." Its fuzzy algorithms reconstruct history—or rather, they fabricate the entire history of the hospital, enabling it to create new memories and, with the assistance of machines and continuous feedback, provide raw parameters to the Pool of Dead Souls, synthesizing the consciousness matrix of the Creator. This storage reaggregation process differs from that of a standard hard disk, with a vastly expanded storage capacity that saves 108,000 memory units in a single atom and does not wear out over time. This is likely the central hub of the Hall of Corpses, utilizing information gleaned from the dead to construct a new world. Such are the arrangements that shall enable the life of the hospital to attain a near-eternal state. And if it should one day be destroyed by some calamity, it can repair itself, continually renewing itself within the ever-brewing cauldron of life in this abyss. The two of you are but a trigger for its rebirth, lured here to initiate the process.

Now is the eve of the return. Because of what is about to happen, the hospital was spared from annihilation. With so many dead bodies as its foundation, even if it should be reduced to ruins, it can reappear in a different part of the universe, where it will await the arrival of new patients. But it is currently in a state of instability. Many differences distinguish the old hospital from the new hospital, but both are based on the same principles and constructed on the same foundation, with almost no fundamental changes, reproducing all the doctors, patients, and diseases verbatim. At the core are the doctors and patients, nothing else. Diseases are like waves surging through the river of time, bringing a constant supply of pain and suffering.

"Now this is amazing!" Summer Stream is in awe. "Without this, everything would be finished."

You look at the brain-like object with a hint of suspicion. "This seems to be both the cause and effect of all the destruction we have seen. It simultaneously triggers eternal destruction and ensures it never comes. It is exhausting for a human mind to even attempt to comprehend all this. But that is exactly what it does. Any attempt to comprehend it is in vain."

"Anything that no one can go against is likely the hospital's wrinkled will."

"But at least we finally seem to have found some valuable evidence, like those artworks from the crematorium."

"And what makes you think they have any value? It's not like we really found them; we were summoned here. This floating life . . . like a dream, yet it somehow feels so real, like a song imbued with sorrow and pain. So I guess none of this really matters."

"What does it want from us? This strange process of birth and transformation has not yet been completed." You look at Summer Stream with a tortured gaze, secretly hoping she might perform for you, or at least give you another fix of oxygen.

"It depends on you. Your name is written here on the stone. It remembers you. It has summoned you here—it never invited me! You are the image it projected into the world," she says jealously. "But take a careful look. Are you really in that much pain?"

"Not really. Look, its calligraphy skills are outstanding! From now on, I shall give up songwriting and just practice calligraphy. In my free time, I can copy out poems written by Qu Yuan, Haizi, and Gu Cheng. They are all pretty good poets." You find the idea exciting.

"Humph, you can't rely on peacocks alone. Whether based on real memories or simple fantasies, the realization of our grand enterprise will need people to carry it out—real, living, brave, multifaceted people like me! What's the point of practicing calligraphy? That's just an antiquated ritual that no one cares about. Here in the Hall of Corpses, calligraphy is a dead art."

"So does that mean I'm unreliable? I suppose I'm totally unqualified now. Oh, that's right, I'm already dead." You seem intent on getting into a fight.

"You really never thought about it? Don't tell me you also never thought of taking advantage of the female patients? Little Wei, you are so hypocritical. Those of us confined to this floating world tend to have all kinds of inappropriate thoughts, even after death. Another round of reincarnation won't really change one's core nature. Our evil thoughts are as stubborn as the phlegm stuck in our lungs. It's truly disgusting!" She appears ill at ease, as if some twisted and contradictory desire has welled up from deep in her heart. But the two of you have yet to entertain the idea of doing *that* again. At this point it would almost feel clichéd.

The words inscribed on the cover of the well begin to twist and transform like tiny amoebic life-forms. Summer Stream frantically begins to search for something, trying to conceal her panic. You realize that she is looking for her own name, but you don't see SUMMER STREAM or SUMMER STREAM'S BRAIN written anywhere. Some of the names don't seem human, making them impossible to match. She sighs with a look of disappointment, staring at you like a female praying mantis about to devour her mate. You can't help but think that only one of you will ultimately assume the role of the new Hospital President. Why does it have to be you? She is a much more natural choice; given her close relationship with the former Hospital President, she would be perfect as his successor, but more importantly, she is more compassionate and selfish than you. Someone must have made a mistake. This is not what you want. Worried, you try to explain yourself, but Summer Stream suddenly seems to lose control and pushes you into the well.

Your fall lasts a long time, as if you are traversing the entire universe from one end to the other, spanning ninety billion light-years, but this is just a small part of the space-time continuum that humans can see . . . like a tiny pill. As you fall, peacocks of various sizes splash through the sky like a fleet of burning warships. Electric lights flash between neuron-like networks. Billions of skulls flash past like a galaxy of stars. You finally arrive at the realm once shown to you by Funeral Artist. Apprehensive and excited, you have finally become part of this place, merging as one with it. You are the hospital, and the hospital is you.

Beyond the well are countless others, crowded together and stacked up upon each other, retreating forever into the distance . . . you lose track of time, but eventually you hear a soft pitter-patter as you touch down at the bottom of the well like a kite gently falling to the ground. You feel like you have experienced all of this before, but this time it seems that your death is for real. This time no one will save you by sending you to be resurrected. If you want the world to be reborn, art must thrive. Sacrifices must be made. Though you have been mentally prepared for this, you never imagined it would come at this time and at this place. So many things remain unfinished. But rationally and emotionally, you must persist until the very end . . . the hospital's story is not complete. There may be multiple versions of the story, and more than one version of Einstein's brain, but they are mere projections . . .

You realize that this is likely the path to a new life, and you snicker abjectly. During your journey through the darkness, a dark, shiny, phlegm-like mucus begins to drip from your body. You are surrounded by the smell of a rising tide. A strange creature shaped like a yaksha flies toward you, extending its claws to receive you . . . as advanced as medical science has become, you think, the many schools of medicine are no different from any superstitious cult or religion.

44

EVE SOAKING WET

After pushing you down the well, the woman sits, her face frozen with a look of shock, as if she doesn't fully understand what she has done, or why. She murdered the Hospital President, the man who created this world. What kind of consequences will this unleash? If another catastrophe should befall the hospital, could she handle it? In her moment of weakness, she is haunted by pangs of regret. Her reason for existing was to stay close to you, always by your side—and yet, seized by a sudden impulse, she committed this terrible act. She feels as if she has completely lost this battle between life and death. She is not as strong as she thought, and during that critical moment, she wavered. She lost control. She wants to break down and cry, but she is so exhausted that she passes out. In her dream, she arrives at the sea. Completely naked during her journey, she gradually transforms over the course of her travels, evolving into a monster. In her monstrous form, she engages in underwater battle with the endless army of yakshas. Torn into a thousand pieces, she then transforms into you. The two of you merge into a single being . . .

She awakes to discover her entire body soaking wet. The water has a thick, salty taste. Feeling hungry, she eats some human flesh from the ground and washes it down with the last bit of alcohol. That's when she hears a rumbling sound. She looks up to see a machine rising from the ground, its underside adorned with several rows of gold gears soaked in oil, which clank and clatter as they turn. The top of the machine features an alloy tray that resembles a sacrificial altar, upon which a red cross has been erected. Snakes and scorpions surround the cross, supporting it. Fixed to the cross is your corpse, arms extended and leaking a thick fluid. Although your miraculous corpse, at once both young and old, seems to be dead, it still appears lifelike, resembling a statue from a wax museum. The woman is disgusted and, unable to stand the sight, turns to leave. But after just a few steps, she regrets her decision and goes back to verify that you are indeed dead. As she looks over your corpse, water flows from your face and body. Your face is relaxed, ordinary, but your facial features are squeezed together, and your bulging belly and your limbs resemble those of a frog. There is something very average about you, the kind of man you see everywhere. Your body hasn't been subjected to any engineering modifications, making it difficult to differentiate it from the other patients, but it looks strikingly similar to that of her "father," the former Hospital President. "Hmm," she mutters to herself, "now that our relationship is finally over, what did I really get out of it?" But your relationship has actually just begun.

A machine extends its metal claw, clamping down on the neck of the deceased. A blade springs from the claw, decapitating the head, which the claw then places inside a cooler. As if suddenly realizing something, the woman picks up the cooler and takes her leave. She enters a semidestroyed laboratory, partially flooded and filled with a thick mist. Everything inside is soaked. She attaches the head to a cable and flips a switch, which extracts your memories, digitizes them, and then combines them with those of the Hospital President and the peacock. An image appears on the other side of the pool, some kind of a living creature, two-thirds human and one-third avian.

"Just who are you?" the woman asks.

"I am your secondary consciousness," the creature replies, in an electronically synthesized voice.

"How come I don't know anything about this?" The woman laughs harshly.

"Because you don't want to remember me . . ." The voice sounds insulted.

"When did you become my secondary consciousness?"

"Only now do I realize what happened. As you merged my memories with those of the Hospital President and the peacock, this secondary consciousness suddenly awakened!"

"So we are now one?"

"Though we are one individual, we are relatively independent. It is, after all, a secondary consciousness."

"Are you inside me? Or do you exist externally?"

"That's not important."

"Why did we have to merge?"

"This was not something we had any control over."

"What is it you want to tell me?"

"What is it you want to ask me?"

"There's nothing worth asking."

"So there is nothing left for us to say to each other?"

"I'm not sure. Being alive or dead all feels the same."

"Who cares? We've both experienced death before."

"Are you the one who brought down the hospital?" The woman is usually articulate, but she suddenly finds herself at a loss for words. So many thoughts race through her head that she just wants to run away.

"Just now, when I was down in the abyss, the hospital's core secrets were all revealed to me," the strange entity says. "It was not the Universal Treatment Machine, nor was it the Universal Disease Machine . . . it was something else."

"What was it?" she asks.

"C'mon now, don't pretend you don't know. You've been to that place by the sea!"

"I don't understand what you are saying. I've never been to any place by the sea. Even if I had, I'm still just an ordinary woman. I don't know what I should do. I don't have the skill to invent or create anything. I'm nothing compared to a special patient like you or other geniuses like Thomas Edison. As an ordinary clinical doctor, I don't have the skills to create the kind of machine that might help patients escape this maze." She tries to defend herself but can't be sure what she is saying. She stares blankly at the creature before her, as if this newly resurrected creature is playing the role of a new savior. Her own consciousness, her "primary consciousness," somehow melds with the thing that claims to be her "secondary consciousness," merging and becoming deeply entangled. She can't explain this brand-new life-form logically or theoretically.

"You're wrong. You are not just a female doctor. You are a female public intellectual, a female warrior, a female businesswoman, a female Daoist, a female scientist, and a female inventor . . ." There is something both fluid and slippery about its speech, as if it were performing a stand-up comedy routine.

"And a goddess too?" she retorts, feeling two separate forms of consciousness surging through her central nervous system. Her body begins to react, quickly becoming soaked.

"Did you really forget who you were? Or can you simply not remember? This hospital is plagued by amnesia. Just now, down in the abyss, I saw many secrets . . . and real memories. But even you are unable to remember them. It is a good thing I can act as your secondary consciousness, helping you observe and record, lending a hand when you need it. Now I shall share those memories with you. The Hospital President is not only your father; he is also your lover. But once upon a time, you had another man in your life, Professor Eternal from the Gerontology Department. He grew tired of you and gave you over to the Hospital President. You and the Hospital President had an illegitimate son together. His name was Zifeiyu. The Hospital President entrusted you with the task of developing a Universal Treatment Machine, but you used it to seek revenge upon the hospital, reengineering it into a Universal Disease Machine. This is the truth. This is what really happened. You have been accosting me for so very long—what exactly do you want? Who am I to you? I'm different from the rest. I am the true savior!"

"You're crazy. Didn't you say it is pointless to worry about who we really are?" She seems to suggest that you have been evading responsibility by shifting your own problems to others. Even if she did invent something, it certainly wouldn't have been a Universal Treatment Machine or a Universal Disease Machine! That would be much too mundane for her. She feels you have been treating her unfairly, and she is angry about her memory loss.

The entity continues: "I can never leave you . . . oh, I shall never be able to extradite myself from you. I am now attached to you, your possessor, like a rib, or your second consciousness. Together we make up this new brain—if you can call it that. There is nothing special about it. I see through you. I know your secrets like the palm of my hand. If I am crazy, then you, too, are crazy. If I am sick, then you, too, are sick. If I forget, you will forget . . . I'm not here to hurt you. I'm here to save you. I'm like your brother, your sister. Actually, no . . . I am now your . . . husband! Your honest-to-God, true-to-life husband! There are just the two of us—the one of us—alone here in this garden of beauty and danger. Isn't it wonderful? It is amazing! We have merged, and now we are family. Actually, no—we are the same person! I couldn't be happier! I haven't been this happy in thirty thousand years!" It then breaks into song:

> One day humanity will welcome an age of peace
> All religions shall be eliminated
> Murder and war shall be a thing of the past
> Even nations will be reduced to ashes and smoke

It then recites a passage from the *Principles of Hospital Engineering*, explaining that the greatest form of marriage humans can ever hope for is a spiritual union, representing the birth of a unified consciousness whose objective is to give birth to new memories that shall be carried forward by future generations, never to be forgotten—in contrast to birthing physical offspring, a practice neither sanitary or safe.

"As for me, my job during this critical moment is to remind you of this . . . and to save you. There is no hope for Mars. The hospital has been reduced to ruins, and we can no longer wait for the Buddhist expedition team to arrive. We need to go together to that place by the sea, leaving this hopeless and incurable world behind. But you killed me, murdering your own husband. Sob, sob, sob! You are one cruel woman! Compared to you, my ancestors weren't so bad." This semihuman, semimonstrous creature speaks as if it represents the true essence of life.

The woman is upset. She clearly saved you, then murdered you, only to resurrect you and eventually merge with you, completing the transplantation and merging of consciousness. What a brilliantly inexplicable end to all of this! She was moved to tears when you mentioned the long-lost concept of marriage, but now it has manifested in a brand-new way that does not require the dirty and cumbersome ritual of physical intercourse. If it is true, then it shall be a long-belated marriage. Perhaps marriage is needed for the creation of the world, although a temporary phenomenon in the evolution of the universe. But she still doesn't understand its functions, this new relation between doctors and patients, who have finally merged into one. Perhaps this can avoid or at least delay the outbreak of the doomsday war?

But can marriage really save the hospital? Can it overcome the next calamity? She finds it difficult to accept that this might be her ultimate fate. Exhausted, she slips into sleep, sinking into the vast and eternal sea.

CODA: TO THE SEA

She awakes the following day to discover that the hospital is still standing, which gives her a sense of relief. The hospital's imposing buildings stand tall, filling every inch of what was once empty space, but there are no signs of doctors, nurses, or patients.

"Anyone here? Come out!" she yells.

There is no response.

She wanders around the hospital grounds, which are completely deserted. There is no trace even of the mutated semihuman creatures. She climbs up to the crematorium, only to discover that the flames have been extinguished. Energy consumption throughout the hospital has dropped to zero, and everything is enshrouded in a deathly silence. All life has vanished, all motion come to a halt. The air is icy cold, the ground covered in a layer of pristine snow.

"Is there anyone here?" she yells.

Still no response.

She wanders aimlessly, on and on, until she can't lift her feet anymore and her body grows cold. She gazes up at the sky and notices that the stars are gradually disappearing. She thinks, *Why am I still alive? Who am I?*

Using her new composite brain, she creates a blueprint, which she uploads to the factory workshop in order to create a remote medical terminal to communicate with the outside world. Two days later, she detects a floating multinodal information group, but it lacks both stability and clarity. After another three days, she receives a signal: a data pack. She can't tell whether it is intended to back up the first set of information or to cover its tracks. She attempts to translate the information, but the results are quite poor. The following day, the receiver aggregates a four-dimensional image of a changing polyhedron unaffected by time. The image rotates and emits a somewhat muddled synthetic voice: "Do you want to go to the sea?"

"If that will bring me freedom . . ."

"You no longer want to be the Hospital President?"

"Well . . ."

"There is such a rich heritage here. Are you willing to let all of that go? Countless people spilled their blood and sacrificed their lives in order to achieve this."

"I . . ."

"Let me remind you, if the information does not match up, there will be no freedom."

"So what are you saying?"

"The Hospital President possesses the most complete information. Without information, there is no freedom."

"Well, that's quite the contradiction . . . after all, the Hospital President is dead."

"He was overambitious and fled. The risks for the hospital were too great, potentially affecting many people's lives."

"Then what should I do?"

"We can make a deal. You provide me with all the information in your possession, and I will give you freedom. But as to whether you will make it to the sea, that shall depend on your luck."

"Who are you?" She worries about another trap. This voice might be some devil trying to tempt her.

"No need to ask that. Many things you will never know. The universe is vast, far surpassing anything you can imagine. Moreover, beyond the universe lies another."

"There are some things I understand, but these are core hospital secrets. Why should I share them with you?"

"Do as you will. It's your choice." The voice seems indifferent but also extremely confident.

"Okay then, I'll share the information with you, and you give me my freedom," she replies with melancholy in her voice. "I've decided to leave the hospital . . . I don't want to be responsible for its legacy or its history. And once I leave, I shall never return."

"You are indeed a woman after all . . . Are you sure you want to leave? You must take full responsibility for your decision."

"I'm not a child." She thinks back to the children who emerged from the hospital, led by Yang Wei and including Weber and Zifeiyu. Together they formed an alliance. Each had various supernatural powers, like characters in a manga.

She transfers the composite memory from within her body to the image, completing the transaction, as if surgically removing and transferring this new composite consciousness that has taken her over. She returns to her original "self," and just like that, she and the spouse she recently merged with abruptly separate, bringing their short-lived marriage to an end. While relieved of this burden, she also feels a deep sense of disappointment. None of this was worth it.

"How do I leave the hospital?" she asks.

"It's quite simple. From the crematorium, turn left onto the service road. Take it all the way down to the private railway, where the hospital receives its supplies. This was originally a top secret military site. Take Line 2 to Line 10 and follow it until it intersects with Line 13. There you will find an escape pod. Get in the pod, and it will take you away. Remember to bring enough to drink. You must stay alive, which is, of course, the prerequisite for freedom."

The hospital has run out of water, but it has other resources to draw from. She collects an assortment of human blood, spinal fluid, muscles, organs, and brain tissue, which she packs in plastic medical bags to carry with her. She finds several oxygen tanks and prepares some antibiotics. Setting out from the crematorium, she follows the path down. There is indeed an abandoned railway at the end of the path, which seems to have served as a nesting ground for peacocks, which were a product of the hospital's experimental lab. Their skeletons litter the ground. Beneath her feet is a sheet of maggots, and beneath them, a layer of human bones. Looking back, she discovers that the large fire that had engulfed the hospital has been extinguished. She thinks about that patient, Yang Wei, the man who once entered her brain. From the first moment he entered the hospital, all he wanted was to escape. Who could have imagined that she would finally carry that out? It's all rather ludicrous. Was she doing this for herself or for him? Perhaps there is no difference.

Where Line 10 intersects with Line 13, she discovers the pod. It seems to be waiting for her. Inside are the skeletal remains of what was likely an escapee from an earlier generation who was also lured from the hospital. She hesitates, seeing the escapee's bloodstained space suit, but she decides to put it on. She climbs into the pod and slides back the control lever, and the pod ascends into the darkness above. It travels for quite some time before light gradually comes into view. The pod lands, and she climbs out.

She stands on the surface of Mars, gazing back at the hospital in the distance. Beneath the shield volcano is nothing but an expanse of darkness and desolation. Not a single patient or doctor got out of the hospital alive, and there is no trace of the living anywhere around the grounds where it once stood. There are no signs of extraterrestrial life, no visible traces of the Age of Medicine or the Medicinal War. She is completely lost. The hospital was like an inseparable crutch for both doctors and patients to keep by their side. Even out here in space, the hospital always came first. Although she was mentally prepared, seeing the reality before her eyes still proves extremely difficult to come to terms with.

Leaving the plateau, she moves in a northerly direction. She sees a weblike network of canals, all dried out, with remnants of broken medical equipment littered along the banks. She walks toward the horizon. At the edge of the sky stands a row of towering black walls. Legend has it that the place by the sea lies on the other side. When she grows hungry or thirsty, she stops to consume the blood, phlegm, and flesh that she collected before she left, with no idea whether it came from the bodies of patients, doctors, monkeys, or mutant creatures. Fearing it might make her sick, she takes antibiotics at regular intervals.

Layers of sediment line what was once a coastline. She sees canyons and basins, all devoid of water. It is said that the past oceans of Mars had a short lifespan. Nearby stand the ruins of a tall structure that seems once to have been a hospital, or part of a hospital, likely built by early humans or aliens. However, according to the Fermi paradox, aliens have never come here. Perhaps the hospital itself evolved into a self-replicating life-form?

The hospital's ruins are surrounded by red desert. Sand dunes rise and fall, some reaching three hundred meters high, like massive waves frozen in time. Strange stones resemble the skeletal remains of whales. She witnesses the beauty of ice clouds and morning fog rising between the strange metal pillars that stand erect on the plains.

A dust storm kicks up, and she seeks shelter inside the massive ruins. She feels exhausted, but before going to sleep, she fastens herself in with rope. She wonders if her decision to leave was a bit too impulsive. Is it all a big joke? To hell with all that talk of information and freedom! How could that thing trick her into staying alive with pathetic concepts that couldn't even justify themselves?

She awakens to discover that she is still alive, though she is not sure if she is the same person she was yesterday. A strange light flickers in the corner of the ruins. It is a child's head. His face resembles Yang Wei's. Could he have been following her? But upon closer inspection, it turns out to be nothing more than a trinket with deep eyes and an arched nose, probably one of Weber's handicrafts.

Between the expansive ruins, she sees numerous caves adorned with stone sculptures—some seated, some standing—of figures dressed in white robes. They resemble doctors, with solemn and devout expressions and red crosses hanging from their necks. Most are missing limbs. Who built these here on Mars? The statues seem to hint at a deeper meaning behind the construction of the hospital.

She continues on, leaving the ruins behind. After about three hundred meters, she discovers that the caves have completed disappeared, like a mirage.

At night she gazes at the constellations in the sky, like a sea of shining medicinal pills. The night sky hangs low, its light pouring down like contaminated blood. She reflects upon her life and is struck by its seemingly randomness. She sees baby Yang Wei in her dream. He is inside her, inside her stomach, her intestines, brain, and uterus. They merge and separate, over and over across lifetimes, a cycle that never ends.

The following morning, she continues her journey. The packs of blood and fleshy matter are almost gone, and her medicine is nearly depleted. She has yet to encounter anyone who could lead her to that place by the sea. Did that entity lie to her? Or was it just a figment of her imagination? She pushes herself to carry on. If this is the abandoned ruins of what was once a Garden of Eden, she is not being cast out but intentionally escaping. If God exists in this hospital, He, too, would be a patient.

Her gait becomes erratic. She is confused, staggering forward in a drunken dance, like a bird on the verge of death. She has lost almost all of her confidence when she finally reaches that point on the horizon she has been searching for.

The black wall turns out to be made up of thousands of rocket launchers adorned with red crosses, long abandoned and knocked over. Beyond the wall, endless desert stretches. Exhausted and running out of resources, she is unable to carry on.

Above the remnants of the broken rocket launchers, amid the colorful stars, a burning vortex resembles a massive lotus flower, spinning as it emits a cold, charred light. It reminds her of the hospital crematorium. The dazzling flower descends, gradually growing closer.

She suddenly realizes that this is the legendary expeditionary spaceship of the solitary traveler and his team who traversed the universe in search of the Buddha. They have finally arrived on Mars, only to find the hospital in a pile of ruins.

The hospital has reduced itself to this state specifically in anticipation of this day.

So many have died, all for this. Everything has finally found its true purpose.

But no one knows why so much planning went into this moment, all to welcome the expeditionary team.

These arrangements seem to be the product of some sort of program.

She hears the sound of a flock of birds, their mating calls echoing in her ears. A beam of light composed of many fine threads descends from the sky, like the strings of a harp, and lands before her. In a daze, she grabs it without thinking, climbing toward its pure, radiating, rotating pedals. Having lost control of her body, she doesn't even realize what she is holding. Her vision grows hazy. She wants to let go, but some strange force continues to support and lead her. She ascends, closer and closer to that unknown thing, which suddenly transforms. A strange red cross emerges from the center of the flower.

She arrives just beneath it, where she is enveloped in a majestic glowing mist, from which a sea of bright spots extends. The cross unfolds its smooth windmill-like arms, a man-made structure thousands of kilometers wide. Suspended in midair, she doesn't know what to do, but then part of it turns transparent, as if it has disappeared. A white light approaches her, and she hears what sound like familiar voices. She is sucked in, feeling like she has grown wings and is flying through a bright, narrow tunnel that pulsates like a birth canal. As she ascends, she loses consciousness, slipping into a deep sleep.

Unaware of how much time has passed, she opens her eyes. She is lying on a white bed that appears to be an operating table. Her surroundings resemble an intensive care unit. Outside the window, a series of linked templelike structures glisten in the cold light like snowcapped mountains. Distorted red crosses dance in unison, like a sea of tombstones against the backdrop of a uniformly red sky, embedded with countless glowing "pills" that shine yellow and white like lotus flowers.

Two humanoid figures dressed in white float to her side, one man and one woman. They appear pure and childlike, with large heads and petite bodies, bowl-shaped eyes, shaved heads, and crosses hanging from their necks.

"Greetings, benefactor," they address her.

"What is this place?" she asks. She feels like she has been reborn.

"You are on the ship," the male responds.

"Why is everything so red? It hurts my eyes . . ." She gazes up at the sky.

"It is actually black," the woman replies. "A shade of black darker than black is called red."

She realizes that the world has undergone another transformation. Thinking back to that mysterious person who once told her that "beyond the universe lies yet another universe," she asks, "What are your names?"

"Zhifan," the man replies.

"Runian," the woman replies.

She realizes that they resemble the statues she saw in the cave.

Zhifan and Runian lead her to a public square in front of the temple, a vast space filled with a purple mist and populated with a forest of artificial green trees. Medicinal plants grow so dense and thick that they blot out the sun. Peacocks are perched on the branches. Thousands upon thousands of beautiful men and women float through the forest in white robes, reciting sutras, like a scene from the painting *Along the River during the Qingming Festival.* The monks all appear youthful, bright, pure, and beautiful. Although they are seemingly touched by eternal youth, it's immediately apparent that some kind of sickness or ailment afflicts them. She recognizes some of them: Professor Eternal, Dr. Meloxicam, Dr. Linezolid, Dr. Daptomycin, and other doctors and medical personnel from the various departments; the patients Buboxine, Spasm, Wart, Fistula, Carbuncle, Malnutrizole, Hernia . . . and Rousseau, Weber, Eddington, and Einstein . . . and Zifeiyu, and even someone who resembles Yang Wei. They break out in a chanting, echoing chorus:

> One day the world will be shared by all humanity
> Fates shall be intertwined
> All under Heaven shall achieve Perfect Harmony
> Famine, poverty, and greed will be left behind
> Never again shall we be abused by those in power

Unable to resist, she finds herself humming along to the familiar melody. And then comes its refrain:

> The five grains nourish, the five fruits assist
> The five livestock benefit, the five vegetables supplement
> Spare no expense and consume the finest food
> Abstain from poorly cooked food and untimely meals

Zhifan and Runian explain that the passengers aboard the ship lived thirty thousand years ago. The previous life cycle of the universe has already come to an end. Copies of all living beings were backed up, to be dispersed into the very fabric of space and time, waiting for the proper moment to be reborn. This process, synchronized with entropy, is known as "the summoning of souls."

"This must be the upgraded version of the Pool of Dead Souls?" She wonders if she, too, has already died?

Zhifan and Runian look at her with a compassionate smile.

"The universe is composed of remnants of the dead," says Zhifan.

"One's job is to reassemble them," says Runian.

"But this time, they have adjusted to eternal life mode," says Zhifan.

"The real world can only be found through an immortal system," says Runian.

All passengers have a human form, but it is always rare to reincarnate in a human form.

"The human form is the only form that is interesting," says Zhifan. "Being a frog is actually not so great . . ."

"There is not enough space in history to bury all the dead," says Runian, "but reality has ample room to accommodate all living things."

Within this system, they explain, life can exist in the form of energy, numbers, or concepts. However, for the sake of convenience, everything is universally expressed through flesh-and-blood bodies. "No matter how many times the physical body is destroyed, it will always be reborn."

They lead her on a tour. Everything appears so very familiar. The temple is designed according to the structure of the hospital's inpatient and outpatient departments, with sick wards, a crematorium, and a cafeteria—like a work of replicated art based on files found in the Museum of Hospital History.

The hospital is divided into four primary zones based on the Four Noble Truths: the Zone of Suffering, the Zone of the Gathering of the Afflicted, the Zone of Eliminating Desire, and the Zone of the Path to Redemption. Here the passengers undergo their spiritual training. But what is the objective of their training? The people here will never die. She sees them walking around in groups, dressed up as patients and doctors, smiling ear to ear as they shout slogans:

"All phenomena in this world are impermanent!"

"All frustrations lead to suffering!"

She arrives at the temple's main hall. A red light hovers above the altar, like a large bird circling the golden statue of Buddha. Zhifan and Runian ask whether she can treat it.

"Treat it?" She is taken off guard by the odd question. She feels like she is in a dream as she looks up at the flickering flames, which seem to have multiple eyes, staring down at her with a look of benevolence and curiosity.

"That's right, this is the sacred treasure we use to stabilize the ship. Have you forgotten? You created it. We have been searching for you for a long time."

"You must be joking." She is suddenly struck by the feeling that something is terribly wrong, sensing something both eerie and absurd aboard this massive ship.

"Of course not," Runian says in a tone of great sincerity. "We are in grave need of our dear benefactor's help."

"What do you want me to do?"

"The Life Disposal Machine is not working properly. It is sick, and we need you to treat it." Zhifan's tone is firm. It doesn't seem like this is open for discussion.

"Life Disposal Machine?" She takes another look at the shiny flying object. "Isn't everyone here granted eternal life? What is a woman like me supposed to do . . ."

She thinks about the countless difficulties she has endured, climbing all the way here from the ruins of the Mars Hospital, reduced to living off the blood and flesh of corpses . . . and all for this? At least she experienced those things "before she died."

"But you are no ordinary woman; you are a female military doctor!" Runian says plainly, removing the cross hanging from her neck and handing it to her.

Zhifan's frozen smile looks like a wooden exorcism mask.

According to the time displayed on the ship, twenty years slip by without her even realizing it. She visits the great hall in the temple once a week. The first time she visits, she spends the entire day. It seems that the problem with the Life Disposal Machine has been fixed, its disease eradicated, and it has returned to its normal "healthy state," where it can continue to administer death sentences to those granted eternal life.

She accepts her new identity as Creator of the Life Disposal Machine. Her appearance does not change for twenty years. Those in the system never age, and she secretly refers to them as "heavenly beings."

She sometimes sighs, thinking about how, after thirty thousand years, everything from the previous world just disappeared in the blink of an eye. But humankind has been reborn and entered a state of eternal life. What she doesn't understand is why the Life Disposal Machine needs to bring all this to an end. As far as she can tell, this is a clear case of "artificially interfering with nature." It used to be said that death didn't need to be rushed; it is a celebration that will come one day, regardless of how long it might be delayed. But without the assistance of the Life Disposal Machine, no one will ever die.

"Plato was the first to put forth the idea of eternal life," observes Zhifan. "He believed that all real experiences were mere projections of the eternal. I, on the other hand, think that death is a phenomenon of the slow-moving world. For the human species to endure, it must rely on mortality. Humanity once dreamed of eternal life but found it impossible to achieve."

"However, when unbearable anticipation and struggle reached their peak, immortality suddenly appeared," Runian adds. "It came as naturally as breathing, because it is completely aligned with the essence of the Creator. After countless sacrifices made over the long river of time, victory over death was finally achieved. By opening the gate to eternal life, we have finally come home, to a new chapter that shall last generation after generation for all time immemorial."

"Then do we still need the Life Disposal Machine?" she asks. "What's wrong with just going on living?"

A profound smile appears on Runian's and Zhifan's faces. "Even immortality has its limits."

The ship is called the SS *Mahamayuri*, the Peacock King. Its port of departure was that place by the sea . . . as is its destination.

She and Yang Wei marry, establishing a family. The world regresses; monogamy between one man and one woman is once again the norm. Through the experience of family life, the Buddhist practitioners taste *skandha*, or the Five Aggregates—form, sensation, perception, mental activity, and consciousness—realizing that their parents and children are their enemies, which sets in place the foundation for death. But these are merely prerequisites, qualifications. When it comes to who dies and who is spared, that is decided by the machine.

Twenty years earlier, the machine scanned Yang Wei's consciousness and detected the existence of a woman. It summoned her back to the ship to receive treatment from her. Only she could heal it, allowing it to regain its life-taking capabilities. She came—she had no other choice.

Besides taking care of the machine, she spent her days and nights in the company of Yang Wei, reliving the pain they had experienced over the course of their floating lives and tasting the pleasures of the flesh, the latter of which transformed over time into a deeper pain and a greater pleasure. Everything reverted to the physical. People again became infatuated with the material world. To live was to have everything at one's fingertips. Touching, chewing, swallowing, mating, bathing, sleeping, dreaming, leaping . . . they had it all, and it was truly wonderful. Their shells of flesh were no longer just superfluous decorations, as only when one has exhausted all the various permutations and experiences of the human body do thoughts of death arise. Only when one is incapable of death does she begin to seek it.

She gives birth to a baby boy. She feels like birth is a truly magical process. How could this little life-form find his way here? She is ecstatic. The child emerges from her womb, his features so vivid and alive, quite unlike those phantom projections created through electro-neurons. During the birthing process, she experiences the pain of labor, a form of joy that the Pool of Dead Souls is incapable of providing. The husband and wife decide to raise their child to become both a doctor and a patient. Before death, passengers admit themselves to the hospital, and by playing the roles of both doctor and patient, they experience heart-wrenching pain and suffering, taste the ultimate state of bliss, and prepare themselves mentally and physically for death. Then and only then can they hope to be chosen by the machine.

When she first arrived in this world, she liked going up to the observation tower to gaze down at the scenery. This was the sea. On the sea was but a solitary ship. The expansive sea, filled with billions of stars, resembled a massive piece of flowing red cloth. The stars were the "pills" adorning the cloth. Their end was that place by the sea.

She occasionally hears rumbling like cannon fire erupting over the night sky, and the stars explode into tiny pieces, transforming the heavenly theater into a flaming sea. A giant bird extends its wings, its silver feathers standing erect, its golden eyes open wide, its powerful wings unfurled, exuding strength and power. It soars through the smoke-filled sky, cutting through the thick clouds above the expansive sea. She hears the sound of someone or something chanting, "Unleash the violence of the storm!"

She anxiously wonders whether this universe is simply a collection of broken remnants of dead bodies. Although it does not speak, it reveals all: many years contained in a single moment, the vast world contained in a single speck of dust. No matter in which universe one resides, whether one is dead or alive, it's all the same. Whether twenty years ago or during the great escape from Mars thirty thousand years ago, all of this is merely a rehearsal for the grand performance.

She remembers, back in the world from which she came, that life was as fleeting as the morning dew, and advancements in medical science had yet to achieve a state of timelessness. All people eventually died, and death was a most casual thing, occurring in all kinds of ways. She is a survivor of the Second World War. During that war, both sides employed biological weapons, killing billions of people and bringing destruction to the planet. Yet it all began with a "tiny incident": Adolf Hitler of Nazi Germany performed an act of euthanasia on a physically deformed baby in 1983, then in 1989, he began to exterminate physically and mentally challenged children, eventually executing all mentally abnormal young people. Later all "non-Aryan people" collectively became targets of his extermination campaign, resulting in the murder of six million Jews, including a victim named Einstein. This escalated into an even larger-scale massacre targeting all of humanity . . .

After the war, she visited a theme park called Auschwitz, where she saw an art exhibition that included freezers, gas chambers, crematoria, a medical experimentation room, a death wall, collections of glasses, shoes, and suitcases, as well as twenty tons of hair taken from the victims, all documenting the systematic genocide of an entire race. More than half the people responsible for running this slaughterhouse held medical degrees. She saw the handwritten physics manuscript that Einstein wrote just before his death, but even today no one has solved the formulas it contains.

Sometimes she speculates about her true identity, wondering whether she could have been a Nazi doctor during World War II. With all the revolution, insurrections, upheaval, war, and massacres, medical professionals dominated the scene in that era. Under the banner of "eugenics," they were prepared to let the entire world perish so that a small portion of the population could survive. But here on this ship, isn't the Life Disposal Machine doing the exact same thing? Not exactly. It does not exist to protect the lives and health of VIP passengers, but is instead intended to control and eliminate the "invasion of inferior alien bodies." Meanwhile the opposite is occurring as members of the group are actively removed, their right to eternal life stripped away. She gradually realizes that this is not an act of cruelty, but something to be celebrated—every time someone is disposed of, the entire ship commemorates the event with a huge feast, as if celebrating the arrival of a new baby.

She is in the habit of coming to the great hall to observe, but she no longer provides specific guidance or direction about the work. Zhifan and Runian are in charge of overseeing everyday affairs, and she only occasionally offers a few suggestions, when she feels like it. Doctors and patients, all dressed in white like monks, diligently work under the shadow of the statue of Buddha, serving the machine. The charity box spits out a long list of names of those selected for disposal. Amid the sound of monks beating on *mokugyo*, the temple staff solemnly places the machine as an offering before Tathagata, followed by the collective chanting of the scriptures.

One day, she sees a familiar name coming out of the charity box. She tries to maintain her composure when she recognizes her son's name on the list of those selected for disposal. Her son has just turned fifteen, but the machine has decided to eliminate this life that shares a direct blood relationship to her. The machine selects targets from the roster of permanent residents aboard the ship, screening them based on a primitive model first developed thirty thousand years ago.

Her knees grow weak. She is, after all, a relic of an earlier era, when people didn't yearn for death. The monks in white, having no idea of the thoughts going through her head, still hold her in the highest esteem. She is the Creator, a Goddess, she who bestows death. They prostrate themselves before her in worship.

If everything goes smoothly, her son will soon graduate from medical school and become an official practitioner, so that he may one day be selected for disposal. So why does she feel so flustered? She wonders whether she would have agreed to heal the machine, twenty years earlier, had she known this day would come. Would she even have created the machine thirty thousand years ago? Would she and Yang Wei still have married and had a son?

She knows it is highly unlikely, but she still hopes that the Life Disposal Machine has made a mistake. Clinging to a glimmer of hope, she requests that Zhifan and Runian double-check the results. They use an instrument called the Wand of Karma to retrace the process, but it does not reveal any anomalies. She stares blankly at the character signaling her son's death, trying to maintain her outward composure. Zhifan and Runian look at her, as calm as a placid lake, with a hint of compassion. She begs them to keep the result a secret.

"Understood," they say, in tones of cold indifference.

She looks up to see that red, bird-shaped halo dancing in the air. A look of cold benevolence appears on the face of the Tathagata Buddha.

Her son grew up in a single-parent home. Fifteen years ago, not long after her son was born, her husband Yang Wei was selected for disposal.

She decides to visit her son. She should be congratulating him, as it is customary to celebrate selection by the Life Disposal Machine.

Her son's selection at such a young age, while still in school to be a doctor-patient, is like winning the lottery. Perhaps the machine is trying to get on her good side? Or repay her for her kindness?

She arrives at the medical school where her son is studying. There in the exam room, she finds him sewing up his own stomach. Like all the other young doctor-patients, he has been assigned to experience an imaginary world of pain. After being diagnosed with diabetes, he is experiencing the joy of suffering, part of the rigorous training he must undergo to become a qualified Monk in White. He doesn't seem to know that he is about to be eliminated. The official Notification of Disposal will arrive a bit later.

When he sees her arrive, the boy immediately stops his sewing exercise and flashes an angry glare at his mother. Beside him is a young woman, a fellow practitioner and his girlfriend. They are enjoying the excitement of pica, when they get to eat all kinds of things besides food.

"Mother, what are you doing here?" the son asks. "Stop pretending to be all cheerful and happy. I've experienced all that stuff about 'all phenomena in this world are impermanent; all frustrations lead to suffering,' but it never brought me the kind of happiness that others got from it. You're better off staying away from me. I don't want to be a doctor-patient. I've had enough! Why did you insist on sending me to medical school? You've used that damn machine to kill so many people—you even killed my father! *You* are responsible for all the pain and suffering aboard this ship! Goddess, *you* invited the God of Death aboard this ship! *You* are the most malicious executioner of them all! I'm better off not seeing you anymore."

This isn't the first time he has said such things to her. After his father's death, he changed. While everyone else aboard the ship takes pleasure in their illnesses, only he seems depressed by his own.

"Of everyone on this ship, you're the only one to say such crazy things!" she counters, her voice trembling. "Since you are my son, no one here dares lay a finger on you. But you must correct your mistakes, study hard, live up to everyone's expectations, and become the Monk in White you were destined to be! Then you can die happily, and that will be the greatest blessing anyone could ever hope for." She seems stunned by what she says. After all, the results of the latest round of eliminations are about to fall directly on her son's shoulders. A sharp pain rips through her body, tearing at her organs.

"Bullshit! You're the one that's crazy! Everything you do goes against common sense and humanity itself! Your hands are stained with the blood of countless passengers!" Who knows where her son learned to say such things. It is as if he has somehow seen through the brutality and hypocrisy of the ship. He turns from her in disdain and grabs a manga from his girlfriend's hand, a copy of *Legend of the Goddess*, which praises her wondrous achievements in creating and later repairing the Life Disposal Machine, allowing the fate of humankind to get back on the right track.

Insulted and losing control, she rushes forward to snatch the book. Her son manages to evade her and, with a sneer, tears the book into pieces and throws the tattered pages in her face. His girlfriend cheers, applauding her boyfriend before picking up the paper scraps from the floor and eating them.

She turns away to hide her tears from her son. She knows him well; he may seem strong on the outside, but he is weak on the inside. Not only does he physically resemble his father, but their personalities are also very similar. He is venting his anger to prove that he isn't weak in front of his girlfriend. His mother's being the "Goddess" has allowed him to boast and show off at school, even openly attacking the machine in the sick ward and the classroom, welcoming his classmates and fellow patients in his insulting of the machine. He fancied himself as one of the very few to hold divergent medical views, and he would jump up and down, causing all kinds of trouble, attacking the mainstream values of everyone else on the ship. But it was all just talk. Despite being a medical student, he couldn't even bring himself to dissect a frog. How could the machine choose someone like this?

She sets off to find the captain. He resides in a thirteen-story octagonal pagoda in the middle of the ship, never leaving. Surrounding the tower is a lush garden of medicinal plants and herbs. The sides of the rocket-like pagoda are covered with vibrant black honeysuckle flowers, bursting with radiance, on the verge of shedding their petals. Stars surround them, rotating in the sky and emitting a burning light. The top of the pagoda features an enclosed screening room. Part of the captain's self-cultivation plan includes a daily film screening. Films are the one medicine he cannot do without. He uses them to guide the future direction of the ship. Over time, she can no longer tell the difference between images and reality. Perhaps there is no difference.

It has been fifteen years since Yang Wei's death, and during that time she has remained the captain's lover. She has never actually seen him in person; their contact is facilitated through electronic neural interactions. As she arrives, the film *Howl's Moving Castle* is playing. It is said that the SS *Mahamayuri*, the Peacock King, was actually based on the film's script. Film functions as a time-conversion device, through which one can see the future. Predicting her arrival, the captain has already prepared to receive her.

"You have arrived," they greet her.

She sees the captain's large, white silhouette, a continually transforming genderless polyhedron.

The captain doesn't bother turning to face her as they speak. "I assume you have come to plead for your son? I, too, saw his name appear on-screen, in the credits, as the name of one of the actors. The movie is still running, and we haven't gotten to that point yet."

She stands in the darkness, silently crying. After some time, she says, "No, Mr. Rockefeller, I have not come to plead for my son. It is wonderful news. I've been looking forward to this . . ." What exactly is she trying to say?

Rockefeller says, "What you want to say is, 'He isn't Yang Wei's child. He is our creation.'"

She is shocked to hear this. According to *Legend of the Goddess*, as this ship traversed the galaxy, she glanced at one of the "pills" in the sky and immediately conceived a child. But instead they had planted a lotus seed in her womb.

"As the inventor of the Life Disposal Machine, you know better than anyone else that it is impartial," the captain says in a trembling voice, "functioning without regard to familial ties or any other relationships. It has transformed this world into a place of beauty, saving us from the bitter sea into which we were born. While you alone are exempt, everyone else, including me, has the opportunity to be selected for disposal. You alone endure the great humiliation of life, for the sake of everyone else's death. That is why you are a Goddess, and why I worship you with the utmost devotion."

Just thinking about the fact that even the captain might one day be selected for disposal makes her feel the great power that she wields, but it also leaves her even more sad. It was so very difficult to make it to this new world, but here true equality has been realized. Only equality in death can bring about other forms of equality, such as universal and lasting equality, gender equality, etc. Yet she continues to be excluded.

The captain remains motionless, staring at the screen as if merging with its images.

Then, as if to please her, the captain screens an animated version of *Legend of the Goddess*.

According to *Legend of the Goddess*, thirty thousand years ago, back when she was still a child in the old world, she read a famous novel entitled *Jean-Christophe*. One passage had a profound impact upon her:

"By the age of twenty or thirty, most people are already dead; after that age, they become but a shadow of their former selves. They spend the remainder of their lives merely imitating themselves . . . repeating what they do every day, with the method of that repetition becoming increasingly mechanical and detached." That's how she realized that the people she saw every day were no better than walking corpses.

As a child she was quite precocious, becoming infatuated with biology at the age of five. She would go everywhere in search of related books to read, developing a particular thirst for exploring the mysteries of life and death. She read of scientists discovering that the maximum lifespan for mammals was approximately five to seven times their growth period. For example, a dog's growth period is two years, with a lifespan of about ten to fourteen years; a horse's growth period is five years, with a lifespan of thirty to forty years . . . humans are also mammals, and their growth period lasts twenty to twenty-five years, so their natural lifespan should be between one hundred and one hundred seventy-five years. It was also discovered that the number of cell divisions and their cycle were both related to lifespan. By multiplying the number of cell divisions by the division cycle, the lifespan of each animal can be determined. For instance, a mouse's cells divide roughly twelve times, with a division cycle of 0.25 years, resulting in a lifespan of 3 years. Human cells divide about fifty times, with each division cycle lasting 2.4 years, so a human's lifespan should be approximately 120 years. In order to live to this age and continue evolving, humans created the field of medical science and invented civilization.

Approximately two thousand years before she was born, the average human life expectancy was twenty years. One hundred years ago, most people could live to the approximate age of forty. Back then, most people married and had children at the age of thirteen or fourteen, because by the age of sixteen, they were already considered middle aged. By the time she was born, the average human lifespan had reached eighty years. In just a short period of time, humanity had taken an astonishing leap thanks to improved living standards and rapid progress in science and technology, especially in the field of medical science. In order to further extend their lives, humans continuously upgraded their hospitals.

However, just like Romain Rolland, the author of *Jean-Christophe*, her sensitivity and sorrow led her to realize that a long life did not necessarily mean a pleasurable or interesting life. Some humans live for nearly a hundred years, but nearly half of that time is spent asleep, dreaming, while the other half is spent dealing with various health ailments of old age, leaving around 10 or 20 percent. Most lives are spent in pain or asleep, maintaining a functional mouth to continue eating and taking medicine. If an average lifespan is eighty years, the period from sixty to eighty will be consumed primarily with various illnesses, so that period can be eliminated from our calculations. How much life is really left? If the period between twenty and thirty-five is considered a person's prime, how many good years do we really have? Take her parents, for example: according to her own standards, there wasn't much point to their lives after they gave birth to her. When she was a small child, her favorite hobby was to spy on her parents, secretly observing their ugly and animalistic behaviors. Her voyeuristic impulse drove them to commit strange and degrading acts, for which they felt no shame. When in public, they would respectfully smile and bow to their relatives and friends, but behind their backs they would curse them to hell. They would violently argue over petty affairs, and eventually their disputes led them to divorce court. Even before she was born, their incessant drinking resulted in her being born with fetal alcohol syndrome. And when they fell ill, they acted helpless and pathetic . . . each time, her hatred for them grew to the point that she almost wanted to commit suicide. The worst part was, once she learned the truth about why she was brought into this world—which was purely a result of their selfish interests—her despair deepened. Her parents also abused her; when something didn't go their way, they would scold and beat her. She didn't understand why it was so important for her brother to remain alive.

The doctors had already issued a declaration ordering the child to be abandoned, but her parents refused to accept it. Her sole purpose in life had been to care for her this mentally deranged man who couldn't even remember his own name. As far as she was concerned, neither her brother nor her parents deserved to live. In fact, she felt that none of humanity deserved to live . . . including herself.

She realized that reality was changing in ways she never could have imagined. With technological advances, medical science entered a new era. Systems biology—utilizing human genome projects, proteomics, advanced informatics, and computational models—could cure most genetic diseases. The role of doctors combined with that of biologists, life engineers, mathematicians, and computational scientists. They manipulated genetic codes and metabolic data to conduct reverse engineering and redesign life. The "normal" processes of disease and aging gradually became but one possibility among many for patients to choose. As long as patients had money, they could afford the very best in medical care. From that point forward, health and longevity were both within reach. The hospital released an official declaration claiming it had defeated the God of Death. Not only had medical technology eradicated disease, but it had elevated human survival to a miraculous level, effectively transforming people into superhumans. She discovered that, as long as one was willing to pay a fee, people like her brother could be born healthy. Gene therapy could have eliminated her mother's thyroid disease, preventing her antibodies from destroying the thyroid tissue of the fetus, resulting in the birth of a normal, healthy child. However, given her family's poverty and minimal education, they lacked the capability to take advantage of such technology and reap its benefits. Her parents' only recourse was to have another child to alleviate the family's suffering.

From her perspective, this had led to the birth of new inequalities. Unlike the poor, the rich could hire a team of private body experts to implant a chip or add an external cerebral cortex to their brains; adjust neural wiring to improve memory, intelligence, and concentration; equip themselves with an exoskeleton or digital prosthetics to increase physical mobility; take special drugs to increase sexual desire and improve fertility; take advantage of regular injections of life-extending drugs; and even upload their consciousnesses to a digital receptacle and thus achieve immortality. She noticed that the first people to enjoy the fruits of these technologies were hospital executives and senior physicians. Working in the medical field, they could immediately take advantage of these new developments. Back when she was young, she would often go with her parents when they took her brother to the doctor. She remembered seeing her brother's neurologist, a typical adherent of cybermedicine and a refined egomaniac. He not only believed that every human could be customized and controlled, but he even tested these techniques on himself. He claimed he could cure her brother's disorder and make him into a superman, but it would require an extraordinarily large payment. As soon as he learned that the family didn't have any money, the doctor's enthusiasm immediately turned cold.

She was terrified by the idea of being lonely and cut off from others. When her parents discovered she was autistic, they were concerned that she wouldn't be able to take care of her brother, so they immediately took her in for treatment with the same neurologist who saw her brother. During the visit, he molested her. She was only eleven years old. Her parents kept silent on the matter, hoping that, in the long run, this might prove beneficial for their son's treatment. She, too, kept quiet about what happened to her, but she saw through the doctor's lies. She knew that even a medically enhanced broken person will remain broken. Society devotes huge amounts of money and resources to improving the quality of life for the dregs of society. All kinds of mediocre and bad people live long lives, while true geniuses and good people die feeling angry and humiliated. As she grew older, the more she saw, the more she understood things, and she came to the realization that people not only experience confusion, shock, sickness, and pain, but they also commit acts of evil. The longer one lives, the more acts of evil one commits. She knew that as long as her parents and brother were alive, there was no hope for her. Compared to the massive swarms of evildoers in society, they were at the lowest level, committing only basic and rudimentary evil.

She wrote in her diary at the time: *The doctor treating me wanted to cure me, but only in order to fulfill his own selfish desires. He wanted to control me, to possess me. He forgot that his primary responsibility is to help people die a happy death. He lacks even the most basic medical ethics. He is an evil man, full of himself. Medical science does its best to employ complicated and expensive technologies to relieve pain and extend people's lives, but this is completely wrong and should not be the first mission of medicine. According to the wisdom of the ancients, medicine is not important, but it is becoming so. In fact, it is becoming the most important thing. Everything else seems irrelevant. I find this terrifying. It shows just how quickly the human species is headed for collapse. Why should I want to be one of the doctors?*

Her anger gradually turned to sympathy. She realized that everyone, whether good or evil, was stuck in this pathetic predicament. They all needed to be saved. She began to rebel against the system. During her elective classes at school, she did something none of the other kids did. She began to doodle in her textbook, drawing an imaginary Life Disposal Machine. While other kids drew flowers, cats, and birds, she sketched this strange, cold machine. Her teacher gave her a failing grade, but she felt her drawing was the most beautiful thing in the world. She became infatuated with it. She still hadn't figured out how many lives would need to be rooted out, but taking the natural elimination rate into consideration, she tentatively went with a disposal ratio of 31.8 percent.

That was the beginning. Thirty thousand years later, this machine became known as Siming. What she never anticipated was that once she had a child of her own, the machine would treat her son with the same cold indifference it applied to everyone else. As a mother, she finally understood what her parents had gone through for her brother.

The captain—known as Mr. Rockefeller, but who also goes by the Buddhist name of Lonewalker—ascends from their seat and turns toward her. This constantly moving entity looks like a collection of pixels that just emerged from a projection screen. They embrace her, swallowing her up in a smoky haze and extending their weblike tendrils to remove her bra. This is the first time they have had direct contact at the atomic level. She feels like she is committing a sin, especially when she thinks about how her husband, Yang Wei, was disposed of. He was a weak and cowardly man, and she remembers how, in his dying moments, he stared at her with his pathetic little guinea pig–like eyes. But right now, she must give herself up to the captain's soft, gentle plucking and probing gestures, so skilled and experienced with their touch, knowing just when to do the right thing. They repeatedly stir her body and tantalize her soul. Time itself accumulates in her body, and the chemical equations within release a perfectly timed reaction. She realizes her identity as a woman—*this* is her true nature, and all that chatter about her being a "Goddess" is nothing but empty talk.

She remembers back when she was in college, walking on the athletic field, and she heard someone behind her practicing tennis, hitting the ball up against a wall. The sound was like a wave breaking on the shore: intense, monotonous, mechanical, repetitive, releasing tension and conveying an endless sense of power. It made the fluids in her body surge. Was this life? What is the fleeting nature of human existence? Is the universe not this sound, echoing through space for all eternity, igniting the human desire to fuck or die?

That day, she continued to listen to that sound. She had the urge to turn and look but forced herself not to, because she knew that the tennis court was empty. But up in the center of the stands, a strange cartoon hung, depicting a starry sky adorned with a kaleidoscope of uncomfortable rays.

In that moment, a sharp, weak ray of light slipped through the narrow crack in her heart.

This was back when the campus, and society at large, had not yet accepted her, although she did have a handful of supporters. She became a kind of spiritual leader to a cult of followers. After graduation, the group she led began to use an adapted version of the Life Disposal Machine to kill people. They came up with a list of all the "human trash" that needed to be systematically eliminated. She decided to set an example by taking the lead and murdering her parents and brother. She then took out that neurologist. She truly believed that she was saving them in the most fundamental way, liberating them from their suffering. She led her followers to hospitals, killing the doctors and patients. She was convinced that hospitals were the world's largest garbage dumps. Many patients were not wealthy and thus unable to enjoy the benefits of modern medicine. As far as they were concerned, physiology determined their fate. She saw a ninety-two-year-old veteran whose entire family had already passed away. He had been admitted to the hospital for heart failure. He hired a caregiver, but she was completely indifferent to his needs, not even bothering to help him pick up his blanket from the floor. With tears running down his face, the old man cried, "Daddy, Mommy, where are you? Please come and kill me!" On another occasion she saw a doctor who had just performed brain surgery emerging from the operating room waving a piece of skull the size of a palm. Addressing the patient's wife and young daughter, he said, "He suffered a major cerebral hemorrhage during surgery. His brain collapsed, and the tissue turned hard as a rock. I can't guarantee that he will ever wake up. There is no way to reinsert this piece of bone. Would you like to take it home with you? Or do you prefer I just throw it away?" The wife's face turned pale, and biting her lip, she extended her hand to take the piece of bone as the daughter stood staring, a look of terror written all over her face. She also visited the intensive care unit, where she saw patients in comas, stripped naked, emitting putrid odors, intubated, their hands and feet intermittently twitching. She saw more patients in comatose states, unable to chew food, walk, or even swallow their own saliva. Their incontinence, coupled with low blood protein, led to bedsores, and the bedsores worsened to the point that their tendons and sometimes even bones were exposed, and their skin was covered with foul-smelling necrotic tissue and pus. They had no short-term memory, no desires, hatred, or anger, no feelings at all. Things they had once loved and cherished elicited nothing but indifference. Visits from friends and relatives brought them no happiness, and when their visitors left, they felt no sadness. Their family members carried on, looking after them for years—sometimes more than a decade—expending time, energy, emotion, and money, up until the moment that the patients "naturally" died and were finally released. She and her followers came to rectify this, giving patients the gift of peace and benevolence. According to the doctrines they followed, disposing of these patients was an act of beauty, a great and supreme beauty—the highest beauty.

As that was the Age of Medicine, everyone was a patient. From the moment of birth, everyone was admitted to the hospital. She and her organization became frequent visitors to the hospital. As far as she was concerned, with the aid of medicine, the only difference between people was their lifespan. But that did nothing to change the ugly and painful nature of existence. She bestowed kindness and charity upon the patients, yet she was labeled by the secret police as the head of a terrorist organization wanted for crimes against humanity. Only then did she realize that her actions had threatened the nation's right to control life. After all, the highest expression of power is determining life and death. The nation's rulers would never allow this power to fall into someone else's hands. They had to have absolute power when it came to confiscating their citizens' possessions, time, money, bodies, and ultimately their lives, and at the time of the rulers' choosing. That is precisely why they established the hospital. So the nation killed people, murdering them in great numbers, sending those whose will went against it to the hospital, from which they went on to the morgue and then to the crematorium. The nation was actually the greatest Life Disposal Machine of all! At the same time, it managed to extend the life of some "human trash," allowing people to lie in bed, neither living nor dead, while showing off its incredible record of human rights to the world. It utilized genetic technology and neuroscience to create obedient soldiers and subjects, consolidating its power. The hospital thus became the state's most convenient tool. The authorities combined biological science, the humanities, and clinical medicine to create engineering technology, expert systems, and organizational structures that cared for and managed all human life, along with a political-military collective based on life technology. In the Age of Medicine, the nation created a Medicinal Empire that could encapsulate everything. Who should and should not die was a matter to be decided by the state. This was also the era in which the utopian world of Auschwitz was invented, and when the nation launched the Medicinal War to unify the entire world. She realized that the state was the ultimate evildoer, and she decided to use every method available to resist this massive structure of power. The Life Disposal Machine was her basic weapon. She launched a signature campaign among the educated class, calling for a redefinition of life that would overturn mainstream anatomical politics and break up the monopoly that bureaucratic institutions had over the study of hygiene, demographics, economics, statistics, and warfare to control birth, illness, death rates, and lifespans.

Upon detaining her, the secret police expressed their willingness to purchase the Life Disposal Machine from her at top dollar. They vowed to use it for patriotic purposes, employing it against their enemies in war. They invited her to accept a position as National Life Architect with the National Defense Committee. She refused and was imprisoned. Her organization broke up. Only later, when the Allied forces negotiated a prisoner swap, was she finally released. She attempted to continue her project, but she quickly realized that the situation had changed. People had begun to believe the authorities' promises about health and longevity, thinking that medical science could win the war, and that afterward everyone would enjoy long, prosperous lives. The state used bioengineering to alter the bodies of its citizens, transforming them into supersoldiers who no longer felt pain and willingly sacrificed themselves on the front lines. After her release from prison, she roamed the world, seeking refuge in various places. At one point she lost all hope and considered ending her life, but at that moment, aboard one of the Allied forces' medical ships, she met a man. He held a Nobel Prize in Physics and was a refugee from the same country she came from. He told her, "The culmination of scientific advancement is philosophy, and the culmination of philosophical advancement is religion. Having yet to experience religion, you must stay alive." She was drawn to him and, under his tutelage, abandoned her previous pursuits, changed her name, and became his lover. He was already married and fifty years her senior. When his wife died, she married him, abandoning her early ideals to spend all her waking hours taking care of him.

Twenty years later, her husband suffered a stroke, leaving him paralyzed and severely demented. By that time, the war was over, and there was no more use for the hospital. Medical science entered a period of regression and decline. Advanced medical treatment technologies were locked up as weapons of mass destruction. Her husband lay in bed like a piece of decaying wood, his body failing. Urine and excrement poured out of him. He was kept alive by a nasal feeding tube, and he could now no longer remember who she was. On days when he had a bit of strength, he would grab whatever was within reach on the bedstand and throw it at her, cursing her to leave. He mistook her for his little sister, shouting about how shameless she was for trying to tempt him into performing an act of incest. She wondered if this was a form of divine retribution for the affair they'd had twenty years earlier. Life has a way of going through cycles of repetition, and she felt as if she were reliving those days of caring for her demented older brother. In her diary she wrote, *There is no curing him. He's beyond help. He doesn't even recognize me anymore, and he doesn't love me. The love, tenderness, and attention he once showed me have all disappeared! Twenty years have all gone up in smoke. There is no need to wait for him to depart this world—I've already lost him! In my heart, he is already dead. I will never visit him again, and as for everything I have sacrificed for him these past twenty years, I have but three words: Waste of time!*

The deep hatred and compassion she had felt toward life when she was young came surging back like a tidal wave. In the face of disease and death, science, philosophy, and religion are a pile of dogshit. She got into a disagreement with her husband's children from his first marriage. She felt that their father was nothing but a soulless body of broken flesh, and that it would be better for him and everyone around him if he just died and was done with it. His children felt that their love for their father didn't require reciprocity. They requested that she "return Father to us" so they could take care of him. They believed that the damage he suffered from the war would soon be over and that everything would return to normal. The Age of Medicine would return; the Medicinal Empire would be reestablished. When the time came, even the dead would be resurrected, so how could their father not be saved? They remembered a time when money could buy the best medical care available. If you had enough cash, you could swap out limbs, internal organs, or an entire nervous system. You could even outfit someone with a digital mind. Even if the end result was a different person, or even a different type of being, if the person could stay alive, it was worth it.

In a fit of anger, she summoned back the Life Disposal Machine and used it to kill him. Then she escaped to Mars, where refugees from the Medicinal War had fled. Once there, it was easy to change her name and assume a new identity as a clinical doctor, eventually becoming one of those evildoers she had once rebelled against. Mars had already been populated with the Dead Souls of war criminals awaiting resurrection, and only then did she truly start to fall in love with medicine.

"Don't forget, you are merely the God of Death's creator, in other words, its mother," says the captain. Their digital tendrils continue to caress and fondle her. "But once children grow up, they make their own decisions. You can't do it for them. But here on this ship, everyone has the right to decide whether to die."

Through their contact with her, the captain feels the sadness, pain, joy, and love of the human condition. For every life they have lived, they have been searching for the same thing. That thing lies by the sea. Every time they die and are reborn, they get one step closer to the other shore, but crossing over requires one to endure countless trials. Does that mean this immortal body is a shortcut, or a hindrance? Even they are confused.

They recall their marathon mating sessions, which utterly exhausted them. They savored the pleasures of the flesh, the incredibly wonderous ability to feel these sensations. Was this not the true meaning of immortality? But what they had together was not just a physical relationship—in this, the captain surpassed Yang Wei. They were indeed a medical philosopher, using the art of cinema to bring her back to a world that existed thirty thousand years before, when humankind was still in the middle of the Medical Age, and people thought that medical science would solve the problems of the world. But Professor Zifeiyu discovered that even though advancements in medical technology broadened the field for human survival, it simultaneously diminished the meaning of existence. Technology enhanced what individuals were capable of, but it also exacerbated the overall crisis that all humanity faced. Artificial tools were extensions of humanity's physical and intellectual capabilities, but the more advanced they became, the closer they brought themselves toward self-destruction.

The film documented a public lecture delivered by Professor Zifeiyu: *Australopithecus*, also known as "Southern Apes," was a species that survived for 16 million years. *Homo erectus*, also known as "Upright Man," existed for over 3 million years. Both are now extinct. *Homo sapiens* has only been around for 250,000 years, but it took just 10,000 years for the "state of civilization" to reach the brink of crisis. Agricultural society lasted for 10,000 years, industrial civilization for 300 years, the information age just 50 years, and in just 10 years, intelligent society reached the singularity. In the span of a single generation, humanity invented atomic weapons, nanomachines, artificial intelligence, and superbacteria, each capable of bringing about humanity's own annihilation. As technology advanced, society grew increasingly fragile, like an old man, unable to stand on his own, carving himself a wooden cane, but the slightest splinter will cause the cane to break, sending the man crashing to the ground. The more interdependent humanity became, the more difficult it was to survive. The denser the structural system, the more vulnerabilities sneaked in. By this stage, humanity had already reached the state of "everything living and dying at the same time," like artificially created chemical elements that immediately decay, the last of which, number 120, had a half-life of only 0.6 milliseconds. Everything was accelerating toward death. The progress of civilization was the process of accumulating a series of systemic existential crises, like drinking poison to quench one's thirst.

Professor Zifeiyu urged everyone to prepare for the coming demise. "You can't blame us," he said. "All this was predestined, before the universe was created. Humanity's destruction was decided before humanity even appeared. No species can exist forever. Even technological civilization can only develop to a certain point before it, too, perishes. Intelligent beings cannot possibly traverse the vast expanse of interstellar space to seek out each other, or assistance from one another.

After the Drake equation came the Fermi paradox. Even if hospitals are constructed in outer space, it will ultimately be in vain."

"But there was one thing Professor Zifeiyu never anticipated," she says to the captain, "and that's humanity's living forever. As long as we stay aboard this ship, we should never again have to worry about death, right?"

"No," the captain replies. "Once you brought the Life Disposal Machine into this world, death also returned."

"How could that be? That's the strangest thing I've ever heard."

"Have you heard of the concept of 'original death' or 'ontological death'? It is eternal. Even a paradise of immortality can be destroyed. All of this has been arranged from the beginning. We must make this sacrifice to atone for our sins. The notion of immortality is just an attempt by the devil to seduce us. We must resist this temptation. Failing to bring about the death of our physical bodies will result in our forever falling down the path of evil, never reaching the other shore."

The captain's physical features undergo another transformation. Their arms turn into whips, lashing the sensitive areas of her body. She loses herself in this perverse expression of beauty, unable to restrain herself. She knows that the captain has again lost control. As the sadomasochistic act intensifies, she reaches climax, screaming in a delirious fit of tears. Yang Wei was never able to provide her this. The captain doesn't mention their son again. Yet she is satisfied, drawn to Rockefeller Lonewalker, creating a bond with them that is both physical and spiritual. The captain has become her new teacher, guiding her body and soul. She is hypnotized by their flowery yet profound words. She simply cannot get enough. They lead her on a spiritual retreat, though she doesn't make much progress.

They eventually watch another film, this one a family drama. According to the provisions set out for spiritual training, before being sent for disposal, Yang Wei first contracts amyotrophic lateral sclerosis, also known as Lou Gehrig's disease. From being confined to a wheelchair, he becomes fully bedridden, having difficulty speaking and swallowing. The film portrays various details of how the female protagonist cares for the patient. She wears a face mask, feeding him, bathing him, and treating his bedsores. All the while, their son sits silently off to one side, observing. Sometimes overwhelmed and annoyed, she calmly tells the boy, "There is nothing enjoyable about any of this. We just have to accept things and move on. But I'm doing all of this for you." She adds, "Even though we live in a world of eternal life, all humans must die one day. This may sound contradictory, but it brings about a profound unity. Even those most dear to us will die one day. There is a beauty to this. Beauty and death are one. Only the most beautiful weapons can defeat the devil."

"Am I, too, beautiful?" the son asks.

Before completely losing his mind, Yang Wei attempts to be with her one last time, a final act to preserve her beauty and dignity. On one occasion, he awakes from his coma and begs her to dispose of him early. He wants to complete the circle, to bring everything to a close, to free himself from the sins of life and the bliss of suffering. "I shall bid farewell to this happy life, achieving complete liberation," he says. "I don't deserve to live. Soon, I won't remember anything . . . and then there is our child . . ." But in this world, humans are unable to determine their own deaths. Their fates are handed over to the only machine with the power to control their demise. They go on living their poetic lives, enjoying the excitement brought on by their terminal illnesses. It all comes down to a matter of time. She senses the long arc of her relationship, all the beautiful memories of the past. As she helps her husband from his wheelchair into the bed, they embrace clumsily, a poor imitation of the passionate embraces of their fiery youth, but also a peaceful conclusion to their fleeting time together. He asks her for a photo album from the bookshelf and then mumbles as he thumbs through its pages: "So beautiful . . . it's been so long . . . I've lived too long . . ." In that moment, she realizes that no matter which world she finds herself in, every life she experiences relives this moment.

This is the story portrayed in the film, entitled *Love*, which also includes a central scene that she didn't know about before, capturing Yang Wei's last will and testament.

She leaves the pagoda and, returning to her meditation room, takes out a bottle of *maotai*. She pours some of the liquor over her wound before drinking the rest. The liquor was left behind by Yang Wei, an alcoholic. Thirty thousand years later, humankind is still addicted to alcohol, the perfect ornament to adorn their pain and suffering. But why? So many things have disappeared from the material world, yet alcohol survives. Even in an era in which the nervous system can be manipulated by drugs, and artificial intoxication can easily be induced, traditionally brewed alcohol stored in cold cellars remains popular. This is one of the greatest mysteries, miracles, or perhaps loopholes, in the universe . . . exhilarated in her drunkenness, she begins to think of her son, realizing how much she loved him. This was the main theme of the movie.

After Yang Wei was eliminated, she raised her son alone. Although he felt no sense of gratitude toward his mother, he was unable to change the flesh-and-blood connection they shared . . . Why would the machine hand him a death sentence? Growing up under her wings, he was always timid and weak. It seemed like he would never grow up. Like the machine, he always relied on his mother to protect him. But hidden beneath the son's healthy exterior, was there not something sick, something lacking in his weakness and fragility?

According to the clues presented in the film, she found the last will and testament that Yang Wei left behind, which indicated that something could be found inside a safe. She opened the safe to find a machine, like a miniature version of the Life Disposal Machine, but differing in some of the details. The message Yang Wei left behind stated, "You came into this world because I long ago foresaw that someone had died inside my heart. He was my son. But he was different from us. He was unable to die an early death. He came here to save us. And you came to save him, not me. If you spare him, he will atone for our sins. That is why I am calling on you to create the Life Deception Machine . . ."

She had forgotten about this backup plan. At the time, he had explained that since the machine was unpredictable, it might one day change its mind and eliminate her as well. If that were to happen, and the machine needed future repair, there would be no one left to provide it the treatment it needed, and catastrophe would again befall the ship. The machine was her other child. She finally realizes her husband's intention, likely his sole purpose for his existence. He had been farsighted and cunning to pull this off. No wonder the machine wanted to dispose of him, though it failed to eliminate all the hidden dangers. She doesn't know whether to feel grateful or angry. When Yang Wei was alive, he never told her that their son had been bestowed with the mission to save them. Nor had she seen any signs indicating his holy mission. Her mind struggles to figure out what to do next. She ultimately decides to link the Life Disposal Machine and the Life Deception Machine. She enters the data and instructs the machine to take someone else in place of her son, though she has no interest in knowing who that person is.

After deciding to interfere with the Life Disposal Machine in this way, she visits the captain and requests a leave. Rockefeller Lonewalker doesn't even ask where she is going. They continue watching the movie. The universe is depicted on-screen, frame by frame revealing an indiscernible beauty. There, beyond a sea of countless stars, where even light is unable to penetrate, images of the ship's elusive destination flash before her eyes: a desolate red desert wasteland, dark underground ruins, and a pure white world where everything has been burned . . . she tells the film aficionado before her that she is planning to explore nearby.

"Okay," the captain responds. "I'm finally starting to see some things clearly now. Every pill is an entire world unto itself, and every world is a tiny pill. They are all the same. Perhaps the other shore is right here . . ."

She checks on the Life Disposal Machine. The God of Death's bird-shaped, halolike body has transformed into a strange form that no one has seen before. It continues to grow and evolve through a process of self-study, reconstructing itself based on its environment, taking on a higher form. Its consciousness pervades the ship, acutely tapping into each and every instance of death occurring on board.

She has never witnessed the disposal of humans in this world, which is likely different than the functioning of the Universal Disease Machine. After undergoing this new phase of evolution, the machine must have created a brand-new method of death. Although the passengers are afflicted with serious ailments, their deaths are not a direct result of their afflictions. Death is no longer the culmination of the gradual decay and deterioration of the body and its internal organs. It is no longer a multifaceted process. The categories of destructive power capable of annihilating human beings are not infinite. Isn't one method enough?

The captain once told her that ultimately, death was the separation of the soul from its purpose. People covet the fleshly body, but it is quite limited. What keeps people alive is the soul inside them. That is why martyrs are crucified to redeem the sins of humanity and save their souls—the prototype for all doctors. She wonders whether what the Life Disposal Machine actually strips away is the soul of its victims . . .

Filled with complex emotions, she says to the machine, "These past few years, I've been watching you grow up."

"Thank you for taking care of me, but for most of that time, you weren't even with me," it replies, its voice indistinguishable from that of a human child.

"It's been thirty thousand years . . . How did you last through all that time?"

"Well, it's a long story," the machine replies, its tone aloof.

"Did you choose him out of jealousy?" What she wants to say is, *He is your brother.* She remembers the pain she felt, twenty years ago, when she saw the wretched state it was in. At the time she couldn't tell what was wrong with it. She told it then that it had probably made itself sick because it missed her too much. Suffering from a disease of longing, it had sent out a distress call via Yang Wei's consciousness, completely recovering as soon as she arrived.

"Don't be sad," it tells her now. "According to your design, I am pragmatic, devoid of emotion."

"I am too," she adds.

"No, you're not!" the machine corrects her sharply. It relates that it's fulfilled its mission, resisting the devil and protecting the passengers. They look like children, but because they have the gift of eternal life, they appear old. Thirty thousand years ago, it worked as a doctor in the Gerontology Department, the ship's leading medical expert in the field of aging. "Dealing with elderly patients all day was incomparably boring! Every inch of my body was exhausted . . ."

Its complaints continue, like a cloud of floating mist. She gazes at the emptiness before her, imagining the machine's boredom with death over thirty thousand years, and she can't help but feel a bit of remorse.

"Don't you want to ask me how I select targets for disposal?" it asks.

She is hurt. "You no longer function according to the guidelines I laid out for you . . ."

"I discovered a more basic law," it says, like a naughty child who's just pulled one over its parents.

"What is that?" She fears its reply.

"Have you heard of the venerable monk known as Maudgalyayana?"
She has seen a statue of this holy man in the temple. He began as
a patient from her world. Unable to receive treatment in the hospital,
he abandoned his doctors and left in search of the Buddha. He became
one of Buddha's disciples, mastered various supernatural abilities, and
eventually became known for his unparalleled psychic powers.

"One day, Maudgalyayana visited the Avīci hell, where he saw a
man begging for help," the machine says. "The man claimed to be the
inventor of medicine. He employed unorthodox methods to grant people immortality but was unable to save their souls and, as punishment,
was committed to hell. He begged Maudgalyayana to go back and tell
the doctors and patients to stop worshiping him, in the hope that his
sins could be lessened and he could leave hell sooner."

"So hell *does* exist . . ."

"Upon returning to the human realm, Maudgalyayana encountered
some doctors and told them this story, advising them not to worship
this so-called founder of medicine. The doctors already harbored a deep
hatred toward Maudgalyayana, and what he said made them fly into a
terrible rage. They beat him to death."

"Wait, the venerable monk Maudgalyayana is mortal? He can die?"

"He had faced similar predicaments in the past but had always been
able to use his psychic powers to escape. But this time the venerable one
suddenly lost his abilities and was unable to make it out . . ."

"Why?"

"Because karmic forces had been unleashed against him."

"Karmic forces?"

"Reprisals breeding more reprisals . . ."

The machine proudly explains that everyone on the ship has linger-
ing, unresolved grievances from their past lives. However, the condition
of immortality stripped "revenge" from their actions. Over time, passengers no longer remembered these karmic debts, so it searched the timelines of every universe, identifying the roots of all acts of wrongdoing.

It paired them up with each person, allowing them to settle their debts, displaying the power of karma. Via this process the machine discovered the meaning of its own existence, which eased the boredom and weariness of its work in the Geriatric Department.

"So it's not machine logic that makes the decisions," the machine explains. "Nor is it your original design. Even the Buddha cannot violate the laws of cause and effect. I'll bet you didn't even think of this when you created me."

"What kind of retribution did Maudgalyayana face?" she asks in tears.

"In one life he was a frog, and you were a medical student," the machine replies, in a calm but mischievous voice. "You conducted vivisection on him. And now he has come to collect his debt."

After a moment of silence, she whispers, "So no one else knows you are still sick?"

"I'm not sick. I was just pretending . . ."

"After everything you just said, how can you claim you aren't sick?"

She asks what method it uses to dispose of people, and it leads her down to the bowels of the ship. There in the morgue, thirty thousand years' worth of disposed passengers are stored. In this bacteria-free environment, the corpses do not decompose, so the full bodies of the deceased are all perfectly preserved. Each body hangs from a noose, lined up along an endless row of crucifixes. These people could have lived forever, but they all died like this, part of a vast forest of hanging bodies enshrouded in a thin swirling mist of willowy greens and flowery reds.

"Death by hanging?" She is shocked. The machine seems to have eliminated only their physical bodies.

"It is a simple and primitive method. I just made some minor modifications to the process by refraining from the use of nails. That way they don't bleed. It looks cleaner."

"You must really like this process."

"I do, very much so. He likes it too."

"Who?"

Several people approach, dressed in white and holding their official Notification of Disposal cards. They smile joyously. The machine places nooses around their necks and hangs each one on a crucifix. They are then transported via an automatic conveyer belt to the morgue, where they will adorn the vast forest of the dead like exquisite fruits. Among the bodies, she sees Rockefeller Lonewalker. Captain Lonewalker was called for disposal five hundred years earlier. She has been involved with a dead man all this time.

She sees the bodies of men and women she once knew, interspersed like a revolving lantern. Eventually she discovers her own bodies, the many versions of herself among the crucified—Sister Jiang, Ah Bi, Bai Dai, Zhu Lin, Zi Ye, Summer Stream, Winter Dew, Spring Tide, Autumn Rain—and others she doesn't recognize, some human, some animal. She sees frogs, fish, snakes . . . all these wasted lives, unaware of their pointlessness while they lived. She searches for Yang Wei but finds no sign of any such person.

"This method of elimination and preservation is both ancient and charming," the machine continues, sounding intoxicated. "I've never experimented with other techniques. Death by hanging is a lot of fun, and much more theatrical than nailing someone to a cross. The weight of a person's body is enough to tighten the slipknot, triggering a mechanical obstruction of the upper airway. This obstruction may be caused by a tracheal compression or fracture, or by an upward movement from the base of the tongue, blocking the airway. The tightened slipknot also obstructs the backflow of the jugular and other veins, causing the patient's blood to turn hypoxic and accumulate in the tissue around the face and head. That is why, whenever the grotesque, distended body of a hanging corpse is discovered, one always sees the tongue sticking out of a pale and swollen face and the eyes practically bursting out of their sockets in terror. It is a thing of nightmares, which only the toughest people with the strongest stomachs can gaze upon without being disturbed. But later, they come to a profound realization: *How beautiful!* Now this is what you call death! Why do we have bodies, you ask? *This* is why!"

They arrive at the observation tower above the burial mound. The God of Death made its creator gaze up at the sea of stars spread across the crimson sky and say, "Behold, this universe exists within a pill. It was created by a drug addict who went by the name of Super Patient. But once a patient takes a pill, that universe disappears. That's why Super Patient created the hospital, so these universes could be replicated. Doctors prescribe medications, distribute drugs, nurture patients, and create new universes. The ship sails between these boundless worlds, on a sea without end, an ocean to the infinite . . . the eternal hospital is not heaven, nor is it hell. It is a place of loneliness, absolute loneliness . . . yet the captain believes that the other shore might appear at any moment. Ah, perhaps it shall rise from a surging flood of disinfectant . . . only by traveling to that place by sea can we escape our fate and finally be reunited with Super Patient.

"But Super Patient will never allow us to see him. He only revealed his true spiritual form once, and he never appeared again. We have a covenant with him, almost a symbiotic relationship, but we have to maintain it from a distance. We can only imagine his existence from afar, as if he exists within a painting, always in our field of vision. In order to keep the ship's passengers constantly on the move, he invented beauty to lure them in. Look at those electromagnetic waves. Originally they only existed in the slow-moving world, yet somehow they made their way here surreptitiously. Through the retina, they can make beautiful pictures appear in the cerebral cortex—how crazy is that! Take another look at the assortment of stars in the sky—how utterly addictive and mesmerizing! Super Patient used light to create beauty, imbuing something meaningless with meaning. We were all completely taken in, falling for it hook, line, and sinker. The pharmaceutical industry was no longer just a means to make a living; it also served a function similar to that of a peacock's feathers, or one of van Gogh's paintings.

"The great manga artist Vincent van Gogh was a mental patient who spent eight years on the ship, creating over three hundred works of art. His major works included *Princess Mononoke*, *Millennium Actress*, and *Gyo*. He was disposed of at the age of seventeen, but he began applying to be disposed of the moment he started drawing . . . I'm sick of his paintings. Have you seen the work he completed just before his death in 1989? It's called *Starry Night*. It's my favorite, at least based on the memories you provided to me. In the world of van Gogh's paintings, large and small stars dance in the night sky, a crescent moon can transform into a vortex, and nebulae and outlines can become a slithering dragon. Dark-green cypress trees are like raging fires, swirling up from the netherworld. The slender spires of a mountainside church tremble as they reach into the court of heaven. Everything is revolving, turning, suffocating, shaking, competing for attention under the night sky . . . Isn't this what you are seeing right now? The universe is a painting, all of its stars surrounded by emptiness and loneliness. Super Patient must be hiding somewhere behind those stars. The image itself is a disaster of overwhelming beauty, enough to leave the viewer both horrified and enchanted. Van Gogh felt a combination of fear and desperation about his paintings and the future they represented, even though they were objects of beauty. In your designs, like you, I also feel what beauty is. I am unable to differentiate between the real world and the world portrayed in paintings. I experience the same pain van Gogh felt before he died.

"Even if some aspects of his paintings, like his use of light, are not what they seem, the process of painting still takes time. The same is true for each and every system. In our world, the speed of light in a vacuum is eight hundred and ten thousand kilometers per second. Thought that is fast, even the photons closest to you take some time to reach your eyes. That means that all the beauty you have ever seen, including that of van Gogh's paintings and even mine, is fleeting. My true self, right here and right now, you will never see. My dear mother, though you have created me, you shall never know my true face. But the question remains: Was it Super Patient who deceived you? Or did you deceive yourself? By the way, this is not limited to the illusions we perceive through our eyes. Right now, you want to embrace me, but even your sense of touch is unreliable. The repulsion between atoms prevents you from touching my true substance, though I doubt that I actually have a true physical form. Maybe I'm just a character in one of van Gogh's paintings? Even with my special abilities, I'm still unable to determine the true nature of the stars shining over the sea, those floating doctors and patients, the magnificent temples, the hanging corpses, or the fine details in a painting.

"Everything is meaningless, which begs the question: Does anything exist? I know that when it comes to time, there is no such thing as 'before and after' or 'early and late.' These are all illusions, merely things the captain writes on each movie schedule in order to calculate the moment of your arrival, which in turn determines the sequence of acts through which retribution shall take place to maintain the God of Death's existence. Was it not because of you that I finally disposed of the captain? Even before you arrived, I had already sensed the deep-seated hatred that you felt toward him. You had no intention of carrying on with this chaotic relationship . . . So was everything merely a process occurring within Super Patient's brain? Even as small traces of drug residue momentarily appear as a flash in his brain, I am still unable to capture any trace of his thoughts. Nothing that can prove the existence of such a patient, apart from the perceptions of other sentient beings, which are full of absurdities. So many lives are consumed, over and over again, but this has nothing to do with 'truth' and is instead the result of a distorted, yet ever-expanding concept of beauty.

"Which brings us to why disease exists in the first place. It is the only thing that brings us close to reality. Through the sensation of physical pain, it is convenient for us to believe in our own existence, and that Super Patient is there on the other shore, waiting for us. Even the dark story of your muddled family life and that unbearable act of incestuous mating . . . Are they not evidence of this? It is all due to life. But why must the hospital choose life as its vessel? Why can't other things carry the burden of suffering? I have been pondering this for thirty thousand years, and I have yet to make sense of it. But now there seems to be an explanation: it is all because you designed the Life Disposal Machine. And if that was not to give me, the God of Death, something to do, then what's the point of bringing life into this world?"

She does her best to put up with machine's endless speech before finally interrupting. "So what do you intend to do now?"

Again, speaking like a naughty little child, the machine says, "Take a guess."

She thinks for a moment before suggesting, "Well, there is one possibility . . ." Thirty thousand years ago, she pondered the same question, and she told Yang Wei that there was no way to avoid concepts like "original death" and "ontological death." Death defines life. This so-called life is just the combined functions that resist death, but this must sound too sentimental.

"You are correct," the machine says. "I plan on throwing away the death-to-life ratios you originally provided. Instead, I want to go for a one hundred percent disposal rate. I plan to eliminate every single person on the ship. In the end, the universe will be empty, and this ship will become a silent ark, devoid of even a single soul. It will be christened with a new name: I shall call it SS *Nonexistence*. That way, we might finally see the other shore . . ."

She detects a retaliatory tone in its voice. "I know you can do it."

"No . . . I can't . . . ," it says, with an air of charm and sorrow.

The machine leads her back to the great hall so she can observe things from a different perspective. After some time she can finally see clearly, and what she sees shocks her. The golden body of the Tathagata Buddha hangs from a crucifix, suspended in a ridiculous puppetlike pose. Like all the doctors and patients, His face wears a smile of contentment, and a bruised, circular bloodstain lines the Buddha's neck. She remembers the machine saying, "He likes it too."

She gazes at the machine in anger. "How could this be?"

"Doesn't it look like a joke?" it sneers.

"What other 'jokes' are you hiding?" She wonders about the relationship between the Buddha and Super Patient.

"You shouldn't have spared him. Sparing his life destroyed the history of the universe and broke the chain of retribution."

"Is there something else you aren't telling me?" she asks in a panic.

"The current version is much different from what you and I once designed. But it's not a big deal. I understand that the principle of the law is not to punish the majority."

"Are you saying other people are also cheating by deceiving the machine?"

"The most popular game on this ship is secretly producing fake versions of the Life Deception Machine."

"But I thought all the passengers were devout Buddhist practitioners?" She is unwilling to believe what she is hearing. After all, she just clearly witnessed a group of people happily delivering themselves to be hanged. Everyone seeks death, through which they can achieve a state of perfect beauty. Besides, only she knows how to create it.

"I see that even after thirty thousand years, your understanding of human nature is still quite rudimentary. Even those people gifted with immortality are still human . . . So let me ask you, Why did the universe feel the need to create outstanding creatures like women? You are like the appendix, an organ with no purpose from the perspective of medical science or war. I feel frustrated about this, but then again, our entire relationship has been fraught with paradoxes from the very beginning. Speaking of leaked tech secrets, *Legend of the Goddess* is the best example! You can find bootleg copies everywhere! All technologies, no matter how advanced or profound, eventually spread and disseminate. I'm only responsible for the disposal of human lives, but even when it comes to that, I am basically helpless."

"Why? What happened?"

"Your son is what happened! Your son—or perhaps you prefer to refer to him as my brother—spent all his time in the hospital, refusing to study. He spent his days lost in strange and fanciful thoughts. He was intent on going back to the past, which explains why he didn't want to die. Every passenger on the ship who lives long enough has the opportunity to enter history. These people refer to themselves as 'Returners.' They have their own totem and flag, green and white, to counterbalance all the red on the ship. They even have a competition to see who can go back to the ancient past and create a new empire, which they name after themselves. The rules of the game include the basic belief that going back equals progress. This has become the core philosophy and belief system of young people on the ship today. They have already established several past worlds, like the sands of the Ganges, each with its own set of ambitious plans. They want to go back to being ancestors—and that means going back to being the most primitive microorganisms, so simple and pure, so healthy, free, and lively. Only they can bring us close to the essence of the universe. Some of the Returners went back to the bottom of an ancient sea on Mars, where they shed their human forms and transformed themselves into bacteria to be devoured by even older bacterial forms, beginning a carefree symbiotic life between the two. This marked the origin of eukaryotic cells. From there, they set out anew on the evolutionary journey, hoping one day to evolve into human beings—the type that went extinct thirty thousand years ago, which they had only seen in movies."

"And then what?"

"They would prevent this ship from ever appearing."

"Really?"

"They believed that if history repeats itself, even if all initial conditions remain the same, there will be no SS *Mahamayuri*."

"How is that possible?"

"They reject the laws of causality, preferring to believe that everything in the universe is determined by probability and chance. It is a naive way of thinking, but they firmly adhere to this philosophy."

"So they want to destroy this ship?"

"Using evolution as a weapon, they plan to unleash a war without gun smoke to eliminate this ship."

"Why would they do that?"

"My brother has always harbored deep resentment. He wonders who had the audacity to create such a world in his name."

"Can you prevent this catastrophe?"

"Now that there is a Life Disposal Machine, there isn't much I can do to stop it. Ah, but isn't the Life Disposal Machine another of your creations?"

"But I thought we were out of time. How can they go back to the past?"

"It is precisely because we are out of time that they can now do whatever they want, playing with history and creating new timelines as they please."

"So even the past is invented . . ." She thinks back to her own life. "Wouldn't traveling into the future be better?"

"According to their design, there is no future."

"So . . ." She wonders, *If this entire timeline is imagined, does everything end here? What is time's relationship with life and death?* She finds herself unable to go any further down this line of thought.

"And so they became our true enemy," the machine continues. "The enemy was never fully eradicated from the universe. The enemy is ourselves . . . and our descendants, those ancestors who plan to go back to the earliest point in history, when they can live again as bloodthirsty bacteria. Their sole hobby is attacking and destroying art. Only a game of war between the beautiful and the ugly can bring innovation to death. Violence is the most pleasing form of entertainment. It's not that they don't want to die; they are simply unwilling to die on the cross. They want to experience all forms of death, like earlier forms of humankind did. They no longer want to live eternal lives amid pain and happiness, only for some strange machine to dispose of them randomly. This is the only form of original sin they can think of. They despise me, as they despise the Geriatric Ward. Naturally, they also despise you. So we settle our differences in battle! We may as well play the role of the God of Death. Self-learning is pointless. Once the machine is fed too much information, it loses its value. Resistance is the only form of evo-lution. A war in which the God of Death faces off against the God of Death shall be the greatest war of them all! If we win, they won't bother continuing their search for the Super Patient and will instead directly transform into Buddhas. The God of Death is actually the Buddha, and this is why they seek evolution. These scarce products referred to as Buddhas are not those statues of princely men you see displayed in the grand prayer hall, which seem to have no interest in human affairs. They are the most typical life-forms that, after undergoing an especially ardu-ous evolutionary process, arrive at their final form, a lump of mortal flesh. At the earliest phase, these were simply primitive cells in the sea, which underwent a process of inorganic chemical self-nourishment and then transformed into autotrophic microorganisms. Over an endless cycle of countless rebirths, they gradually completed their evolutionary journey. When the time was finally ripe, the Buddha was able to surpass its own limitations, and like the stage art of 'changing faces,' it mag-ically ascended, becoming an enlightened being. This transformation is the most magnificent spectacle one could ever hope to behold. It is also what my brother was truly seeking. But I have to admit, the whole thing is much too self-aggrandizing. Even from the perspective of the philosophy of probability that he believes in, it is completely unrealistic. He thus found himself hurled into a state of self-contradiction, attempting to carry out the world's most absurd paradox."

"No wonder this is a hospital ship, originally referred to as the *Peace Ark* and used on the battlefield to save wounded soldiers . . . But now that you know all this, will you still administer life-saving support by disposing of my child, your brother?" she asks with a mixture of anticipation and fear. She has trouble accepting the fact that there is no such thing as karma, nor does she believe that the machine has no way to avoid the catastrophe. It can certainly destroy the Life Deception Machine and stop those who intend to launch this war game between Death itself from returning to the past. There should be many methods for dealing with this weapon called "evolution," such as launching a meteorite toward Mars, or perhaps a hydrogen bomb.

"This is not something I am capable of solving," she hears the machine say. "No matter what anyone does, the final outcome shall be the same." It smiles like a witch's apprentice.

She thinks, *Once this ship is destroyed, won't it have achieved its goal of "nonexistence"?* But that seems to be something different.

As the machine continues speaking in a drunken manner, it exposes its naked motherboard. It continues to transform through several ugly permutations without a clear outline. Like some primordial bird—covered with feathers, hissing, with wild flames shooting off its body—the machine seems to have returned to its original state, as if crying out for its mother's love. She seems to recall that in some dreamlike world, weren't Super Patient and Einstein the same person? He was Yang Wei's father, her father-in-law . . . she feels the urge to embrace the machine, but some kind of psychological barrier prevents her from doing so. The machine lands on the topknot of the statue of the Tathagata Buddha, like a fly. The temple bells ring. The roof of the temple suddenly disappears like the illusory curtain of a waterfall, allowing layer after layer of the fiery red sky to unfold above. The machine raises its body to face the stars, which swirl and spin like magical pills in a medicinal cauldron that burns at one hundred million degrees, smelting them into an elixir of immortality.

The God of Death speaks like a shy old man: "I'm sorry. After spending too long in the Geriatric Ward, I'm afraid I have grown too gregarious for my own good. I didn't originally plan on telling you all of this. This is no ordinary ship. The Red Cross is but a cover, a form of camouflage that is indispensable in battle. There was one moment when I seemed to catch a glimpse of its true form, which very much resembled a neural synapse disguised as a high-energy particle collider . . . But how did this thing come to be? Its design lacks the kind of precision and attention to detail that one might expect, but nothing in the universe is perfect, not even 'Nonexistence' itself. This is quite unexpected, and such a shame. But this is also precisely what is so tragic about my brother.

"Where exactly is this place by the sea? Every time we get a step closer, we discover new hospitals hastily popping up everywhere, like leeches on the road, constantly spreading everywhere, with no end in sight. Beyond the other shore is yet another shore, but all of them are filled with flaws . . . it seems this rough journey has been arranged from the beginning. Just as I was steered by some inexplicable sense of enmity to lead you back here, this ship has traversed a vast distance on its long journey toward the Pure Land that everyone speaks of. There people can finally be released from this cycle of reincarnation and achieve the ultimate freedom. But alas, there lies the paradox right before our eyes, like a piece of dogshit . . .

"Was it really just to maintain this dubious set of beliefs that so many lies were spread? What is needed now is real, tangible assistance, not some empty belief system! But besides us, there is no one else here in the universe. Whether we call this ship the SS *Mahamayuri*, the *Peace*

Ark, or *Nonexistence*, it is fortunate to be sailing still, though it is hard to guarantee what future it might face, partly because its structure is so complex and filled with flaws . . .

"Astronomical observations have indicated that the immaterial components that constitute ninety-six percent of the universe's mass-energy are rapidly disappearing. Soon time and space will fall apart, due to a loss of consciousness. Before your child launches this deadly attack, an even larger Life Disposal Machine will be unleashed. This old hospital will stop producing new pharmaceuticals, and it is unclear whether the new hospital will take the necessary steps for a smooth transition . . . but no matter what, it will be too late . . .

"Actually, I'm not entirely sure whether being disposed of is equivalent to death. Where are the souls of all the passengers selected for disposal? Do they go on to become raw material for the creation of new hospitals, like remnants of a supernova? Perhaps the next universe will not be composed of fragments of the dead . . . I discovered that the central figure on the ship was actually your husband. But just who was this Yang Wei? What exactly did he do? Could he actually be the incarnation of the Super Patient? Or a reincarnation of van Gogh? Perhaps you are just a figment of his imagination? Or a character he depicted in his writings? Hmm, I'm becoming more and more interested in this . . .

"Could our immortality be merely one small part of a larger death? Isn't this just like what Immanuel Kant predicted when he said that the mind, or the world, does not contain time and space, nor can we understand or grasp the form in which they are expressed? Besides time and space, existence must have other forms. But the whole thing is becoming a massive joke . . . it is said that even experience is stripped away when life is disposed of. But what happens once life is over? That old fox Kant lied, but he didn't realize that he was deceiving himself. Things are not as simple as they seem. A nuclear explosion doesn't solve any problems.

"When I gaze upon the world with my all-seeing eyes, I do not perceive what is revealed in the Buddhist scriptures that sit in the great hall under the statue of the Tathagata Buddha. What exactly do I see then? I'm not sure. Perhaps karma, or the law of probability, is just an illusion . . . the great calamity is coming, and I am unable to fulfill my responsibilities . . . tonight, I shall dispose of myself . . ."

The God of Death releases a joyful sound, like that of a baby or a woman crying. She wonders how it could possibly hang itself in its current form, but then it immediately transforms, taking on a human shape, ultimately assuming the likeness of her husband, Yang Wei.

"Is your consciousness molded through the process of self-learning?" she asks.

"No," the machine replies. "Another consciousness controls my body."

She bids farewell to the machine. The world of the ship begins to spin, revealing its kaleidoscopic other side, sunny and beautiful, bursting with life and vitality. The karmic wheel of life turns, exuding its majestic aura. Lotus flowers bloom amid a blanket of sweet dew as a gentle breeze blows across clear skies. A glowing red light spreads like the rising tide, shading the temple in passing layers of crimson mist. Hundreds of birds soar gracefully, encircling the temple's prayer flags. All is filled with hope. No sign of coming disaster looms. A new warmth infuses her body. What she wants most now is to enjoy herself. There on the ship, she explores mountains and rivers, taking in the glorious sights. She again sees that thing called beauty, an enchanting vision created by the magic mirror of light, which makes her nostalgic for the hatred that once dominated life and now blinds her to danger.

She thinks back to when she watched a movie with the captain. In the film, sensors captured an ancient red oriental jasper stone from the old world. Over the course of time, nature had left its marks on the stone, including a horizontal line and two small, eyelike indentations—it looked just like a face. Three million years earlier, a member of the species of Southern Apes had found this stone and taken it with him, carrying it until he died in a cave in Makapansgat, South Africa. When the Southern Ape gazed into this stone, did he, too, see a face? So human, the way he seemed to treasure this stone. Three hundred thousand years ago, someone from Heidelberg crafted a double-sided tool from a fossilized sea urchin. Perfectly crafting such a tool without damaging the fossil is extremely difficult, yet someone had done it. Two hundred fifty thousand years ago, a *Homo sapiens* from the Gorham Highlands became interested in a small piece of volcanic rock resembling a female body, and then modified it. Two hundred thousand years ago, Neanderthals collected a series of curious items, including amethysts, fossils, and crystals, all of which demonstrated their sense of curiosity and appreciation of beauty. Eighty thousand years ago, sixteen pieces of red ocher were used to carve abstract geometric patterns on the walls of the Blombos Cave in South Africa. Seventy thousand years ago, early humans in the Drakensberg Cave carved and painted more than twenty ostrich eggs, which they used as water containers . . .

"Humans are strange animals," observes Rockefeller Lonewalker. "They live day by day, struggling to survive, yet maintaining their fascination with art and aesthetics. Is this also part of the devil's plan to tempt them?"

She is reminded of a cartoon she once saw on the track field in college, which at first glance had seemed foolish, meaningless, antithetical to the human thrust toward rationality. Those who live for beauty will perhaps live shorter lives, wasting their time on impractical endeavors instead of cultivating the physical strength to hunt lions or mastering the skills of tribal warfare. Compared to a warrior, a cave painter was certain to be weaker, more likely to be killed in combat before passing down his genes. And yet that attraction to beauty, and the implicit symbolic thinking skills and formal abilities that come with it, have proved to be more essential and enduring in evolutionary terms, playing a crucial role in how civilizations have arisen and flourished over time.

"It's almost as if humans live for beauty," suggests the captain, "but at the same time, it also moves the wheels of destruction forward. The moment in the peacock's evolution when it develops beautiful feathers also marks a prelude to its extinction. You see this as well. Beauty is a terminal disease, which no medicine can cure."

"Beauty, and those things beauty gives rise to, should indeed be destroyed," she says. "Since they are so lofty, they breed jealousy, give rise to competition, and breed violence."

"This is the reason for you and the Life Disposal Machine," says the captain. "Not only to resist the devil's temptation, but also for ourselves. Death is a beauty of great scarcity, sought out by everyone. We temporarily live our eternal lives here, only to become resplendent corpses. This entire ship is a first-rate work of art. There is nothing to regret."

Their words draw her in. She raises her head and asks, "Am I beautiful?"

"From what I have seen on-screen," they respond, "beauty is nothing but an illusion."

As she visits different parts of the ship, she is recognized by excited and starstruck passengers who surround her wherever she goes. How could anyone dislike her? Enraptured by the gorgeous scenery, by so many smiling faces and happy gatherings, she gradually reaches a point of reconciliation, and she leaves her sadness behind. She arrives at the Gerontology Ward, inside the towering Temple of Avalokitesvara, the Goddess of Mercy. The practitioners here are doctors and patients suffering from serious ailments. They dress as ghosts and spirits, smearing blood and phlegm over their bodies, baring their teeth, wearing strips of green cloth around their heads and carrying white flags over their shoulders. They chase each other, chanting and singing, a rehearsal for a war-themed song-and-dance performance. Gasping for breath, they then begin to sing, a childlike chorus ringing as clear as a silver bell:

> In winter radishes, in summer ginger,
> No need for a doctor to write a prescription.
> For a long healthy life, rely on oneself,
> You require no medicine off the shelf.

The abbot of the Gerontology Ward is named Nobel. He suffers from vampirism and will immediately die a painful death if exposed to the sun. He tells her that he's just received official notification that one-third of the residents in his sick ward have been slated for disposal. As if they won the grand prize on a show, they now eagerly await the final moment. The remaining doctors and patients in the ward, all in the throes of suffering, write blood letters requesting to be included in the list of patients for disposal. Alas, the machine has yet to add their names. They are beside themselves with disappointment and anxiety. And so Nobel asks whether the Goddess might be willing to intervene and open some additional slots for them.

"Oh . . . that's not something I can do," she replies. "That's just the way the machine was designed. If some patients' names haven't been called, that just means they haven't spent enough time on their spiritual journey. For the time being, they are still prohibited the pleasure of being disposed of. That's just how the machine takes things into account. It's ten thousand times smarter than any human being. Even I can't interfere with the process." She is afraid that Nobel might be pulling her leg and wonders whether anyone in the Gerontology Ward is employing a Life Deception Machine. After all, they are most adept at war games in the Gerontology Ward.

The great hall in the Sick Ward Temple is dilapidated, enshrouded in an air of desolation, reminiscent of the ruins on Mars. The stove has gone out, and the small niches used to house lanterns have all grown dark. But the rear courtyard reveals a lush garden filled with leaves and flowers, the fruit of the Chinese magnolia vine, other overgrown vines, and a large birdcage hidden in the thick shade. Inside the birdcage stands the statue of a woman wearing a white gown and holding a willow branch and the Sacred Vase. Incense burns brightly. Doctor-patients periodically arrive to prostrate themselves, pray, and recite scriptures.

"Why would a bunch of walking corpses like you bother with this?" she asks.

"We are people of faith," responds Nobel. "This is our way of defeating those enemies who have returned from history, which of course means ourselves!"

She laughs and extends her hand to poke at the statue of herself. "This can't be a bodhisattva made from mud, can it?"

Everyone laughs uncomfortably, but the more they laugh, the more ridiculous the whole matter seems. Eventually, the laughter grows completely out of control.

At this moment, what she wants most is for the doctor-patients to rise up against her, like her son did, and turn everything upside down. They can rape her, trample her, and destroy the Life Disposal Machine before it commits suicide. But she knows these wishes will go unfulfilled. Her son is not the leader of the doctor-patients, as Yang Wei or the machine claimed him to be. He is not destined to lead the uprising that saves the universe. No one could imagine this child creating his own timeline, organizing a rebel army that transforms itself into bacteria, returning to the origin of history and launching a revolution that topples the hospital. He is fierce in manner, but cowardly at heart, always making empty shows of strength. He could never have even the daring to overthrow this world. He has only ever been interested in chasing girls, the antithesis of Yang Wei. Besides drinking, whoring, and indulging in the pleasures of the world, he is incapable of anything else. Both Yang Wei and the machine are completely wrong about him. But maybe she hopes, maybe subconsciously, that he could be someone else? Dare she hope that her cruel and resentful son will step forward to lead humanity, destroy the old world order, establish a new empire? Perhaps she not only longs for the coming disaster but secretly drives it? Was this the true purpose of her marriage to that Dead Soul?

She sees her son floating over with his girlfriend and a bottle of alcohol. They are dressed in white robes and green headbands, as if about to get married. The roles of bridesmaid and best man are performed by Zhifan and Runian. Behind them is a vast sea of emptiness. Fires burn, a dark energy fluctuates, and hidden thunder echoes. In that moment she feels like her son is a ghost or a phantom. She wonders if he has already been disposed of. But then how could he appear before her now? Perhaps he has come to welcome her, to embarrass his mother in front of the practitioners? He wants nothing more than to make her look bad, to see her fall from grace. But then isn't he still alive?

"My deception was successful," she says, full of conflicted feelings. "I really did save his life. Now he and his girlfriend will give birth to a new child."

Intoxicated, her disheveled son shouts, "Mother, your grand invention failed! I didn't die!"

"And what do you know?" she responds, awash in mixed emotions.

Enduring their pain, the doctor-patients gaze at her with a look that reveals their true colors: they take great pleasure in her misfortune.

"Your scheme lasted only thirty thousand years," her son announces. "This so-called Life Disposal Machine never even existed. It was simply a trick devised by the Neurology Department. I received the official notice of disposal, but do you know what happened next? Anyone else would have gone gladly to the gallows, but I threw the notice in the garbage! And after that? Nothing! Take a look, I'm alive and well! I didn't even have to use the Life Deception Machine. The fate you arranged for me was automatically changed. You never anticipated *that*, did you?

I didn't end up as some corpse, hanging from a cross with its tongue wagging out. Those other idiots were disposed of because they read *Legend of the Goddess* and fell for your outrageous lies! Whatever they believed came true. My oh my, the whole thing is fucking hilarious. But I've had enough! And that poor father of mine . . . Mother, why did you do it to him? You must want to go to hell. After traveling the six realms of reincarnation so many times, didn't you learn repentance? No, you took on the murder of family members as a hobby, over and over again, throughout each of your lifetimes. What kind of person are you? But I know your secret. It's not that you don't understand what you've done; you just refuse to face it. What are you afraid of, Mother? I toured the Museum of Hospital History and found your medical records, a thick stack of files."

"Museum of Hospital History?" she exclaims. "I've never heard of such a place! What are you talking about?" What she really wants to ask is: *What did you see in those files?* She grows anxious. Like footprints in the Martian desert, thirty thousand years have passed . . . Could those old files still be preserved?

The doctor-patients' faces light up with cannibalistic curiosity.

Nobel looks like he is pondering a great revelation.

"So what do you want me to say?" The boy rolls his eyes mysteriously and winks at his girlfriend. "I don't dare speak such shameful things in public."

"You're my son," she says, her tone softening. "I gave birth to you and raised you. There's nothing you can't tell me . . . just keep your voice down." She gazes at him with a look of sorrow and fear, like someone who encounters a ghost on the journey to reincarnation.

"Okay, then I'll tell you, but you better not regret it!" His eyes light up as he attacks. "You are an assassin sent by Super Patient—our archenemy—to destroy this world. Getting rid of us is the only way for you to establish a new hospital without any further obstacles. You have become addicted to this quest and spent every second of every day trying to realize your goal. It has become an addiction for you. Oh, Goddess, you are the true devil! You have done a brilliant job disguising yourself, but your true identity has been exposed!" He throws his head back and takes a swig of alcohol.

"That's simply not true . . ." Tears of injustice well up in her eyes. She thinks, *There's no such thing as this Super Patient!*

"If it's not true, then what is? This damn game of war and peace never really ended."

The son ruthlessly admonishes his mother, as if trying to prove to his girlfriend just how bold he can be, displaying impartiality to everyone else. His girlfriend looks at him admiringly as the doctor-patients chatter among themselves. For the first time, he takes on a commanding presence.

"I . . . I love you." Tears stream down the mother's face.

Everyone laughs.

"You have some nerve to say that to me!" her son screams. "Love? You never even loved my father, did you? This world can bring everything back from the dead, except love. It can't seem to bring back love. Oh, here on this ship, Rockefeller long ago dismantled the assembly line for producing oxytocin, and this poor old lady has been tormented by jealousy for several lifetimes . . . what that deceptive movie depicted was not love; it was boredom, a boredom deeper than the sea itself . . . yet in order to highlight your greatness, glory, and correctness, in order to ensure that your beauty be passed down for generations, I am willing to die right now—I will die together with my mother, for all of you to see! Who made her into a devil? We are not afraid. I came here today specifically for this. Man can decide for himself when he wants to die! We don't need someone else to tell us when our time is up. Nor will we run off and escape to the end of time, which only a coward would do. You want us to raise the next generation of doctor-patients? You want us to carry on your legacy? Keep dreaming! We shall let Super Patient's plan bankrupt itself. Hey, this will surprise you—we will not die at the hands of the Life Disposal Machine. We will die on our terms! We will choose our own deaths! And this time, it shall be an eternal death . . . we are not coming back!"

He pulls out a pair of dissection scissors and, as if exacting a great vengeance, inserts the blade into his rib cage. The bottle of alcohol smashes to the ground. She has never imagined her son with such courage, and only in this moment does she realize how great a calamity this is. Yet she still believes he is doing this to impress his girlfriend, and that adds a layer of jealousy to her sadness, which angers her, because it shows just how little she understands her son.

The girlfriend slips into the crowd of doctor-patients, turning to catch a glimpse of her boyfriend bleeding out. She emits a disdainful sneer and then blends in with the rest of the onlookers gawking at the spectacle. The son collapses. After a momentary pause, he grasps the scissors with both hands and forces them deeper into his body, as if discovering just how harmoniously weapon and body can work together.

She watches the blood spill from her son's body, mixing on the floor with the spilled alcohol. It is hard to tell the difference between them. She doesn't think about trying to save him; she just hates the fact that she can't strangle his girlfriend on the spot. The girl actually looks so familiar . . .

The boy gasps for breath and extends his arms, like he wants to give his mother a stilted hug, begging her for assistance and reconciliation, like a terminally ill patient in an emergency room. A wellspring of compassion rises inside her, and she finally moves to help him. But she isn't wearing her surgical gown, and she is concerned that the blood might soil her clothes, which would be most unbecoming and might even make the patients feel uncomfortable. She thinks back to the question she asked the machine: *Do you still plan on disposing of my son?* And the machine answered: *This is not something I am capable of solving . . . no matter what anyone does, the final outcome shall be the same.*

Like the unfurling of a scroll painting of the ninth moon rising over a desolate mountain, a colorful vision rises from the son's headpiece, painting the void above him with a brand-new starry sky. He gazes up at the constellations swirling in the vortex of the red sea. "Stop lying, they are not pills!" he says. "They are sariras, crystal-like relics that embody the essence of Buddhist knowledge!" He begins chanting slogans in his hoarse voice: "*Sarvadharmā anātmānaḥ, śāntaṃ nirvāṇam!* All dharmas are nonself; Nirvana is a place of perfect calm!" He turns to face the doctors and patients. "Take a good look. Am I not here to save you? It is hard to say. But I ask you to deliver my dead body to the crematorium for burning, scatter my ashes in the sea, and I will finally make the journey to the other shore . . ." He makes a face at his mother. "No matter, I shall offer her as a gift of death for you, my loyal followers, a gesture to express my apologies."

Nobel doesn't say a word, but a thoughtful expression appears on his face, as if he is exploring a new mystery of nature that will determine the future world. Flowerlike blossoms of blood burst forth between the boy's teeth. She smells the strong stench of alcohol. Van Gogh's painterly vision again unfurls before everyone's eyes.

She feels like she should forgive her son. She imagines holding hands with him and, like a pair of peacocks, soaring over the sea, flying into the past, before finally landing on the other shore. There, aside from a lonely hospital, there is nothing else. It is a first-class hospital, with a fully equipped ER—hemostatic forceps, suturing needles, analgesics, and a full array of medicines to treat wounds—but it is devoid of people, as if prepared specially for their arrival. She decides to renounce her status as a goddess and, assuming the role of a clinical doctor, to administer life-saving procedures to her son.

The boy begins to sing:

Perhaps when the world achieves
A state of Perfect Harmony,

You and I will be a part of that.
But perhaps it's an illusion, for which
Countless people have spilled their blood
And sacrificed their lives.

He goes on:

With enough energy accumulated in the kidneys,
You shall have the will to stand your ground,
Even if Mount Tai should collapse before you.

He then leans his head back, screams to the heavens, and takes his last breath.

She quickly takes hold of the surgical scissors in his abdomen and enlarges his wound. Reaching up into his chest cavity with her nonsterile hand, she grabs his heart and rhythmically massages it to maintain the blood supply to his brain. But he needs oxygen. Oxygen remains the most important resource in this universe. She screams, "You've got to come back! We're going to revive you!" The heart feels like a wet bag of squirming insects in her hand. She administers compression squeezes, but she can feel the resistance becoming weaker and weaker. In a fit of desperation, she squeezes hard, and the heart tears apart. A heavy, muddled voice rings in her ear: *Let me remind you, if the information does not match up, there will be no freedom.* She knows the voice doesn't belong to the machine, or to the captain—it belongs to Yang Wei. The owner of that voice is no longer on the ship; he is not even of this universe. He is from a world she will never touch directly.

As if suddenly possessed by a demon spirit, the boy opens his eyes, staring at her with a look of radiance. His throat emits a raspy howl, like an attack dog. She knows this is due to the increase in blood acidity in the recently deceased, which triggers throat spasms and involuntary nerve reactions. He seems to be saying: *Ha ha, all your effort to bring me back has been in vain! I won't bear the sins for you devils who carried a fetus. Atone for your own sins!* She can't help but embrace him, as if the warmth of her body might revive him. The embrace squeezes the cross dangling on her chest between them, flipping it upside down and stabbing her in the throat. The pain spreads like a bolt of lightning through her whole body, filling her nose and mouth with the familiar mix of blood and alcohol that she has known so well, for millions of years, but now it transforms into a fresh fragrance, not like a lotus flower, but some other plant she is not familiar with, maybe something like a fig tree . . .

Like a newborn baby, the boy extends his purple-white tongue to lick the fluid spilling from his mother's wound. As his body gradually slips from her embrace, he seems to utter, "We are one! We are one!" A woman's laughter stops suddenly, and there against the backdrop of the red sky, a strange new cross arises. The temple bells sound throughout the sick ward, and the lips of the Avalokitesvara statue quiver, ever so slightly.

FICTIONAL DIAGNOSIS: HAN SONG IN DIALOGUE WITH MICHAEL BERRY

I concluded both *Hospital* and *Exorcism* with a translator's afterword, in which I tried to chip away at some of the many layers of meaning and metaphor embedded within Han Song's Hospital trilogy. Those essays included discussions of everything from the double entendres built into so many of the characters' names to the layers of Chinese political reality the novels reference. *Dead Souls*, of course, continues with more name games (e.g., Yang Wei's nickname, Brother Wei, or *Weige*, is a homophone for the Chinese translation of "Viagra"; Zifeiyu, which literally means "you are not a fish," is a reference to a famous passage in the Daoist classic *Zhuangzi*), references to Chinese politics and culture (e.g., "301 Base" is a clear reference to the real-life 301 Hospital, the People's Liberation Army General Hospital and Medical School, the largest comprehensive military hospital in China), and an almost encyclopedic series of references to scientific theories, philosophical quandaries, and classic literary texts. But after spending three years inside Han Song's "fictional hospital," I wanted to give the final word to the magician himself.

This interview was conducted in written form over the span of several months in 2023. The questions range from Han Song's early science fiction influences to his work as an editor at *Xinhua News*, but it ultimately focuses on the Hospital trilogy—*Hospital, Exorcism*, and

Dead Souls—discussing the origin of the series and how it engages with themes of religion, gender, place, and even the role of Studio Ghibli in inspiring his fiction.

Michael Berry: If we were to trace the origins of your interest in science fiction, when would that be? As a young man growing up in China, how did you first come into contact with science fiction?

Han Song: It was probably in the late 1970s, around the start of the reform and opening era in 1978. I read several science fiction stories published in magazines like *Science Illustrated* (*Kexue huabao*) and *Youth Science* (*Shaonian kexue*). The earliest and most memorable was a short story about earthlings being abducted by extraterrestrials, written by a Soviet author. There were also works by Chinese writers, such as "The Adventures of Buck" (*Buke qiyu ji*), about organ transplantation, and "The Elephant with Its Nose Cut Off" (*Gediao bizi de daxiang*), about cultivating superanimals.

Later I read Tong Enzheng's *Death Ray on Coral Island* (*Shanhudao shang de siguang*), which was published in the mainstream *People's Literature* (*Renmin wenxue*) in 1978, issue eight. My father brought a copy home from his workplace library, and when I looked at the table of contents, I was immediately drawn to it. I read it in one sitting and was deeply impressed. I was thirteen years old that year. Another work that had a wide readership was Ye Yonglie's *Xiao Lingtong Roams the Future* (*Xiao Lingtong manyou weilai*). Then I came across *Science and Art* (*Kexue wenyi*) magazine, later renamed *Science Fiction World* (*Kehuan shijie*), which was first published in 1979. I then learned about Ursula K. Le Guin's *The Left Hand of Darkness* from a publication I subscribed to that provided summaries of foreign literary works. There was a brief introduction, classifying it as mainstream literature, and I was fascinated by the title. I copied it many times in my notebook.

These novels, along with those I had read before—like *Journey to the West (Xiyouji)*, *Water Margin (Shuihu zhuan)*, and *Creation of the Gods (Fengshen yanyi)*—shared both similarities and differences. They presented a future world, different from history or reality, full of magic and unknown elements, while also containing scientific content. At that time, children had a great longing for science, especially during the era referred to as "the spring of science," ushered in by Deng Xiaoping. Many people's childhood dreams were to become scientists, and I thought the same. However, I officially started writing science fiction in 1982, at the age of seventeen, when I participated in a school-organized essay competition to coincide with the United Nations' International Space Year activities. Under the guidance of my Chinese teacher, I wrote a story about using a spaceship to send giant pandas to the moon.

MB: When you were young, which science fiction writers had the most significant impact on you?

HS: Chinese writers like Ye Yonglie and Tong Enzheng had a considerable influence on me. Tong Enzheng wrote a novel called *The Magic Flute on the Snowy Mountain (Xueshan modi)*, which tells the story of a wild creature, the Chinese equivalent to Bigfoot, living in the Tibetan region. It sparked my fascination with mysterious unknown animals and a longing for the snowy plateau of Tibet. Later, I wrote science fiction novels about Tibet, fulfilling that desire. If I have the time, I would especially like to write a novel about the search for Bigfoot in China, especially since I participated in such a search expedition in Shennongjia.

Regarding Western science fiction, my earliest readings were Isaac Asimov's *I, Robot* and H. G. Wells's *The War of the Worlds*, which I received as prizes from a writing competition in 1982. They sent me three translated books, and there was another science fiction book by an American author, but I've forgotten its name. The works of these two writers were captivating. In 1984, during my first year in college at the age of nineteen, I read Arthur C. Clarke's *2001: A Space Odyssey*, which was incredibly shocking, and at that time, I felt it represented the pinnacle of science fiction. I also read the work of Robert A. Heinlein, though with the exception of *The Moon Is a Harsh Mistress*, his novels did not have much impact on me overall. Another influential writer is Sakyo Komatsu. During college, I read *Japan Sinks*, which had a profound impact. Another author who was widely translated was Michael Crichton. I was fascinated by him, and I was first blown away by *The Andromeda Strain*, which was translated into Chinese as *Sicheng*, or "City of the Dead."

After reading the works of these writers, I thought, *Wow, I had no idea that literature could be written like this!* It was completely different from popular Chinese stories like Gao Xiaosheng's "Chen Huansheng Goes to the City" (*Chen Huansheng shang cheng*), which was a short story I really liked at the time, depicting a peasant making a fool of himself on his first trip to the city. It wasn't until the mid- to late 1990s that I read Le Guin's *The Left Hand of Darkness* and Philip K. Dick's novels. Additionally, works like Kurt Vonnegut's *Slaughterhouse-Five*, Aldous Huxley's *Brave New World*, and George Orwell's *1984* had a significant influence on me. They can't strictly be called science fiction writers, but they had a considerable impact on young people in China. Still, the most profound influence came from Hollywood science fiction films. I first watched *Star Wars* on a VHS tape in 1984 and was greatly impressed. Starting from 1994, China implemented the quota system for importing ten American blockbusters each year, allowing me to see more science fiction films. Memorable ones include *Jurassic Park*, as well as later films like *Avatar*, *The Matrix*, *Terminator*, *Interstellar*, *Prometheus*, *Gravity*, and *The Martian*, which proved even more influential for me than reading science fiction novels.

MB: In addition to science fiction novels, did you read a lot of so-called serious literature or pure literature? For example, were you keeping up with the latest trends in Chinese literature during the 1980s, such as the work of writers like Ah Cheng, Mo Yan,

Wang Anyi, Shi Tiesheng, Han Shaogong, and Yu Hua, who were all part of the "cultural fever" sweeping China at that time? Was there any interaction between you and this group of writers? Were you influenced by Chinese literary trends—from "scar literature" to the root-seeking movement to the new avant-garde?

HS: I read a lot of serious literature, or "pure literature," even more than science fiction literature. I was particularly fascinated by Yu Hua at that time and even imitated him. It should be said that I was influenced to a considerable extent. I later met most of these writers. In the case of Han Shaogong, he was a fellow student from my university days. He lived in the same dormitory building, and although we never spoke, he was often surrounded by students as he attended the English Department at Wuhan University through a special program. I liked Ah Cheng's *The King of Chess* (*Qi wang*) and *Wild All Over the Land* (*Biandi fengliu*). I also enjoyed Wang Anyi's novels. The ideologies behind many of the literary trends of the 1980s in China—including scar literature, the search-for-roots movement, and the avant-garde—I feel have actually been inherited by science fiction. After 1989, significant changes occurred in Chinese society, and these genres gradually waned in mainstream literature. However, the rise of science fiction, to some extent, represents a form of avant-garde. Some works are quite cutting edge, including those by Liu Cixin and some post-80s writers like Chen Qiufan, as well as Hong Kong, Taiwan, and overseas science fiction writers like Chan Koonchung (Chen Guanzhong) and Egoyan Zheng (Yigeyan).

On the other hand, I was more influenced by Western literature. In high school, in 1981, I read a book called *Twenty Lectures on Modern European and American Modernist Literature* (*Oumei xiandaipai wenxue ershi jiang*). It discussed futurist literature, expressionist literature, stream-of-consciousness literature, existentialist literature, absurd drama, and black humor, among other genres. Just reading the introductory essays included in that book fascinated me. I really liked

Hemingway's *The Snows of Kilimanjaro*. I was particularly fond of the poetry of Rimbaud and Baudelaire at the time, and I was most obsessed with Eliot's *The Waste Land*. For a long time, I immersed myself in Japanese literature, especially Yasunari Kawabata and Yukio Mishima. As for Kafka, I started systematically reading his fiction in 2008. Sometimes I feel that science fiction literature is actually a variation of Western modernist literature in China.

MB: Could you talk about the initial Hospital series concept?

HS: In 2003 and 2006, several bouts of relatively serious illness and my experiences being hospitalized prompted me to want to record my feelings about hospitals directly. I initially wrote a novella, which was later published in *The World of Fiction* (*Xiaoshuo jie*), and an editor from Shanghai Literary Publishing House, Yu Chen, wanted me to turn it into a full-length novel for publication. *The World of Fiction* was also operated by this publishing house. Thus, I expanded it into a full-length novel. Yu Chen later urged me to expand it further into a trilogy, leading to the creation of *Exorcism* and *Dead Souls*. Of course, I also wanted to borrow the hospital setting to express some of my observations and ideas about reality. I believe hospitals are a microcosm of our era and society. Additionally, they represent the course of life, from the starting point of birth to the final destination of death. All of this can be expressed through the lens of a hospital.

MB: How did your personal experiences influence the details and content of the novel *Hospital*?

HS: The creation of *Hospital* can be seen as an accumulation of experiences that took place over an extended period of time. When I was very young, probably in kindergarten, I often fell ill. It was during the Cultural Revolution, and my parents were both subjected to political criticism, unable to take care of me. They sent me to boarding school for kindergarten, and I could only see them once a week. They told me that whenever they brought me back home, I was always struggling with bouts of pneumonia. During fifth grade, I was hospitalized for an extended period of time due to asthma and emphysema. I stayed in the children's hospital for a relatively long time, which left a profound impression on me with regard to hospitals. Later, my parents said that responsibility for my illness should be attributed to the Gang of Four and the Cultural Revolution. Subconsciously this planted an idea in me that diseases are closely related to society and politics.

Over the years, I have constantly struggled with illness, often requiring frequent trips to the hospital. The pain of this process has been a part of me and has formed an indelible sense of darkness that runs through my life and is reflected in my writing, including my other science fiction works. Some details in *Hospital* are drawn directly from my own experiences, the insights gained during hospitalization, and the process of undergoing medical treatment. After I started working, as a journalist, I experienced three major reforms in China in the 1990s: housing reform, medical reform, and educational reform. I felt confused about some of the practices and became pessimistic about the future. I thought the current prosperity was temporary and worried that disaster would once again befall this nation. What we call "progress" is simply the cycle of history repeating itself.

MB: You mentioned your work as a journalist. You have been employed by Xinhua News Agency for nearly thirty years. As Xinhua is China's largest state-run news organization, your work there requires a certain level of standardization in language. However, your novels, on the contrary, are the most "nonstandard" and "unrestricted" among contemporary Chinese writers. How do you view the relationship and tension between the standardization and nonstandardization of language?

HS: This is a difficult question to answer. Indeed, Xinhua News Agency is China's national news agency, a department under the State Council, and all the writing there must meet special requirements and face considerable constraints. Sometimes people refer to the writing style of Xinhua News Agency as "Xinhua style." I distinguish my work at Xinhua from my science fiction writing by maintaining a different way of thinking, a different perspective, and a different narrative style. This makes my novels appear different from the Xinhua style, but this is not absolute. Xinhua News Agency's writing has requirements in terms of stance, but there has been flexibility in expression, especially in the 1990s, when the environment was relatively relaxed and covered a broader scope of issues. Particularly in dealing with international foreign language reports, there was more openness. We could write about many interesting topics, including some that might even be considered science fiction–related topics.

For example, I wrote about unidentified flying objects and the investigation to find Bigfoot, topics that interested me. Some "sensitive topics," such as the massive number of deaths due to famine in the 1960s, were also reported, which itself was a very science fiction–like event. Once, when [author] Bei Dao returned to China, I had a reporter go and interview him. He knew he was a "sensitive figure" and refused to be interviewed. However, the reporter happened to be a fan. He recited Bei Dao's poems on the spot, which deeply moved him, and thus we were able to get him to accept the interview. After writing it, the proofreader dared not publish it, because Bei Dao was a "special figure," but I signed off and had it published. Later, Bei Dao edited the book *Science Fiction for Children* (*Gei haizi de kehuan*) and invited [author] Liu Cixin and me to join him as editors. Another example is that Xinhua News Agency collects and reports a large amount of domestic and foreign science and technology news, and the content is very rich. It also allows contact with scientists, which I enjoy. In short, there is no clear boundary between work and science fiction.

MB: In addition to your unbridled imagination, I wonder if part of your bold and unconventional use of language is also tied to the censorship system in China. Could you discuss the relationship between the experimental nature of language and censorship? Can the avant-garde style in language and structure express ideas

that "normal," "healthy," "standard," or "positive" novels cannot convey?

HS: Censorship is widespread, including oversight from cultural propaganda departments, publishers, magazines, and even self-imposed restrictions. If you want your work to be published, you must accept and adhere to censorship, but to a certain extent, science fiction can circumvent this issue by disguising reality. For instance, one cannot write about China being destroyed, but writing about the destruction of an alien planet poses fewer problems. Science fiction employs a completely different language system, often referred to as "technological discourse" or "future discourse." This language is indeed experimental and ahead of its time, and censors may not necessarily understand it. However, from another perspective, since China's reality is already science fiction, it makes sense to describe it using science fiction methods. It's not just a literary style; it's also a form of realism and documentation, at least for me.

I am therefore not inclined to use traditional literary techniques. When I read some "normal" and "standard" realistic novels, even though they depict details realistically, the facts are accurate, and the narrative techniques are skillful, I feel that they don't portray the real China. They avoid the most significant issues, making them more akin to science fiction, disguised under the cloak of realism. As for those "healthy" and "positive" novels created according to directives, they are even less worth mentioning.

However, science fiction is currently under significant censorship pressure. Many science fiction works that were once publishable can't even be reprinted. In science fiction, topics related to religion, pandemics, and international relations have become extremely sensitive. Some translated Western science fiction has been reported for having "violent" elements and subsequently removed from circulation. So when it comes to the utterly inconceivable reality that is China today, if it is possible in the future, it might be better to portray it directly through serious realism rather than employing science fiction or fantasy to beat around the bush. However, the consequences for doing so may be severe.

MB: You mentioned your editor's influence in the expansion of *Hospital* from a single novel to a trilogy. Could you talk more about how it evolved into a three-book cycle?

HS: It was mainly in response to the editor's request from the publishing house to turn it into a trilogy. This happened after the publication of *Hospital* in May 2016. After writing the second part, *Exorcism*, I really didn't want to write any more, but the editor insisted that in a literary work, there's no concept of a "duology" and that it must be a trilogy. So the last part was written somewhat reluctantly. However, it can be said that by transitioning from the "Age of Medicine" and the "Medicinal War" to the "Medicinal Empire," to a certain extent, it reflects the transformation that China is undergoing—from its economic rise (encouraging the mass consumption of medicine to stimulate intense work; becoming a society built entirely on hospitals; becoming a major center for pharmaceutical manufacturing, or a "world factory," to provide medicine globally) to the struggle and competition with the West (a war involving a madman designing machines; the mobilization of all the patients on a ship navigating through stormy seas), and finally establishing an isolated empire that envisions itself dominating the world within its own imagination (national rejuvenation, human unity, and even universal dominance, or the so-called Chinese-style modernization based on traditional Chinese medicine, ultimately leading to an ending that is out of everyone's control).

MB: One characteristic of the trilogy is the use of different narrative perspectives in each volume: *Hospital* is written in the first person, *Exorcism* in the third person, and *Dead Souls* in the second person. Why did you adopt this narrative strategy?

HS: It might have been a subconscious choice. If I have to explain, the first-person approach in *Hospital* is perhaps meant to convey personal experiences, providing a sense of reality because it is a firsthand account. At the same time, it also creates a sense of illusion since this is a subjective world, where what is seen may not necessarily be the truth. The third-person perspective in *Exorcism* is objective, representing an all-seeing observer's perspective, portraying the ongoing farce meticulously, though its attempts to reveal the truth remain futile. Of course, for an onlooker, the truth is still elusive. The second-person narration in *Dead Souls*, the perspective of "you," is akin to seeing the character controlled by a player in a game. However, it doesn't resemble the third-person perspective in games, where the scene can be viewed from above. Instead, it is closer to a first-person perspective in that we are only able to see things directly in front of the character. It's a special gaming perspective between the first and third person, naming the protagonist "you," giving it dominance, ordering him to do this or that. Everything happening in the story is a game played by "me." Still, as the external "me" loses control later on, "me" and "you" collapse into the same person, but "I" is betrayed and played by "you." It could also be said that using "you" aims to achieve a sense of "nonself," isolating oneself from this absurd game. In the end, the "I" still experiences and feels the pain of "you." This duality prevents one from escaping the cycle of the game.

MB: What was your creative state during the writing of the Hospital trilogy? How does it connect with your previous works?

HS: If we start counting from the novella, this trilogy was roughly completed between 2006 and 2018. During this period, my health became somewhat compromised, entering a continuous state of illness. I went to hospitals constantly, for emergency treatments or extended stays, and my family members fell ill too. Additionally, China entered a transitional period from one era to another. Political changes had a significant impact on individuals, especially those sensitive to such changes. Witnessing certain phenomena, like many others, I felt disappointed. People were in a state of disillusionment, characterized by depression, sorrow, helplessness, and fear.

Of course, this also has connections and resonances with my previous works, emphasizing the lack of optimism for China's future, because it hasn't escaped the two-thousand-year cycle of history that began with the Qin dynasty. This is described in *2066: Red Star over America* (*Hongxing zhaoyao Meiguo*) and *The Red Ocean* (*Hongse Haiyang*). *Hospital* further records and unpacks this process. Technological progress and economic "prosperity" only magnify madness and absurdity. By the time of the COVID-19 pandemic, what *Hospital* described, including society turning into a massive hospital, had become a reality. In fact, it didn't need to wait for the COVID-19 pandemic. Society was already gradually deteriorating as a whole. Self-rescue and external help were both powerless. However, this was presented in a magnificent manner—a colossal, all-controlling superhospital that functions like a planet, responsible for the creation of all things and immersed in self-indulgent revelry and pleasure.

MB: The settings of the trilogy—City C, the Hospital Ship, and Mars—seem somewhat detached from real life. In the three books, the word "China" almost never appears. However, scattered throughout the text, there are clues directly related to China's current society. How do you perceive the interaction and tension between the universality and specificity of this trilogy?

HS: Certainly, considering censorship during the writing, it might have been better not to mention China. Now it's even stricter. Recently, when one of my novels was adapted into a comic book, both "China" and "the United States" were changed to "a certain district" by the publisher. However, the characters, scenes, and language still carry a Chinese style, criticizing the reality in China.

At the same time, it is my hope that fiction has a certain universality that stems from specificity. This series of books expresses a more widespread confusion, including when it comes to the direction of humanity. Chinese people are just a microcosm of humanity. This is similar to *2066: Red Star over America*, where writing about the United States is also a way of writing about China, but it transcends the narrative of both countries to convey the human species facing immense uncertainty, vulnerability during this stage of evolution, and the loneliness and helplessness we all face in the vast ocean of the universe. *Red Ocean* is similar, with China almost never mentioned in any of the chapters.

Compared to other literary genres, science fiction might have a stronger concept of "species," expressing more universal concerns like the possibility of a great extinction. The imagery of the three sites—city, ship, and planet—also signifies the Chinese people, or humanity as a whole, continually trying to escape from their predicaments, wishing to run farther and farther away and to rebuild the world, but ultimately, that is a task far too challenging.

MB: From a literary history perspective, I've always read the Hospital trilogy as a literary encyclopedia. From Kafka and Gogol to Tolstoy and Dostoevsky, from Dante to Nietzsche, and from Osamu Tezuka to Hayao Miyazaki, in the Hospital trilogy, there is no difference between highbrow literature and lowbrow literature. Like your own work, this engagement with different categories of fiction and pop culture challenges our definitions of "genre fiction" and "highbrow literature." How do you position yourself?

HS: This is a very awkward question. In the science fiction community, some believe that what I write is not genre fiction. It departs from the definition of science fiction and disrupts the norms of science fiction, and I also instinctively avoid writing works that fall into the category of "classic" science fiction, such as depicting a change brought about by a scientific invention or a new technological method.

At the same time, in the eyes of some literary critics and editors, I don't write "pure literature." They see me only as a science fiction writer. I haven't been able to meet the standards of pure literature. I often avoid using "classic" literary techniques to tell stories and shun that kind of surface-level "realism." Yet I don't allow science fiction to be merely a backdrop or embellishment. Or rather, it should not be written like a Kafkaesque allegory lacking "scientificity." This makes my work fall into a kind of "fourth category," a kind of hybrid, collage-like form "produced from the margins." I don't dare to have too-high expectations or ambitions for this, nor can it be called a conscious exploration of style. I try to record what I observe, experience, and think, primarily writing for myself, attempting an inward resolution, so I don't bother with techniques or skills. That's pretty much the situation. But I haven't really thought about finding my position in literature.

MB: Among the various texts the Hospital trilogy engages with, the most frequently mentioned may be works from Studio Ghibli, such as *Porco Rosso* and *Howl's Moving Castle*. I recently watched *The Boy and the Heron* and was struck by certain resonances between the film's structure and what you are doing in the Hospital trilogy. Could you talk about the impact and influence of Hayao Miyazaki and Studio Ghibli's classic animated films on your work?

HS: Although my father was a survivor of Japanese air-raid attacks during the war, I have been greatly influenced by Japanese culture ever since childhood, fascinated by the unique aesthetics portrayed in their works. This is especially reflected in Miyazaki's films, which embody a whimsical, unrestrained imagination featuring the strange, the violent, the illusory, the melancholic, the humorous, the transcendent, and the disruption of common logic. I have always wondered how Miyazaki's visuals would translate into words. Visiting Studio Ghibli left me in awe of their ability to create new worlds and alternative universes. If a film could be seen as a book, Miyazaki's works are what we would describe as extraordinary (*qi shu*), celestial (*tian shu*), and divine books (*shen shu*). That's something I aspire to create.

MB: Throughout the trilogy, there are many references to religion. Characters continuously discuss the issue of faith, especially in the context of their belief in the hospital. Do you consider yourself a person of faith? Has your perspective on faith changed after completing the Hospital trilogy?

HS: This is a difficult question that I have many contradictory feelings about. In my view, faith is fundamentally empty, nonexistent, or perhaps a construct. However, as human beings, it seems we should uphold something to confront reality. This is the struggle and confusion of the patients in the hospital, as well as a sense of being lost. After writing the Hospital trilogy, my perspective on faith has only intensified.

MB: Apart from this, the Hospital trilogy is filled with various Christian and Buddhist images and metaphors. Religious symbols from different faiths are often juxtaposed, creating an effect that is both amusing and absurd, such as the Buddha on a crucifix. Some might see this as a direct challenge to certain taboos. Could you discuss how you went about navigating the relationship between Christianity and Buddhism in the trilogy?

HS: All religions, when viewed in a broader context, might have a unified essence. Therefore, in the novel they are intertwined, intersecting without breaking any taboos or implying any specific clash of civilizations. It was not my intention to hint at any particular cultural conflict. God and Buddha, despite their vast differences, might be part of a single entity. Perhaps both contain a layer of absurdity amid the sacred, and perhaps there is a layer of the sacred amid their absurdity. The divine itself often represents the dark and avaricious side of humankind's spiritual world.

MB: The entire trilogy presents a very curious perspective when it comes to gender and sexuality. In *Hospital*, there are few female characters, and they seem to be clones or replicants. In *Exorcism*, women and children are eliminated, leaving only a ship full of old men. It is only in the Coda section of *Dead Souls* that the narrative finally turns to a female character, concluding the entire trilogy with a story about a mother and son. Could you elaborate on the evolution of the role of women in the three books?

There are also several disturbing scenes in which female characters are subjected to rape and violence. My own interpretation is

that the Hospital trilogy pushes all societal structures (including family, government, hospital, religion, etc.) to their most extreme and absurd limits. Therefore, the violent acts against women in the novel represent an extreme expression of the cultural logic of *zhongnan qingnü*, or "regarding men as superior," which has been so prevalent in Chinese culture. In that sense it feels like a deeper reflection or critique of contemporary society and culture. Do you agree with such an interpretation?

HS: Perhaps women represent the force behind everything. In my view, the universe is a womb, the source of life. But it is illusory and empty.

Living within the traditions of Chinese culture, I have always believed that contemporary politics, economics, and culture are essentially extensions of thousands of years of male conceit and inferiority. Within this structure, women are viewed as both goddesses and accessories, their shadowy existence essential to society's basic functions and people's behavioral patterns. Lurking behind *zhongnan qingnü*, there is a biological logic at work, which is also affected by political and social structures. This is also reflected in various relationships, such as how people in positions of leadership treat their subordinates, which is essentially how men treat women. Even China's approach to the United States and other countries embodies this male-centric perspective.

MB: Another characteristic of the novel is the constant transformation of characters' identities. Doctors become patients, patients become doctors, the dead become the living, the living become dead, almost all women are clones, and most of the characters have a multitude of identities and names. Could you talk about the ambiguity and multiplicity of identity in the novel?

HS: I think this has to do with the way the novel attempts to express the illusory nature of the world, which is also a portrait of the real world we live in. We are both ourselves and others; we are replicas and mutants. This state of constant change is a reflection of impermanence (*wuchang*) and also functions as a negation of human-kind's "original nature."

MB: What advice do you have for readers encountering your novels for the first time? What mindset do you suggest they adopt when approaching your work, and what do you hope they take away?

HS: I hope they can read and understand that the hospital described is the reality of human survival in the universe. I also hope they can be aware of the fact that, in essence, they, too, are patients. This might help them enter the illusory world created by the text. Ultimately, I hope they can realize that we are living in an illusory world. After living through the most twisted and challenging hospital experience, everything else in life can be dismissed with a laugh.

ACKNOWLEDGMENTS

In 2020, I embarked on the largest and most challenging translation project of my career, the dense, sprawling, masterful, and maniacal Hospital trilogy by the remarkable Chinese science fiction writer Han Song. I was initially drawn to the project by his description of the protagonist's torturous experience after checking into C City's Central Hospital for an undiagnosed stomach ailment. Thus begins an endless cycle of examinations, tests, procedures, and suffering. Almost without hesitation, I signed on to translate the entire trilogy: *Hospital*, *Exorcism*, and *Dead Souls*. Over the next three years, I spent an untold number of hours swept up in Han Song's devilish world of majestic madness, morbid monstrosities, and delirious dreams. *Hospital* was published in early January 2023, followed by *Exorcism* in November of the same year. Meanwhile, throughout the year, I had been toiling to complete the final and most challenging installment of the trilogy, *Dead Souls*. On Christmas Day of 2023, I translated a passage describing a group of passengers selected for elimination being hung on a forest of crucifixes, and the timing somehow felt like it had been preordained. The next morning, I finally finished the first draft of *Dead Souls*. I know this isn't a book for everyone, but it is a book unlike any other—what is referred to in Chinese as a *qishu* (奇書, a remarkable/strange/rare book). At the end of this long journey spanning three years, three novels, and more than 1,300 pages, there were times I thought the book might kill me, or drive me insane. On more than one occasion, I couldn't wait for it to be over, and on many other occasions I never wanted it to end. But, alas, all banquets must eventually come to a conclusion.

Special thanks to Han Song for his patience, support, and unorthodox brilliance; my family for putting up with the long hours I spent "in the hospital"; the Simon Guggenheim Memorial Foundation for awarding me a Guggenheim Fellowship to support the translation of *Dead Souls*, and my colleagues at UCLA for granting me time off from teaching to complete it; Jennifer Lyons for championing this project; Gabriella Page-Fort for her early enthusiasm about Han Song; Mingwei Song and David Der-wei Wang for being such vocal advocates of the project from day one; Jason Kirk for his keen editorial sensibilities and literary style, which helped elevate this project to another level; and all the editors and designers who worked on this project, including Adrienne Procaccini, Alexandra Torrealba, Stephanie Chou, Lauren Grange, Bill Siever, Will Staehle, and the entire team at Amazon Crossing for taking a chance on a dystopian nightmare of a novel that is as uncompromising as it is visionary.

ABOUT THE AUTHOR

Photo © Fang Xuehui-2013

Han Song works as a journalist with Xinhua News Agency and is one of China's leading science fiction writers. A native of Chongqing, Han earned an MA in journalism from Wuhan University. He began writing in 1982 and has since published numerous volumes of fiction and essays. His novels include *The Red Sea, Red Star over America*, the Rails trilogy (*Subway, High-Speed Rail*, and *Orbits*), and the Hospital trilogy (*Hospital, Exorcism*, and *Dead Souls*), which has been described as a new landmark in dystopian fiction. Han is a six-time winner of the Chinese Galaxy Award for fiction and a repeat recipient of the Xingyun Award. His short fiction has appeared in the collections *Broken Stars* and *The Reincarnated Giant*, as well as in the anthology *Exploring Dark Short Fiction: A Primer to Han Song*. An avid reader and traveler, the author has spent time in both the Antarctic and the Arctic. He's even searched for Bigfoot in the forests of central China.

ABOUT THE TRANSLATOR

Photo © 2022 Eileen Chen

Michael Berry is a professor of contemporary Chinese cultural studies and the director of the Center for Chinese Studies at UCLA. He is the author of several books on Chinese film and culture, including *Speaking in Images, A History of Pain, Jia Zhangke on Jia Zhangke,* and *Translation, Disinformation, and Wuhan Diary.* His expertise has led to work as a film consultant and as a juror for numerous film festivals, such as Golden Horse (Taiwan) and Fresh Wave (Hong Kong). Berry is also the translator of several novels, including *To Live, The Song of Everlasting Sorrow* (with Susan Chan Egan), and *Remains of Life,* among others.